"*Pulling Through* is an exciting, page-turning novel, but it is more than that. It is a preview of where four decades of arms buildup and foreign-policy adventuring is leading us. If you read Dean Ing's brilliant novel you will see how, with only moderately optimistic assumptions, perhaps as many as one-third of the American people can survive a nuclear war and enter into an existence of twelve-hour, seven-day drudgery, with few amenities and an excellent chance of grisly disease. What it does not discuss is how arms reductions and a genuine attempt at finding peaceful solutions could allow all three-thirds of the American people to survive, with technology and amenities intact. Since we go on electing machismo addicts to high office, probably Ing regards this possibility as pure fantasy, not worth discussing. Unfortunately for all of us, the available evidence suggests he is right."

—Fred Pohl

"Can anyone pull through a nuclear war? If it is an 'all-out' exchange, I doubt it. If it is 'limited,' some will live. I've heard people say they wouldn't *want* to live. I doubt that, too. Finding themselves alive after a holocaust, survivors would do what they've always done: try to survive a bit longer. They would fare better if they had read *Pulling Through*. In an engrossing fiction and a series of practical articles, Dean Ing has given us a survivors' handbook crammed with the lore of the post-nuke world. There's no way to make it pretty. Still . . . you *might* survive—and *then* what would you do?"

—John Varley

PULLING THROUGH

DEAN ING

SF
ACE BOOKS, NEW YORK

For
Dave Shumway
. . . who has pulled me through
more than once.

Contents

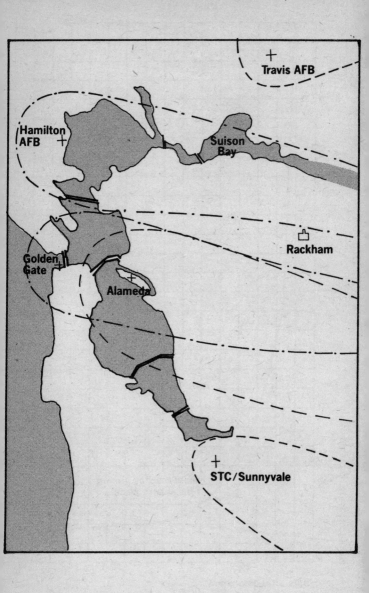

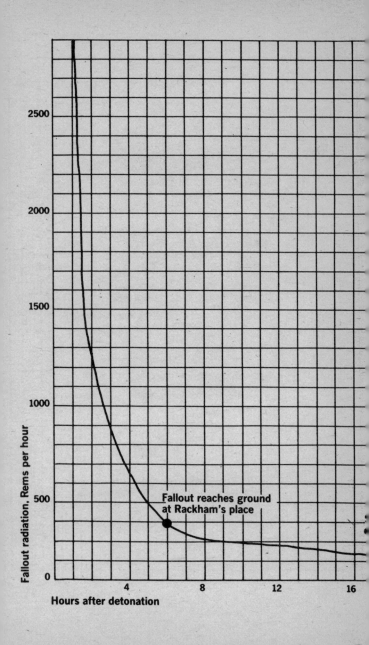

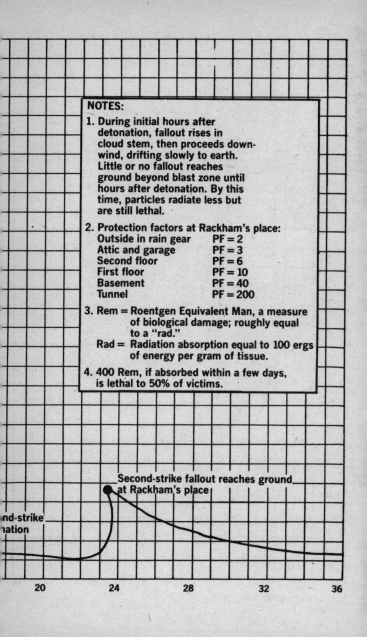

NOTES:

1. During initial hours after detonation, fallout rises in cloud stem, then proceeds downwind, drifting slowly to earth. Little or no fallout reaches ground beyond blast zone until hours after detonation. By this time, particles radiate less but are still lethal.

2. Protection factors at Rackham's place:

Outside in rain gear	PF = 2
Attic and garage	PF = 3
Second floor	PF = 6
First floor	PF = 10
Basement	PF = 40
Tunnel	PF = 200

3. Rem = Roentgen Equivalent Man, a measure of biological damage; roughly equal to a "rad."

   Rad = Radiation absorption equal to 100 ergs of energy per gram of tissue.

4. 400 Rem, if absorbed within a few days, is lethal to 50% of victims.

Second-strike fallout reaches ground at Rackham's place

nd-strike
nation

20   24   28   32   36

INTRODUCTION

By Spider Robinson

When asked to do an introduction for a book by another writer, I usually go for the metaphor, and more often than not I find it. I once characterized Gordon R. Dickson, for instance, as a quiet giant: you might live with him in an enclosed space for *years* before noticing how *big* he is. Edgar Pangborn, that overlooked Mark Twain, I think of as a country with undefended borders, a place in which you are always welcome. If I'm ever asked to do an intro for Harlan Ellison, I'll probably describe him as an arm-breaker who gets a lot of repeat business—and so forth.

I've been worrying about Dean Ing since I accepted this assignment, and all I come up with so far is Cruise Director on a deepwater supership, one of those suckers so big and so laden with cargo that they can only dock in a port the size of Halifax, my home. Dean Ing stories carry freight of that kind of magnitude—and yet he keeps you so busy with shuffleboard and dancing and swimming and happy chatter, he is so damned *entertaining,* that you will disembark from the voyage convinced that it was a pure pleasure cruise, and a steal at the price. It may be months later before you realize that you unloaded most of that heavy freight with your own hands, and brought it home with you—and that you are glad to have it around.

I remember my first Dean Ing story very well. I was in Bellevue Hospital at the time, and I was stoned to the eyeballs on morphine. A few days before, a couple of very talented fellows in white suits had sawed open half my ribs and done drastic but therapeutic things to one of my favorite lungs. While I was reflecting on this, my second-best friend Ben Bova (I am married to my best friend) brought me a book to read: a copy of the soon-to-be released *Analog Annual,* which contained a story of mine. Of course, I turned first to that story—and such is the effect of Sister Morphine that I was two or three pages into the tale before I realized that I had misread the Table of Contents and was reading the story *before* mine, something called "Malf" by someone named Dean Ing. But I was having so much fun by that time that I just kept reading. I was enjoying the story as much as I would have enjoyed one of my own. I don't know if I can convey to a non-writer what high praise that is.

I had, in fact, so much fun that it would be several months before I realized that "Malf" had taught me some subtle and important truths. (No, I won't name them here. Go read the story—it's in one of Dean's collections.)

So the next time Ben came to visit I brought up the story. "Hey, where'd you find this new kid? He's terrific."

"New kid?" said Ben. "John Campbell bought his first story when you were six years old. He just took a twenty-year vacation."

"Geeze. I'm glad he's back."

"Me too," Ben said sincerely.

I've since gone back and looked up that first story, "Tight Squeeze," published in *Astounding* in 1954, back when Dean was an Air Force interceptor crew chief. It's a good story, but I see why he soon decided to stop writing for a while. He has always had messages to deliver, sermons to preach, and perhaps there is at least a core of truth in the tired old dictum that messages should go by Western Union. While you'd never know it to judge from this book which you hold in your hands, Dean Ing was *not* a "born entertainer," not a "natural." He had to *teach* himself how to make his nutritious mindfood taste so damn good that people would voluntarily wolf it down as if it were junkfood. He was, it seems, both wise enough to realize this, and tough-minded enough to keep his mouth shut until he had mastered his lessons. To my mind this is more impressive than any achievement of a natural storyteller who got his talent as a gift from God—Dean worked for his, for over twenty years.

Of course, he did other things over those two decades, becoming, in rapid succession, father of two girls, technical writer, rocket designer, senior research engineer in aerospace, racer of lightweight Porsche-powered "specials," father of another brace of daughters with his second wife Gina (Dean and Gina are listed in the phone book as $^{D\ Ing}_{G\ L\ Ing}$, and I can't help but wonder if that influenced their marriage plans), holder of master's and then doctorate degrees, university professor, backpacker, survivalist, and slayer of trout.

Oh, I nearly forgot: he ... uh ... dabbled in automobile design. That is to say, twenty years ago he built a sportscar which looks like it won't be built before 1999, as a hobby, just to demonstrate that Detroit could build good cars if it wanted to. The Magnum, as originally powered by a standard VW engine (and you must bear in mind that this was in the late fifties), got just over 50 miles per gallon on the highway—although of course in city traffic it fell off to 40 mpg. To test its Ing-designed crash bumpers and 70-gee restraint harness, Dean ran it into a wall at 30 mph. He broke a headlight bulb. The car would go 1400 miles on a tank of gas.

No one seemed to give a damn.

But by now Dean was beginning to learn about sugar-coating your message. He pulled the VW engine, installed a Corvair mill, a Ferrari differential, a one-of-a-kind Porsche tranny, all kinds of sexy stuff like that, with the end result that the Magnum II will do 55 mph in low gear. Of course, now he only gets 30 mpg—but the new version was a long feature in *Road & Track*, the central exhibit in a San Francisco exhibition, and is to this day something of a legend around Dean's home state, Oregon. Wouldn't you like to get 30 mpg? Not in a squat, ugly little foreign box made of sheet-metal and scaled to the size of a cut-rate coffin, mind you, but in a chariot that looks like what Luke Skywalker wants for Christmas?

While all this was going on, Dean was marinating in communications theory, both studying it and teaching it. As he put it in a letter to me a few years ago, "Media theory gave me insights into things that needed saying, and suggestions on how to say them entertainingly. So I started writing fiction again, while my wife and eldest daughter were both taking their degrees *summa cum laude*. Now, thank God, we're back on the West Coast where my wife hauls home steady bacon while I write, keep house, and stalk trout ... I make no apology for didactic writing unless I fail to entertain as well."

In short, Dean Ing has had nothing to apologize for for several years now.

Apparent digression: author and critic John Gardner was

killed in a motorcycle crash last week. Why this is germane here is that Gardner's death inspired me to dig out and re-read his wonderful book, *On Moral Fiction* (which, like Galileo, he was later pressured into renouncing). Allow me to quote you a brief section:

"True art is moral: it seeks to improve life, not debase it. It seeks to hold off, at least for a while, the twilight of the gods and us. I do not deny that art . . . may legitimately celebrate the trifling. It may joke, or mock, or while away the time. But trivial art has no meaning or value except in the shadow of more serious art, the kind of art that beats back the monsters and, if you will, makes the world safe for triviality . . . Art builds temporary walls against life's leveling force, the ruin of what is splendidly unnatural in us, consciousness, the state in which not all atoms are equal. In corpses, entropy has won; the brain and the toenails have equal say. Art asserts and reasserts those values which hold off dissolution, struggling to keep the mind intact and preserve the city, the mind's safe preserve. Art rediscovers, generation by generation, what is necessary to humanness."

Or, as Dean himself puts it, "I write science fiction because I think a lot about the quality of life, and experiment with improving it, and find sf a ready forum for the topic. I have enough arrogance to think I can provide some worthwhile innovations. I put high value on academics, but to many academicians 'speculation' is a dirty word. It is, however, the soul of induction—and induction is the key to innovation. To put it another way: sf is my insulator against future shock."

Even more important, Dean is willing to share his insulator, and most important of all, he has rendered it so attractive, so stylishly cut, so pleasant to the skin, that you can get away with wearing it as a leisure garment.

Furthermore, the specimen you now hold in your hands is, in my opinion as a longtime student of sf, his most impeccable work to date, the best book he has yet produced. For a long time now, over thirty years, it has been customary to refer to Robert A. Heinlein as "the dean of science fiction writers." On the strength of this volume, I'm prepared to call Dean a Robert Heinlein of a science fiction writer, and that is the highest praise I own.

One last thing before I turn you over to Dean:

You are about to have a wonderful time with a novel called *Pulling Through*. But at some indeterminate point, you—even the dullest of you—are liable to notice that the informational subtext being imparted is information *so* vital to you own personal survival potential, that you will be tempted to start taking notes while you read. Please don't bother; it would inhibit and impede your enjoyment of an extremely fast-paced story—and besides, Dean has taken the notes for you. Every survival datum in the story, and many that didn't fit there, will be found in one of the accompanying essays at the back of the book.

I do suggest that you store this book somewhere where you and your family can find it in a hell of a hurry in the dark. Near a radio in the basement, say.

And now I hand you over to one of the most moral fictioneers I've ever met. Enjoy!

—Spider Robinson
Halifax, 1982

PULLING THROUGH

I. Doomsday

I found her thirty miles north of Oakland at Sears Point—the international raceway, to be exact, where headstrong car freaks of all sexes liked to hang out before the war. She looked smaller than eighteen. Also older. I had no trouble recognizing her from mug shots and, from the bail bondsman, glossies from her days as a teen model. But the glossies were before she'd gone pro in the worst sense, the sense that brought me into it. My name's Harve Rackham; I was a bounty hunter.

My first problem was isolating her from the quiet machos who ran Sears Point on autumn weekdays, teaching chauffeurs evasive driving and making a show of unconcern to the pit popsies—or whatever they called wistful jailbait in those days. I hadn't kept up on pit jargon since my weight climbed into the two-fifty range and I let my competition license lapse. You can't give away sixty pounds to other drivers when you drive the little cars. My Lotus Cellular wasn't tiny, but it weighed next to nothing; just the thing to drive when some bail jumper tried to sideswipe you, because the air-cushion fans could literally jump you over the big bad Buicks. And the plastic chassis cells in an off-road Lotus would absorb a handgun slug as— but I was talking about the girl. Like most sportscar nuts, she could be hypnotized by certain phrases: my Ferrari, my Lotus, my classic DeLorean; but you had to be ready to put up or shut up.

The girl had a very direct way about her, and in five minutes while I watched she was left standing at the Armco pit barrier twice by guys who didn't need whatever she was offering. She was making it easy for me.

Instead of sidling up to her—ever see anybody six foot two *sidle?* Ridiculous . . . I waved her back, adopting a proprietary

3

air. "These are private practice sessions, miss. And you're in a bad spot; if one of these four-door Bimmers kisses the Armco barrier it'll be spitting hunks of mag all down the pit apron." It wasn't likely, but it sounded good.

Her voice was a surprise, as sunny blonde as her Mediterranean features were dark. "I wasn't thinking," she said, "thanks. Uh—d'you know if any of those big limos," she paused, drowned out as a long BMW limousine howled around the last turn and then accelerated up the straight with a muted *thrummm*, "will be going home today or tomorrow?"

"A couple," I said, just as if I had the foggiest idea. "Why?"

I could see *what's it to you* in her sultry, too-experienced young face, but she erased it after a moment's thought. "I've never copped a ride in fifty thousand bucks' worth of limo," she said with a shrug.

By God, but she had cute ideas! Chauffeurs trained in the limos they drove from Denver or L.A., and the evasive training took a week. So an enterprising wench on the run might cop a ride out of the Bay Area without showing her lush tush at bus depots or freeway on-ramps, where some plainclothesman might recognize her. And she could pay off in the oldest coin of all.

A big Jag sedan sailed past, its Pirellis squalling. Its plate prefixes told me it was from L.A.; in my business you memorized that kind of trivia for the times when it might not be trivial. "He'll be heading for Pasadena," I said into the ensuing quiet—it might even be true—"and I expect I'll beat him there by two hours in my Cellular."

Quick, suspicious: "You're taking a Lotus to Pasadena?"

"Nope. To Palm Springs," I lied, and sighed a rich man's self-indulgent sigh. "A limo's okay, but they always put me to sleep." I pulled my Frisbee-size pocket watch out, though I already knew the time. A wrist chrono hangs up on clothing sometimes, and my ancient eighteen-jewel Hamilton was rugged as hell. It also carried the same false hint of money as a Rolex. I flipped the Hamilton's protective cover up, studied the dial, sighed again, put the thing away. "Enjoy your trip," I said and turned away.

For an instant I thought she had spurned the bait. Then, "I don't believe it," she said to my back.

I turned my head. "Shall I hover and wave?"

She hurried to catch up. "You just don't look like a man

who drives superlight cars," she said brightly. "A Lotus Cellular? Can it really outrun the Porsches?"

"Outjump, yes. Outrun? No," I said truthfully. Now we approached the glass-walled anterooms where staff members made their low-key pitches to interested execs.

She was so intent on peering through the glass to spot my car in the parking lot, she didn't notice much else. Two young men stood in the anteroom in much-laundered driving coveralls labeled "Mitch" and "Jerry." I'd never seen either of them before. "See you next time, Jer," I rumbled on my way out, for the girl's benefit. Every little scam helps.

When she saw my car, her suspicion fled. I slid the half-door aside, shoehorned my gut in with me. She ran her hand along the sand-tinted door sill opposite. "Feels rubbery," she said.

"Stealth coating. Plays hell with fuzz radar," I said, winked, fired up the engine, and made an unnecessary check of the system's digitals.

She had to talk louder, so she did. "My name's Kathy." I knew it was Kate Gallo. "You really going to Palm Springs? Right now?"

One good lie deserves another. "Right now," I said, and let the hover fans burp a puff of dust from beneath the Cellular's skirts.

"Aren't you even going to ask me if I want a ride?"

"Nope. Haven't time for you to collect luggage. And young girls are trouble." I blipped the engine.

She held up her shoulder bag, the kind that you could swing a cat in; the kind that alerts shopkeepers. "I travel light. And I'm free and twenty-one." She licked her lips, forced a desperate smile: "And I can be very friendly."

"I'll settle for repartee that keeps me awake on Interstate Five," I replied and waved her in as if already regretting my bigheartedness.

She piled in with a goodly flash of leg; levered her torso safety cushion into place as I backed in wheel-mode onto macadam. No sense in leaving a ground-effects dust pall behind. Then I eased onto the highway, ran the Lotus up through her gears manually and cut in the fans again for that lovely up-and-over sensation, nosing upward until we could have soared over anything but a big semi rig, before I settled us down again to a legal pace on wheels. All to give Kathy-Kate a wee thrill.

It was the least I could do; she didn't know I'd locked her torso restraint. She couldn't get out if she wanted to, and that would've given her something entirely different. A wiwi thrill.

So far it had been so easy I was ashamed of myself. I hadn't needed cuffs on her. She didn't even know my name, or that she was headed for the Oakland jug—and she wasn't, but *I* didn't know *that*, of course. I got my first inkling of it as we passed the new bridge that led to Mare Island Shipyard.

Mare Island wasn't just fenced off: it boasted two men in civvies carrying Ingrams with the tubular stocks extended and thirty-round magazines. No suppressors. Those guys commanded real respect; not even an armored Mercedes could get past them, much less fat Harve with his puddle-jumping Lotus. But I intended to pass them by anyhow, over the Carquinez bridge and down to Oakland before rush hour with my unsuspecting "suspect."

So much for my intentions. Carquinez bridge was closed to southerly traffic—and patrolled. I didn't understand until, diverted toward the Martinez bridge some miles away, I noted the wall-to-wall traffic heading north from the Oakland area. I pulled up near a uniformed Vallejo officer who was directing traffic. I bawled, "What's the trouble over Carquinez?"

He looked at me as though I were an idiot. "You must be kidding," he called, but saw from my expression that I wasn't. "You got a radio in that thing?" I nodded. "Use it. And if you're thinking of heading south, think again," he shouted, and jumped at the dull gong of a minor collision behind him.

I punched the radio on and exchanged shrugs with the girl. In my rearview I could see the officer waving the fender-benders aside with no effort to ascertain injuries or to take videotapes. It was a bad intersection, already littered with glass and fluids from other recent collisions. Evidently the officer had special orders to keep the roadway clear at all costs.

"Okay," I said to myself as much as to the girl, "we'll detour east to Martinez," and squirted the Lotus ahead at a speed that should've put a black-and-white on my tail.

But long before I reached the Martinez bridge, the radio had told me why that was wishful thinking. A nervous announcer was saying, ". . . at the request of the White House, to participate in the Emergency Broadcast System. During this emergency most stations will remain on the air, broadcasting news and official information to the public in assigned areas.

This is Station KCBS, San Francisco; we will remain on the air to serve the San Francisco County area. If you are not in this area, you should tune to other stations until you hear one broadcasting news and information in your area.

"You are listening to the Emergency Broadcast System serving the San Francisco County area. Do not use your telephone. The telephone lines should be kept open for emergency use. The Emergency Broadcast System has been activated—" Flick. The girl beat me to it, seeking another station.

". . . is Station KABL, Oakland. This station will broadcast news, official information and instruction for the Alameda County area—" Flick. This time I made the change.

I got KWUN, a Concord station. The girl couldn't have known it, but Concord was within ten miles of my place and by now I had no other goal but that fenced five-acre plot of mine on the backside of Mount Diablo. The announcer seemed disbelieving of his own news. "Radio Damascus claims that the Syrian attack on elements of the US Sixth Fleet was a legitimate response to violations of Syria's air space by our carrier-based aircraft. In Washington the Secretary of Defense defended the policy of hot pursuit against the bases from which Soviet-built Syrian fighter-bombers sank the US tender *Bloomsbury* about fifty miles west of Beirut early this morning. There has been no official response from Washington to the Syrian claim that the supercarrier *Nimitz* lies capsized in the Mediterranean after a nuclear near-miss by a Syrian cruise missile—"

"Oh shit," the girl and I said simultaneously.

We soon learned that most stations were simply repeating the prefabricated EBS messages we'd heard earlier, awaiting an official White House announcement. Little KWUN soon fell back on the same script as the others, but it had already told me enough. Syria's cruise birds were Soviet-made; her nukes probably Libyan. It no longer mattered whether the Soviets had known that Syria could screw nuclear tips onto those weapons. Far more important was the battle raging between our Sixth Fleet and the fast Soviet hoverships we had engaged as they poured from the Black Sea into the Aegean. I figured the *Nimitz* for a supercasualty, and I was right; once the Navy lost that big vulnerable beauty they'd be shooting at everything that moved. Our media weren't telling us, yet, that things were moving toward West Germany, too, on clanking caterpillar treads.

We found the Martinez bridge blocked, its southbound lanes choked with the solid stream of northbound traffic. Cursing, I took the road past the old Benicia historical monument because I knew it led to the water. "I hope you can swim, Kate," I called over the wail of the engine, "in case we get a malf halfway across Suisun Bay."

"Stop this thing," she screamed. I did. "We'd never make Palm Springs in traffic like this," she said, her dark eyes very round and smokily Sicilian. *"And why did you call me Kate?"*

"I know all my property," I said. "Legally, Kate Gallo, you are my temporary chattel property by California law. I can slap you around if I need to, or put you in handcuffs and gag you."

Her eyes became almost circular. "Bounty hunter," she accused.

"You got it, and it's got you. But I'm not taking you back to Oakland now, Kate. I'm heading for my home in Contra Costa County, which has a nice deep basement and all of Mount Diablo to protect us against whatever ails the Bay Area." She was struggling against her torso restraint. "Are you listening?"

In answer she turned toward me with claws flashing; raked my jacket sleeve in lightning swipes that almost drew blood through the Dacron; shifted her aim toward my face. It was not a move calculated to bring out my gentlemanly instincts.

I cuffed her with my gloved hand, lightly, twice—just enough to make her draw back to protect those lovely strong cheekbones. "You can go," I said, and repeated it as she gazed at me through defensive hands. I triggered the release on the torso restraint and, while she surged up from the seat, I added, "While you lie dying, remember I gave you a chance."

She hadn't panicked because she was still thinking ahead. She paused astraddle the door sill. "A Berkeley whizkid told me once that the only smart way out of Oakland, in an evacuation, was north along the coast. I'll make it."

"So will a million others." I jerked my head back toward the clogged arterials. "Did he also mention that you might starve? Did he mention the very few people there who might be willing to share food and drinkable water? I may take chances, Kate, but I haven't been stupid."

While she stood there undecided, for all I knew, heavyweight Soviet rockets might've been thundering up from Semipalatinsk—and from Nevada, for that matter. I jazzed the engine. "I asked if you can swim, Kate."

"Damn right," she shot back, and twinkletoed back into my Lotus. "You just make sure I don't have to haul *your* fat ass ashore."

And that was how I chose to spend Doomsday with a beautiful felon.

If I'd had a true unfettered choice, I'd have chosen someone other than Kate Gallo for a nuclear survival companion. And I probably would've chosen worse; Kate was no survivalist, but a born survivor—as I learned. As for Doomsday: you can't split a planet with a few gigatons of explosive, but you can sure doom a lot of its inhabitants.

I muttered something to that effect while keeping the Lotus above small, languid whitecaps in Suisun Bay. Kate Gallo stayed scrunched down, scanning the October sky as if by sheer willpower she could keep it clear of hostile weapons. Halfway across the two-mile stretch of water she showed optimistic colors. "So what do you do with me if this turns out to be a false alarm?"

"Hadn't thought about it," I said, shouting to compete with the fan noises. "Let you give yourself up, maybe, if you can convince me you're through making dumb decisions. But don't count on—oh, *Jeez*-us," I finished, glancing to my left toward the soaring bridge structure a mile distant.

Near the bridge center, vaulting the rail of concrete and steel, a tiny oblong of four-door sedan climbed aloft, etched on a hard sapphire sky, propelled from behind by a determined eighteen-wheeler. Shards of concrete and metal sparkled. A minuscule fire-bloom trailed the sedan as it cartwheeled nearly two hunderd feet to the water. When the big rig jackknifed, its trailer found the same hole in the rail and (okay, admit it, Rackham) I had the satisfaction of seeing the bully ooze through the gap and begin a one-and-a-half pike into the bay. The rig moved so slowly that I saw its driver, ant-size from my view, leap to the safety of the bridge. However small his chances, they were better than those of anybody a few miles behind him in Oakland.

I guessed that the bridge incident was being multiplied by drivers made mindless by terror from San José to Norfolk. We couldn't hear the truck caterwaul past the railing, nor even its splash, and our distance somehow insulated us. In minutes we'd be nosing into the reality of waterfront chaos in Martinez.

The dashboard map display reminded me we'd have to cross one major arterial, then skirt the Concord NavWep station en route to the winding roads near my place. With traffic like we were seeing, those odds had no appeal whatever. Our chances would be better with the bay itself as our conduit—but not if I kept the Lotus's engine near redline for much longer. "Don't worry if you feel water," I called to Kate Gallo, and eased back on the pedal while turning the wheel.

The worry was all mine. I passed under the highway bridge heading up the bay, fully aware that an errant wave could toss a gallon of water into the fan intakes and send us skating like a flat rock; a rock that would disintegrate before it sank, at the speed we were crossing. A dozen big powerboats and twice that many smaller ones crisscrossed the bay, creating a nightmarish chop that slapped our bottom. Twice I heard strangled surges as bits of spray entered the fan intakes. I'd destroyed an off-road Porsche that way once, and my sphincter didn't unpucker until we droned up the mouth of the San Joaquin River.

I took the first boat ramp that wasn't clogged, which was on the outskirts of tatty little Pittsburg, and ignored the outraged yells of folks who were trying to clog it as the Lotus wheels found purchase. We fled from the waterfront, eastward through town, between rows of Pittsburg's down-at-the-heel date palms that, like the tall, rawboned strippers in Vallejo, promised a lot but never put out much.

Kate called to me between gear changes: "Why is the traffic so light here?"

"Just guessing," I replied, "but Pittsburg and Antioch have been small towns so long, they don't realize how near they are to ground zero." I still don't know if that's the right answer. I just know a hell of a lot of nice folks died thinking a nuclear strike was a respecter of city limits.

At the outskirts of Antioch, with the brush-dotted hump of Mount Diablo looming nearly a mile high ahead of us, I turned south and passed wrecks at several intersections before turning onto Lone Tree Way. The power lines hadn't yet fallen across this broad boulevard, but some poor bastard's old highwing Luscombe was hung up like a bat on a clothesline between two highline towers, smoking and sparking as it dribbled molten

aluminum ninety feet to the dry grass below. To wrench Kate's
attention from the grisly clinkers that jerked in the cockpit, I
pointed ahead. "Just past the airport we hit Deer Valley Road.
No more towns now." I pulled the phone from under the dash,
coded a number, gave the handset to Kate. "I need both hands;
this road becomes a gymkhana up ahead. See if you can get
through."

"We're not supposed to use the phone," she said. "Your
wife?"

"My sister Sharon, in a San José suburb. If I'm any judge,
she and Ernie and the kids'll be at my place before we are."
Which just goes to show I'm a lousy judge.

Relaxing too soon can be suicide. In the years since the '81
depression, when I lucked into some cash and bought my country place, I'd driven the Deer Valley–Marsh Creek route a
thousand times—before this always enjoying the extravagant
curlicues of two-lane blacktop winding between slopes so steep
they hid the major bulk of Mount Diablo. I hadn't met a single
car since turning onto the creek road; I knew every ripple on
the road shoulder; and I was so near home that I'd begun to
worry about Shar, taking my own safety for granted. That was
when the old black Lincoln slewed around a blind bend, fish-
tailing toward us.

My midbrain made its subconscious guess. If we were lucky,
the Continental would regain enough traction to lurch back so
that we could pass on the shoulder.

We weren't lucky. Neither was he. This was no gimmicked
limo with tuned shocks and suspension but your truly classic
two-ton turd, and it began to spin at us just past the bend. But
a mass that size does everything in slow motion; by the time
its overlong rump swung around, my hand was on the fan lever.

The trick to a Cellular's jackrabbit leap is in slapping the
gear selector to neutral a split second before you engage the
fans, so that all the engine's torque is available to energize
those big air impellers inside the body shell. It doesn't halt
your forward motion; in fact, removing your tires from macadam, it relinquishes all braking and steering control to the
fan vents, so you can't obtain any strong side forces. With fans
moaning, we soared over the trunk of the Lincoln by a two-
foot margin, only to sideswipe the branches of a pinoak that
showered us with twigs as my airborne Lotus tilted and veered

back over the road. I kept my foot off the brake, let the fan vents remedy the tilt, chopped back on the impellers and didn't engage third gear until I felt the tires touch the road. After that I kept busy getting through the bend and decided to slow down a bit.

"Aren't we going to stop?" Kate was white-faced, her neck craned backward.

I hadn't risked a backward glance. "What for?"

"He rolled and hit a big sycamore next to the creek!"

I slowed while thinking it over, then let my biases show and pressed on. "If he was driving that kind of fat-cat barge with that kind of disregard," I growled, "the hell with him."

She started to reply, then gave me a judgmental headshake and tried the phone again. But communication lines, like other traffic, had become overloaded to the point of paralysis. When I ducked off the macadam onto the gravel access road to my place, the girl was still trying Shar's number fruitlessly.

I remoted the gate in the cyclone fence surrounding my place as we approached and caught sight of my friend Spot, whose ears could always discriminate between the sounds of my Lotus and any other machine. Kate studied the sign on the eight-foot fence, one of several around my five-acre spread that proclaimed:

CHEETAH ON PATROL

and she gave me a smirk as the gate swung shut behind us. "You don't expect anyone to believe that," she chided.

I drove slowly toward the garage, a partly converted smithy behind the house, and smirked right back. "Just so long as *he* believes it," I said, and jerked my thumb toward her door sill.

Kate's brow furrowed and then she turned and stared full into the dappled half-feline face of Spot, whose lanky stride kept his blunt muzzle almost even with hers. Her whole bod stiffened. Then she faced straight ahead, swallowed convulsively, and slid far down into her seat. Her knuckles on the torso restraint were bone-white, but, tough little bimbo that she was, Kate never whimpered.

I drove into the garage and killed the engine and delivered a long sigh, then traded obligatory ear sniffs with Spot while my head was still level with his. His yellow eyes kept straying to my passenger, more a question than a warning; I rarely brought nonfamily guests to my place. "Company, Spot," I said, and reached over to scratch Kate behind the ear.

— She sat rigid. "Does that mean I'm one of your pets, too?"

"It means you're his peer; he'll let you take the first swipe. But Spot's no pet; he's my friend and a damn good watchcat. My Captive Breeding Permit from the Department of the Interior says I own him—but nobody's told *him* that."

"So how do I behave? No sudden moves?" I caught the tremor in her voice.

"Neither of us could possibly make a move he'd consider sudden," I said, and proved it by pushing my door aside abruptly. Spot, of course, pulled back untouched as I grunted my way out of the Lotus and waved for Kate to do the same.

But: "Don't leopards turn against people sometimes?"

"I wouldn't know. Spot isn't a leopard; he's a male cheetah in his prime and he stays healthy on farina mix and horsemeat. He's the nearest thing to a link between cats and dogs; his claws aren't fully retractile and he wasn't born with the usual feline hunting instincts. Even has coarse hair like a dog, as you'll find out when you pat him."

"Fat chance." At least she was getting out of the car.

"Or you can panic and run wild and wave your arms and scream," I said, "and he'll frisk circles around you and laugh at the funny lady. Come on, I need to check my incoming messages," I added, and let them both follow me to the tunnel while she stared at my house.

My white clapboard two-story house, I told her, was a basket case when I bought it. I reroofed it, then found myself shopping for antique wallpaper patterns and reflectors for kerosene lamps, and ended with an outlay of fifty thou and two hundred gallons of sweat only when the house was furnished a la 1910 from the foundation up. The basement and part of the old smithy were something else again: you can't maintain a Cellular, or an automated cheetah feeder, or a bounty hunter's hardware, amid dust and mildew.

I led Kate past gray shreds of wooden doors that led to my root cellar. The doors lay agape on an earth mound, flanking the dark stairs fifty feet from my back door. "Let there be light," I said on the stairs, and there was light. I could've said "Keep it dark," and the tunnel lights would've come on anyway. It was my voiceprint, and Shar's and Ern's, that the system reacted to. It didn't recognize Spot's sound effects. For all his wolfen ways, Spot had a purr like God's stomach rumbling. Plus a dozen other calls, from a tabby's meow to yips and even a ludicrous birdy chirp.

Kate Gallo negotiated the turn behind me. "Curiouser and curiouser, cried Alice," she gibed. "I can't decide whether you're behind the times or ahead of 'em, Mr. Rackham."

It was my turn to register surprise, and I stopped. So did she. "You didn't lift my wallet, so how'd you know my name?"

"You told me."

I merely shook my head, very slowly. Smiling.

"Okay, if your ego needs stroking: most people on the scam in the Bay Area know about you. You're seven feet tall and weigh four hundred pounds and leap tall buildings, et cetera, and inside that rough exterior beats a heart of pure granite. You've got no friends, no family, no home, and anybody who tries to negotiate with you had better do it with silver bullets. I suspect you invented some of that crap yourself. Satisfied?"

"Eminently," I said and laughed. "So why didn't you peel off when you first saw me?"

"Lots of fa—uh, heavyset men around," she amended, glancing at my backlit paneling. "Let's just say I'm stupid."

"Not me. You've suckered too many bright solid citizens into the badger game for me to make that mistake, Kate." She just grinned an impudent grin and, for good measure, deliberately laid her hand on Spot's patient head. I pressed on: "I know your family has money. Why'd you do it?"

"*Because* of my family—and because I damn well like making men squirm. If you knew my mother you wouldn't have to ask."

I nodded. Raised in a strict household where females were expected to keep the Sabbath holy, the pasta tender, and the men on pedestals, Kate Gallo had learned too much about the rest of the world; had cast aside her illusions and her virginity before reflecting that both had their good points; had decided she would make the system pay. And men ran the system, so-o-o.... "Ever meet a male who didn't undervalue your gender?" I asked.

"A few."

"Well, you've just met another one. Two, if you count him," I said, nodding at Spot. Who just sat there with his tongue showing in a doggy leer. "Time's awasting, Kate; and quit laughing, you skinny sonofabitch," I said to Spot.

• • •

Long before I'd asked Ern McKay to critique my ideas on "the place"—we seldom called my fenced homestead anything else. With twenty years at NASA's Ames wind tunnel in the south Bay Area, master modeler Ernest McKay was what the Navy called a mustang engineer; no degree, but bagsful of expertise. Ern had taught me about parsimony, i.e., keeping it simple. Why require two codes for my tunnel lights and basement door lock when a unique voiceprint was the key to both functions? It was my idea to hang the steel-faced door into my underground office so that gravity swung it open, and Ern's dictum to avoid an automatic door closer. That would've required a selenium cell, pressure plate, or capacitance switch— all fallible—when all I needed, quoth ol' Ern, was a handle. While helping me convert a basement into a livable modern apartment and office, Ern had briefed me on a lot of NASA's design philosophy.

The result was a subterranean Bauhaus living area without many partitions, where everything worked with a minimum of bells and whistles—and when something didn't work, like a clogged drain, it was easy to get at. You can carp all you like about exposed, color-coded conduits, but I liked knowing which plastic pipes were air vents and which one led from my basement john to my septic tank down the hill. *You* guess which was painted a rich brown.

Kate Gallo stepped onto the linolamat of my office and gawked while I heaved the door shut. "Up those stairs"—I pointed to the freestanding steel steps that melded into old-fashioned wooden stairs halfway up—"is the kitchen, and just off the kitchen is a screen porch. Grab the antique galvanized tub off the porch wall and all the pans in the kitchen, bring 'em down here to the john, and fill 'em with water."

I strode around the apartment divider, a rough masonry interior wall that served as a central crossbeam under the floor above, grabbed my remotable comm system handset from my computer carrel, and headed for the john while querying for incoming messages. In the back of my head was envy for Kate, who was evidently slender enough that she didn't make those top stairs squeak on her way upstairs.

The first message was from a bail bondsman, who assured me positively that Kate Gallo had run to Sacramento. I muttered an anatomical instruction for him under my breath while readying my oversize bathtub for filling; started back to my office as the second message pinged; stopped dead as I saw why Signorina Katerina hadn't made squeaky music on my stairs. She was still standing on my linolamat, arms crossed in defiance. We traded hard stares as the message began, and Spot's ears twitched in recognition of the voice from my speaker.

"We're on the way, Harve, at—uh, eleven fifteen or so. Ernie and Cammie are putting bikes in the vanwagon and Lance is clearing out the freezer. I dumped our medicines and toilet things into a box and I'm checking off everything, and we'll take the Livermore route to avoid freewayitis. In case you haven't heard, Ernie says tell you somebody at Ames got word from Satellite Test Center at Lockheed: they're monitoring evacuation out of Leningrad and Moscow..."

Then we caught part of a McKay tradition in the background, young Lance throwing one of his patented tantrums. "... but he's not taking mine and he *knows* I gotta have it, he can fix it; I know it, Iknowitiknowit—" and then a slam of something. I knew it wasn't the impact of Shar's palm on Lance's butt; that was beyond reasonable hope.

My sis again: "Poor Lance, his bike is broken so he's been using Cammie's in spite of everything we've —well, Ernie isn't packing it so of course the child is broken up," she went on quickly, ending with a breezy, "Well, we'll cope. We always do. Oh! You said to be specific, so: we're taking Route Six-Eighty toward Livermore, then the old Morgan Road to your place. Don't worry, bubba, we should be at your place by three pee-em unless we have to fire the second-stage. Coming, hon," she called to someone, and then the line went dead.

"Poor Lance," I snarled, tossing my handset control and catching it instead of hurling it against a wall. "Little bastard beats the bejeezus out of his bike, too lazy to fix it, and now that he realizes why Ern nagged him to keep it in shape it's too late, so he takes his frustration out on everybody else. And why the fuck aren't you collecting water containers," I shot at Kate.

"Because the fuck," she said, sweetly enunciating it to extract its maximum gross-out potential, "I didn't relish being ordered around like a servant. What was all that stuff in the garage about peers, mister?"

I took two long breaths; stared at my reproduction of Bierstadt's *Rocky Mountains* near the stairwell for solace. "I believe

I said you're Spot's peer, Kate. Not a pet but a working part.
He keeps the place free of swagmen and rabbits, and if he
didn't, he wouldn't have any place here. I'll be as democratic
as I can—which means not very, when it's my place and I
know the drill and you don't, and since there has to be a leader
it is going to be the one who knows what must be done.

"That was my sister Shar, on tape. They're two hours late
and I don't like wondering why, and if you think I'm stuck
with you here, you should know that you are exactly one more
smart-ass refusal away from getting tossed over my cyclone
fence." My one office window gave me a veiw of Mount Diablo
and, reluctantly, I cranked its wire-reinforced outer panels
closed. I hated the thought of shoveling dirt against those panels,
since it would block off the only natural light into my basement.
But that was part of the original drill we'd worked out long
ago, after Shar inexplicably signed up for an urban survival
course at a community college.

I went back to the john and shut off the water, painfully
aware that I'd given the girl a galling choice; also aware that
I meant every word. When I glanced at her again she had aged
astonishingly, arms hanging loosely, no longer the pert rebel—
maybe ever again. "All right," she choked, and went up the
stairs. "You know I don't have any choice."

Following her, I said, "Neither do I. I hope you can be part
of the solution, Kate—and I can't afford you as part of my
problem. Cheer up, kid, maybe this is all just—"

"Please," she said, looking around her at my turn-of-the-
century kitchen, "just leave me alone. Please?" Then, spotting
the squat bulk of my cast-iron wood stove, she allowed a piece
of a chuckle to escape as she passed it. "Boy, you are really
weird—don't do that," she added suddenly.

I removed the hand I'd put on her shoulder, intending to
convey something—hope, camaraderie, understanding; hell, I
don't know what—but obviously I *didn't* understand her.
"Right," I mumbled, and sloped outside to get a shovel. Swinging up in a long arc from Travis AFB was one of our new
heavies under rocket boost. I heard several more while digging,
and while I didn't stop to watch them, I wondered what they
were up to. I don't wonder anymore.

Working up a fast sweat, I shoveled a ramp of turf against
my office window until it almost matched the slope of the
earthen ramp that surrounded the house about to the level of

the first floor. I tried not to tally the minutes by which Shar and Ern and the kids were overdue. The tally came unbidden, since it was nearly five pee-em, two hours past Shar's estimate.

Muted thunks and sloshes reached me as Kate filled my kitchenware with water. I was ruminating along the lines of, *Even if this false alarm costs a thousand lives, it may eventually save fifty million*, when a vast white light filled the sky, more pitiless than any summer noon, and did not fade for many seconds.

In my hurry, I hadn't followed my own drill; hadn't kept two radios tuned to different stations; and so I didn't hear the President's brief, self-serving spiel that called for crisis relo- cation and, by implication, admitted that we could expect a "limited" nuclear response to the tactical weapons we were unleashing on the wave of Soviet tanks that had lashed across the border into West Germany. "Crisis relocation" was an old weasel phrase for "evacuation;" our Office of Technology As- sessment and thinktanks like the Hudson Institute had solemnly agreed that Americans would have between twenty-four and seventy-two hours of warning before any crisis developed into a nuclear exchange.

Actually, from the moment our Navy engaged Russkis in the Aegean until the first wave of nuke-tipped MIRVs streaked up from Soviet hard sites, we'd had about fifteen hours. It might've been halfway adequate if we'd planned for it as So- viet-bloc countries had done—or even as one solitary local government had done in Lane County, Oregon.

Everybody joked about the jog-crazy, mist-maddened tokers around the University of Oregon in Eugene, so the media had its fun upon learning that city and county officials there were serious about evac—I mean, crisis relocation. Some poly sci professor, in a lecture about legal diversion of funds, pointed out that most federal funding for crisis relocation was turned over to emergency-services groups in sheriffs' departments. And that those funds—all over the country, not just in Ore- gon—were being diverted by perfectly legal means to other uses. The overall plan for a quarter-million people in the Eugene area was orderly movement to the touristy strip along the coast.

Then an undergrad checked out the routes and nervously reported that the wildest optimist wouldn't believe that many people could drive out of firestorm range in two days' time

through a bottleneck consisting of a solitary two-lane highway
and a pair of unimproved hold-your-breath gravel roads. County
maps showed several more old roads. They hadn't existed for
thirty years.

Firestorm in Eugene bloody *Orygun?* A strong possibility,
since the Southern Pacific's main switching yards in the coastal
Northwest sprawled out along the little city's outskirts. No
prime target, certainly, but all too likely as a secondary or
tertiary strike victim. In a county commission meeting, some
citizen asked, Why worry? We'll just get on the capacious
Interstate 5 freeway and drive south.

The hell you will, replied a state patrol official. We have
orders to keep that corridor clear for special traffic running
south from Portland and the state capital. There'll be riot guns
at the barricades; sorry 'bout that, but Eugeneans were scheduled to the coast and if they didn't like that, they could stay
home and watch the firestorm from inside it, har har.

When local politicos realized how many feisty folks in the
Eugene-Springfield area were clamoring for a solution, one of
them hit on a rationale that couldn't be faulted. Eugene could
be a target because the railroad had such tremendous load-
carrying capacity, right?

Right. And SP's rolling stock, flatcars for milled lumber
and boxcars slated for Portland and Seattle, often sat waiting
on sidings all over the place, right?

Right. And the SP had a branch railway straight to the coast
and a small yard for turnarounds only two hours away by slow
freight. A hastily assembled train could haul fifty thousand
people and all the survival gear each could lift from Eugene
in a single trip, then return for more.

And that was right, too. With public subscriptions helping
to fund their studies, SP troubleshooters found that they could
make up such a train in about twelve hours. They even tried
it once, billed as an outing for subscribers who'd paid SP to
do the groundwork, and though two drunks were injured falling
off a flatcar, it made a lighthearted tag end to the eleven o'clock
news across the nation. That had been two years ago.

Eugene's solitary preparations flashed through my head as,
groveling flat on my belly, shouting into the eerie silence and
seemingly endless flashbulb glare, I protected my eyes and
called to Kate to do the same. I'd always thought an enemy
would choose, as ground zero, the Alameda naval facility to

my west. Ern had said STC, the satellite control nexus south of me in Sunnyvale, would be the spot. Occasional news pieces had suggested Travis AFB, a reactivated base twenty-five miles north of me; or Hamilton AFB, thirty-five miles northeast.

And we were all absolutely correct. The ghastly efficiency of a MIRV lay in each big missile's handful of warheads, and each warhead could be aimed at a different target. Travis disappeared in a ground burst, perhaps to take out our bombers and deep-stored nukes there.. That was the deadly flower that blossomed first in hellish silence over the hills north of my place. The others were only moments behind.

When the light through my eyelids dwindled to something like normal afternoon brightness, I heaved myself up and pounded back into the house. On my way downstairs I saw my dining room wallpaper reflect another actinic dazzle from the windows, coming from the low airburst over Hamilton to our west. The fluorescents in my office below seemed pale for a moment. "Come on," I called, unable to find Kate. "Our best protection is in the tunnel!"

She rolled from beneath my desk; yelped, "Don't *do* that," as Spot darted ahead of her while *she* was darting ahead of *me*. I shut the big door, slapping the light plate to keep the tunnel lit, and sat down on the tough yielding linolamat.

"Spot, come," I said as his languid trot carried him toward the root cellar entrance. Another burst of energy lit the root cellar from the distant entrance, making Spot wheel back quickly.

"That's three," I said. But I was wrong, having missed the light show of Alameda's airburst. We were seeing cloud reflections of the ground-pounder that took out Sunnyvale, Palo Alto, and much of San José.

In a very small voice Kate said, "The air is bad in here," and slumped against the wall. Spot nuzzled her ear as I got down on one knee and propped her into a sitting position.

Her breath was quick and shallow, pulse racing but strong, and Spot wasn't sneezing or showing any of the discomfort he shows in foul air. She wasn't shocky cold either, and suddenly I realized she'd been hyperventilating—not the deliberate deep whiffs of a free diver but the slow oxygen starvation you could experience when quiet panic and rigid self-control made a battleground of your hindbrain. "Head between your knees, Kate," I murmured to her trembles. "Try breathing slowly; all the way out, then all the way in."

At that moment a sharp rumble whacked the house and my
ears, not very hard. But a softer rumble continued for what
seemed a full minute; the Travis shock wave and its retinue of
thunders. Spot's white-tipped tail flicked, his ears at half-mast.
He showed his teeth in a hiss at the doorjamb, which was
buzzing in sympathy with a vibration that shook the earth re-
morselessly.

When the second shock came it hit sharply, with a clatter
of my fine Bavarian china as obbligato upstairs.

The third jolt hit five seconds later, the one from Alameda.
A freak shock front raced through Concord, making lethal
Frisbees of every glass pane and marble false-front in town.
My western windows blew in and, with a pistol's report, one
of my sturdy old roof beams ended nearly a century of use-
fulness. My ears popped with a faint pressure change; popped
again. I could hear bricks falling from my chimney onto the
roof, sliding off, but couldn't at first identify the snap-crack
that came more and more rapidly until it became a guttural
rising groan. It had to be my handsome old water tower, though,
because that was what toppled near my kitchen, splintering
porch stairs as it struck.

My electric pump was probably whining furiously to refill
it, but I couldn't shut it off right then, thanks. The tank, strap-
bound like a wine cask, had held several hundred gallons of
water twenty feet in the air for gravity flow—probably the
only overloaded structure on my place.

Well, it was overloaded no longer. One of Ern's old NASA
bromides was that highly stressed structures have a way of
unstressing themselves for you—but wouldn't you really rather
do it yourself?

The last shock wave, from Sunnyvale near San José, was
almost negligible for us in the lee of Mount Diablo. I tried to
recall the crucial time sequences: the initial long flash that
distributed heat and hard radiation at the speed of light and
could have temporarily flash-blinded me if I'd had a line-of-
sight view of the initial moment; the shock waves, one through
the ground and a slower one through air that pulverized concrete
near ground zero; a momentary underpressure a moment later
near the blast that could suck lungs or houses apart; another
machwave that could flatten a forest or a skyscraper. Fires and
cave-ins were my most likely failure modes during those first
long moments. If we came through all that alive, *then* it was

time to worry about the fallout that could destroy live tissue through a brick wall.

Yet Shar's classroom work had taught us something vital, something most of the doomsday books ignored: *if you were twenty miles or so from ground zero, you got several hours of "king's X" between blast and fallout.*

My tunnel lights were still on, and we hadn't felt any suction after the blast waves. That suggested the nearest detonation had been many miles distant. According to Shar's texts, the fallout of deadly radioactive ash and grit moved upward into the stem of the mushroom cloud to an altitude of several miles within ten minutes, then more slowly upward and laterally with the wind. Usually the wind speed was fifteen to forty miles an hour. While it was cooling, the stuff fell heavily from the mushroom cloud, which, at first, moved laterally at great speed. But if you were directly beneath that initial cloud you would've already taken enough thermal and shock damage so that only a miracle or a deep, hermetically sealed hideyhole would've made it of any interest to you.

I didn't know where the blasts had occurred. If they had been more than fifteen miles away, I'd probably have a few hours in which to assess damage, fight fires, or pray before the slowly descending ashfall dropped several miles downward to begin frying everything it fell on.

Kate seemed to be improving. "We made it through the first round," I told her, huffing to my feet: "Now we've gotta make sure the place isn't burning up or falling down. You up to it?"

Her olive skin was sallow but, "We'll know if I keel over," she said, and let me help her up.

I led her back to my office, touched my liquor cabinet where I'd hidden the detent, swung back the bottle-laden shelf. I fingered the detent for her to see. "Just a simple pressure latch. Always keep it shut when you're not using what's in here. And never pick up anything you don't know how to use."

"Jesu bambino," she breathed, goggling at the tools of my trade: "I thought alcohol and firearms didn't mix. Is all that stuff legal?"

"Perfectly," I lied, and pointed out the few things she might need. "Malonitrile spray up here—better than Mace; the target pistol over here, the twenty-two longs for its magazine down there," I pointed among the ammo boxes. The extra sunglasses and thin leather gloves were self-explanatory. I'm always losing the damn things so I keep a dozen pairs of each on hand.

"What on earth is that thing in the middle, a cannon?"

"Near enough," I grunted, swinging the liquor shelf back. She'd seen my heavyweight, the sawed-off twelve-gauge auto shotgun with two pistol grips and a vertical magazine as thick as a two-by-four. That fat magazine held sixteen cartridges filled with double-ought buckshot, and the thoroughly illegal twelve-inch barrel fired a pattern that couldn't miss at ten yards. I could also hide it inside a coat front. Frankly, I didn't like the thing and had flashed it only once, at a man whose own emm-oh included concealable shotguns. He had just blinked and then had gone down on his face without a word. "That's one of the gadgets you *don't* want to pick up," I told her. "If you weigh under two hundred pounds it'll knock you on your can."

"I'll take your word for it." She put on her glasses and we went upstairs.

I first studied the kitchen ceiling and walls, which showed no cracks or wrinkles, and then bobbed my head up to window level for a fast glance outside, taking care with the splinters of glass on the floor. I saw nothing unusual, but the nearby hills impeded my view. "Sweep up this stuff before it dices us, will you?" I crunched my way into the spacious old dining room, mourning the shambles where window glass had speared into my glass-fronted china cabinet. The living room seemed undamaged and I saw no sign of danger through the intact multipaned north and east windows. The parlor windows had held, too. They revealed a sky innocent of intent to kill. I took the stairs two at a time to check on the second floor.

My first glance out the splinter-framed bathroom window upstairs made me duck by reflex action. Boiling into the stratosphere many miles north, an enormous dirty ball of cloud writhed on the skyline above my neighboring hilltops, showing streaks of red, like blood oozing out through crevices in burned fat. I risked another look; realized the target had been either the old mothball fleet anchored in Suisun Bay or Travis AFB, twice as far away. For all its agonized motion, the top of that cloud did not seem to be climbing very quickly, but from all reports it *had* to be. That meant it must be twenty miles or so away from us, and the prevailing winds were west to east. That hideous maelstrom of consumed rock and organic matter—

including ash that had been trees, homes, human flesh—would scatter downwind for hundreds of miles but might miss us entirely. Given a direction and approximate distance, I knew the target had been Travis.

In retrospect I keep juggling ideas about preparation and luck. The Travis bomb was a ground-pounder which vaporized a million tons of dirt and, irradiating it in the cloud stem, lifted it to be flung in a lethal plume beyond Sacramento into the Sierra. Bad luck for anyone in that plume, my good luck to be out of its path. Nor could I have affected some Russki decision to kill Hamilton AFB and Alameda with low airbursts, which started vast firestorms but scooped up relatively little debris to add to their fallout plumes. From my view, that was all luck.

Yet our understanding wasn't luck; it was the result of Shar's classwork and Ern's inside knowledge. I knew it was likely that a ground-pounder was more likely to be used against hardened targets: missile silos, underground munitions, control centers under concrete and bedrock. And I knew what else I needed to find out, such as the locations of those other detonations and the extent of the damage to my roof. I climbed the attic stairs, pushed the door aside, and let my flashbeam play across an immediate problem.

My central roof beam, a rough-sawn timber supported by A-frames, had buckled halfway between its slanting supports. No telling how soon it might completely collapse without a jury-rigged support, but I couldn't see light through the roof and wanted it to stay that way. An intact roof would keep fallout particles from drifting down into the attic—a little more distance between our heads and hard radiation. I had laid fiberglass batts between the attic joists for insulation, but it wasn't much protection against fallout; too fluffy and porous.

I called for Kate to accompany me and puffed out to the garage, pausing on the screen porch to snap the circuit breaker to my water pump. The garage and smithy hadn't come through unscathed. A pressure wave had slanted the clapboard west wall, taking the window out. I had two things in mind: checking for damage to the structure lest it fall on the Lotus, and collecting tools to dismantle the child's swing set I'd erected outside, years before, for Cammie and Lance. The tubular A-frame of the swing set were rusty but ideal for propping up that broken beam in my attic. Now a dozen other problems intervened, each clamoring for top priority.

I stopped and looked around, breathing hard. Some things Kate could do alone—I hoped. But she didn't know where I kept my tools, so I'd have to collect things. Rummaging for my necessaries, I explained. "Kate, in the root cellar are two rolls of clear polyethylene wrap, about knee-high, the kind of plastic you can unwrap and nail over broken windows. It may have a brand name on it—Visqueen, I think. One roll is two-mil—uh, too flimsy. Get the ten-mil stuff and haul it out here. It's eight feet wide when you unfold it. Cut a piece and stretch it across outside this broken window, and then do the same on all the house windows, upstairs and down, okay?"

She was already sprinting for the root cellar. I found the short, big-headed roofing nails and hammer, placed snips next to them, then snatched up penetrating oil, wrenches, and my other hammer and hauled my freight into the yard. I met Kate on the way, toting her milk-white roll of plastic film. I pointed to her tools and then attacked the swing set's rusty bolts with oil.

Kate looked into the sky—wishing, I supposed, for an umbrella. "Why not nail the plastic over the windows from the inside?" she asked.

"Makes a better seal on the outside," I hollered, more snappish than I intended. "You're trying to keep the wind from blowing tiny particles of radioactive ash indoors. If a breeze slaps a plastic sheet that's on the outside, it'll only make the edges hug tighter instead of bulging open between the nails."

I found it hard to explain one thing while doing another, and it made me clumsy. Naturally I ripped my sleeve while detaching the chains of the two little swings. It occurred to me that those sturdy chains could serve as guy wires if I drove nails into the links, so I piled the chains where I wouldn't forget. And forgot. One bolt hung up, and I was in the act of swinging the hammer when I recalled that if I put one little dent in the tube, most of its stiffness would be lost. I managed to ease the blow, and with that, the whole tubular framework squealed and collapsed, and I bundled the pieces so I could carry them over my shoulders.

Kate was spacing her nails only at the corners. "You need a nail head every six inches," I shouted.

"I've been thinking about the way people use this stuff on unfinished houses," she called back. "They nail strips of wood all the way around the edges."

She was right. "I don't have any furring strips," I began, then remembered. "Yes I do! Some old strips of wooden molding on the floor against the smithy wall. Break 'em up as you need 'em and go to it! If you need more, just—just use the hammer's claw and pull the molding loose in the rooms upstairs." That hurt; I'd mashed many a finger installing the stuff. I carried the tubing up to the attic, wondering how much of my place we'd have to cannibalize while securing its basement.

In my haste I'd removed bolts I hadn't needed to remove, wasting time instead of thinking it through. It was hot work in the attic without much light, and only when I'd reassembled the A-frames did I notice that they were too long by a foot. And I'd need those chains, and big twenty-penny nails to help anchor the tubular legs and the chains. What I needed most was another set of hands and a heaping dose of calm. I was starting to act suspiciously like a panic-stricken klutz.

Okay, so I might have to cut the ends of the tubes off. My list of hardware lengthened: swings with chains attached, hacksaw, nails, battery-powered lamp (my three-way emergency flasher from the Lotus would do), and stubs of two-by-four. If the steel A-frames simply didn't work, I might have to break into an upstairs interior wall for wooden supports. That meant I'd need a pry-bar and wood saw. Dashing downstairs and outside, I called to Kate: "Great; neater than I'd have done it!" She had woman-handled my telescoping ladder from the garage and was stretching a sheet of poly film across my kitchen window.

I dumped trash from a hefty cardboard box in the garage; placed nails, pry-bar, and saws inside; then simply swept an array of hand tools from their places over my workbench and added them to the load. I grabbed my flasher lamp from the Lotus and grinned in spite of everything as Spot plopped down in the passenger seat with a little falsetto yawp. It was his way of begging a ride. Poor fool cat, he was infected by all this hurry and could think of nothing more exciting than a nice little rip down the road. Which was the last thing in the world I intended to do. Or was it?

"Sorry, fella," I told him, returning with the box to get the chains. Kate was trying to lengthen the ladder, having finished with the broken first-floor windows. I parked my load on the screen porch and helped her.

"I'll have to steal that molding upstairs," she said, hoisting her shoulder bag by its sling. Bright girl: she'd dumped her bag and used it now to tote hammer and nails up the ladder. The scissors she was using to slit the plastic weren't mine; a matched set of stilettos so sharp she didn't need to snip with them. I wondered how near I'd been to getting them between my ribs earlier in the day, then thought again about her ability to fend for herself. Kate was street-smart; more so than my sis and her family.

"Kate, it's five thirty, roughly a half-hour since the bombs. More could hit any minute and you know where to take cover if they do. Judging by those clouds," I stabbed a finger to the west, then north, "we may have only a few hours before fine gritty ash starts falling here."

"Tell me later," she grunted with another fine leg show as she leaned out to my upstairs bathroom window.

"I may not be here later." She stopped, frowned down at me, her brows asking her question, so I answered it. "I intended to bring all my tools and stored fuel from the garage to the tunnel, but I can't do that and check on my sis, too. If I hadn't listened to Shar, I wouldn't be any better prepared for this than your average bozo. Her family is somewhere out there," I nodded at the southern skyline, "and you can see parts of the road from where I'm going. Believe me, I intend to be back soon, but I've got to do this. I've *got* to," I repeated as though arguing with somebody, which I was: my own sense of self-preservation. I started to give her more instructions but there would be no end to them, so I shut my trap and turned away toward the garage.

"It's only fair to tell you," she called after me. "When I lock myself up in that basement without you, it won't be with a full-grown cheetah."

A clutch of scenarios fled past me as I headed for the garage with Spot at my side. Each scene led to some innocent act on Kate's part that would cause Spot to show her a modest warning. Not that his threats are loud, as big cats go, but a raised ruff and an ears-back show of *his* front scissors will scare the piss out of a Doberman pinscher. Who would blame Kate for unlimbering my target pistol against him the instant his spinal ridge fur came erect?

For that matter, I wasn't sure how well Spot could accept a week of confinement, and I worried about that as I fired up the Lotus and eased it from the garage. I told Spot to stay, sizzled toward the closed gate, then shouted, "Spot: *come*," before engaging the fans to leap the fence. I was twenty yards ahead of him when I called out. Would you believe the lanky bugger beat my Cellular over an eight-foot fence?

It had been a silly stunt, I saw, as Spot's half-canine claws raked the paint of my rear deck. But I was only doing thirty-five at the moment—half-speed for him across open ground. Spot scrabbled into the seat and placed a forepaw against the dash, settling his chin onto the door sill, sniffing the air. I hurled the Lotus along an access path leading to the fire lane up the mountain.

Every few years a brush fire proved the wisdom of fire lanes, bulldozed paths along ridge tops that cleared away brush and grass as a barrier against wildfire. A four-wheel-drive vehicle or a ground-effects car like my Cellular could follow a fire lane all the way to the top, if you avoided the occasional boulder. And the new obstacles that I should've counted on, but hadn't. People.

For the first five minutes I had to dodge only a farmer and his cream-yellow Charolais cattle along the lower slopes. The man didn't even disfavor me with a glance. Whatever errand took me over his property, the responsibility for his dairy herd made him single-minded. I hoped he could keep them all under a roof for many days since (Shar had told me) cattle and dogs aren't as resistant to radiation as, say, swine and poultry.

Then a middle-aged man passed me on a scrambler bike at a suicidal pace, bounding down from the fire lane. Jesus, but he was good! The *burrrp* and *snarlll* of his engine vied with my Lotus for only a moment, making me realize how much noise I was making on my way up. Spot's senses beggared mine; the quick jerk of his head revealed a young fellow who was evidently prying debris from the drive chain of his bike. Then a girl Kate's age slithered and slewed downhill on a trail motorbike, hair flying, riding point for a half-dozen others who were taking their half of the fire lane right down the middle. I like to think it was a family making good on their preparations for urban disaster. I didn't enjoy taking evasive action, but I couldn't expect amateur bikers to maintain much control down such a grade.

The first lone hiker I spied was trying to blend into the

scrub, a biker's leather pack slung from one shoulder, his right hand thrust into it as he watched me pass. No doubt he'd heard me coming, and if he'd had more time, I suspect I'd have seen a handgun. Pure defense? A 'jacking? He probably couldn't have controlled the Lotus in ground-effects mode, but when a man's eyes are as wild as his were, you can't expect him to give a whole lot of thought to his actions. More bikers appeared on my skyline, bobbing toward me; then a few single hikers, all with small packs or none at all. I wondered why until I saw the logic of it.

On the other side of the ridge top lay the entire south and east Bay Areas, a series of forested ridges becoming rolling open meadows with farms and, in the valleys, bedroom communities: San Ramon, Danville, Dublin, Pleasanton. To the southwest stretched Oakland and other big population centers that would be feeding terrified throngs into the imagined safety of the hills. The vast nuclear hammer blows had struck forty minutes before—any people fleeing up the highland roads might've abandoned the roads when the great shocks came, especially those who were most highly mobile. And nothing but a baja-rigged sportscar was as mobile as a tough lightweight scrambler bike. No wonder the first wave of evacuees down the fire lane consisted almost wholly of bikers!

More bikers passed. One bike lay in the edge of the scrub, its front wheel fork ruined, and I guessed that the guy who was afoot with the saddlebag and the frightened eyes had abandoned it. Then Spot's attention drew mine to tiny figures that bobbed across open heights; people afoot who had abandoned the fire lane, perhaps fearful of the onrushing bikers. I saw a half-dozen of them in the next few minutes, one squatting over another who lay face-down. I couldn't tell if it was a mugging, but in my work you tend to infer the worst and I figured the rough stuff was only beginning among people who would need each other damned soon.

I topped out on the last ridge near state park property, staring down to locate the road from Livermore, then let my gaze sweep to the cities along San Francisco Bay. I said, "Oh— my— God."

Parking the car just off the fire lane, I made Spot stay as my sentry, retrieving the snub-nose little piece I kept clipped under the dash with its cutaway holster. Twenty miles away, where Oakland fronts the bay, was—had been—Alameda. Now the entire region, miles across, lay half-obscured under a gray pall like dirty fog. Winking through it were literally thousands of fires, some of them running together by now. Black plumes roiled up from oil storage dumps, and as I watched, a white star glared in the bay, hurling debris up and away in all directions. Even faster than the debris, flying away in what seemed a mathematically precise pattern, a ghostly shock wave expanded through the smoke, fading as it spread from its epicenter. In the paths of the debris, spidery white traceries of smoke fattened into a snowy mile-wide chrysanthemum that hid the source of that mighty blast. It looked like one of the old phosphorus shells from an earlier war, but an incredibly enormous one. I guessed it had been a shipload of munitions.

All the smoke over Oakland seemed drawn toward Alameda; in fact, sucked toward the broad foot of the smoke column we'd been taught to call a mushroom cloud. But this mushroom had a ring around it and several heads, the top one so unimaginably high that it seemed nearly above me. The mind-numbing quantity of energy released by that airburst had heated every square inch below it so that the very earth, like incandescent lava, heated the surrounding air and triggered leviathan updrafts that fed the stem of the cloud. I was watching a city consumed by fire, the updrafts creating winds that howled across skeletal buildings and fed flames that would rage until nothing burnable remained.

Nothing could live in or under that hellish heat unless far down in some airtight subbasement. Even after everything on the surface was consumed, the heat, baking down into the earth below fried macadam, would linger for many hours to slowly cook the juices from any organic tissue that might have somehow survived the first hour of firestorm. In a few hours there would not be a child—a tree root—an amoeba—living within miles of ground zero.

Far to the south another deadly column climbed through the stratosphere. Its shape was different, its pedestal and ring of smoke broader, with one well-defined globular head that was beginning to topple, so it seemed, eastward, blown by prevailing high-altitude winds. I wondered if any USAF personnel had bunkers in Sunnyvale deep enough to live through that ground-level wallop. The firestorm raging into San José was too distant for me to see flames, but the smoke suggested low-level winds blowing east to west toward Sunnyvale.

Nearer to me, some traffic moved, but for the most part the arterials were simply clotted into stagnation. A faint boom, horn bleats, and beneath it a soft whispering rumble told me of a million lethal scenes being played out below me against a backdrop of Armageddon. A pair of bikes *braapped* past me fifty yards off, and a dozen hikers labored up the slopes, reminding me of a crowd straggling away from the site of some vast sporting event after the fun was all over.

Short stretches of Morgan Road were visible from a promontory some distance away, and I turned to get my stubby 7-by-50 monocular from the glove box only to see a man in a half-crouch trading eye contact with Spot. He hadn't seen me. The man wore a business suit and expensive shoes and he was motionless except for his right hand, which was drawing a medium-caliber automatic, very slowly, from a hip pocket.

"I wouldn't," I said. He jerked his head around, saw me holding my little .38 in approved two-handed police stance, and wisely decided that he wouldn't, either. "Just put it back in your pocket, Jasper, and don't look back. I don't want to kill you—but I don't much want *not* to at the moment."

The handgun disappeared. He tried to smile but his sweat-streaked face wanted to cry instead. "Lotus and cheetah," he enumerated, licking dust-caked lips. "I know you. Can't recall the name, but word gets around. My name's Hollinger; I'm an attorney." And I will be damned if he didn't two-finger a little embossed card from his vest!

I ignored it, watching his hands as I moved to the car and fumbled for my gadgetry. "I haven't time to chat and neither do you, Mr. Hollinger." I waved him away with the revolver as I came up with the monocular, not wanting him near while I peered through it.

"Look, my car's two miles back, on the shoulder. No fuel. Cadillac. I'll sign it over to you for a lift to Santa Rosa."

I chuckled. "Tried to sandbag us, and now you want to plea-bargain. You're a lawyer, all right." I motioned him away.

He wasn't used to summary judgments. "The emerald in this ring is worth five big ones, buddy. It's yours for a lift. You won't get many offers this good."

"In two weeks there may be emeralds available for anybody who likes 'em. God Almighty couldn't get you to Santa Rosa right now; you waited too long. Put the fucking ring in your

pocket, stay off the fire lanes, and look for shelter in Antioch."
He crossed his arms, threw his head back, and inhaled. "Or I
can put you out of your misery right now because you're starting
to bug me," I finished, thumbing the hammer.

He turned and ran; limping, cursing, and sobbing, ignoring
my free advice. I scratched Spot between the ears as I watched
the man scramble down, and stuck my convincer away as a
fortyish couple approached. They were both rangy, with small
scruffy-looking packs, Aussie hats, and high-top hiking boots;
and the man saluted me casually as they passed. They didn't
seem panicky and their faces were weathered from many a day
in the open. They weren't breathing as hard as I was and I was
glad for them, hoping they could translate their readiness into
long-term survival. If only Shar and Ern had kept up their daily
two-mile runs—one of the many fads she'd badgered him into
during the past years—I'd have felt more confident about them.
Now, they were probably somewhere below me to the southwest, waiting for a road to unclog or pedaling their second-
stage vehicles, or maybe lying in a ditch with bullets in their
heads while some business-suited opportunist pedaled away
with their survival packs.

I knew my kinfolk; they'd all reach me together or not at
all. Scanning the road, I saw that something had blocked it in
one of the ravines beyond my view, for a solid line of traffic
formed a chain that wound for miles to the south, perhaps to
Livermore. Nothing larger than a big bike traversed the road
nearby, and for every citizen who headed for my ridge, twenty
kept to the roadway. I hoped they didn't expect too much when
they got to Concord, and hoped I was wrong about that, though
I wasn't. Singletons moved faster than groups, a moving pan-
oply of Americana. One old guy trundled a wheeled golf bag
along; not, I hoped, stuffed with putters. Most evacuees carried
something and most showed that they hadn't given their evacuation much thought until the last possible moment. When I
saw the man, woman, and two kids loping along my heart did
a samba stumble-beat, but it wasn't my family after all. I
guessed they were active in scouting because they walked fifty
paces, trotted fifty, then walked again. They were the only
group that overtook most singletons.

Maybe, I thought, I should drive along the ridge, stopping
to scan the road from time to time; in for a penny, in for a
pound. Then I glanced toward the Travis cloud and saw, slightly

to the north of west, the enormous dark thunderhead approaching from Hamilton AFB. It loomed higher than the evening cirrus, curling up and toward me from where San Rafael must have been. Its lower half hid behind the flank of the nearby mountain but it was obviously, lethally, a fallout-laden megacloud heading in my direction.

I might be in for a pound, but not for the full ton. I didn't know how long it would take the dust to fall forty thousand feet. Not long enough to let me backtrack to Livermore, for damn sure. Ern had brought me a fax copy of a manual that showed how to build an honest-to-God fallout meter, but I hadn't built the effing thing, and in any case it wasn't enough to know you were frying in radiation. You had to get away from it.

I stepped into the car again, sorrowing for all the people who, walking in the shadowed flank of Mount Diablo, could not see that they were moving straight into another shadow that could banish all their future sunshine forever. I started my engine before I saw the youngster hauling his trail-rigged moped upslope.

"If it's broken, leave it," I called to him.

"Just out of gas," he said with a grin, puffing. His moped was one of the good four-cycle, one-horse jobs that didn't need oil mixed with its fuel.

What I did then shamed me, but at least I didn't con the kid. "See that cloud?" I pointed toward the dull gray enormity curving toward us across the heavens. "Fallout. Those people won't know it until too late, unless you tell 'em."

"Me? Mister, my tongue is just about hanging down into my front wheel spokes." Impudence and good humor: I wanted to hug him.

"If you'll do it, I'll fill that little tank of yours. Get somebody to erect a sign or something. Tell 'em"—I glanced at my watch and swallowed hard—"that fallout will be raining down from San Rafael in a few hours. They must find shelter before then. Deal?"

He nodded. I got my spare coil of fuel hose from the tool compartment. One nice thing about an electric fuel pump is that you can quick-disconnect its output line and slip another hose on, then turn on the car's ignition and let it pump a stream of fuel from your fuel line to someone else's tank. The kid had his tank cap off in seconds and tried to stammer his thanks.

"I'm letting you take chances for me," I admitted. "It could cost you."

"My aunt in Walnut Creek has a deep basement," he replied. "With this refill I can stay on the road and get there in an hour." He was priming his little flitter as I reattached my fuel line. "Is that a real cheetah?"

"Yep, and a good one. I can never catch him cheating."

He laughed and bounced away, refitting his goggles, and didn't look back. Neither did I. If he didn't stop to warn others on the road below me, I didn't want to know. I also did not want to scan the carnage again that stretched across the dying megalopolis. I no longer felt anger; only profound pity for good honest people whose chief transgression lay in thirty years of refusal to prepare for a disaster so monstrous that no government could save them from it. I hadn't felt tears on my cheeks for years, but as I nosed the Lotus downhill toward my place, I decided these didn't count. They were mostly self-pity, in advance, for the loss of my little sis and her family. They were my family, too.

I didn't feel like shooing Spot out to lighten the car's load for another fence-jump. Besides, there was always the chance of a miscalculation, which could snag a tire and throw the Lotus off balance, and I was beginning to consider every screw-up in context of a total moratorium on medical help. So I toggled the automatic gate control. Nothing. Usually at this hour of lengthening shadow—it was past six—I could see distant lights from a few places up and down the road from my place. Not now. The power from Antioch had failed. It was a little late for me to wish I'd installed a wind-powered alternator or even an engine-driven rig. I hadn't.

I unlocked the gate using the manual combination, let Spot in, pushed the damn car through because it was such a chore to get my lardbutt in and out, then relocked the gate, wondering if Ern would recall that combination; wondered if he'd get the chance to. I saw honey-gold hair flying, the girl running to meet me as I scooted for the garage, and thought it was Kate until I remembered Kate's hair was black. Ern wouldn't have to remember any combination because the girl embracing Spot on the shadowed lawn was my niece, Camille!

She gave me a big smack as I left the car. "Scared the heh-heh-*hell* out of us, Uncle Harve," she scolded, starting to snif-fle, trying to get an arm all the way across my shoulders as we headed for the root cellar.

"Just taking a look around," I lied as Shar met me on the steps.

I got a quick tearful hug and kiss from my sis, whose dark Rackham hair was tied back from her round, attractively plumpish features. In response Shar had a faint upcurl at one corner of her mouth that tended to make a man check his fly for gaposis. In action she was a doer, an organizer; and I saw that the upcurl was now only part of a thin line. "Ernie and Lance are making a fallout meter in your office," she said and added darkly, "while your cutie-pie tapes around doors and windows upstairs. Harve, I thought you said we wouldn't turn the place into a public shelter."

"So everybody's here, and you've met Kate." I sighed my relief, letting my arms drop, realizing I was already tired and getting hungry. "Sis, we need to bring in everything movable from the garage and smithy storage and stack it in the tunnel."

"Done, thanks to your little flesh," Cammie cracked, and I needed a moment to translate her high-school jargon. She was linking me to Kate.

Before I could protest, Shar put in: "Your friend seemed ready to fight us off until Ernie told her who we were and proved he had your gate combination. That young lady runs a taut ship."

"She's led a rough life," I said and shrugged, then saw the welter of materials where Shar had been working in the root cellar. "What's all this?"

Shar's irritated headshake made her ponytail bounce. Like me, Shar inherited a tendency toward overweight. Unlike me, she had fought it to keep some vestige of a youthful figure, and diets were among her fads. They kept her bod merely on the *zoftig* side but also made her snappish and hyperactive. Now she was both. "I know you kept those outside cellar doors decrepit just for atmosphere," she said, bending in the gloom to choose a strip of plywood. "But they're no seal against fallout. If we intend to use the tunnel, someone has to stretch plastic film over these doors before we tape them shut. As they are now with all those cracks, they're hopeless. Just hopeless," she repeated with a sigh that richly expressed Why Mothers Got Gray.

My root cellar was so crowded with stuff from the garage that there was barely room for my sis to work. Obviously the whole bunch had arrived shortly after I'd left, because they'd done half a day's toting in half an hour. "You'll need light in here," I said in passing.

"You're in the way, Uncle Harve," said Cammie, and I saw that she was perched on her bike at the tunnel mouth. Ern had talked about rigging old-style bike stands, the kind that elevated the rear wheel and swiveled up like a wide rear bumper for riding; but he hadn't built them. Instead someone had taken two of my old folding chairs, put them back to back a foot apart, and strapped wooden sticks between them so that they formed a support frame to elevate the bike's rear wheel. As I stepped aside, Cammie began to pedal and the fist-size headlamp of her bike glowed, then dazzled, illuminating Shar's work. "Sonofabitch," I chortled. "Score one point for cottage industry."

The tiny DC generator on the rear wheel whined quietly, and I noticed that Cammie had removed the red lens from the puny little tail lamp. In the gathering dark of the tunnel, its glow wasn't all that puny. I trotted through the tunnel, every muscle protesting, feeling every ounce of my extra flab.

Soft creaks above me said that someone was hurrying between windows, taping around the edges to keep out the finest dust particles. Since I hadn't told Kate how to do it or showed her where I kept the inch-wide masking tape, I figured Shar had done it for me. The dozen rolls of tape in cool dark storage had been Shar's idea in the first place. I moved around the stone divider that defined my office to find my brother-in-law, his reading glasses halfway down his nose, his light blue eyes peering at the manual he'd left with me long before. His massive red-haired forearms were crossed on my desk top.

Ern McKay's calves and forearms had been designed for a larger man. In other physical details he was medium, with short carroty hair balding in front and stubby fingers that should've been clumsy. They were, in fact, so adroit that Ern made his living with them at Ames. Or had until this day. Ern saved all his clumsiness for social uses; he wasn't the demonstrative sort.

"Hi." He gave me his shy grin over the specs. "Heard you come in. Lance is upstairs looking for your fishing vest. That where you keep your two-pound filament?"

"As you bloody well know," I said, squeezing his shoulder lightly as I studied the pages before him. That was all the greeting either of us needed. Ern was the tyer of dry flies in the family, but I'm the one who got to use them. Two-pound-test monofilament nylon is very thin stuff, the kind I used for leader on scrappy little trout in Sierra streams.

Ern's stumpy forefinger indicated a passage in the manual. "Says here that thin mono is hard to work with though it's otherwise perfect for the electroscope." "

"I thought this was a fallout meter, Ern."

He turned his head, vented a two-grunt chuckle typical of his humor: underplayed. "You've had this damn manual five years and never read it once. Got half a mind to tell Shar on you."

"Christ, Ern, have a heart," I mumbled.

He held up the clean empty eight-ounce tin can from among other junk he had collected on my desk: adhesive bandage, razor blade, an oblong of thin aluminum foil, a bottle cork through which he'd forced a hefty needle. "Some guys doped this out years ago at Union Carbide; even got it published through Oak Ridge National Lab, including pages any newspaper could copy, free of charge! Any high school sophomore can build the thing from stuff lying around in the kitchen. If he can read," Ern qualified it.

I had assumed from the official-looking document number, ORNL-5040, that it wasn't kosher to copy it. Apparently the reverse was true, but I'd never read it carefully. The damned manual was in the public domain!

"Fellow named Kearny ramrodded several projects at Oak Ridge oriented toward nuke survival," Ern said, "and his team deserves top marks. The Kearny Fallout Meter is just a capacitor, a foil electroscope really, that's calibrated by the time it takes to lose its static charge after you feed that little charge to it. It loses that charge in an environment of ionizing radiation—the kind that makes fallout such a killer—and you can recharge it by rubbing a piece of plexiglass with paper to build up another charge."

"I understand only about half of what you just said," I complained.

"That's the point: you don't have to. Follow the instructions, learn to read the simple chart here, and you can use it *without* knowing why it works."

"Is it the kind of thing that only tells you when you're as good as dead? I mean, hell, Ern, it can't have much of a range of sensitivity."

"Take an F in guesswork. It works through four orders of magnitude," Ern replied, flipping pages to a sheet with a chart meant to be glued around that tin can. "From point-oh-three rems per hour—which is hardly worth worrying about—to *forty-three* rems per hour," he said with feeling.

"Which means kiss your ass good-bye," I hazarded.

"That's the layman's phrase," he harrumphed, subtly playing the quarrelsome scientist for me. "At NASA we say 'anus.' Ten rems at forty rems an hour and it's an even bet you won't live long."

"You're a little ray of sunshine."

"Just be glad," he said, tapping the pages, "that Kearny's elves realized nobody would buy expensive radiation counters until it was too late. They engineered this thing so well even you could build it for thirty cents—and why didn't you? And where the devil is Lance? I'm ready for that monofilament line."

"My fishing vest is in the screen porch closet," I said, and trotted upstairs. Only it wasn't in the closet. I called Lance.

From somewhere on the second floor came his muffled eleven-year-old tenor: "Come find me."

Sometimes Lance was eleven going on thirty, and sometimes going on seven. What rankled most was that he looked so much like I did at his age; beefy, shock of black hair, insolent button-black eyes under heavy brows. But mom hadn't spoiled me, hadn't let me hurl tantrums. I'd grown up with due respect for dad's belt. That was where Lance and I differed; my sis had figured her youngest for a genius since he began talking so much, so soon, and ruled against breaking his spirit. In that, at least, she'd succeeded. "We can play later, Lance," I called up. "Bring my fishing vest if you have it."

"I have it," his voice floated tantalizingly down the stairs. "Come find me."

Kate Gallo paused while tearing a strip of tape with her teeth; smiled at me. "Welcome back, boss." The evening light through the film-covered windows was a dusty pink, tinting the gloom in which she worked.

"Some boss," I said and bellowed, "Goddamnit, Lance, this is life and death!"

"I don't think you'll make much of an impression on that one," Kate murmured and continued working.

"Come fi-i-ind meee," quavered in the air.

So I climbed the stairs and found him in the closet of the guest bedroom his parents sometimes used. "You win," he chirruped and held up my many-pocketed, fish-scented old vest. Then, "You better watch out," he wailed.

My vest in one hand, Lance's belt and trouser back in my other, I carried him like a duffel bag to the window. Kate hadn't sealed it yet but had put the plastic over it outside. "You know why the sunset's so red, Lance?"

"Those smoky clouds. You're hurting my stummick."

"Those clouds are full of poison. The poison will be falling on us tonight and for a long time after. It'll kill us if we don't get ready, Lance. Your help could make the difference."

Sullen, short of breath with his belt impeding it: "Better put me down." Then as I did so, he folded his arms and faced me. "I think that's a lot of crap about clouds being poison. How come airplanes fly through 'em all the time?"

I waved him ahead of me down the stairs. "Haven't you paid any attention to what your folks told you about fallout?"

"Some. Mostly I have better things to do. That stuff is dull." I knew what his better things were; I'd found his caches of comics and kidporn. "Anyway, if any poison comes down, the roof'll stop it."

The roof! I pushed him aside and took the rest of the stairs fast, tossing my vest to Ern. "I'd completely forgot," I said to him, trying to recall where I'd stashed my tools. "The central roof beam buckled from concussion. We've got to shore it up, Ern. Could you finish that thing later?"

He tapped the little cork with the needle in it; only the tip of the needle was exposed. He'd made several tiny holes in the tin can that way, following the manual but using amateur model-builders' tricks to do a neater job. "Guess the roof is top priority," he mused, then arose and called into the tunnel. "Shar, when you're finished, will you and Cammie haul mattresses and bedding down here?"

"Another few minutes," Shar's voice echoed.

Cammie, faintly: "Isn't sealing the tunnel more important?"

"Yes," Ern and I chorused. Bedding or no bedding, the tunnel was the safest spot on my place. I'd had it dug with a backhoe as a deep, broad trench years before, a passageway from the old farmhouse to the root cellar. Then, by hand, I had dug a shoulder a foot wide and three feet deep on each side, running the length of the tunnel. Finally I laid cheap discarded railroad ties across that shoulder with a layer of heavy tar paper between the cross-tie roof and the dirt I shoveled onto it.

During one rainy season the tunnel had stood three inches deep in water, thanks to my incompetence. After that I dug a smaller, foot-deep trench along one side of the bottom of the tunnel, laying perforated plastic pipe in the hole with gravel around it before I installed a floor and wall paneling. The perforated pipe took ground water that percolated into the gravel. I had to dig another trench by hand around the old concrete foundation of the house so I could install more drainage pipe to carry ground water downhill from the tunnel and the house— but that kept the basement dryer, too. With that mod, my old place no longer had the dank, musty, moldy basement common to many old homes. I'd be lying if I claimed it was all done for nuclear survival, but my dry tunnel beneath cross ties and three feet of damp soil provided protection you could beat only in a mine shaft. According to Shar's texts, the tunnel had a fallout protection factor several times greater than the basement itself.

In Shar's jargon, the basement under my two-story house was rated at a PF of over 30; that is, over thirty times as much protection as you'd get walking around outside in shirt sleeves, which is no protection to speak of. The PF got better when I blocked off my one basement window with dirt; that's why I did it. It would've been better still had I thrown a ramp of earth up against the exposed concrete foundation, which was visible for a foot or so below the clapboard siding.

Shar estimated that with the window blocked off (and the long, hinged trapdoor lowered over the stairwell so that it became, in best farmhouse tradition, a segment of my kitchen floor), my basement could have a PF of nearly fifty. If fallout radiation got as high as a hundred rems per hour outside, it might be only two rems per hour in the basement.

Of course, two rems an hour weren't good for you. If you absorbed that much radiation steadily for a week, your body would get a total exposure of 336 rems during that time. Chances were one in three that you'd die in a month or so from such a dose.

The operative word there was "steadily": fallout particles radiate so much during the first day or so, they're only emitting ten percent as strongly seven hours after the blast; *one* percent as strongly after two days. After fifteen days that emission rate is only *one tenth of one percent* as much as it was during the first moments of that monstrous fireball.

That dwindling radiation rate was the rationale for staying put awhile—and for optimism. If radiation rose to deadly levels outside, we would experience only a small fraction of it in my basement. Sure, it was still dangerous. We might get sick; we might even contract cancer and die in a few years. In my book a few years beats hell out of a few days.

But Shar's hundred-rem-per-hour estimate had been wildly optimistic. As Ern chased me up to the attic, we had no idea that the particles slowly drifting down toward us from forty-thousand-foot altitude were from the very center of the Hamilton cloud, so ferociously lethal they should've glowed in the dark. They didn't, of course.

Stepping carefully to avoid fiberglass insulation, we still got it in our eyes and cussed it as we worked. Ern had a better understanding of structures than I did; he judged we could make a four-legged pyramid from the A-frame tubes. We used up ten minutes putting the A-frames in place with only my lamp to illuminate us, straddling the tube butts on joists and nailing stubs of two-by-four to keep the butt ends from skating away. Then I braced my legs, put my head and both forearms under the cracked roofbeam, and Ern helped me lift.

A pain like an electric shock banged alongside my spine. I'd half-expected it. Given plenty of time, Ern would've jacked the beam up by an old expedient: a sturdy vertical timber under the roof beam with overlapping hardwood wedges under the vertical piece. By driving the wedges toward each other with a hammer, a slender housewife could elevate that timber by the thickness of both wedges; several inches, in fact. Well, we didn't have the time. We did have a tall, heavy-boned idiot with an old back injury—me.

The joists groaned underfoot. Dust and splinters fell from the roof beam. With a great dry groan the center of the beam rose within an inch or so of horizontal. Ern, standing on different joists, panted, "Can you hold?"

"Do it," I grunted, and he rushed to lean the tops of the tubes into place, apexes nearly together under the roof beam.

"Let down easy," he said, holding the tops of the tubes in place. As I did, the tubes bit a half-inch up into the beam—a good thing, since they wanted to slip aside. Ern saw the problem, grabbed the hammer and nails, and drove nails into the beam so their protruding heads held the tube lips from moving. Then, "I still don't like it, but it'll do," he said, and I staggered back. "We should span the break with plywood and screws, Harve, but we don't have the time."

"What if we nailed chains across the bottom of the beam?"

He saw what I meant. If we stretched a chain across the bottom face of the beam, nailing through several links where the wood wasn't split, the beam couldn't sag again without snapping chain or very sturdy nails. "Smart," he agreed, and we did it in two minutes flat. Now he was happy. Ours was a stronger repair than a simple vertical post resting in the middle of a joist, since that lone joist might give way. I suggested that we clear out.

"Oh hell, we didn't block the attic vents," Ern said then as we collected our tools. The little screened vents weren't large, but a strong updraft under the eaves could sift dust into the attic. Ern saw me kneading the muscles near my kidney, told me to wait, and scrambled downstairs. He was back moments later with newspapers I had put in the bedrooms for atmosphere. The front pages were expensive fakes with historic headlines like FIRE RAVAGING SAN FRANCISCO—an appalling irony now— and LUSITANIA TORPEDOED. We thrust the paper, a dozen thicknesses at each vent, flat against the holes and nailed them in place. Then we abandoned the attic and taped the door edges.

Kate and Cammie were rechecking their tape job around upstairs window edges while Shar, with some help from Lance, wrestled mattresses downstairs to the basement. Ern and I shucked off our clothes in my old-fashioned second-floor bathroom and used perfectly clean water from the toilet tank to sponge-bathe, scrubbing off the itchy insulation as well as we could.

On our way downstairs for fresh clothes, Ern tried joking about the picture we made, two middle-aged naked guys scratching where it itched.

"I'll laugh tomorrow," I promised glumly.

Then while he retrieved a coverall he'd left at my place, Ern called to me. "Who's that outside?"

I paused with one foot in my size 46 jeans. "Beats me; we're all inside."

"Spot isn't," he rejoined.

"Why the hell isn't he," I stormed, and pounded out to the back porch while buttoning a long-sleeve shirt.

The back of my roof overhung the screen porch by three feet, but the faint breeze on my cheeks told me the place wouldn't be safe for long. We hadn't stretched film over the screen. Now I heard, from beyond my perimeter fence, a voice either female or falsetto. "Get down, Richard, *there's a lion in there!*"

This was followed by a male whoop and cries that faded into the distance. I called Spot and waited, peering into a rosy semi-darkness that obscured all but silhouettes of trees and skyline. The glow over the mass of mountain was red on rose. I wondered if fires would spread from Oakland to leap the fire lanes; to engulf us all before dawn. I wondered if I should've let those poor devils in. And I wondered if Spot was radioactive by now.

I finally got my dumb cheetah inside and made him understand that he was to stay in the tunnel. When I returned to my office and told Ern what I'd heard outside, I was too exhausted to ream anyone out for letting Spot roam loose. It was hard to believe that it was only eight o'clock.

Ern, who had to be more weary than I, sat with my battery lamp and sipped from a glass of my brandy as he trimmed rectangles of aluminum foil. "Another hour and I'll know if this one works," he said as I sat on the edge of my waterbed, twenty feet away in my unpartitioned sleeping area. Then he must've heard me grunt. "Hurt your back up there, didn't you?"

My old vertebra compression fracture was an enemy I had to live with. "Just a muscle spasm," I said, and eased myself onto the floor where I could lie flat on the carpet. Sometimes, by forcing myself to relax while lying full-length, I could feel the flutter-crunch of vertebrae unpopping in the small of my back. I closed my eyes. "We had room for those two out there, you know," I said softly.

"Two? It may have been twenty," he replied. "We made that decision a long time back."

"I know."

"When would we stop, Harve? How many could we take?"

I didn't answer. Ours was the classic crowded-lifeboat dilemma: how to decide when taking one more swimmer meant reducing the odds of the lucky occupants. My cop-out was accidental, but no less an avoidance. I fell asleep the instant those vertebrae unkinked.

• • •

I awoke to feel fingers massaging my scalp so I knew it was Cammie bending over me, speaking softly, urgently. ". . . to get up now. We can't carry you."

I peered into almost total darkness; came up on one elbow, flooded with the sudden awareness of where I was, and why. My forty-by-twenty-foot basement was lit by a single candle, its wick trimmed, that squatted on a low bookshelf in my lounging area. "I can walk," I protested, and saw Ern's bulk disappearing into my tunnel, dragging mattresses. "Whatthe-hell? Another bomb?"

"It's hot in here, Harve," called my sis, who was lugging a tub of water into the tunnel.

"I don't feel very—" I said, then realized what she meant. "Fallout?"

"Yes, and getting heavier," Cammie said. She hurried off to help carry things to the tunnel as I creaked upright.

My watch was still in the clothes I'd discarded. My digital clock didn't glow because the power was off, and if it hadn't been for that candle, that basement would've been dark as Satan's soul. I learned while blundering into people with books and boxes that I'd slept only three hours, but that little bit had done my back lots of good.

"Wish we could get that damn waterbed in here," Ern groused as I swung the tunnel door closed. He busied himself by passing armloads of books to Shar and Kate, who were restacking them on a bookshelf they'd scrounged from my office. Cammie was on her bike, pedaling to provide enough light for our needs. Lance was sitting on a mattress. And what the hell was I doing? Nothing useful. I didn't have to ask why they were making a barrier of books at the foot of the stairs in the root cellar; instead, I hurried back to the basement and lifted my entire small bookcase of *Britannicas,* hauling it through the tunnel to help create the book barrier.

If fallout was intense enough to warrant our moving into the tunnel, the radiation through the puny film-covered doors of my root cellar would be high at that end of the tunnel. Distance alone was some help. The right-angle turn into the tunnel helped, too. But thick, dense stacks of paper make an excellent barrier against ionizing radiation—and a shelf of books, Shar's texts claimed, was better than a steel-faced door. She had begun the book barrier directly in front of the root cellar steps and used scraps of lumber nailed across the wooden stairway framing to keep the rickety barrier from toppling.

I leaned against the bookcase to help Shar and watched as Ern rubbed an antique phonograph record against the fur rim of my old parka. The light in the tunnel was dim enough to reveal the blue crackles of static sparkling in the fur. "Ern, what the hell are you—oh," I subsided as he brought the record disc near a whiskery piece of wire that protruded from the top of the tin can in his other hand. He'd finished his fallout meter.

A small spark jumped to the wire. Ern snapped on my lamp, stared down at the tin can, which now had a clear plastic film cover through which the wire protruded. He moved the wire gently. He glanced at his wristwatch, gnawing his lip—and Ern chews that lip only in extremis.

He glared through the plastic cover into the tin can, holding it in the light as if daring it to do him wrong. After a minute he glanced up at me, and his smile was an act of bravery. "The manual tells you to charge the leaves of foil by rubbing a hunk of plexiglass with paper," he said, trying to sound unconcerned. "I remembered how old vinyl records sometimes took a hellacious static charge from wool or fur and stole one of your old LPs and—sure 'nough," he said and shrugged, squinting down into the can again, checking his watch.

I whispered it: "Don't kid me, Ern: how we doin'?"

His reading glasses gleamed as he muttered, "Lots better here." He pointed down into the tin can to show me. "Those little foil leaves are suspended by nylon monofilament. See the inked paper scale I pasted on the plastic top? You center the scale so its zero mark is exactly between the foil leaves, and then see how far out the bottom of each leaf is from zero." Anxiety infiltrated his low baritone. "No, don't lean so close; your eye must be one foot from the scale to give the right parallax—uh, anyway, after a little practice you can get it pretty close without a ruler."

Though I was older than Ern, my eyes haven't yet gone farsighted on me. I could see that the suspended leaves of foil stood slightly apart, defying gravity since their static charges made them repel each other. "I get a reading of two," I said.

He pulled the can back in a hurry, stared at it, glared at me. "Scare the living shit out of a feller," he grumbled. "Two millimeters for one leaf and nearly three on the other. That makes five, Harve. I started about four minutes ago with readings of seven and eight millimeters on the scale. Now"—he checked his watch and nodded—"I read it as two and three. So the bottom edges of the foil leaves have swung nearer by a total of ten millimeters in four minutes. Look at the paper chart on the side of the can."

I did, knowing Ern was *not* going to tell me how much radiation we were taking because he wanted me to do it myself. "Ten millimeters in four minutes: two rems. In four minutes?"

"Jesus, no! Two rems per *hour;* you read the dose rate in rems per hour, you nik-nik. Why didn't you build one of these years ago?"

"Because I'm an idiot," I concluded. "And you?"

"Built mine so long ago I forgot half the details. But Lance tore it up trying to get at the hunks of dessicant in the bottom of the can. He was only five. Thought it was candy." Ern tried to make it seem a clever ploy by a blameless child, but I knew his disappointment with Lance was marrow-deep even if he rarely showed it.

To realign the topic away from Lance I said, "Those little hunks of rocks in the bottom are dessicant? Where'd you get it?"

"Knocked a corner from a piece of wallboard under your stairwell," he confessed. "The crumbly stuff in wallboard is gypsum. Kate heated the little hunks inside a tin cup over a candle for a half-hour to make sure they were dry before I put 'em in. You can't afford moisture in this can, and dry gypsum is a dessicant—soaks up the water vapor from the air in the can. It's all in the manual."

I watched Shar and Kate finish their work, conscious of the close quarters and of the muffled echoes in the tunnel. Only Spot and Lance seemed capable of sleep. "Hey, a two-rem reading in here is pretty high, isn't it?"

Ern snorted. "Try it on your porch. For the first two hours I didn't notice the foil leaves relaxing. Then when I wasn't looking, they lost their charge in a hurry. When I charged 'em up again, they sagged by twelve millimeters in one minute flat, which is nearly ten rems an hour. Just to check, I took your lamp and wore your parka out to the porch with a handkerchief over my mouth, and tried to get a reading." His long single headshake was eloquent. "I could actually *see* the damn aluminum leaves wilting down, and the best spark I can make gives about a sixteen-millimeter reading to start with, and the static charge decayed to zilch, buddy—*zero*—in just a few seconds."

I stared at the chart pasted on his fallout meter. "That's completely off scale, Ern. Over fifty rems per hour on my porch! Any chance the meter is wrong?"

"Sure there's a chance. You feel like taking that chance?"

"Maybe some other time," I husked. "What do you think the dose rate would be for anyone out in the open?"

"If the protection factors we estimated are any guide, Harve," and now he was whispering, "they could be taking hundreds."

"And their chances after an hour or so—"

"No chance, buddy. Maybe a ghost of one if they got to shelter right after that. But they'd probably be the walking dead, and not walking for long."

I glanced at that steel-faced door, then down the tunnel as Shar moved toward us. "I'm wondering if we'd get a different reading right up against that door, or by the book barrier," I said.

"What could we do about it?"

"If there's a radiation gradient along the tunnel, we could stay in the safest part of it."

"I'm getting stupid with exhaustion," Ern admitted. "You're right." He started past Shar; kissed her forehead.

She was too preoccupied to respond. "All right, girls," she said, "now we must lie down and relax. There's only so much air in here, and the less we exercise, the less we foul the air." Kate had a snippish reply on her face but glanced at me, shrugged, and chose a mattress.

"Until we get our flashlights it's gonna be dark, mom," said Cammie, and slowed her pedaling to prove it.

"Your father has Harve's lamp," my sis replied, and saw Ern nod in confirmation. Moments later the only source of light was my lamp, which Ern conserved as much as possible. The women settled quietly among blankets they didn't really need, and I sat almost as quietly, avoiding exertion.

Ern took readings at the book barrier, then backtracked down the tunnel to the basement door. It took him quite a while because the longer he waited for a reading, the more accurate it was. When he finished at the basement door, I was nearly asleep on the mattress I shared with Kate, who was snoring gently, and no wonder.

He walked to us, roughly midway down the tunnel, and switched off the lamp as he sat next to Shar. "Looks like we did something right by sheerest intuition. Hon? Harve? You awake?"

My sis and I acknowledged it.

Softly he asked, "You awake, Kate?" Silence, if you discounted the mezzo-soprano of her snores. "Cammie?" No answer. "Lance?" No answer. "Okay, team, it's midnight; time for a progress report."

In his travels down the tunnel, Ern had also made sure our food and water were not only present but out of the way. The root cellar was a jumble that we would have to straighten out, because we might be living in these cramped quarters for quite a while.

Near the steel-faced door, he said, the reading was roughly three rems per hour. At the book barrier it was over four. At the midpoint of the tunnel it was only two, maybe a shade less. Without any question, my half-assed root-cellar-door arrangement could have killed us all—might still be killing us, depending on how much dust might get through the sealing job Shar had done with such desperate speed. "The good news is, the radiation level must be dropping," he reminded us. "At least it *should* be. We'll know for sure in an hour or so." He stopped, listening. Rain drummed against the plastic that covered the root cellar doors, reminding me of a stampede of small animals. Those drops must've been as big as marbles. To my relief, it didn't last long.

"I wonder how fast we're using up the air in here," Shar muttered in the darkness. "Harve, how many cubic feet of air are in the tunnel?"

I made a rough calculation. Seven feet high, four and a half wide, sixty from end to end, plus the volume of the root cellar itself. "Maybe two thousand," I said.

"Not enough," she said with a catch in her voice. "Not even half enough. We're exhaling carbon dioxide into it, fouling what we have, and we need three or four hundred cubic feet an hour *each*. I'm trying not to panic, but if we fall asleep now, it's possible we'd never wake up."

I could hear their movements and imagined Ern trying, in his diffident way, to comfort my sis. Finally he said, "So we pump fresh air in here somehow."

"My hand-cranked blower in the smithy might do it," I said.

"It might as well be at the North Pole," he rejoined. "It'd take you an hour to detach it and bring it back. You'd be dead in a few days, so forget it. Hold on: your forced-draft furnace blower in the basement has a filter, doesn't it?"

Not much use, I said, when the power was off.

"But we could tap into the air source if we had an air pump. Look, team, I'm having a brainstorm. If we can locate a big sturdy cardboard box, I think I could build a bellows pump with it. A bellows will suck air through a filter better than a squirrel-cage blower does."

Shar said, "It's dangerous, hon. Who's going to stand in the basement and pump it all night?"

But Ern was already up, groaning with fatigue, the lamp shining toward the disorder of the root cellar. "We can run a pipe from the filter box to the tunnel and pump from in here," he insisted, starting to rummage between the bikes. "If either of you has a better idea or can figure where we'll get—um—thirty feet of pipe as wide as your fist, let me know. We need it for an air conduit."

My modern forced-air furnace system sat under the stairs in the basement, linked to sheet-metal conduits. I had no pipe and no ideas. For a long moment I considered just relaxing, taking my chances. Which weren't good, and I'd be whittling away at the chances of three young sleepers and Spot as well. I grunted to my feet and followed Shar, who'd already had a lifesaving idea.

Ern chose a corrugated carton big as a two-drawer file cabinet and worked without visible blueprints. He thought Shar's pipe might be too flimsy but had no better answer, and I helped her when I saw what my sis had in mind. Shar just took a stack of old newspaper and started rolling tubes, each tube made from a dozen sheets. I taped the seams. Ern suggested we cover the paper tubes with latex paint to seal the pores in the paper, then countermanded his own idea; it'd take too long to dry. Instead we unrolled my thin two-mil roll of plastic film and sheathed each paper tube with it, taped on the seam. The first two were pretty sorry specimens, wrinkled and repaired with too much tape, but we got better at it. By the time I noticed the muggy, oppressive atmosphere, Shar and I had finished over a dozen knee-high lengths of air pipe made from newsprint.

Ern muttered, "We're going to have to open that basement door soon." Sweat stood on his face. He was breathing a bit too quickly, and so was I. "Shar, you remember how to read the fallout meter from the one I built before?"

She did, but didn't know how to charge it up. I said I'd show her. It was necessary to align that protruding wire with the foil leaves, then move the wire away again after its spark charged the foil. We crowded near my lamp—all hail to the guy who invented rechargeable dry cells—and after a few tries we got it right.

"I'm still getting three rems an hour here in the root cellar," she announced softly after timing it with her watch, then fumbled in the bag strapped to her bike. She withdrew a two-cell flashlight, reminding me that those little second-stage evacuation kits contained everything from raisins to razor blades. I still had no idea what problems they'd had getting to my place—but there'd be plenty of time for those stories in the next week. Assuming we lived that long. Judging from the way our bodies were laboring in that clammy air, I couldn't assume we'd pull through.

Shar went into the basement and closed the door again to take fresh readings; not that we had much choice about them. We would have to go in there and punch into my sheet-metal furnace filter box and insert the air pipe whether we liked the readings or not. Meanwhile I held a heavy polyfilm trapezoid in place while Ern double-taped it onto the big cardboard box.

The box was now cut away so it had a steep wedge shape in side view, with thick polyfilm replacing the trapezoid of cardboard he had cut away. He had cut two holes through the rectangular back of the box, cut a thin-walled mailing tube into two shorter pieces, and taped them firmly into the holes. As we taped polyfilm on, I could see through it into the box. A hastily cut rectangle of cardboard was taped over the mouth of one segment of mailing tube, but only at the top so that the rectangle could flap loose. "You didn't find any more mailing tubes, did you?" I asked.

"Nope. Wish I had. The partial vacuum when I lift this bellows will probably collapse Shar's air pipe—no it won't, either!" He put down the big box and upended another smaller cardboard carton, letting food cans spill onto shelves in the root cellar. "Harve, you cut this box into strips, maybe three inches wide—just so they'll slip into the airpipe. We'll need twice as many inches of cardboard strip as we have of pipe."

I grabbed tin snips, a shitty tool but better than nothing,

and began cutting without knowing what Ern had in mind. I saw, though, while cutting the third strip. Ern grabbed the two I had cut, used his keen-edged pocketknife to cut slits length-wise halfway down the center of each, then forced the slit wider by prying and reversed one strip so the mouths of the slits matched. Then he merely shoved them together so that, seen from the end, the two strips had an X shape. "There, damnit, shove that down the air pipe and it won't collapse." It was good to hear the satisfaction in his tone. It said he wasn't licked yet.

Shar returned with guarded optimism as Ern attacked his project again. He was making a handle from the folded widths of cardboard but looked up expectantly. "What reading did you get in the basement, honey?"

"About fifteen rems an hour at the desk."

"That's a shade less than I got."

"Funny thing, though: I get about eight at the stairwell, and the same at the other end of the room near the waterbed."

We considered this in silence. Shar cooed in delight when she saw how my cardboard strips stiffened her air pipes and began assembling the things as I cut them. Then, "Hon, you're stumbling like a wino," she warned Ern. "And my headache is definitely worse."

Without a word he lifted his bellows pump, tape, and tools; staggered down the tunnel; managed to get the door open. We were gradually asphyxiating in the root cellar's stagnant air, and it wasn't much past midnight.

I grabbed a double armload of air pipe and caromed off the paneling en route to the basement, leaving Shar to bring what I'd left. Ern helped me to the stairwell. Though I was dizzy, I had no headache and said as much.

Ern, breathing deeply in the basement, located the filter intake box of my furnace system and selected the large blade of his bulky Swiss pocketknife, then jabbed hard into the bottom face of the thin sheet-metal box. Using the heel of his hand to hammer the blade in, he glanced at me. "Foul air doesn't affect everyone the same, Harve. Tell me: what's twelve times eleven?"

I blinked, swayed. "Uh—look it up," I said.

"Headache or not, you're rocky. Just keep breathin', and bring the kids to the basement doorway. I can do this without you."

I grabbed mattresses and pulled them, kids and all, toward

the basement. I was already recuperating enough to wonder how long the basement air would last when we were sealed in. If only we had a column of clean air to draw from—*the chimney!*

Spot was awake and curious. I settled him with a pat and a "stay," and hurried to where Ern was folding thin metal tabs back on the underside of my furnace air intake box. "I know why the fallout's worse near my desk, Ern," I said, not wanting to say it. "We should've blocked the chimney at the top while we could still get to it."

Shar, holding a segment of air pipe ready, frowned and then understood. "Of course! The dust box at the foot of the chimney is right outside the foundation near your desk. A little fallout is dropping straight down the chimney. It can't be much."

"Enough, though," Ern grunted. "Nothing we can do about it right now except stay away from that part of the basement. Here, hon; try it now."

She thrust the air pipe past the bent tabs; let Ern tape it in place. She said, "Let's hope the furnace filter's a good one."

It wasn't, but we wouldn't learn that for another fifteen minutes.

Our primitive air pipe looked like hell, but lying along the floor from stairwell to tunnel entrance, it looked like salvation, too. Ern finished taping a square of cardboard over the outside "exhaust" piece of mailing tube protruding from the pump and lifted the handle atop the bellows.

The whole thing tried to lift. "Wedge it down for me," he said and pulled again. The box heaved a might sigh as its top came up, the polyfilm unwrinkling at its full extension, and then Ern pushed down. I heard a *clack* inside the bellows— that cardboard flapper operating, the simplest kind of valve you can make.

But more important, a solid *whooosh* emerged from the exhaust tube, its flapper flying up until Ern started another intake cycle. He kept lifting and shoving for a minute or more, and squatting there in the tunnel, we could not mistake the change in the air quality.

Ern saw the tears of relief in Shar's eyes. "Hon, get something to wedge this bellows box in place; takes more force to lift it than I thought, but it's farting nearly two cubic feet of fresh air every time it cycles. Where are you going, Harve?"

"Not far, that's for sure," I said instead of telling him. I wanted to use the fallout meter to be sure the air was free of fallout.

It wasn't as easy to get a static charge transferred to the foil leaves as it looked. When I touched the uninsulated end of the charging wire, the foil lost some of its charge. I tried again, and after several fumble-fingered tries I had the foil-leaf capacitor properly charged up.

All these goddamn details! They were driving me around the bend. But my brother-in-law had known details that let him build a high-volume bellows pump from scratch, and in an hour. My flibbertigibbet sis had saved my very considerable bacon with air pipes made from fucking *news*paper, of all things. But I knew some details I didn't like.

Item: I hadn't changed that furnace filter in a year.
Item: The furnace filter drew air from a standpipe buried in the wall, which poked up through my roof.
Item: Ern's bellows pump sucked so hard you could see the air pipes flexing, even with the cruciform stiffeners inside them. Would it also suck fallout particles in *sideways* under the raincap on my roof?
Item: If it did, would the dirty furnace filter trap them?

I found out a few minutes later, eyeing the fallout meter in front of the bellows exhaust. "Stop the damn pump, Ern," I said.

He'd worked up a sweat. "Gladly. You want to take a turn?"

"No. The meter is reading over thirty rems an hour. We're sucking fallout in past the filter."

"Oh dear God," Shar moaned, and covered the sleeping body of Lance with her own.

In the glow of Shar's flashlight I took another reading just inside the tunnel, aware of Ern's eyes on me and of our mutual exhaustion. From many nights of stakeouts, waiting for some bail jumper to poke his nose up, I knew you felt most like cashing it all in when your body was at its lowest ebb. "Twelve rems now, maybe just residual from what we pulled in through the filter," I said, as chipper as possible. I went to the door, fanned it back and forth a few times, then saw the obvious and untaped the air pipe halfway across the floor. "This damn

basement must have six or seven thousand cubic feet of air,"
I growled. "Try pumping again."

Shar saw her husband trying to rise and pushed him back;
knelt at the bellows as if venerating it—and why not?—then
cycled it slowly. Noting with regret that the old LP record Ern
had chosen to generate a static charge was my rare old ten-
inch Tom Lehrer album, I recharged the meter again and waited
a long time to get my reading. We were too tired to cheer when
I concluded that we were taking only two or three rems an hour
lying in the tunnel, its door open only enough to admit the
airpipe, drawing air from the basement.

I flicked the flashlight off. "We just may make it through,"
I said.

Ern, almost dreamily: "I've been thinking. The dose we
take is cumulative, but that fallout couldn't have reached us
much before eleven or so. Maybe we took ten rems before we
got to the tunnel, but we haven't taken over a few more in
here. Then another five or so in the basement, another couple
while pumping shit through your lousy furnace filter—I'm
sorry, Harve, and anyway it was my own idea—and I come
up with a grand total of less than twenty rems. We have a
fighting chance to pull through."

"Unless we run out of air," I reminded him.

"Bubba," panted Shar in the darkness near me, "I am going
to—pull every single hair—out of your body." Thirty-five
years before, that had been her darkest threat to a brother twice
her size. I started to chuckle and heard Ern's soft laugh warming
me, and we squeezed that moment of merriment dry.

Sometime after one A.M. I took over the pumping chores.
We hadn't set up any official sequence, but when a cautious
whisk of the flashlight beam told me Shar and Ern were both
asleep, I decided they needed it. I pumped the bellows every
ten seconds and rested in between, and figured after four hundred
cycles that an hour had passed. Then I roused Kate, calmed
her sudden outbreak of fear; told her we were going to make
it if she would do three hundred slow pumps of this bizarre
gadget before waking Cammie to take her place.

"And who does Cammie wake?"

"Me," I said.

After a moment's thought in the blackness she said, "That
won't do, boss. If anybody plays the sacrificial lamb now, we
can all be sorry later. And," she said teasingly but with damning

accuracy, "you're the one dude in this menagerie that nobody can lift if he collapses. Now we'll try it again: Cammie wakes who?"

"Her old man," I said, and laid my hand on her shoulder before I thought about it.

I think she said, "Thanks," but I was already drifting away to Lilliput, where, according to my synapses, evil homunculi amused themselves by driving pickaxes between my vertebrae for the next few hours.

II: Doomsday Plus One

Around six in the morning my sis roused me. Thanks to the work I chose, when awakened by rough handling I tended to come up with elbow sweeps. Of all those dear to me, only Cammie had intuited that a gentle scalp massage defused the reflex that had soured some relationships with ladies over the years. Shar just squatted near my feet and tugged at my trouser legs until I sat up and said something akin to, "Who'sit?"

"Shar, bubba; can you take over at the pump?"

With my mental cobwebs torn asunder I reckoned that I could, and asked about the radiation level. She lent me her wristwatch; told me it now took four minutes to get a decent reading, which was roughly one rem on the chart.

As I took the little flashlight and sat down before Ern's pump, I noticed that my plastic film was now taped down the slit where the basement door stood open enough to admit the air pipe. I played the flashbeam up and down the new mod. "Trouble, sis?"

"Huh? Oh; no, Ern did it, thinking we could raise the air pressure in here by a smidgin and gradually flush the foul air out past holes in those *des*picable doors above the root cellar."

"Shouldn't be any holes," I said.

"Maybe; but when you pump, you can see the plastic bulge at the doorway, and Ern says the root-cellar air smelled okay to him just before he waked me. Spot was sniffing around in there a few minutes ago. Would he advance into foul air? Well, you two argue about it later, Harve; I'm simply dead." And she curled up and proved it.

I began the hour by worrying about falling asleep but found enough worries to keep me awake. My back still ached; I resented the fact that Lance weighed almost as much as Kate

56

but couldn't be trusted to man the pump; realized that Spot was freeloading in the same way and worried about justifying his presence. Finally I thought about the frozen horsemeat in Spot's automatic feeder in a corner of the root cellar and realized that all my frozen food upstairs would soon be at room temperature; and how the goddamn, et cetera, hell could we avoid all that spoilage?

For one thing, we could avoid opening a freezer door until the moment we needed something. Maybe tape polyfilm over the opening when we opened it, cut a hand-size slit, and minimize the heat transfer every time we opened that compartment.

Spot's feeder could be manually triggered without opening its horsemeat compartment—and it contained thirty pounds or so of ground dobbin in one-pound discs. The stuff might stay frozen three days if we didn't open the top, and by then we might be ready to eat horsemeat. The feeder's defrost coil, of course, no longer would warm the disc. We'd have to cook it somehow, and Spot could damn well eat farina mix.

He could also stink the place up until we were ready to embrace a fallout cloud, or to shoo him outside, which was obviously the more logical answer. I didn't smell cat shit until, halfway through my stint, I toured the tunnel and got to the root cellar. Like most cats, Spot had fastidious ideas about taking his dumps. In the flashbeam I saw clawmarks where he'd tried to get around the book barrier. But it was intact; he hadn't forced the issue. My nose told me he'd done his doo-dahs somewhere near instead, and since I hadn't spread lino-lamat under the cellar shelves, it was still packed dirt.

So why couldn't cheetahs defecate like other cats and cover it up? They don't. They're choosy, yes—but they choose high places.

So voilà, and damn, and cat shit at the back of the top shelf a yard from the ancient timbered ceiling. I scooped it onto a hunk of plastic film, folded the fair-size bilivit neatly, and left it nearby.

Back at the pump, doubling the cycle rate to make up for lost time, I thought some more about elimination. Cats weren't the only folks who shat. People who underrate that function as one of life's little pleasures should do without it, and without sex, for a week—and see which one they crave the more. I'd heard that homey observation as a kid and still couldn't fault it. We would have to solve another problem soon.

The best answer was *not* my basement john; it required several gallons of water per flush. My waterbed, the one thing after my tunnel that Shar had praised most as nuclear survival advantage, was as outsize as I was: six feet by seven, eight inches thick. Twenty-eight cubic feet of water was roughly two hundred and thirty gallons.

I reflected on the evenings when we'd sat by my fire upstairs and toyed with the ghastly math of obliteration, comfy and cheerful with our beer and popcorn—Ern's version, corn popped in olive oil and spiced with garlic and oregano. Armed with her texts, my sis knew a lot of disquieting facts. Water, for one: locked in a basement, we might consume nearly a gallon a day each, plus what we cooked with. Plus what we washed in, and that might be a lot. If we needed to decontaminate ourselves after a foray outdoors, we would each use eight or ten gallons per wash. Discounting Spot, the six of us could empty my waterbed in a few days if we weren't careful.

We didn't expect to emerge from the basement in less than a week or so.

There simply wouldn't be enough water for niceties; we would have to skimp. And I hadn't even figured on the water needed to flush the Thomas Crapper. Ern had said once that a portapotty was a simple rig. I hoped he hadn't forgotten his mental blueprint.

Urination was no real problem if we were willing to do it in my basement john, because you can pee endlessly into a toilet bowl and it will maintain its fluid level. But as I roused Kate again to take her place at the pump, I felt a familiar abdominal urge. I denied it and let sleep return, knowing that in a few hours we would have to face a problem in, ah, solid-waste management.

It must've been the shock that woke me, about nine-thirty in the morning; whacked me right through the mattress. I sat up, hearing familiar voices under stress in the near distance, peering through the open basement door toward faint illumination. Kate lay at my side, and I managed to get up without waking her. From what I gathered, Master Lance had innocently made use of my toilet before anybody discussed it with him.

With all my muscles tight from the previous day, I still felt vaguely humanoid. In my lounge area Cammie was setting up a cold breakfast. "The kid didn't know," I called as I shambled my way to the candlelit area. "And it's the day after doomsday, and we're still vertical, team."

Ern came out of my john with a "why me" look, asking if I had felt an earth tremor. He added, "Sharp jolt, not the usual shuddery shakes we get in the Bay Area."

"A quake," Kate said and yawned, standing in the doorway. "Goody, just what we need now."

Shar, after explaining the facts of water conservation to Lance, exited my john and went straight to my coffee table to criticize Cammie's choice of food. "Pineapple juice and stewed tomatoes for breakfast?" She lifted her hands in helplessness.

"That's what Uncle Harve had the most of. I thought these big quart-and-a-half cans would be about right for a meal."

Then the second shock hit, the sonic clap that set crockery and nerves ajangle and, judging from the sound of it, blew out one of my windows. "God*damn,*" I said.

Lance, jaw stuck out in defiance, voiced for all of us as he latched his belt: "They better not be atom-bombing us again."

Ern: "Roughly two minutes between ground shock and air shock; thirty miles or so. But in which direction?"

Everybody had frozen in place. Into this still-life Shar said, "If it's south, we may be okay. In any case, we have several hours. The radiation reading in the bathroom is about four rems, but Lord knows what it will be later if that *was* another bomb."

"I suggest we all, uh, tinkle in the john and hold our heavy stuff until we get a portable rig fixed," Ern said as Cammie started toward my john. To me, he said, "We can't keep drawing air from the basement forever, Harve. Got to make a decent filter."

"I don't suppose the Lotus air-intake filter would do."

After a moment, half-listening to Shar arrange a repair party to the upstairs window: "No—but its twelve-volt battery would sure boost the tunnel lights without making us sweat for it. And you just gave me an idea," he added, grabbing up the empty pineapple juice can. "How long would you need to get the battery?"

"Five minutes. It's no biggie, and I know the drill."

"Wear your stream waders, raincoat, hat, gloves, and a scarf to breathe through. Near as I can figure, Harve, there's still a hundred and fifty rems an hour firing away at anybody outside."

I dressed for my mission, dreading it. I would absorb another ten rems in five minutes—maybe less in the garage, if I used the scarf to breathe through and buttoned my rain slicker. The women had already gone upstairs, leaving the trapdoor open so that a gloomy light flooded the basement.

Ern glanced at me at the stairwell. "You're early for Halloween, fella, but that's a great costume."

"Screw you, fumble-fingers," I chortled. In those hip-length rubber waders, with gloves and my wide-brim rain hat as accessories to my slicker, I felt clumsy and absurd; almost as absurd as my brother-in-law, who stood studying a juice can in one hand and a roll of toilet paper in the other.

I stumped upstairs, unsealed the kitchen door, shut it after me, and while crossing the screen porch to the back door, I learned to step lively without scuffing. A thin patina of dust lay on the porch, stuff that had passed through the screen during the night, and I didn't want to breathe it.

The sun's glow on the east ridge fought its way through a grayish yellow haze as I crossed the yard, and I wished I'd dug the tunnel all the way to the garage. A few tiny visible gray flecks drifted down, dislodged from my staunch old sycamores by wisps of breeze, and I tugged the scarf up over my eyes. I had forgotten my sunglasses but could see dimly through the scarf, and I kept an old pair of racing goggles in the Lotus.

Before filching the battery, I tried the Lotus phone, hoping to learn whether we'd been bombed again, feeling sure we had. I couldn't even punch a prefix without a busy signal. Well, what had I expected? In an urban disaster public two-way communication channels are among the surest casualties.

Pliers and screwdrivers are vicious tools, but in ninety seconds I'd used them to wrest the battery terminals loose while trying to identify a putrid odor nearby. I pried the battery up, fearful of the faint dust coat on the car and floor. Then I eased the hood down, lifted the heavy battery, and hurried to get those goggles from the glove box, pausing long enough to pop the glove-box lamp—socket and all—from its niche. Given time, I could've pocketed a dozen twelve-volt bulbs from the car, some with sockets intact.

But I didn't get that time. What I got was a silent thunderclap of emotional shock as I recognized what stood motionless, had stood there while I worked, in a shadowed corner near me.

"You can put the mattock down, son," I managed to say. "Nobody wants to hurt either one of you."

He was a slender seventeen or so, with corn-silk hair falling like a shed roof across his forehead and a wide mouth meant for grinning. His dark windbreaker and jeans were a typical high school uniform; not much protection, yet he was still lively enough to be dangerous. You couldn't say the same for the woman huddled at his feet, draped in a pathetic torn canvas awning. The kid had tucked it around her, unable to find anything in my garage to keep the lethal dust away from himself. "You've gotta help my mom," he croaked, the mattock still on his narrow shoulder.

"We can't do it here," I said, and stared at the mattock. He lowered it in slow suspicion.

"Where, then?"

"In my house," I heard myself say, thrusting aside all the carefully reasoned arguments of an era that had vanished forever under mushroom clouds. "Help me lift her and then take this battery for me."

En route to the house I learned something about masks and goggles; unless they are sealed against your cheeks, goggles quickly fog up when a mask directs your exhalations upward. I had to breathe out through my mouth and still I nearly fell on my ruined back steps, half-blind with my limp burden.

"Only four minutes, Harve," my sis called as she heard us come into the kitchen. "I timed you."

Kate raced down from the second floor, arms loaded with wrapped packs of toilet paper, calling, "I found it, Mr. McKay, in the"—and then she saw the wild eyes of the youth as he pressed himself against the wall, and she gaped at the awning-wrapped woman—"closet, Holy Mary comeseethis," she finished just as loudly. It had the ring of a call to arms.

Kate and the boy regarded each other warily, and I developed a notion that both he and his mother might be so contaminated that, like Rappaccini's daughter, their very bodies were poison. Though that was purest fantasy, their clothes might well be a danger.

I made a command decision then, unwrapping the canvas as I said, "Throw this thing outside, kid, then come upstairs," The woman seemed gossamer, very frail in a short housedress and open-toed flat shoes. I took her upstairs as fast as I could, ignoring the outbursts as Shar and Cammie came into view; ignoring also the awful smell of the woman.

The boy—his name was Devon Baird—found us in my upstairs john and was too scared to protest at the sight of his mother being stripped by a clownishly dressed stranger. "You get every stitch off, boy. Toss it in the tub and rinse your hair with water from the toilet tank."

The mother's straight blond hair and breast were streaked with vomit, but the worst was from her diarrhea. I kept my gloves on while sponging Mrs. Baird's sad little bod with a damp towel, propping her up until young Devon stood by, shivering and naked, to help.

He washed her hair out with loving tenderness, talking to her all the while. "We're gonna be all right, mom," he said; and, "It's *my* turn to take care of *you*," and, "These guy have food and water. You'll be okay." His gaze at mine asked whether he was a liar. I didn't want to give him my opinion.

The Baird woman's breathing had been shallow. Momentarily it became stentorous, and then she retched; long trembling dry heaves. What did come forth came from the other end; a thin trickle that soiled the toilet lid. The boy pressed his mother's face to his stomach and beseeched me wordlessly with tear-filled eyes. Maybe my sis had been waiting for something poignant enough to let her accept these strangers gracefully. In any case, she waited no longer but pulled me aside and began to tend the woman.

I said to the boy, perhaps too gruffly, "Have you been sick like this, too?"

He hesitated, started a negative headshake, swallowed hard, glanced away.

"You have to be strong, and truthful, if we're going to help you," my sis said. It had a threat in it. I wished she'd always been this firm with Lancey-pants.

Mumbling, he said, "She made me wear that damn awning in the culvert while she went to find a better place in the middle of the night and wouldn't let me give it to her until we got over your fence about dawn and then she started puking and—and all. I barfed a little just before you found us. I think it was her being sick that made me sick."

Shar said she hoped he was right and asked why the devil I was still wearing contaminated clothes. While I took my scare costume off in an upstairs bedroom, Shar got the fallout meter and set it between Mrs. Baird's thighs while Devon murmured hopeful things and answered Shar's questions. It seems that Mrs. Baird, a divorcée wary of adult male help, had been panicked by a radio warning at roughly ten the night before; had driven wildly from Concord without the least idea where she was taking her son. She simply took the road of least resistance away from the debris of a shattering, flattening blast wave that had freakishly left their apartment whole while sending storefronts screaming like buzz saws through crowded streets, and through the people composing those crowds. By the time the Bairds drove through it, the massacre of innocents was hours old, and the scenes they passed were silent and dead.

When stopped by a wreck, they had run together up the highway, taking refuge in a culvert for a time. Assuming Ern's estimate was close, she must've taken nearly two thousand rems during those first few hours when the fallout was at its most lethal level, showering its gamma radiation in all directions. Devon's dose might have been survivable as he cowered in that culvert, but Shar's single glance at me endorsed my thoughts about the woman; we were in the presence of death momentarily deferred.

"Her reading is about ten rems per hour," my sis said as I handed an old bathrobe to the youth. "That's about the same as it is everywhere on this floor, maybe a bit more—maybe because of all that," she indicated the pile of clothing in the bathtub. "Let's get her to the basement, Harve, and make her—better." We both knew that was a white lie. We could only try to make her comfortable. But Devon perked up a bit, stumbling along in a robe that swallowed his thin frame. Later Shar presented Devon with her old jeans and sweater from my guest bedroom.

Ern, feverishly slashing precise cuts in cardboard boxes he had pirated from the root cellar, stared in glum silence as we made a pallet for Mrs. Baird near my waterbed. The boy hurriedly visited the john and from the sound of it was trying to muffle his dry heaves. Kate had stashed containers of water in the tub, and I figured Devon knew enough to use it as necessary.

I told Ern how I'd found the pair; watched him work, mystified at the juice tins Lance had emptied into my old stewpot. My nephew was now modifying them in accord with the one Ern had made.

Ern made no complaint about the foundlings, no reproof for

my weak-minded decision to take charity cases I had sworn not to take. He chose another topic. "I hope you got the battery. It's going to get damn tiresome in the dark when those dry cells run down, 'cause we can't afford to keep somebody pedaling a bike all the time. Uses too much oxygen; gives off too much water vapor and carbon dioxide."

Cammie was making a tinned beef sandwich for Devon. I asked, "Cammie, will you bring that battery down from the kitchen?"

My niece stopped assembling the sandwich, glanced at her dad, made no move to comply until he gave her the slightest of nods in the basement gloom. I dug the glove-box lamp from my pocket and gave it to Ern, who recognized its utility without a word being spoken. And then I sat down with Lance and mimicked the things he was doing with juice cans. I had some thinking to do.

This was *my* place. If I chose to get sticky about it, they were all guests subject to my rules. As I'd warned Kate, democracy couldn't reign unchecked when our lives depended on everyone taking some direction. If I made the rules, couldn't I break them?

Well, I had; first with Kate and now by ushering this desperately sick woman and her teenage son into my shelter after agreeing with Ern and Shar that extra people would overcrowd our "lifeboat." Now I sensed that my kinfolk were realigning their ideas about my leadership. That worried me. Was I or wasn't I the one who ran things in my own home?

I compared my work with Lance's and punched holes in the next juice can more like his. Then I realized I was actually letting a spoiled kid show me what to do. I didn't like that one damn bit.

However, Lance was working in accord with our recognized expert: Ern. I could choose to do things differently for the sheer pleasure of self-determination, or I could do them the right way. Seen in this light, my urge for control looked pretty silly. Any leader who leads primarily for the joy of wielding power is a leader ripe for overthrow, especially if he makes too many bad decisions. I couldn't fault that logic. It had brought about the Magna Carta and the Continental Congresses and the Russian revolution and god*damn* if I wasn't denying my own right to run things in my own castle, so to speak.

Had I made a bad decision, bringing the hapless Bairds in?

I knew Shar thought so; suspected the others felt the same way. Yet no one had overtly challenged me for it. Maybe they were giving me another chance—or enough rope. And maybe Ern's mystifying work with toilet paper and tin cans would prove faulty, too, but he had a good track record. The least I could do was give him the freedom to keep improvising, even if that meant my temporarily becoming a peon on his tiny assembly line.

In this way I discovered a rationale of leadership that we seemed to be adopting without endless wrangles about it. I knew where things were; had physical strength the others lacked; and in the economic sense we were living in an investment I had made. On the other hand, my brother-in-law brought technical expertise that I lacked, and at this point our survival was chiefly a matter of technology and its applications.

To some extent my sis also knew more of the technology than I did. I'd be suicidally stupid if I failed to let them guide us while we navigated these nuclear shoals. Like it or lump it, I knew I should accept this erosion of my authority, letting it pass to Ern without making a big deal about it. I neglected the fact that Ern was not the authority figure in his household. Shar was—and she hadn't exercised much authority with Lance.

Kate interrupted my reverie, having taken a sentry position on the second floor. She had used a spatula to pry a few inches of tape loose at several window edges, the better to squint at our horizons without going outside. Anger and dismay filled her voice as she called, "It's another radioactive cloud west of us!"

The Golden Gate bomb needed forty-five minutes to thrust its cloud so high that we could see it over nearby ridges. There's been lots of speculation about the warhead, some claiming it was meant for military reservations near the north end of the bridge, and some insisting it was part of a ragged second-strike volley targeted against cities instead of military sites.

We weren't concerned about strategy but about tactics. That cloud was headed our way, and if we were going to survive another day in the tunnel, we would need something better than the air supply in the house. It might've been adequate for two or three people, but with so much activity by a half-dozen of us, our sealed environment was becoming a hazard.

Shar made herself a poncho from polyfilm and a babushka

to match, taping it together with Kate's help. She wasted no time explaining when I protested her trip outside. "The girls can tell you, bubba," she said, mimed a kiss, and went outside.

"You and Mr. McKay have taken the most radiation so far," Kate told me, "so she's the logical one." For what, I asked. "To make a slit in the film over the cellar doors and tape a flap of film over it, leaving the bottom of the flap untaped. It makes a one-way air-exit valve, to encourage flow of air through the tunnel. I volunteered but I'm not sure I know the best way to do it. Shar claims it'll only take a minute or two."

I nodded. If that new fallout cloud dumped on us, it would soon be too late for outside work. "Kate, can you use the fallout meter?"

She smiled almost shyly. "Cammie showed me. Should I start taking readings here in the kitchen?"

"Right. Uh—you getting along with everybody?"

An instant's hesitation before, "Everybody that counts."

"Everybody counts, Kate. You mean Lance?"

A nod.

"He's a problem. But Shar's the one who keeps him in line. Just wanted you to know you're not alone."

Leading the way to the basement, she stopped, looked back. "No, I'm not. It's a good feeling, boss."

"Not 'boss.' You know my name, Kate. This is no time to be stressing who's boss; we have enough problems without that."

"I noticed," she murmured, and collected the meter materials. By now someone had cut a swatch of fur from my parka to make the process simpler.

Mrs. Baird had not improved, but Cammie had rigged a bedpan from a biscuit tray. She and Devon hovered over the woman, trying to get her to accept a sip of water.

"Don't try to force-feed anyone who's unconscious," I cautioned. "She could strangle."

"Mom said we need to replace the fluids she's losing," Cammie said. "Her skin is flushed but she's trembling all over, Uncle Harve. I don't know whether to cover her up or sponge her with cool water."

I didn't know either, but one look at Devon's drawn features warned me against saying so. I felt his mother's pulse—quick and shallow—and despite her reddened skin, she didn't seem warm. If anything, her body temperature might be a bit low.

I said, "Cover her lightly and keep trying to get her to swallow. There's instant coffee somewhere and I'd say she could use the stimulant. Better if it was warm. Devon, you might nibble on that sandwich whether you want it or not," I finished, spying the food he hadn't touched. I hoped all my guesswork wouldn't do any harm.

Meanwhile I had another job. Ern heard me out and agreed, with a suggestion I hadn't considered. "If you're going to block the chimney flue from the inside, try lightly stuffing a brown paper sack with newspaper and stick a broom head in with it. Then tape the sack's mouth over the broom handle and push like hell. The handle will give you something to pull the plug out with later," he explained.

Kate went to the second-floor fireplace with me and took a fallout reading while I arranged the plug I'd made. I had broken the broom handle off short enough to get it into the fireplace and was kneeling at the hearth when she gasped, "Wait! Isn't some fallout going to get on you when you go poking into that thing?"

I stopped short with a curse, aware that she had saved me from a dose of contamination. "So how else can I do it?"

She hurtled downstairs without answering. I spent the time checking our attic beam repair, which looked good, and came down as Kate unfolded more of my thin polyfilm. Hers was a sloppy-looking answer to the problem: film taped completely across the hearth opening, so loose and voluminous that I could grasp my handmade plug through the film. "Don't breathe," Kate warned, and stepped back sensibly as I began to stuff the paper plug up past the flue damper.

We could hear a cascade of small particles falling like sand; most of it just harmless crud, no doubt, but Kate rushed to retape the edge of film I pulled loose as a puff of dust emerged near me.

The broom head was too wide and I virtually tore it to pieces in thirty breathless seconds, using the handle like a ramrod. When I felt the plug leap upward inside, I knew it was past the damper into the main chimney shaft, and I simply lit out for the stairs. Kate collected our hardware and followed.

My sis had returned from outside. She shooed Cammie away from a very unpleasant moment while Mrs. Baird threw up pale green fluid into a saucepan. Devon himself wasn't having an easy time because I could hear him retching in the john. At least he had something to throw up, having eaten half a sandwich.

Kate reported that her last reading had been twenty-five rems on the second floor. "And we're soaking up too much radiation here in the basement," Shar replied. "Just because it's gradually dropping, we're acting as if we weren't accumulating more damage to our bodies. But we are, and the sooner we return to the tunnel the better off we'll be. Ernest McKay, that means you!"

Ern sighed and agreed. "I can finish this filter arrangement in the tunnel. Kate, will you take readings under the stairs and then in the tunnel?"

I was collecting the hardware for a string of tunnel lights when Kate revealed her findings. The readings were horrific; twenty in the basement, nearly the same in the tunnel.

Ern paused, thunderstruck, his arms full of cardboard and tin cans. "Good God, we're losing the tunnel advantage!"

Then I mentally flashed on the little meter, abandoned near the fireplace upstairs while Kate helped me minimize the leakage of dust through the film. Grabbing a roll of toilet paper, I moistened a few squares of it and wiped the little meter, taking care to clean its entire outer surface. "Try it now, Kate. You may be reading light contamination on the meter itself."

It was true. Dusted by "hot" particles, the meter had given spurious readings. Now, repeating her readings several times to make absolutely sure, Kate got three rems at the stairs, a half-rem in the tunnel. But the low basement reading didn't slow our retreat back to the tunnel. Shar kept reminding us that every additional rem was one too many. Up to a point, a human body repaired its riddled tissues—but who among us wanted to find that point?

Through all these morning antics Spot had stayed out of the way, but with all of us milling around on our hurried errands, he began to pace the length of the tunnel. A cheetah is a great one for pacing when he can't cut loose and run.

I busied myself collecting parts for the portable john, which Ern had explained to me in one breath: "Make a seat by cutting a big hole through several thicknesses of heavy cardboard, tape them together over the mouth of a plastic trash box, and make a plastic bag to fit inside."

I was astonished to see how much polyfilm we'd used. We had started with a pair of fifty-foot rolls, but now only a little of the ten-mil stuff remained. Of the two-mil film perhaps half the roll was available for toilet baggies or whatever. Those two rolls of polyfilm were among the smartest purchases I ever made.

Then I tripped over a mattress in the dark tunnel and nearly fell on Spot, who marched with feline dignity to the root cellar and sat warily watching Lance. The kid was foraging in the bike kits with my big lamp.

"What're you after, Lance?"

"Getting flashlights for mom," he complained, as if I had accused him of something.

"Good. Don't use the big lamp when a little flash will do," I said as pleasantly as I could while moving away. I didn't hear his reply clearly but my palms itched because it sounded suspiciously like "fuck off" to me. Surely, I reflected, there must be some way to pulp a kid without actually harming him.

The subdued light flooding down the stairwell shed enough illumination for most of our basement operations, but I needed a flashlight to ransack my office for a coil of wire. I asked for a light.

"Coming up," Shar responded, then raised her voice in no-nonsense tones: "Lance, if I don't have a light by the count of ten, you will get *no lunch!*" I filed that one for future reference; Lance was with us, displaying two fresh flashlights, at the count of nine.

During the next few minutes we lined the tunnel with our stuff and pulled Mrs. Baird into it, pallet and all, before sealing the stairwell door and filing into the tunnel. Devon still had little to say, though he made optimistic noises each time his mother managed to sip cool coffee. I suppose she was, at most, half-conscious.

Ern's air filter was a trick he borrowed from oil filtration of an earlier era. During the next hour five of us slaved to get it ready. Ern filled empty juice cans with rolls of toilet paper, plugging off the central tube of each roll and punching holes near the bottom of each can. Then he taped the cans into circular holes in a cardboard box so that, when he connected the bellows pump to the filter box, any air that reached the bellows had to be sucked endwise through the toilet paper rolls from edge to edge. According to Ern, any dust particle that found its way through those layers of paper—between the layers, really—had to be a micron or less in size. So much for the good news.

The bad news was that the bellows had to suck like hell to get any air through a single filter element. That was why Ern used six elements, six rolls in juice cans, for the filter box. He had a second filter box half completed, not knowing how long it might be before the filters became clogged and perhaps heavily contaminated with fallout particles. If one clogged, we'd have another ready.

Before going back into the basement, we discussed the job. Shar felt that she should stay with Mrs. Baird, which left me and Ern as the two most adept at placing that filter box. We needed a fifth hand to hold the flashlight, and Lance and Cammie were the two who had taken the least dosage. Of course we chose Cammie; she could also take meter readings out there.

Kate saw the portajohn I'd been making while we talked and put the plastic trashcan between her knees when I relinquished it. "By the time you're finished with that filter out there, this little throne is going to be very popular," she said with a smile that wouldn't stay on straight.

I showed her my palm and she slapped it lightly, and then I shuffled into the basement to make the filter hookup, wondering if a new Kate Gallo would emerge from all this; and if we would all be changed. *If* we emerged.

The hookup went quickly. First we coupled the air tube we'd already linked to my furnace air intake, to the new filter box which had an enclosed front plenum chamber. That way we made sure the filter elements couldn't draw air from the basement. Our next hookup was from the rear plenum chamber of the filter box to the air pipe leading to the pump and took only moments. We secured the connection with tape and went back to the tunnel.

While I sealed up the slit at the tunnel door, Ern was pumping, "Kee-*rist* but it's hard to pump," he muttered. "Cammie, get a reading on the pump exhaust, will you, hon?"

Me: "An obstruction?"

Ern: "No, I checked that. This damn thing just needs a lot of suction, or a little extra time to get through a cycle."

He was understating it. I could see the air pipe trying its best to collapse until he slowed the cycle rate. I counted sixteen cycles a minute and said, "We have two more people but we're pumping at half-speed, and it's harder work. Ungood, Ern."

Cammie knelt with the meter and flashlight, counting *sotto voce,* and registered pleasure. "I get less than a rem," she said.

"No more than we were taking last night during the worst," said Ern, still pumping, studying his handiwork. "You know, we really should be keeping a journal on radiation versus time."

Farther down the tunnel Spot kibitzed as Kate and Devon lugged Cammie's propped-up bike nearer to us. A good sign: the youth was fit for light duty, or thought he was.

"Here, dad, let me," said Cammie, and she settled herself at the pump. "Lordy, and me already sore from working this thing last night," she said but kept at it.

Ern mumbled, "We've got to do better than this," and motioned me to follow him to the root cellar. We could talk there without auditors except for Spot, whose coarse doggy shoulder ruff I scratched as Ern plied a flashbeam around us.

As though to himself he said, "Here it is, then: the valve Shar made at this end of the tunnel might improve airflow enough to offset the addition of two more people. Or it might not."

"I'm sorry, Ern. If I'd had more time I might have made a different decision out there."

"I doubt it. And I probably would've done just what you did. I guess I just didn't expect you to suddenly turn soft on the human race."

"It could be in short supply a week from now," I explained.

In determination that bordered on anger he grated, "Well, we aren't gonna go under here, by God! We *must* build another front plenum for that spare filter box. But we're out of cardboard."

"Why duplicate the one you built?"

"To put twice as many filter elements into the system, which ought to give us almost twice as much air."

I tried to envision it. "You mean put a second filter box out there and draw air from the basement, too?"

"No, no, goddamnit, we need air that we haven't been breathing. The only restriction is through those rolls of asswipe. We'll just have to run crossover tubes between the front intake plenums and between the collector plenums—uh, on the suction side. Got it?"

"Yup." When Ern started cussing, he was either drunk or exceedingly worried; and he hadn't taken a nip that day. As he leaned against my thin wall paneling in the tunnel, I recalled nailing the stuff up. It was thin panel board with a watertight plastic facing. I tapped the panel behind him and said, "Well, here's our front plenum."

In two minutes we had the big panel loose and had used the back of the filter box to scribe a pattern. Though Ern's Swiss knife even had a small saw blade, we found it quicker to make repeated scribe lines with a sharp blade and then snap the panel along the lines. Soon we were trimming sides of the new part and double-taping the seams to make them airtight. Ern used the saw blade to cut a circular hole for an air pipe. We taped our new intake plenum onto the spare filter box and found ourselves ready.

I hefted the thing, which weighed no more than ten pounds, and said, "I'll tote it."

Ern's chin went down against his chest. Firmly: "No you won't, Harve. It's only a one-man job, and I—I'd rather you weren't out there."

So: open dissension. I misunderstood his motive. "I'm not *that* klutzy, Ern. And who's going to stop me?"

"Sweet reason, I hope. You and Shar absorbed some heavy stuff outside today. I didn't. Lance can handle a flashlight, and it's time he pulled some weight." Ern's stance was that of a man expecting a backhand, but he planted himself in front of me like a cornerstone waiting for a bulldozer.

Kate disturbed our tableau, moving toward us with the one-holer she and Cammie had finished. It had a taped-together seat of corrugated cardboard over an inch thick, probably in deference to my great arse, and a film-faced cardboard lid with a tape hinge. The lid wasn't airtight, but the film hung down so it could be lightly taped when we weren't using it. Ern's vanwagon had a real chemical toilet, but they had left their first-stage vehicle somewhere en route. Kate's portaprivy would have to serve.

"I'm on the verge of a—ah—breakthrough, fellas. Mind if I test the thing in privacy?"

I grinned at her, stepped aside, handed the unwieldy filter box to Ern, and sighed. "Lance, huh?"

"He's a big help when he wants to be. Don't sell him short."

"Not me, pal." Consumer-protection laws were invented to balk sales of such products as Lance.

But Lance didn't want to. "Why pick on me? Cammie can do it."

"Let him have his breakfast, hon," Shar said. "He's worked

very well this morning." Her tone suggested there was nothing more to say.

Ern said something anyway, very softly.

"You wouldn't," said my sis in horror. Lance smiled and slurped pineapple juice. Shar went on. "Ernest McKay, I will not let you bully your own son. Childish bullying, that's all it is," she snorted.

Ern stripped tape from the door slit one-handed, shouldering the filter box. "Coming, Cammie?"

My niece's gaze swept across her mother and brother in silent accusation as she stood up, stretching the muscle kinks from her neck. She took the little flashlight and went into the basement with her father.

I took over at the pump, exchanging stolid glances with my sister. She held my gaze for a long moment and then said to Lance, "Why don't you pedal the bike awhile, hon?"

"Pedals are too far away."

"That hasn't stopped you in the past, lamb. And you *do* want lunch, don't you?"

"There's more than one kind of bully," he observed. But he went.

In the stillness we could identify sounds of survival: breathing; the clack of pump valves and the whoosh of air; the ratchety whirr of the bike as Lance pedaled; the whine of a tiny generator. And muffled by distance, the murmur and industry of a new filter emplacement in our primitive little life-support system. Unheard but very much in my mind was the slow-fire hammer of gamma radiation riddling the flesh of Ern and Cammie.

Then we heard Kate in the root cellar, denouncing Spot as a voyeur. I smiled briefly and said to Shar, "Lance is right, you know."

"My bubba siding with Lance! Will wonders never—"

"Don't 'bubba' me; I'm not siding with him. He said there are various kinds of bullying, and he's right. He's an expert at it, Shar; he just uses you as his weapon and his shield."

"Nonsense. Look at the child, pedaling for dear life."

"Bullshit; pedaling for dear lunch, you mean."

"A much better alternative than beating a child," she sniffed.

I considered that, found it apt so long as it worked, then applied the idea to our whole situation—if we were lucky enough to have one—our future. "Maybe the whole country made a mistake by inventing so many alternatives," I mused. "Lower scores on college entrance exams; middle-class druggies in junior high; professional athletics dominated by minorities. Maybe because the average middle-class kid has too many neat alternatives, a lot of 'em never learn to pitch into a shitty job and get it over with. At worst they can just run away from home and crash at a series of halfway houses. We've let our kids replace self-discipline with alternatives. No goddamn wonder divorce rates are still climbing, sis."

Armed with years of adult-ed jargon, Shar jabbed with a favorite: "Simplistic. Cammie's no druggie and she's on the tennis varsity."

"Yep, and she also got your belt across her bottom when she snotted off. She didn't get pleasant alternatives, as I recall."

Fiercely whispered: "Cammie's not the angel everybody thinks she is. She's subtle; winds you around her finger. When I see that, it makes me want to protect Lance."

I knew Cammie could be a vamp. But she knew how to give freely, even when it interfered with what she wanted. Chuckling in spite of myself, I said, "Cammie has to work to wind us around, and if we like being wound it can't be all bad, sis." Suddenly the pump handle became very much easier to lift, and I figured Ern would be back shortly. "Anyway, think about it. From yesterday forward, for the rest of his life, Lance McKay is going to find himself goddamn short on pleasant alternatives. For his sake, I hope he's not too old to learn discipline."

After a long silence Shar mused, "As far back as I can remember, bubba, you prided yourself on finding alternatives. Nearly drove mother crazy, and got your backside tanned to saddle leather. But you've turned out to be one of those people who have *so much* self-discipline, except for feeding your face, that you tend to think of yourself as judge, jury, and . . ."

I'm sure she was about to add "executioner." Despite my best efforts, somehow my little sis had learned about the heroin wholesaler, years before. I rousted him in Ensenada and brought him back after he jumped bail. I'd been naive then, and he was such a mannerly dude, and I didn't know about short ice picks in homburgs until it glanced off a rib on its way in while I was negotiating a slow curve on the coast highway. As I saw it, Mr. Mannerly had executed himself.

"Nolo contendere," I said to my sister.

"Cute," she said gently. "What I was getting at is, why aren't you one of the irresponsibles?"

I said it was a fair question and mulled it over as I pumped. Finally I replied, "Maybe because we were farm kids, though we moved to town before you had chores to do, sis. Sure, I love alternatives; they're fun! But feeding those stupid chickens and collecting eggs were things for which there simply were *no* alternatives on our farm. They wouldn't stop laying on weekends no matter what I told 'em. On a farm you try a lot of alternatives, but you shovel a lot of shit, too. Maybe there's an ideal balance. And maybe that's what I'm trying to steer you toward."

In the dim light her profile and the way she had of lifting one shoulder while she cocked her head took me back many years, to when my little sis consulted me on matters she wouldn't dare bring to mother. Finally she laid a loving hand on my arm. "I'll think on it," she promised. "It certainly won't do to let Lance defy his father in this dreadful cooped-up situation."

At this juncture Kate padded back to announce that the potty had passed her most exacting test. Shar allowed as how she was simply *burst*ing to try it.

"You see," I called as Shar moved away, "indoor plumbing! We've weathered the worst."

Su-u-ure we had . . .

Ern and Cammie returned moments after my exchange with Shar, and they were elated when I showed them how easily the pump operated. They drank some juice, and we agreed for Devon's benefit that his mother seemed better. Obviously her system had rid itself of most available moisture, including bile. There was no point in mentioning an IV with saline solution. We couldn't even boil or distill water, much less get it into her veins. All we could do was urge cold instant coffee down her throat when she was able to swallow. That wasn't often, and her gamma-ravaged body refused to keep it long.

Her reddened skin was perhaps the only thing Shar could treat, by sponging her body with saltwater into which a bit of baking soda was stirred. I can't swear it helped much, except that it kept the silent, hollow-eyed Devon from dwelling on his own condition. If he had a chance it lay in his desire to stay active, and we stressed that he must eat and drink plenty.

Shar's purse held a note pad and ball-point pen, which she

used to begin a tally of events, beginning with the first ground shock. She started it as a running record of radiation versus time, but it soon grew into a series of anecdotes as well. There was something about the sharing of tales that brought our spirits up and drew Kate and Devon into the group. Not that we were idle. We took turns at the honey bucket and the pump, except for Ern. With extension cords and safety pins for test connections, he was busily embarking on an honest-to-God electric power system.

Why hadn't we used the battery-powered radios on hand? Well, we had. Precious little good it had done us.

During the night we'd thought about radio bulletins only when we were in the tunnel, where FM reception was hopeless. I tried to get San Francisco's KGO on the AM dial but found, instead, good ol' XEROK, Juarez, at that frequency. Even with the outrageous transmitter power of the Mexican station, I could hardly make out when they were transmitting in English; a skyful of energetic particles makes hash of most transmissions. From some unidentified station, I heard what may have been a list of local roads still open, but I couldn't spot the locale.

Shar had tried a radio while taping film over my broken window but had quit in a hurry because, she said, the little they did hear was disturbing to the girls. She had gotten KSRO in Santa Rosa, which warned evacuees that the town could not absorb another soul. She got KDFM in Walnut Creek, which begged hysterically for help from a studio buried so deep in rubble that the announcer could not escape. From San Francisco and Oakland she got nothing. And that was when she quit trying.

I decided to try a third time early in the afternoon, and while using the homemade toilet in the root cellar, I poked a little aerial past our book barrier, hoping to tune in and hear something that would make me feel better. I got Santa Rosa's re-broadcast of an EBS bulletin claiming that the Soviet Union had paid with its life for exceeding the parameters of limited nuclear war. The announcer called on Americans to throw open their doors—those who still had doors—to battered victims escaping from target areas. It tried to cheer us with the news that the President was safe, but in my case I'm afraid it failed there. Finally it insisted that many small towns were responding heroically to hordes of evacuees. The Santa Rosa announcer then broke in and reminded all and sundry that Santa Rosa was

not one of those towns. Evacuees from the San Francisco bomb
were reminded that the Golden Gate spans were now in the
bay. I snapped the radio off then. I'd had enough and went
back down the tunnel to my little family, hoping to hear something that would make me feel better.

   During our first long afternoon in the tunnel, we at last had
time to organize and to accept our enforced isolation from the
deadly world outside. Shar suggested our rotation schedule for
air-pump duties and assembled notes to estimate our individual
radiation doses. Meanwhile Ern separated the wires on one end
of an extension cord and, drilling pilot holes into the soft metal
of my Lotus battery terminals with the awl on his knife, inserted
small wood screws as anchors for the bared wire ends. I stapled
extension cords for twenty feet along one wall of the tunnel.
With spare wire and safety pins, Ern soon had a bike headlamp
completing the circuit.
   At that point the kids cheered and abandoned Cammie's
bike, grateful for a source of light they didn't have to work
for. Ern observed dryly, "You kids are lucky; many bike generators are six-volt but these are twelve, so the bulbs are com-
patible with a car battery." Then he hauled the other two bikes
near our cheery little half-amp light and, one by one, stole
their generators and headlamps for the tunnel. During all this
I heard the McKay family's one-day saga.
   Ern had driven to work at Ames that morning, playing a
tape album by the twin-piano Paradox duo instead of listening
to the radio. The traffic was very light. Small wonder! He had
been stunned to find everyone at the shop in a dither over the
news reports, and then had tried to telephone Shar. Their line
was busy because Shar, by this time, was trying to call *him*.
   Long ago they'd agreed that Ern would feign illness and
return home if hostilities seemed near. He couldn't at first
believe things had deteriorated so far, but the model shop at
Ames was operating at less than half-strength that morning.
Ern kept quiet, stayed near his phone, and swore he would not
run for home on the strength of uncomfirmed reports of a tussle
with Syria.
   He had just began checking sensor holes in a specimen wing
section when he overheard his manager on video link talking
with his wife, who worked in the nearby Satellite Test Center;
whatever American citizens might think, Soviet citizens were

streaming into firestorm-proof subways in major cities while
our spy satellites watched.

Ern knew that STC, spymaster of those satellites, would be
a primary target if war came. And STC was only a short walk
across Moffett Field from the Ames complex. Ern was not fool
enough to wait for some official NASA holiday announcement
and was jogging to his car moments later.

At home in their suburb north of San José, the kids were
nearly off to school before Shar caught the first scarifying
bulletins about the capsizing of our leviathan *Nimitz*. Shar called
them back, ordered them both into hiking duds, and started
trying to contact Ern while she consulted her checklists.

My sis had done everything once: EST, Catholicism, a lover,
and a bookkeeping job for a parts supplier in Silicon Gulch. I
suspect that each of those activities included a common side
effect: a knack for compartmenting and categorizing. In Shar's
case it yielded checklists that first became a joke, then a main-
stay in the family.

Her crisis-relocation checklist went further than a vacation
list. In addition to shutting off the water heater and resetting
the thermostat, she included a cleanout of several cabinets that
would fill the vanwagon. Ern had the Ford runabout, but their
vanwagon, with its cavernous storage space on a sturdy light
chassis, squatted in their carport ready to serve as their first-
stage booster vehicle. It was roomy enough for boxes of medicine and food, Ern's tool chest, bedrolls, even a pair of bikes
and the hand-operated winch that could haul them from a ditch.
The other two bikes could fit on racks outside. Each bike had
its own wire basket for the individual survival packs Ern had
assembled. If they became stymied somehow en route to my
place, their plan was to jettison the first-stage (translation: park
the vanwagon) and continue using the bikes as second-stage
vehicles.

Ern squalled his little Ford into the driveway in time to see
Cammie toss the last bedroll into the vanwagon and wasted no
time scrounging some extras: shovel, a roll of aircraft-quality
tow cable, old bleach bottles he'd filled with drinking water,
and the "decorative" blunderbuss from over their mantel.

That funny-looking little period piece had been my gift once
upon a time, a purely defensive household item for Shar. A
do-it-yourself kit from a gunsmith, it was short stocked, a
smoothbore modified from flintlock to percussion cap. Of course

it would fire only a single black powder charge and then had to be reloaded. But its bell mouth spread to an inch and a half diameter, and I loaded it with BBs. You needed two adult hands to cock it. You also needed a good grip when you pulled the trigger, because it had a recoil wallop like a baseball bat. Any intruder who was even in the general direction of that bell mouth would find his world suddenly filled with thunder and smoke and steel pellets, and if it didn't blow him into another dimension it would at least give him serious misgivings about wandering into my sis's home without knocking. Nor would folks a block away sleep through it. The blunderbuss was, I thought, just about perfect for one exclusive purpose: point-blank defense within the home. Anyway, Ern stuck it into the vanwagon.

I couldn't help laughing when Lance interrupted his mother's account of the bike argument. "They wouldn't let me bring my bike," he accused, "so I brung the skateboard. Dad thought I was nuts but I wasn't."

Give the little bugger credit—he was good on a urethane-wheeled skateboard and he knew it, and wore his pads into the vanwagon like a gladiator heading for the arena. In a way, he was.

Shar locked their house and fumed while Ern topped off their fuel tank from his Ford, using the electric fuel pump trick he'd shown me. They left the outskirts north of San José intending to take freeways to Niles Canyon. It didn't take long to see the futility of that idea.

Traffic on Highway Six-Eighty was already stalled clear back to the off ramp. Shar folded their local map under her clipboard and directed Ern to a state road, then to a winding county road when their second choice permitted them only a walking pace. They passed under the freeway presently and saw highway patrolmen with bolt cutters nipping a hole in the freeway fence to let cars leave the hopeless logjam up there.

When Ern spotted a pickup running along the sloping ridge of railroad tracks in Fremont, he followed. The right-of-way led them to the little community of Niles, but a highballing freight with hundreds of hangers-on nearly clipped the van-wagon, and Ern decided they'd played on the railroad tracks long enough. They hit Niles Canyon Road then, seeing that traffic toward the distant town of Livermore was bullying its way across all four lanes in escaping the overcrowded bay region.

Of course they saw the wrecks and quickly learned to look away since neither of the adults had special medical training and their first responsibility was to get their own two kids to safety with a minimum of lost time. A few motorists helped others; a delivery truck dragged one car out of the road with a tow cable while other traffic, including Ern, streamed past. Ern didn't stop until forced to, but he was expecting trouble, and when the chain of rear-enders began ahead, he wisely slowed before he had to, gaining ten feet of maneuvering room.

Standing atop the vanwagon, Ern studied the blockage. Two lanes had been stopped for some time after one car, rear-ended, had spun sideways. The other two lanes had continued, drivers in the balked lanes trying vainly to edge into lanes in which cars moved bumper to bumper. No one would give. Someone finally tried to bluff or force his way in, touching off a chain reaction as cars took to the shoulder trying to pass the new obstruction. As Ern watched, two fistfights erupted. One guy with a knife was sent packing by another flailing tire chains. At that point people began simply to abandon their cars in favor of hoofing it.

"I counted fourteen cars between us and the front of the jam," Ern recalled as he snubbed the third bike generator against Cammie's bike wheel in the tunnel. "I figured with enough people helping, we could get all the wrecks pushed onto the shoulder in fifteen minutes, even if we had to winch some of 'em sideways." Ern figured he was an hour or so from my place if they stuck with the vanwagon but longer if they continued by bike. Besides, they'd be abandoning food, hardware, and protection if they left the vanwagon.

Wearing heavy gloves, winch and tow cable in hand, Ern trotted past other drivers, urging them to help instead of just honking. The owner of the first car in the mess stood at bay with a jack handle, threatening to brain the first guy who touched his car unless they'd help him pull his fender away from his blown-out tire. Someone offered him, instead, a ride in another car, and implied that his most likely alternative was a knot on his head from a dozen determined men.

Ern used the man's jack handle as a pry bar under the crumpled edge of the fender, then hooked his tow cable to the handle. With several men hauling at once, they pulled the fender away from the wheel. The owner drove off very slowly while his blown tire disintegrated on its rim, no longer part of the general problem.

One car, abandoned and locked by its owner, was *hors de combat* simply because the owner had taken his keys. The steering column was locked, so even after smashing a side window, the men couldn't steer the heavy coupe over to the shoulder. Ten men could tip it over on its top to get it out of the way, though, and they did, even while Ern begged them not to. Fuel tanks dribble a lot when a car's wheels are in the air.

The first car to shove its nose past the others was a big sedan, and its driver, a level-headed woman, backed up while others used tire chains as a tow cable from her rear bumper. She pulled two more cars free before charging off down the highway. Ern winched a pair of small cars sideways from the tangle, with help from the owners, anchoring his winch to the base of a steel highway sign. "Played hell with the jack sockets on the cars," Ern said, and grinned, remembering it, "because I had 'em stick their jacks into the chassis sockets to give me something to hook onto." He didn't try that with heavier cars, fearing his winch wouldn't take it.

It took thirty minutes to clear two lanes, and while fifty people struggled to clear other lanes, improvising as they went, Ern sprinted to the vanwagon just as Shar got it started. Soon they overtook the guy riding on his rim. Ern estimated it would've taken the man five minutes to change to his spare, which made that press-on-regardless outlook seem pretty short-sighted.

They left the highway at the outskirts of Livermore, a town experiencing its first-ever taste of terminal traffic constipation. Cammie described it wide-eyed: "Worse than Candlestick Park after a game! You'd see a car go shooting down a side street and then it'd come howling back a few blocks further. People were driving across lawns, pounding on doors, getting stuck in flower beds, you name it."

"Like one of those car movies where they do crazy things," Lance put in. "But in the movies they get away with it." Lance had pegged it nicely; too many citizens imagined they could do the stunts they saw on the screen, and too few realized how much those stunts depended on expertise and hidden preparations.

Once they were across town and headed north toward my place, said Shar, she thought they'd pulled it off. They drove slowly, with frequent horn-toots to warn hikers and bikers who streamed out of Livermore along with many cars. There was some traffic into the town as well, coming down from the hills.

Shortly after the road began its twisting course toward Mount Diablo they saw the other van, a battered relic, its driver approaching with no thought for other traffic but the steady blare of its horn. Ern braked hard. "I didn't think they'd make the turn at the rate they were coming," he said.

They did, but only by taking all the road and forcing a hiker to leap for his life. They didn't make it past Ern, though, sideswiping his left front fender with an impact that threw both vehicles into opposite ditches.

Since all four McKays were harnessed, they sustained nothing worse than the bruise along Ern's muscular forearm. Shar quieted Lance's wails ("I wasn't really scared," he insisted.) and after ascertaining that they weren't injured, Ern found that his door would no longer open. He went out the back of the vanwagon, both kids piling out with him, and then hugged them close in protective reflex. Approaching from the other van was a bruiser in his forties, a semiauto carbine in his hands and murder in his face. Behind him, a younger man limped forward hefting a big crescent wrench.

"Damn fool, didn't you hear me honk? That thing of yours better be drivable," snarled the big one, using his carbine as a deliberate menace.

Ern realized he was being hijacked. "Don't point it at the kids," he pleaded, wondering if either vehicle could be driven. "I'll just get the bikes and—"

"Touch that stuff and you're a dead man," said the bruiser, spying a ten-speed bike in the gloom. "Jimmy, we lucked out."

Jimmy, the younger man, brandished the wrench at Ern, who moved back and started to call a warning to Shar. He never got the chance and in any case he would've been warning the wrong person.

The big man with the carbine stepped up to the vanwagon's open doors and was met in midstride by a thunderous blast. Shar had found the antique fowling piece. The tremendous spread of shot took out a bike spoke, knocked a bedroll out of the cargo area, and snatched the carbine from the man, who cartwheeled end for end. Everyone reeled away from the god-awful roar and the smoke that followed like a bomb burst from inside the vanwagon.

Ern looked wildly for something to throw at Jimmy the wrench man but found the wrench available. Yowling, hands in air, young Jimmy raced back to his damaged van and tumbled inside. Shar emerged from the vanwagon coughing and spitting, the little blunderbuss empty but still in her hands.

The big man came to his knees, stared at his arms through torn shirt sleeves. Ern was near enough to see the bluish welts on his hands; raised knots like some disfiguring disease that began to ooze blood as both watched in silent fascination. Then the big fellow saw my sis march into view; saw her cock the harmless thing as if to fire again. He stumbled to his feet then and ran doubled over, holding his arms across his body and crooning with pain. Ern ran a few paces after him until he saw that the man had no intention of retrieving his weapon. Obviously the old van was drivable, because in seconds the ex-rough type was spewing gravel in it.

The vanwagon was another matter. Its radiator torn loose, steering rod hopelessly bent, it could not be navigated another hundred feet, much less the twenty miles to my place. Ern managed to start it and got it far off the macadam while water poured from ruptured hoses. The McKays then traded relieved kisses all around and started rigging for their second-stage flight. It was then half past two in the afternoon.

That was about the same time, said Kate Gallo, that she first noticed the burly black-haired gonzo at the racetrack. I let her tell it, making me the heavy in her waggish way. She explained she'd been running from a check-kiting spree and I said nothing to contradict her. But when she tried to describe our open-water crossing as literally floating across, I started to hum "It Ain't Necessarily So" and got my laugh before moving over to help Ern.

He was wiring all three tiny bike generators together, positive to positive and negative to negative. That was when I admitted that Ern McKay had truly found a way to *recharge my damn battery!* The output of a single generator was too puny to feed a whopping big car battery, but three generators in parallel? Still a trickle-charge, but a significant trickle.

I thought it might be hard work to pedal with three generators riding against a bike wheel but I was wrong. Ern insisted that we connect the generator's positive terminal to that of the battery only while someone was pedaling. If that circuit was intact while no one pedaled, he said, the battery's energy might trickle *out* through those generators. As it was, we could re-charge the battery with about four hours of pedaling and have twelve hours of light without draining the battery at all. I could've kissed him for that. Kate did it for me, squarely on his forehead.

At length Kate reached the point in her tale where I "abandoned" her to search for my family, and I filled them in with a brief account of my trip along the mountain ridge. "If you had any illusions about the flatlanders around the bay pulling through this," I concluded, "forget 'em. The burn cases in Oakland alone would overload burn-unit facilities from coast to coast."

With a glance toward the comatose Mrs. Baird, Shar muttered, "You might try for a bit of optimism."

"I *am* optimistic, sis. I'm assuming a lot of burn victims will survive the firestorm and fallout long enough to profit from medical treatment. If you've read about the quake and fire in San Francisco back in 1906, you'll recall it was the fire that caused the most casualties. Volunteer crews came from as far as Fresno to help. Trainloads of food and volunteers in, trainloads of refugees out.

"It's not as though there were no precedent for this," I went on, mostly for the benefit of our younger members. "Europeans saw great cities destroyed, whole populations decimated or worse, forty years ago. London, Dresden, Berlin—and don't forget how Japan was plastered. I know it wasn't on such a scale as this, but they did find ways to rebuild."

"It took 'em years," Ern reminded me. "And they had American help."

I nodded. "You're mighty right there, pal. And that's all we can expect, too: American help."

Kate asked in disbelief, "From where? Fresno?"

"No, from us! And millions more like us. Damnit, think! There must be two hundred thousand people schlepping around in Santa Rosa right now, and if the fallout missed 'em they'll probably be outside in shirt sleeves."

"Sure—grubbing for roots," said Cammie. "And I've heard mom talk about the radiation that's spread all over the world now."

"Can't deny that," I said. "We'll probably have higher infant mortality and ten times the cancer we've had in the past. I grant you all that, much as I loathe it. But don't tell me we lack the guts people had in Stalingrad and Texas City and Nagasaki!"

"I wanted to be a golf pro," said young Devon softly. "Looks like I'll be a carpenter or a bricklayer."

Ern: "Could be. Or a cancer researcher. Harve's not promising fun and games, Devon; only hope. We'll all have to bust our butts for a few years, and we have no assurance that we'll ever see things back to normal. Whatever that is," he said and chuckled. "It doesn't take a professor of sociology to predict a sudden change in the American way of life. On the other hand, it might not be so noticeable to farmers in Oregon or a dentist in Napa."

"Oh God," Kate breathe almost inaudibly and quit cycling the air pump.

Cammie asked for us all: "Trouble with the pump?"

Kate took a long shuddering breath, shook her head, began to pump again. "My father has a summer home near Napa. Little acreage just outside of Yountville, which nobody ever heard of. Just a statusy thing. They rarely go there."

"Maybe they're there now," I offered.

Another headshake. "Not them; that's what hurts. You don't know my father. All his clout is in connections with people in the city." No matter where you lived around the bay, when you said "the city" you meant metropolitan San Francisco. "It's just about the only place where he doesn't carry a gun. No, my family will play out their hand right smack in the city."

Of course I'd told them what the Santa Rosa broadcast had said. We knew the approaching fallout was coming from San Francisco itself. Most hands being played out in Baghdad-by-the-Bay were losing hands. It was one thing to reject your family's ways but quite another to envision them all dead in a miles-wide funeral pyre.

"Maybe your folks had a cellar," Cammie said.

Kate brightened. "Wine cellar. Part of the mystique."

"You don't mean *those* Gallos," Lance said in awe.

"No"—Kate managed a wan smile—"but I could lie about it if you insist."

Ern said he didn't care which Gallo she was if she could produce a bottle of sherry, and that reminded me of the stuff in my liquor cabinet. I said to Shar, "We need to take another reading in the basement for that graph you're making. I'll just nip out and do it and bring back a bottle to celebrate our new electric light plant."

It was around four in the afternoon. Shar consulted her graph and calculated that the outside reading should be around a hundred rems, while the basement should read about two or three—if the fallout cloud had missed us. Five minutes in the basement would be a twelfth of that dosage, which laid only a small fraction of a rem on the meter reader. "It's your hide, bubba," said my sis.

I took the meter hardware and fed several sparks to the meter, then chose a half-empty bottle of brandy and some cream sherry the kids could sip with us. I rummaged and found two decks of cards.

The basement stank like an outhouse. We needed the forty gallons of water in the tunnel for drinking, but my waterbed was available so I sloshed some water from the mattress into a pan and filled the toilet tank in three trips. The damned thing had to be flushed of its barf and never-you-mind.

Then, after nearly four minutes, I checked the meter.

The leaves of foil were completely relaxed together.

Fighting jitters, I charged the meter again and took a one-minute reading. Meanwhile I cursed myself for assuming that the reading wouldn't be off scale in four minutes. I got a one-minute reading of over four rems an hour and hightailed it into the tunnel.

Though abashed by my stupid error, I described it to the others, determined that they could profit by my dumbfuckery. Shar's conclusion was simple and direct; the only smart way to read the meter was to watch it closely for the first minute. If you didn't have a useful reading by that time, ambient radiation was roughly one rem or less.

Her second conclusion was borne out as we took readings in the tunnel. Shortly before I'd gone out to the basement, heavy fallout had begun to irradiate my little place.

For the next hour the tunnel was a hotbed of projects. I was urged to do nothing that even smacked of exercise because my great bulk would use up twice as much air as, say, Lance— and I'd give off more cee-oh-two and water vapor. So I sat near the little six-watt bike headlamp and took several long readings on the meter.

Shar turned over the sponge-bath chore to Devon and went to use our temporary john. She sprinkled a shotglassful of bleach into the hole after using it, carefully extracted the half-full bag, and placed it into a big brown paper grocery bag. The taped seams of the plastic bag might give way, but it wouldn't come apart with heavy kraft paper around it. She installed the next plastic bag with the paper sack already surrounding it in the plastic trashcan, and I wondered why Ern hadn't thought of that. It is truly amazing how fast we get smart when faced with a dribble of dookey.

Especially somebody else's.

I also understood how farm and ranch people earn their penchant for earthy humor. Dealing with natural functions like evacuation on such a grand scale, you're often faced with side effects that could outrage a saint. But you can always joke about them, robbing them of their power to beat you down. Maybe that explains the rough jokes we shared while in the tunnel.

Ern read my sister's notes and found little to criticize. At a quarter till five we were reading almost exactly two rems per hour in the tunnel, which scared the hell out of us until we found it subsiding soon afterward. We didn't talk about it to the kids, who were fixing a simulacrum of supper and pedaling the bike.

By six o'clock Shar had a radiation-versus-time graph and an estimate of the total dosage for each of us. For Mrs. Baird, who continued her heaves and diarrhea without losing much fluid, Shar simply put a question mark. I knew the answer in total rems had to be in four figures.

Next to Devon Baird's name she wrote four hundred, with another question mark after it. He seemed to be perking up, even insisting on pedaling the bike and pumping air. Best of all, he was retaining food and liquids now. His question mark was the only valid one, but who was so cruel as to tell him that?

I was next on the list with an estimated forty rems because I'd been in the attic and outside, too. Shar and Ern came next with thirty-five; Kate had taken five less. And below Cammie's twenty-five came Lance with twenty or so. Maybe Lance was young enough at eleven to be one of the "very young" who, like the aged, were supposed to be more vulnerable. I tried not to begrudge him the advantage. In any case it was an arguable set of estimates—in Ern's jargon, strictly paper empiricism.

My sis didn't mention lethal doses in front of Devon Baird. Instead she dwelt on the positive side. "In class we studied the *Lucky Dragon* incident," she said, spooning a portion of tuna and green peas that was not—couldn't possibly be!—half as bad as it sounds. "The entire crew of this Japanese fishing boat was accidentally dosed in 1954; they even ate contaminated food. They took gamma doses of around a hundred and seventy-five rems, and *all of them survived it!* I think one man died months later from some medication, but the rest made it. And they took much higher doses than we're taking here."

Devon, listlessly: "What if they keep dropping bombs near us every day?"

Ern said, "I can't believe there's much more to shoot at around here."

"I hope not," Devon replied, and dubiously addressed his tuna salad.

Presently we finished our meal, and though Spot made overtures to the leftovers, I steered him firmly to his farina mix. A tally of our food told us we'd have enough for two meals a day through ten days without resorting to horsemeat. By then we might be eating farina mix ourselves. At least we wouldn't have to cook it.

Shar urged Kate to be dealer, referee, and sergeant-at-arms for a card game among the younger members, and as soon as Devon got engrossed in the game, my sis motioned me nearer to Ern, who was seated at the air pump. "Let's talk about what we'll have to do next month," she said loudly enough to be overheard, and then much more softly, "Mrs. Baird seems to have a new problem."

The woman was semiconscious now but never spoke and could barely swallow. Shar had noticed the gradual, steady appearance of clear blisters on the woman's skin. Though some blisters were forming on her torso, they predominated in a sprinkle of raised glossy patches on her lower legs, arms, neck, and face. To Devon's query, Shar had only smiled and said we'd have to wait and see. To Ern and me, she said, "I'm afraid it means severe radiation burns, probably direct skin contact with particles only a few hours from the fireball. The blisters are on all sides of her body, so there's no way we can make her comfortable unless—but I guess the waterbed is out of the question."

"In more ways than one," I admitted. "I hate to bring it up, but while stealing some water from it to flush the toilet, I realized that that water will not be drinkable."

They both gaped at me in the gloom. "But we've only got maybe twenty gallons left in the tunnel, Harve," said Ern. "And about the same in your bathroom. What's wrong with waterbed stuff?"

"The chemicals I put in to prevent algae," I said and sighed. "It's not just bleach, guys. Bleach slowly deteriorates a vinyl mattress, so I used a pint of a commercial chemical. It's poison. I'm sorry."

We fell silent for a time. The kids didn't notice because they were talking louder, making noise for noise's sake. I understood why when I heard the Baird kid's spasms from the root cellar. He was losing his dinner into our jury-rigged john. I'd spent years rooting out soured curds of the milk of human kindness from my system because of the work I'd chosen; yet the quiet courage of this slender kid forced a tightening in my throat. I knew why I hadn't befriended him more: I didn't want to mourn if we lost him. That didn't say much for *my* courage.

"That poor boy," Shar murmured, "has diarrhea too. I wish we had some plug-you-uptate."

That was our childhood phrase for diarrhea medicine. I said, "Mom used to have a natural remedy. You remember what it was?"

"Well, she started with an enema of salt and baking soda, but that was to replace lost salt and to clean out the microbes. This isn't the same thing. If anything the Bairds probably don't have *enough* intestinal flora. Anyway, mom also gave us pectin and salty bouillon."

"Why the hell didn't you say so," asked Ern. "We've got a half-dozen bouillon cubes in each bike kit."

I put in, "If it's pectin you need, I doodled around with quince preserves from all those quinces falling off my bushes. There's so much pectin in a quince, you can jell other fruit preserves just by adding diced quince."

"I'd forgotten you make a hobby of food. God knows *how* I could forget, you great lump of bubba."

"Beat your wife, Ern," I begged.

"Just washed her and can't do a thing with her," he said.

As soon as Devon returned to the card game, Ern took a flashlight and went to find the bouillon cubes. Our carefully nurtured good spirits took a dip when he returned with only one tiny foil-wrapped bouillon cube. "I know I put 'em in," he complained, tossing the single cube to Shar.

Lance saw the gleam of foil. "Dibs," he shouted. "I saw it first, mother!" My nephew's tone suggested that he could be severe on infractions of fair play.

Shar regarded him silently for a moment, knowing as we all did that Lance had retrieved flashlights from the bike kits. Mildly: "Lance, you must've eaten at least fifty already."

In extracting confessions my sis had only to exaggerate the offense to have Lance set her straight. "Fifty? Naw, there was only a few."

"How many do you have left?"

"All of 'em. Right here," he said and patted his belly. In the ensuing quiet his grin began to slide into limbo.

"Aw, he's all right, Miz McKay," Devon said in the boy's support.

The point was that Devon himself was *not,* and bouillon could have helped him. Inwardly we writhed with an irony that we must not share with Devon. "Thank you, Devon, but I'll decide that. Lance, come here a minute," said Shar.

Mumbled: "Don't wanta."

"Two meals tomorrow, Lance."

He came bearing the word "Bully."

Shar indicated that he should sit between his parents. Then, in tones of muted mildness, my sis composed music for my ears; a menacing sonata, a brilliant *bel canto* that struck my nephew dumb.

Did Lance recall his father's threat? Shar was ready, even eager now, to endorse it. Lance would touch no food or drink without asking first. He would perform every job we asked without audible or visible complaint. He would use nothing, take nothing, play with nothing unless he got permission first. It was not up to Lance to decide when an infraction might be harmless.

Of course he had an alternative, said Shar with a calm glance toward me. Lance could elect to do as he pleased. He would then be thrashed on his bare butt by parents *and* his uncle (here I saw the whites of his eyes) and would be bound and gagged if need be for as long as necessary.

"By now, dear, you may have thought of claiming you need to go to the bathroom while tied up. Of course you can. In your pants. Since you have no other clothes and you can't wash the ones you have, you may want to think twice before you do that. But it's up to you, sonny boy," Shar gradually crescendoed.

"Finally, I'm sure you don't really believe what I'm saying. You'll just *have* to try some little thing to see where the real limits are, just to test us as you always do. Believe me, dear, I can hardly wait. I want you to try some little bitty thing I can interpret as a little bitty test, so I can blister your big bitty bottom after your father and Harve are through warming it up for me.

"I can't tell you how many times I've considered this, Lance. I've wanted to do it, but I didn't want to stunt your development. Now it's time we all stunted the direction it has taken. What you consider a harmless prank might kill someone. Because you didn't know and didn't care. Those bouillon cubes, for example, were very very important. It's not important that you know why. What *is* important is that you're going to forget and pop off, sneak a bit of food or tinker with something without asking. And when you do, dear, I am going to make up for ten years of coddling your backside. Ern? Harve? Do you have anything to add?"

We thought she had it covered rather well and said so. A long silence followed. Lance opened his mouth a few times but always closed it again. For the first time in my memory, he was not physically leaning in his mother's direction. At last Shar said, "Would you like to go now?"

"Yes'm." It was almost inaudible.

"I recommend it." A chastened Lance scuttled back to the card game. I wondered if Shar had exaggerated her willingness to whale her darling. No doubt Lance wondered, too, but not enough to check it out right then.

Ern asked, "You cold, Shar?"

"My shakes have nothing to do with the temperature," she said. "The more I said to Lance, the more I realized how true it was. I feel ashamed of myself but I want to go over there right now and—and—"

"And whack on him some," I finished for her. "You're okay, sis, but you're right about letting us tan his hide first. If you took first licks you might hurt him."

"We have casualties already." She laughed a bit shakily. "I wish we could go upstairs and get those quince preserves."

"They're in little jars in the root cellar," I said and went in search of the stuff, which didn't need special sealing when I used only honey as sweetener. For some reason honey seemed to dissuade mold; so much so that the fermenting of mead, a honey wine, was an expensive process. I couldn't even get the damned stuff to ferment with added yeast, and I knew a lot of old-timer tricks.

Returning with two jars of preserves under wax, I thought of using a candle as a food warmer. If we lit a candle in the root cellar, it would be downstream of us. Its heated air and carbon dioxide would tend to drift out through the valve Shar had made. Ern thought it worth a try, using an empty bean can with vents punched around its top and bottom as a chimney. For fondue warmers I had a dozen squat votive candles, which quickly became broad puddles of fluid wax unless you had a close-fitting container to keep the puddle from spreading. Ern made one from several thicknesses of foil.

Mrs. Baird's bedpan needed emptying, and Lance performed the chore with the expression of one who has an unexpected mouthful of green persimmon. Ern went to the root cellar with him and tried our little food warmer, which Shar wanted to use for hot water to make a quince-preserve gruel. If the Baird woman could swallow such warm sweet stuff she might—well, it might help. I'm sure my sis was thinking about the tremendous strain I had added to our survival efforts by bringing in a woman who was perhaps better dead than suffering. And who almost certainly would die regardless of anything medical science could have done.

The evening brought its full share of good and bad news. It was good that by nine o'clock the tunnel reading was down to one rem, since that meant the sizzling ferocity of radiation outside had dropped to "merely" two hundred rems an hour—half its level only a few hours previous. It was also nice that Shar remembered my hot-water heater in its insulated niche near the furnace, so much out of sight that I'd forgotten its fifty-gallon supply of clean water just waiting to be drained from its bottom faucet. Seventy gallons of drinking water might last us two weeks, and we could use the waterbed stuff for washing.

If we absolutely had to, we could boil the mattress water and hope the chemical would lose its potency. Ern guessed that a lot of people would be drinking from waterbeds, and with a dilution of one pint of chemical to two hundred gallons of water, the user only swallowed a few drops of mild poison in each gallon of water. Better than dying of thirst; far worse than drinking from your hot-water heater.

I couldn't decide whether it was good or bad news that, if the eleven o'clock news from Santa Rosa could be believed, our government had removed restrictions against the purchase of weapons by expatriate Cubans in Florida. There was no longer any doubt that Cuba had been a launch site for cruise missiles against Miami, Tampa, Eglin, and other targets. Want an Uzi with full auto fire? Bazooka? A few incendiary bombs? See your friendly dealer in the nearest bayou or yacht club, so long as you can say *"Fidel come mierda sin sal"* three times quickly. Castro's radar scopes were already measled with blips that consisted of every known vintage aircraft and surface craft, mostly crewed by disgruntled Cubans who had scores to settle and machismo to spare.

Later we might regret this response. For the moment Soviet Cuba had too much coastline to worry about to mount any further actions against the US. If many of those itchy-fingered expatriates went ashore and stayed there, Fidel's ass was grass. Put it down as good and bad news. Maybe "crazy news" was a better term.

On the bad-news side, the radio announced that grocery sales were suspended nationwide for the next few days, with certain exceptions. Perishable produce and milk could be sold in limited quantities while the government assessed stocks of food, and if you didn't have enough food to last two or three days, you were going to get pretty hungry. This rationing plan was a long-standing preparation by the feds, a decision that few of us had ever heard about. I gathered from the broadcast that the government had funded many studies on nuclear survival but hadn't published them widely, perhaps because so few of us cared to request them through our congressional reps or the Department of Commerce.

The radio claimed that an Oak Ridge study, *Expedient Shelter Construction,* was good news since surviving newspapers were printing millions of copies to be distributed across the land by every available means, including air drops of stapled copies. Was it such good news? I wished I thought so. The

document hadn't reached the public in time. What did we care
if five hundred copies gathered dust in emergency-technology
libraries for a decade?

One news item was almost certainly *not* a government news
release because it suggested that disaster-related documents
could be bought in hard copy or microfiche from an address
they repeated several times:

> National Technical Information Service
> U.S. Department of Commerce
> 5285 Port Royal Road
> Springfield, Virginia 22161

I was sure the item was an ill-advised brainstorm by a local
reporter, since the postal service couldn't possibly be func-
tioning well enough to respond to millions of suddenly fascinated citizens who'd never heard of the NTIS before. If they'd
known and cared years earlier the item might've been of tremendous importance. Now? Much too little, a little too late.

The news of the Bay Area was too awesomely bad for belief
if you listened between the lines. From San Mateo to Palo Alto
and in most of Fremont, fallout was only a few rems per hour,
though unofficial traffic in those areas would be by bike or on
foot. Mill Vally, too, had escaped the brunt of nuke hammer
blows. The main population centers were discussed only as a
list of places declared off limits and subject to martial law,
where deputized crews probed into the debris as far as they
dared: San Rafael, San Francisco, Burlingame, Mountain View,
Sunnyvale, San José, Hayward, Oakland, Vallejo.

Shar jotted down all the details we could recall from the
broadcasts, on the theory that we didn't yet know which detail
might save our collective skin in the long run. We'd have plenty
of time to cobble up notes on the area maps in my office long
before we risked going outside.

Within our own tiny subterranean world we made our own
bad news. Though Devon managed to get his mother to swallow
some lukewarm quince gruel, she couldn't keep it down. He
drank a half-pint of it only after Shar insisted that there would
be plenty for both of them. When Shar brought up the question
of the solitary bouillon cube it seemed a small thing, but it
forced a decision none of us wanted to make.

Despite her youth, Kate Gallo was adult in every practical

sense. That's why, when Shar demanded a committee decision on which of the Bairds would get the pitiful antidiarrhea dose of clear bouillon broth, I insisted that Kate have her say in it. I had to wake her. By then the kids were asleep.

After fifteen minutes of "yes-but," Ern said with a sigh, "It boils down to one likely fact, one agreement, and a hundred conjectures. Probable fact: Mrs. Baird won't be with us much longer, no matter what we do. Anybody disagree with that?" Nobody did. "And we seem to be agreed that if one cup of broth is barely enough to matter, splitting it between them would probably make it a pointless gesture.

"But the boy may be in the same fix as his mother. I've noticed a few blisters on his hands and neck. Still, he may pull through in spite of that. I think it's time for a vote," he finished.

In a small voice Kate asked, "Couldn't we have a secret ballot?"

"Why didn't I think of that," Shar said with a smile and quickly tore four small squares of paper, writing "M" and "F" on each before folding them. "Just circle which should get the broth, male or female," she said, handing the ballots out. Perhaps my sis was trying to make us more objective with this abstraction from names to simple symbols. If so, it didn't work.

Ern took the pen, did something with it in shadow, handed the pen to Kate. I had no doubt with his engineering-determinist's mind, he favored Devon, who had a fighting chance.

Kate needed lots of time. I figured her for the one most likely to favor Mrs. Baird, since the woman, like Kate herself had been, was an underdog.

Shar took the pen and turned away for only a moment before passing the instrument to me. I needed only a moment, too.

Then Shar took the folded squares, shook them between cupped hands, and opened them.

On three of them, neither letter was circled. On the fourth was a circle around the "M." "Three abstentions," Kate snorted. "That's totally unfair!"

"It does provide a decision," said Shar.

"Forced on one of us alone," said Kate, her voice rising until she caught herself. Of course only one of us knew which three had abstained. Kate went on, "If this is to be a committee decision, we should all take part."

The slow precision with which she fashioned another ballot told me that Shar was affronted by this snip of a girl. "Very well, we'll try again," said my sis, her mouth set primly.

We all took longer the second time. When Shar counted the ballots there was no longer any question; there was still one abstention, but the other three votes favored Devon. We all breathed more easily. No one said anything about that abstention, since the abstainer could not have changed the consensus.

Before settling back to sleep Kate muttered, "One lousy bouillon cube. I wish Lance had eaten it."

"No you don't, Kate," Shar said gently. "It may be the tiny nudge that saves a life."

"I hope so. You'll have to claim we found another one and gave it to Mrs. Baird."

"I intended to. Good night, Kate," spoken with respect.

I padded back to the root cellar and warmed some instant coffee that tasted of quince preserves. It was my first warm brew in days, a scent of ripe summer fruit that deepened my anguish over the decisions we had made; unknown decisions we would have to make later; the millions who were no longer alive to puzzle over decisions. Presently the tepid coffee began to taste of salt and I drained it, brewing more for Ern.

But my brother-in-law slumped snoring at the air pump he had contrived, the brandy bottle empty beside him. I roused him and took his place, unwilling to blame him for the dereliction. I had known Ern's mild dependence on booze for a long time, and I'd brought the stuff to him myself.

III. Doomsday Plus Two

It was Devon Baird who woke me before seven in the morning, and he was barely able to shake me after working at the pump. Someone had set the coffee warmer in the open where the candle's glow penetrated the tunnel. You could tell which of us was which but little more than that, since Ern had disconnected my car battery to prevent trickle losses.

Devon fought tears as he admitted, "It's not your time yet, Mr. Rackham, but my arms won't pull that thing anymore. I'm just not worth a durn for anything."

I took Shar's watch from him, hit its glow stud, and saw Devon stumble as I stood up. "You've brought your mother out of an annex of hell," I said gruffly, "and you're doing more than your body can handle. You want a criticism?"

Snuffling, but determined: "Say it."

"We all think you're going to be a great help if you'll take it easy and give your innards a chance to recuperate. You're pushing yourself too hard." I settled down at the air pump and added, "The sooner you get your strength back, the sooner you can do hard work."

His tears began to flow then. He asked if he could sit with me, and I said truthfully that I was honored. Five minutes later he was sleeping, his fuzzy cheek still damp against my back, one slender arm draped over my shoulder so that his hand brushed my face as I moved to operate the pump. Ern was right: Devon was developing blisters on his hands.

Near the end of my shift, Lance awoke and tried to talk to Cammie. "Give her a break," I whispered. "She's been working the pump, Lance. But as long as you're up, you might as well take over for me."

"I'm not up," he said, and then he must have remembered

something because he did as I asked while I carried the sleeping Devon to his makeshift place near his mother. Then I returned and sat near Lance, who squelched his singsong cadence as he worked the pump. Something about, "Columbus had a cabin boy, the dirty little nipper..."

I patted his back the way I used to do when he played outside on the swing set. "How many verses do you know, pal?"

Long silence to prove I wasn't his pal. "Of what?"

"There must be a hundred verses of 'Sonofabitch Columbo.' At your age I knew most of 'em."

"I've heard a few," he acknowledged, softly humming the tune. He didn't sing the words anymore and made sure we didn't touch. Clearly my nephew had changed only to the extent that he was wary of punishment, protecting his flanks. When Lance had worked for a half-hour, I suggested he wake his dad. He was happy enough to do it, happier still to snuggle down against Cammie. As Ern took over at the pump, I settled back near Kate, and as I drifted into sleep, I reflected that I could depend on Lance. He wouldn't be trying to wake the others again if he knew it would earn him an extra stint at the pump.

I don't know whose idea it was to dump the crapsacks up on my screen porch. By the time I was through yawning and blinking late in the morning, Shar had already done it while Ern monitored radiation levels in the basement. Shar reasoned that, since it took only a half-minute to make the round trip to the porch, she'd take only a fractional rem in the process—and any microbe that survived storage on that porch for a week deserved to live. Because the level outside was still upward of two hundred rems.

Ern found two moderately hot spots in the basement. One, near the fireplace foundation, we knew about. The other was very localized at our air filters.

Obviously the filters were collecting fallout. Just as clearly, judging by the negligible readings at the pump, they were stopping that fallout while passing clean air. Still, they made a hot spot that demanded a fix. I helped Ern lug cans of paint, the jerrycan of fuel, and pillowcases full of earth shoveled from the root cellar to make a barrier around the filters. We made a bridge of shelving over the filter boxes and stacked books atop it, which isolated the filter boxes fairly well.

I asked Ern why he poured a gallon of fuel into a double boiler from the jerrycan. "Because we need to cook some food before it spoils," he said, and let me wonder what we'd use for a stove and how we'd get rid of the smoke. I couldn't argue the need for it; we were already tired of canned veggies, and my stock of frozen food was thawing.

Shar had her own solution to the fresh vegetable problem, with the pound of alfalfa seeds I had forgotten in my kitchen. I supposed the stuff was too old to germinate after long storage, but my sis knew better. She dumped a handful of seeds into a one-gallon plastic jug and poured a cupful of water in, then set the jug aside. I would've bet a case of dark Löwenbräu against those seeds sprouting in near-total darkness. And I would've lost.

No matter how stir-crazy we became, the basement reading was still dangerously high—four rems. Shar's graph predicted a flattening out of the radiation curve, and Ern calculated that the radiation in the basement wouldn't drop below one rem for at least another day. During the next twenty-four hours we would absorb a total of ten rems in the tunnel but fifty if we moved into the basement. Enough said. One look at Mrs. Baird was enough to make me shrink from heavy doses.

Kate kept the kids occupied by introducing them to a dreadful card game called I Doubt It that reduced her foursome to tears of laughter while they operated the air pump. At the other end of the tunnel, my sis and I squinted at her notes in the light of a naked bike lamp while Ern sketched and rummaged through junk in the root cellar. Shar also tended the tiny candle stove while it warmed a cup of water for that paltry serving of broth.

"How long do you think the woman has?" We no longer used her name, as though by that means we could depersonalize her.

"She could go anytime, Harve. Her bedpan is showing blood, and the poor thing has lost so much fluid she weighs next to nothing. If only—"

To keep her from saying it, I broke in, "If only I hadn't—"

"If only she'd get it over with!" By voicing assumed guilt, I'd made her say something worse. "It's only a question of *when*. And after that we'll have another problem I don't even want to talk about."

"Telling Devon?"

"No; what do we do with the body?"

It had never crossed my mind. I thought about the way some primitives discarded their dead like so much debris on midden heaps, and our society's equally bizarre rites with embalming fluid and lead-lined caskets. Neither method would serve us, but we couldn't just let a corpse lie in state among us until it began to putrefy. Shallow burial in the tunnel? Removal to the back porch? The—oh, God!—the modest proposal accepted by the Donner party?

Shar crumbled the bouillon cube into hot water and stirred carefully, then called Devon, who weaved with exhaustion as he approached. That kid would have to be mollified with the burial arrangements; desperate as our situation was, we had to demonstrate some difference between our group and mere apes in britches, for the morale of the group itself.

After Shar offered the broth, Devon paused with the pan in his hands, sniffing the exquisite aroma: "My mom needs this more than I do."

Shar busied herself at her notes, unwilling to face him as she replied with her ready lie: his mom had already taken the "other" cupful.

He sipped, sighed, sipped again, then gulped it down. Staring at the empty pan as if it bore an inscription, he said, "Mom isn't going to make it, is she? How could she?"

"I don't know," I said, unsure whether it was better that he be prepared.

In an angry growl: "I think she's made up her mind to die!" He handed the pan to Shar, his glare challenging her to disagree.

It wasn't the first time I'd seen the living rage at the dead for dying. And anger might be a more survival-oriented reaction than hopeless sorrow, I thought. I said, "Whatever she's decided, I can see you've made up your mind to pull through. Join the club." And I stuck my hand out to be shaken.

His grip was as firm as he could make it, his shoulders almost straight as he strode back to the card game. I traded shrugs with Shar; our tunnel contained no experts in the bereavement process.

My voice has a rumble that carries, so I husked it: "One thing we can do is tape up a bodybag, sis. But not until afterward."

"Burial," she said firmly, "is out. A week from now there

will still be too much radiation to dig a grave—unless you can do it in a few minutes. Ernie?"

"I'm listening," he muttered, opening a three-pound can of coffee. "Can't think of a good answer, but I'll mull it over."

Dumping the fresh coffee grains into a plastic bag for storage, he cut wide, shallow tabs around a fourth of the can's lip at the open end. In explanation: "Saw a backpacker's wood stove like this once. Swedish baffles, little telescoping stack. This'll be fed by gasoline, and we'll run its exhaust up your water-heater stack."

I pondered that for a moment. "Won't there be some fallout down that stack?"

"Very little in one that narrow, I suspect. Hell, it's just dust. The stove exhaust should drive it up and out anyway. All the same, Harve, remind me to use gloves when I'm rigging the stack."

I said I would. "But damn' if I know what you'll use for an exhaust stack; you sure can't use paper, Ern."

"I was snooping around your furnace and water heater before you woke up. The water-heater exhaust and some of your forced-draft pipes are wrapped with fiberglass insulation, and the insulation has a thin aluminum skin that clips around like a sleeve. It's that sleeving I'll use for a stack."

I objected that aluminum wouldn't take the heat either.

He countered with a weird solution: pack raw horsemeat around the lowest part of it, with bread or dough around the meat and a jacket of aluminum foil around the whole mess. The meat would absorb the heat, the bread would absorb the grease, and we could cook twice as much at once. It might, he added with a smile, even be edible.

I said the aluminum sleeves were much too wide.

He said fine, he would narrow them with tin snips and curl the sleeve down to whatever diameter we needed, using wire to hold that diameter.

I said somebody would have to stay with it, taking four rems an hour in the basement.

He said like hell; we could leave the tunnel only to take quick peeks at the stuff we were cooking.

I said if he was so goddamn smart why hadn't he thought of using the aluminum sleeves while we were sweating out the air pump.

He said if he'd been *that* smart, we would've smarted ourselves out of a cookstove because there wouldn't be any aluminum left.

I burst out laughing and took my electric lantern to steal those aluminum sleeves from the house ducting.

Spot was as jumpy as I'd ever seen him, no doubt longing for a sprint around the fence perimeter. Before taking pliers to the aluminum sleeving, I went to my office desk and took the little aspirin tin from the back of the top drawer. The tabs inside weren't aspirin. They were what I called comealongs, not as fast as chloral hydrate but capable of turning a flash-tempered goon into a very mellow fellow. I wasn't sure of their effect on a cheetah, but I could always start with a half-tab and increase the dose if necessary.

It was a rotten trick to pull on my friend. So was keeping him cooped up when he was designed to run. I figured that my problem was common to a million people with dogs too big for house pets. I hoped they were working out better solutions than mine—and I doubted it.

Hustling back to the tunnel, I brought three lengths of aluminum sleeving to Ern. Shar was gently treating Mrs. Baird's blistered skin with baking-soda solution, a task made more onerous by the near-certainty that it would all be futile. The woman's eyes were half-open, her breathing almost imperceptible. She was no longer swallowing much.

I steered my thoughts away from the notion of getting a few of my comealongs dissolved in her water. Had our survival demanded it, I would have done it. Instead, I busied myself slicing strips from a roast taken from my freezer the day before. It was no longer frozen, and one thing we didn't need was tainted meat. I also placed a half-dozen discs of horsemeat, still frozen from Spot's dispenser, atop the candle heater for partial thawing. Spot hovered near, ignoring his farina mix, the furry white tip of his tail signaling the gradual abrasion of his patience.

I showed Ern the half-tab I crumbled into the first thawed hunk of ground meat. "I don't get it," he said.

"Mighty right you don't; he does," I replied and placed the meat before Spot. It was gone in seconds.

Ern paused at his job of making a shallow fuel tray from a cut-down tuna can and twisted wire. "I thought you weren't going to give him . . . whoa. It's not aspirin," he accused.

I told him what it was. "The finicky bastard would never

take it in water, I know that. But fool that he is, he trusts me. I intend to keep him half-zonked for the duration, or as long as twenty tabs will last."

Ern nodded, rubbed his temples while squeezing his eyes shut. "Getting a headache—eyestrain, I think. Could the air be going bad on us?"

"I feel clearheaded. I might even tell you what's eleven times twelve, given a calculator and a half-hour start."

"Proof positive," he said with a chuckle and started trimming tabs around the hole he'd made near the flat bottom of the big coffee can. "There's a dozen sure 'nough aspirin in each bike kit, Harve. How about getting me a couple?"

I did, and sniffed out another of Spot's calling cards on the top shelf in the root cellar. Just the thing to shatter an appetite whetted by my rumbling stomach. In any case, Shar had already announced a two-meal day, and if there was one guy alive who could live on his fat for a month, it was yours truly. Well, the more I dieted, the less I'd sweat. Our exhalations had made the tunnel a bit clammy. And that made me think about the moisture in our bodies—which eventually led me to an answer to Shar's unpleasant question about burial.

Ern's little stove became a joke, distinguishable from a comedy of errors only by the fact that no matter how far a comedy goes wrong, it can't kill you. Spot could've been a nuisance when the smell of cooking—yes, and burning—fat began to permeate the tunnel, but the half-tab in his breakfast had made him lackadaisical. Instead of sitting smug and alert like some Egyptian idol, he put his chin on his paws and ignored us. We no longer bothered to seal the door from the basement to the tunnel, since radiation readings were dropping steadily. Besides, we had to run into the basement to adjust the damned stove too often to maintain the seal.

First, the connection between jury-rigged stovepipe and water-heater outlet pipe leaked like a sonofabitch. But Ern's cure was easy: he pulled cottony bits of fiberglass insulation from my air ducts, packed the fluff around the connection, and covered it with kitchen foil lightly bound with wire.

Then the gasoline pan got too hot. We could see fuel boiling just under the flames and hauled the flat pan out to snuff the fire. Then he put dirt into the pan and soaked it with fuel, and covered the little pan with a tuna can through which he punched several holes. That way only a few candlelike flames arose from fumes generated by the heat.

Ern admitted that it was damned dangerous; a nitwit's trick. So was starving or eating raw horsemeat. He finally managed to make the stove work without blowing himself up, but it's not an experiment I recommend.

Under the stove were four inches of dirt we dug from the root cellar, the whole rig sitting in the bottom half of a big turkey baster. Any spattered fuel would soak into the dirt instead of running down onto my carpet. Eventually our noses told us we had managed to include dirt that had soaked up Spot's urine. A male cheetah sprays backward instead of lifting his leg, and some of it had run down the cellar wall into the dirt. Naturally it smelled as though a big cat had peed into a fire. Lovely; just *lovely*.

Then we had a smoke scare when grease managed to find its way out of the foil surrounding the horsemeat we had packed around the base of the smokestack. Ern said that at least we knew the meat was cooking. Shar replied that any housewife knew we could choke the whole place on grease smoke.

Kate had the real solution: she simply made biscuit dough and packed that around the base of the stack with a foil collar. Worked like a champ; sure, the doughnut-shape biscuit blackened on its inner surface, but who the hell cared by that time?

We found that the stove worked best when it was cooking a potful of stuff on its flat top. Over a period of hours we cooked the sliced roast, twelve pounds of horsemeat, and a big pot of stew simmered with finely diced veggies plus a half-pound of bacon. Kate and Cammie seemed to enjoy the slow assembly-line manufacture of biscuits, which we smeared with fruit preserves. Devon got most of the quince preserves; his diarrhea was less, but still a problem. Shar hoped he could build his own personal plug with quince and half-burned biscuit.

After all the damnfoolishness with that stove, most of us had spent an hour in the basement, which was too long for safety. It was late afternoon then, and the others retreated into the tunnel, where Kate promised to read aloud from a collection of Roald Dahl's fiendish little stories. I had something to do upstairs and didn't want to argue about it, so I announced that I intended to find some soup mix that had been overlooked upstairs. The soup mix and some spices were real enough. Only my motive was faked.

I found the mix and spices at the back of a high kitchen shelf, then ran upstairs to get my raincoat and waders. Back in the kitchen, I put on my regalia and unsealed the door to the screen porch, slipping through with a kitchen knife in one gloved hand.

It took me only a minute to saw the long section of screen from its framing, and I slapped dust from the screen while holding my breath. At first I wondered at the faint, pungent odor, like the stink of a generator with worn brushes. It was ozone, a by-product of gamma rays through the air. Hurriedly I rolled the screen into a tube, but before opening the door into the house again, I paused to gaze outside.

Folded gray quilts of cloud spanned the sky over a gray and green world. It wasn't yet time for my oaks to shed, but their leaves were falling. My grape arbor and quince hedge lay under a light dusting of gray stuff, the color and harbinger of death. No magpie or robin patrolled the weeds, no late-season grasshopper crackled across the open places. No distant automobile moaned down the creek road, no farmer's dog barked, no hawk wheeled beneath the ash-gray clouds. I found it possible, inside my protective clothing, to sweat and raise gooseflesh simultaneously. I had gone to the porch for a makeshift burial shroud, only to find that the world had anticipated me with a shroud of its own.

This time I shucked the coat, gloves, and waders in my dining room with the rolled screen and hurried down to the basement, pausing only to reseal the trapdoor tape. I had not been truly frightened of being alone, or of the dank-smelling dark that fills enclosed basements, for many years; yet I fled to the tunnel. I feared no hobgoblin in the shadows. I felt haunted from within, as though death were trying my body on for size.

At his mother's bidding Lance brought me a cup of strong instant coffee while I rubbed briskly at my arms and chest to banish my internal blizzard. My sis had known me for forty years, so I saw no point in bullshitting her when she softly asked what my trouble was.

I thanked Lance for the coffee; waited until he went back to squat, cross-legged, where he could hear Kate's lively rendition of a story called "Parson's Pleasure." Then I told Shar what I'd done and why.

"I hadn't thought of an elevated burial, but it certainly puts the rest of us at minimum risk," Shar mused. "Didn't the Indians do that?"

"Crow, Sioux, Cheyenne," I said and nodded. "Kept animals away. We can strap—the package—outside an upstairs window on the roof, when the time comes. The south exposure gets a lot of sun, and a shroud of screen will let moisture out. It's my guess that a body could simply mummify before it decays very much, given enough sunlight and hard radiation."

"Mm-hmm. Ironic, isn't it, bubba? They've finally made a weapon that not only kills you but keeps you from spoiling."

"Take it further, sis. In cities where they have a half-million dead and no bulldozers to bury them, disposal squads may carry bodies to the hottest spot they dare to reach."

She meditated on me while I slurped coffee. Then: "I never dreamed this sort of awful work would affect you so, Harve."

"Me neither. But that wasn't what sent the wind whistling up my hemorrhoids. Sis, I stood on my porch a few minutes ago and looked and listened, and there's nothing alive out there. No—thing. You know how the effing mosquitoes love to cruise the back porch? Well, not now they don't. Not a bug, not a sight or sound of anything. I know insects are supposed to be resistant to radiation. Maybe it's the ozone in the air; I don't know."

Ern had moved nearer to listen. He said, "Pretty much as we expected, Harve."

"I know. But we also talked about what we'd do as soon as we left the basement. Peeling and canning vegetables that might be in season; jerking and storing meat; planting as soon as possible." I drained the last bitter taste of coffee, envying the innocence of the youngsters twenty feet away. "But it isn't going to happen that way, folks. Don't you understand? *It's all dead out there now.*"

"Not permanently. Surely not the plants," Shar argued.

"Okay, goddammit; if not dead then lost to us. It only has to be hot enough out there to screw a few rems an hour into you every hour for several more weeks. And that it will damn well do!"

"Are you trying to tell us you think it's hopeless?"

"Here? Yes. *Christ,* I hate to think of leaving, but figure it out yourselves. Shar, what do your notes predict in two weeks, after we're completely out of food and safe water?"

"You know as well as I do. Four rems an hour, something like that."

"And seven times longer—fourteen weeks—for it to decay to a half-rem. Let's say we take an average of two rems during every hour we're outside scrounging food and trying to filter water. That means four hours a day or more; eight rems a day. In seven weeks that's a lethal dose.

"And half that dose will make us as sick as those Japanese fishermen, who got expert medical attention, whereas we won't. With all of us in Devon's condition, we won't be able to fend for ourselves here."

Ern, utterly disgusted: "Why the miserable fuck didn't we think about this a long time ago?"

"Maybe it was unthinkable," I replied, "but who expected such hellacious fallout here? It isn't unthinkable now. What we must do—we *have* to!—is plan where to go and the best time to do it."

"That time is certainly not now," Shar said firmly, "unless we know someplace that's free of contamination and that we can reach within a couple of hours."

We thrashed that out for a while. We knew from the radio that safe spots existed across the bay, below San Francisco. But we entertained no illusions about finding a way to get there in a hurry. Roads to the south were probably not navigable anyway.

The fallout pattern eliminated any thought of fleeing east. To our west was the big bay itself, and we thought it unlikely we'd find a boat that would take us all. That left Hobson's choice, northwest past Vallejo into a region without target areas. If we could believe the Santa Rosa broadcasts, their problem was people, not radiation. *Our* problem was getting us across a couple of miles of water onto a road leading north, and doing it in a few hours.

That didn't seem possible. I'd made it with Kate in the Lotus, but it was no freighter. "Ern, could you drive my car over open water? It'd take you and both kids in one hop."

Among Ern's greatest virtues was the ability to face his limitations. "Not a chance, Harve. Anyway, I'd have to leave them and come back for another load, and I wouldn't do that without an armed guard for them. Besides, how would we all get from here to Suisun Bay without walking?"

Shar said it could be done. The McKays had three bikes and a skateboard. With Ern towing Lance and Kate riding double with Cammie, I could take Devon in the Lotus. No one mentioned his mother. We might, said Shar, make it to the narrow neck of the little bay in three hours.

I reminded her that I intended to take Spot, too. "He's a sprinter, not a long-distance runner. If I have to kiss him good-bye I will, sis, but ask yourself where we'll find another guard animal to equal him. You don't have to tell me that people are worth more than animals; I just think we can manage to take him along without tipping the lifeboat over.

"Besides, Spot should be able to go the distance to the water on foot if he goes at the pace of a bike."

"How will you feed him?"

"He may have to work that out himself. My corn patch always gets its share of varmints, and he's learned to snag a raven. He's learned to be wary of a 'coon, but if he's hungry enough he'll make out okay, I think."

An ugly trickling noise told us that Mrs. Baird's body was losing more fluid, a purely mechanical response that we found to be blood instead of fecal material. Shar turned away to attend to the duty she had assumed. Ern and I continued to hammer away at the barriers that stood between us and the north side of Suisun Bay.

I couldn't help ruminating on that day at the racetrack. From a purely selfish standpoint I'd have been smarter to head north instead of coming home. I wondered how often kissable Kate cussed herself for not splitting when she had the chance.

Ern studied Shar's little graph and mused, "One thing's clear: wherever we go, we can't risk it while the radiation count is much over ten rems an hour outside, in case we have to come back. That means we have a week to plan before we run for it."

"Unless we take another heavy dose of fallout," I said. "The damned missilemen are still pounding away at—har, har—'selected targets,' as they put it in the radio bulletins. If we spot another cloud heading for us, we'll have to be ready to jump. Agreed?"

"Shit. Agreed. Boy, could I use a snort."

"Not if it puts you to sleep like it did the other night. Personally I could lay waste to three helpings of abalone supreme. We're just going to have to hobble along without our crutches, Ern."

"Don't remind me." Then he vented a light flutter of laughter, almost a schoolgirl giggle, which I'd learned to identify as delighted surprise. "You know what? We're neglecting the obvious, Harve. If any of the bridges are still spanning Suisun, we can all *walk* across!"

"Well, I'm a dirty sonofabitch."

"Very perceptive," he grinned. Despite the dying woman an arm's reach away, perhaps because laughter was so inapropos, we failed to strangle our mirth. Presently Shar returned with the emptied bedpan, and Ern told her why we were amused.

She perked up, but with a caveat. "Maybe the radio will give us a hint if the bridges can be crossed. If not, one of us may have to risk a solo trip to make sure."

I agreed, no longer amused. The Lotus was the only fast way to make that reconnaissance. And the only one who could drive it well was fat ol' Harve.

IV. Doomsday Plus Three

Maybe the Plains Indians were more in tune with their psyches using calendar hides than we were using our almanacs. Lacking written language, they made annual decisions on the most memorable event of the year and drew a small picture on a tanned hide adjacent to the last year's picture. In that way a calendar hide became a history of the tribe. The outstanding event for our tiny tribe, on the third day after the initial nuclear strikes, was the death of Mrs. Baird.

None of us could say when her body finally yielded to hopeless odds. It happened during the night, the thread of her life parting as silently as a single strand of cobweb. She was already cold at seven in the morning when Devon awoke for his turn at the pump. He must've mourned through the entire hour, unwilling to wake the rest of us, because he was all cried out by the time I woke up.

Though I could have carried her body out to the basement alone, Devon insisted on helping; his right, his duty. I almost had to fight him to prevent him from going outside to dig a grave.

"She took the chances she did," I reminded him, "because she wanted you to live. Don't make hers a wasted sacrifice, Devon."

Shar convinced him that several hours outside, especially with the dose he had already sustained, would positively kill him. "Anyway, we've got a better way. We can preserve her remains until we can give her a proper burial," she said with a motherly hug.

I didn't dwell on the mechanisms of dehydration or putrefaction; only told him we should follow the ways of early Americans with an elevated burial and claimed a false certainty

110

that the body would be well preserved. Devon Baird honored me by pretending to be wholly convinced.

By midmorning Shar and Devon had done the best they could with the emaciated, stiffening body, sprinkling it with cologne I never used anyway. The most grotesque moment came when we carried the body upstairs to my maple dining table and began to roll it into its shroud of screen. Ern had the presence of mind to take a reading in the dining room—about four rems, a reminder that we must not let our pitiful service become a drawn-out affair—and he had the good sense to stand aside until the precise instant when the body rolled off the table.

Ern kept the body from thumping the floor. Devon reacted quickly enough but was so weak that he sat down hard on the floor, his mother's head in his lap. "I'm sorry, mom," he whispered, and caressed the dead face. He was unable to rise without help. The kid was much closer to total physical collapse than I'd thought; running on sheer guts.

At last we got the screen rolled around the body and snugged it with wire, and while it may seem ludicrous to hold a funeral service over a roll of screen, that's what we did, holding lit candles. Shar had told me it was my job to say the right words. Devon would want a man to do it, and Ernest McKay would've frozen solid trying.

I said: "Lord, You've heard it all before. You must be hearing it from a hundred million throats today. For which we give no thanks."

I saw Shar's startled frown, her silently mouthed "Oh," or maybe it was "no." But I saw Devon nod, eyes closed, knuckles white on the fists at his sides. I continued.

"You gave this good woman the terrible gift of free choice, Lord, and she exercised it to keep her son alive, knowing it might kill her.

"And it did. Greater love than this hath no man and no woman, and for this alone we would ask You to cherish her. It's said that you can't take it with you, but Mrs. Baird beat the odds. She takes with her our greatest respect, and our hopes for her everlasting grace.

"If I misquote Khayyám, I crave Your understanding:

Oh Thou who woman of earth didst make,
And in her paradise devised the snake,

> For all the freely-chosen horror with which
>   the face of mankind is blackened,
> Our forgiveness give. *And take*.

Into-Your-hands-O-Lord-we-commend-her-spirit-Amen," I
ended quickly. I half-expected a lightning bolt before I finished.
I didn't care.

We persuaded Devon that it wasn't strictly proper for him
to act as pallbearer; that Ern and I wanted that honor. That
way he didn't have to watch us hauling the screened bundle to
an upstairs window, where, after a little cursing and prying,
we got the old-fashioned window raised enough to slide our
burden onto the gentle slope of the roof. We bound the screen
in place with baling wire, working as fast as we could. It
would've been more coldly sensible to place Mrs. Baird's body
on insulation in the attic, but it seemed necessary, somehow,
that we place the dead outside the lair of the living.

And then we resealed the window and went back to the
tunnel with a side trip to get a bottle for the wake we held.
And yes, I got shit-faced and no, not too shit-faced to take my
turn at the pump. Devon got his chance at the bottle, too, and
he was more sensible about it than I was.

It seems that I had a meal that day, a soupy stew with half-
cooked veggies and more carbonized biscuits. I suppose Shar
or the girls cooked more horsemeat, because the following day
there was plenty of it, sprinkled with brine and folded in film.
My last clear recollection was of Shar draining the water from
that jugful of damp alfalfa seeds and putting them away again.

I don't justify getting drunk; I merely record it. If we'd had
another emergency that afternoon, I probably would've paid
for it with my hide. As it was, the big trouble came later.

V. Doomsday Plus Four,
Five, Six, Seven

My next few days began with a hangover that segued to a powerful thirst, which I tried to slake with tomato juice. Shar said it was fine with her if I drank everything in my liquor cabinet since it kept me from eating much. My head detonated every time the kids whooped during the joke festival Cammie initiated, and my tongue felt like a squirrel's tail. I straggled back to the root cellar and listened to the radio.

The world news was surprising only in its details. Chinese troops had surged across the Sino-Soviet border to the great trans-Siberian railroad and there they had stopped, daring the Russkis to trade nukes. NATO forces were as good as their word; they had stopped Soviet armor before the lumbering red-starred tanks got more than a toehold in West Germany. But not with neutron bombs. They had done it with a bewildering array of small antiarmor missiles; some laser directed, some wire guided, and some with sensors that guided them straight down onto the thin topside armor of the tanks.

The Soviets had staked a lot on that self-propelled artillery of theirs, and they lost the bet. It was a whole lot easier to replace a German infantryman with his braçe of cheap, auto-mated, tank-killer missiles than to replace a seventy-ton Soviet tank with its trained crew.

To my surprise, Radio Damascus was still 'casting. They didn't know whose little kiloton-size neutron warheads had depopulated most of their military bases and wasted no breath on it. Instead Damascus called on the Muslim world to defend Syrian honor with instant cessation of oil shipments to the US and its friends. I was willing to bet that every supertanker in existence was hugging a breakwater somewhere.

Our national news comprised remotely fed bulletins from

the EBS, carefully upbeat in tone, claiming we had weathered the worst. I nearly failed to catch the implication of one report from Alaska. The Soviet raid on our pipeline had been squashed, with only scattered remnants of the raiders still afoot in Alaska. That meant US soil had been invaded, and since no one mentioned the condition of our petroleum pipeline, I figured it was blown in a dozen places. Those "scattered remnants" of Russkis were probably much better equipped for Arctic warfare than our own people; shortchanging the defense of our largest state is virtually an American tradition.

On Doomsday plus five, we began to move back into the basement. We had a frightening hour when Ern's readings told him we were taking heavy radiation in the tunnel. But the basement reading was roughly the same, which told us something was wrong with the meter.

So Ern did some meter maintenance. He removed the plastic top, fished the little dessicant lumps out, and baked them on our little stove—while Cammie and Kate made more biscuits. Using cotton swabs, Ern gently wiped the inside of the meter clean, taking special care to remove the dusting of tiny flecks of gypsum that clung to the aluminum leaves and monofilament.

Then he deposited the dried dessicant back in the can, resealed it, and took fresh readings. It said we were taking only two tenths of a rem in the tunnel and slightly under one rem in the basement. That made sense. It also told us the clammy humidity of the tunnel had finally worked its way into the fallout meter, giving high but spurious readings.

By now I was a believer in alfalfa sprouts. Shar merely added a quart of water and swirled it in the jug to wash the growing sprouts once a day, then drained the water for soup and capped the jug again. Long white tendrils extended from the seeds, a growing, spongy mass that thrived even in the gloom of the basement. I wasn't eating a lot, and when my pants got loose, I just tightened my belt a notch.

Shar made a little speech after brunch—Devon had christened our second meal "lunper"—reminding us that when we had no good reason to be in the basement we should creep back to the safety of "Rackham's lair"—another of Devon's phrases. Shar made her point: did we want to absorb twenty rems a day or only four?

Spot made the most of his freedom to pace the tunnel while

the rest of us were busy in the basement. We took the rest of the drinking water from the john, partly drained my waterbed, then took sponge baths in my tub. Kate, first to bathe, was stunned at the way the rest of us stank. Of course she had smelled just as ripe a few minutes before. Each of us then shared Kate's dismay, but soon our noses gave up and quit complaining. The whole basement reeked of bodies.

Ern caught a radio broadcast that mentioned bridges. The long span to San Rafael was down; the San Mateo bridge was limited to military traffic and you could get shot or run down trying to walk it. The Carquinez and Benicia bridges would be cleared soon, which told us that they still spanned the narrows of Suisun Bay.

We began to hope that "soon" might mean the bridges would be navigable within a few days. At worst, said Ern, we could clamber around stalled cars and cross the Benicia bridge to the north. That sounded reasonable to me, because neither of us realized how the Corps of Engineers intended to clear those bridges.

On Doomsday plus six we uncelebrated a week of underground exile and Ern volunteered to give us sunlight in the basement. Among the things Cammie had lugged from my garage was my so-called surface plate. A surface plate is just a slab, usually of granite, polished so perfectly flat that you can use it to measure the exact amount of warp on a race car's cylinder head. But I'm cheap. I bought an old jet fighter's front windshield at a surplus shop, knowing that it had to be optically flat, a surface plate of glass.

The thing was two feet long, a foot wide, and two inches thick; heavy as guilt and solid as virtue. Ern surmised that it might stop gamma rays while letting light through.

His scheme was simple. He toted the glass slab outside, galumphing in my protective outfit though it swallowed him whole. Then he shoveled dirt away from the top of my basement window, waving as he heard us cheer the light that burst into the basement. Finally he dropped the glass plate against the window and replaced some of the dirt so that the only light reaching us was through that thick windshield.

While he took another sponge bath, we learned that his scheme was flawed, since the radiation reading jumped a bit near the window. We took more readings and found that my stone divider wall made a big difference. Near my office area the reading, and the light, were highest. In my lounge area behind the stone wall, the radiation level was "normal," less than a rem, and enough light reflected from my walls to make us happy.

That little oblong of light had a beneficial side effect. We no longer needed to pedal the bike as much, and pedaling had released a lot of water vapor and carbon dioxide, which were still a problem.

On D + 7—we had coined enough jargon terms to confuse a linguist by them—we ran out of horsemeat. I used the last pinch of it to hide a half-tab of comealong for Spot, who must've wondered if he was becoming a manic-depressive.

We still had enough food for another two days, and my water heater's drain spigot was still yielding drinkable water. Shar had already started her second batch of alfalfa sprouts in a stainless steel bowl and served up that first batch to the music of general applause. She harvested three pints of sprouts in a few days, from a half-cupful of seed and without direct sunlight. That was our nearest approach to a green salad, very popular with soy sauce.

The same day was marked by the remainder of the McKay family saga. I record it at this point because I didn't hear it until eight days after it happened. The kids were bored by my hunting stories, and the playing cards were so badly creased that they might as well have had faces on both sides. We were sharing raisins and onion soup when I thought to ask Shar how they had got from their wrecked vanwagon to my place.

Their first decision, said my sis, was to travel light. They took maps, cheese, and tinned meat, and wore jackets. Ern locked the vehicle in the vain hope that he might return to it, then mounted his bike and tried towing Lance. He found it rough going uphill and let Lance fend for himself as soon as they passed the overturned truck. The truck, of course, blocked off other cars, so that bikes and pedestrians didn't need to dodge speeders.

Lance, like many kids, often went to and from school on his skateboard. The fat urethane wheels ran amazingly well over macadam, and on the first downslope, Ern found Lance spurting ahead with a few kicks. The skateboard was more maneuverable than an expert's bike, but after a near-collision with a motorcyclist, my nephew went to the rear of the McKay procession to avoid becoming what he termed a "street pizza."

After two hours they neared exhaustion, but their path led chiefly downhill then and they finally reached the road that doubled back toward my place. They were on the safe side of Mount Diablo at last, and Shar coasted to rest at the foot of a short, tree-lined uphill stretch. Panting, they rested and watched a collegiate youth who sat at the roadside with a wheel dismantled from his expensive lightweight bike.

"What's the trouble?" Cammie asked.

"Picked up a nail," said the young man. "Can you believe I didn't think to bring a cold-patch kit?"

Ern had placed one of the tiny cold-patch packages in each bike bag. He saw the tubular pump clipped to the youngster's bike frame and dug the cold-patch kit from the vinyl bag on his bike. "What am I bid for this?"

Big eyed: "A box of chocolate bars?"

Ern: "We'll settle for one apiece." He was making the trade when the first great flash backlit his skyline.

"Don't look! Hide your eyes," Shar screamed, ignoring her own advice as she grabbed for Lance, who stared at the sky in rapt fascination. A biker and several hikers went full-length onto the shoulder, perhaps expecting a heavy concussion.

The second flash seemed nearer, coming as it did from a direction with lower hilltops and less masking of the initial dazzle. The third and fourth flashes were also distinct and they felt the jolts, the sudden bucking of the earth itself, conducting shock for many miles beyond ground zero. Leaves showered around them.

Cammie was first to seize her bike, pedaling past a gas station and grocery store well in advance of her family. The first airborne rumble didn't seem loud. But scarcely had Ern turned onto the road toward my place when he, like the others, felt the solid slap on his back from the second blast, the errant shock wave that crossed the bay to macerate Concord before funneling up the narrow valley to blow my windows out.

By great luck they were headed away from it in a declivity of Marsh Creek Valley and felt only a peppering of grit and twigs. But Ern saw the multipaned front window of the gas station disintegrate as if sucked into the little building, a polychrome implosion more deadly than a high-velocity shower of razor blades.

"You should've seen what it did to Concord," Devon spoke up. "No, I take it back." Shake of the blond tasseled head.

Everyone likes to think he's seen the worst. "Didn't hurt you any," Lance sniffed.

"It killed Concord. I was in a downstairs apartment," said Devon, "and don't ask me why all our windows got sucked out, 'stead of blown in. But later I saw what happened to people who got caught in the open." He glanced guiltily at us, cleared his throat, shrugged. "A glove, with a hand still in it. People with branches sticking out of them. Slabs of marble knocked off a building, one with a little kid's legs poking from under it. Like that," he trailed off in embarrassment.

I think Cammie already had a special soft spot for Devon by this time. To ward off further memories of that sort she said, "I'm convinced, Devon. We were lucky. After that shock wave all we did was go like crazy for Uncle Harve's place."

"And we were luckier still that we didn't get hit by the cars that passed us," Ern injected. "You could hear an engine winding up from around the bends behind us, and I made Lance ride double with Shar since he couldn't make good time on the shoulder, and those people were driving like maniacs.

"One guy especially, driving a county jail-farm bus full of inmates. I could see a guard in the rear seat, holding a riot gun and staring back at us, looking scareder than I was. I couldn't decide whether he was more afraid of the bombs or the way his driver was smoking his tires."

The Contra Costa County jail farm was only a few miles from my place. I had helped put a couple of scufflers on that work farm. Inmates ranged from hapless schlemiels and harmless dopers to hard-eyed repeaters who, in my opinion, should've been across the bay in Quentin. I empathized with the guard on that bus; if that vehicle turned over, he'd have a score of two-legged bombs to worry about.

"I don't envy him, or the inmates," I said. "The county farm must've taken the same radiation dose we did. But some of the buildings could be pretty good protection. I gather you were pretty near here by then, eh?"

"Half-hour or so. We got here soon after you left, Harve. Thanks for trying to find us. We owe you a lot."

"*Owe* me? Good God, Ern," I fumed, then pointed at the fallout meter. "Think of yourself as an investment that's paid off a thousand percent. Fallout meter, air pump, filters, even a rechargeable light plant! Nobody owes me. You've done too much for me to owe me."

"We've still got a lot to do for each other," said Kate, perhaps for Devon's benefit. "I can't afford to worry about how much I owe, but I'll pay off as well as I can."

"Strange you should mention that," I said, grinning at her. "Because we've been wondering when you'd extend us an invitation."

Blank look from Kate. "For what?"

Ern, softly: "For the use of your summer place in, uh, where is it again?"

"Yountville," she replied. "There's always a chance that my folks got there. If they did, I can't swear they'd take me in, much less the rest of us." After a moment's thought: "And if it's all the same with you guys, I'll stick with you regardless."

Shar smiled indulgently. "We wouldn't hold you to that."

A snort from Kate: "I'm not saying that to be nice! I just don't think my chances would be as good with anybody else. And by the way, I suspect you've been talking it over when I wasn't listening. Isn't it time you let me in on the plans? After all"—she smiled with disarming shyness—"I might be the landlady."

The evening passed with argument and explanation. Of our younger members, only Kate had ever missed two meals in a row. The kids couldn't believe they'd begin to weaken after a day or so without food and thought we could just buy whatever we needed. I was adamant; we'd be crazy to set out for Yountville on bellies that had been empty for two days. And I didn't think a twenty-dollar bill would buy a meal anywhere in California.

Shar's notebook put our exodus on a no-nonsense footing, with figures to support the notion of northerly escape. We knew the fallout extended to Vallejo from radio broadcasts, and the same source said it did not extend as far north as Napa.

Yet we couldn't figure a way to get us from my place to the Napa County line in less than five hours without taking indefensible chances. I meant "indefensible" in more ways than one. We didn't want to make more than one trip in the Lotus, because I'd already seen how readily some folks would knock you over for the shoes on your feet. Leaving two or three of us near the bridge and retracing nearly thirty miles to my place was a clear case of dividing forces. Like Custer. No thanks. I couldn't defend an arrangement that left any of us more vulnerable than necessary.

It was possible that I was exaggerating the lawlessness we'd be dealing with. But whatever the state of the union, it didn't seem healthy enough in our locale for us to count on anything like business as usual. If we found a place to buy fuel and food, fine. I had a stock of pennies—coppers, at that—and quarters for just such a contingency. But another contingency forced itself on us, heralded as Ern outlined some of the preparations we would have to make. He stopped in midsentence to listen.

In the distance we heard a car pass, the unmistakable *thrumm* of a husky V-eight prowling the creek road. The event took twelve seconds or so, and we strained at the echoes like music lovers catching the faint final overtones of a lute. Such a familiar, homey racket; and now such an anomaly that we fantasized about it. We agreed at last that it must've been some official vehicle checking the road, its driver marvelously tricked out in some kind of space suit, invulnerable to the silent, invisible hail of gamma rays that sought his soft tissues.

A half-hour later Devon interrupted Shar to comment on the backfires he heard far away. Even government cars, he joked, got out of tune.

I laughed because I didn't want to break his mood. I'd heard that brief rattle too. From such a distance, muffled by earth, I might've chosen to think of it as backfires. But it had been a sudden, steady series of sharp reports; perhaps on one of the dairy farms nearby. I hoped it was a farmer killing moribund livestock. Sure as hell it was no backfire.

Shar must have caught the pensive look on my face and she continued outlining the proposed trip with a brief aside. We would have to travel at the pace of the slowest, all together, and we mustn't expect any help—in fact, must be ready for trouble without asking for it, she said.

She figured the bike group could get to the bridge in three hours, Kate and Devon riding with me, and Spot (she sighed) loping alongside the bikes. Then we'd need a half-hour to cross the bridge, strapping the bikes on my Lotus so I could ferry them across the water if necessary. Another hour or two getting around the mess we expected in Vallejo. The best we could hope for was a full five hours in gamma country.

Kate saw the crucial variable immediately. "What does that amount to in rems?"

"If we go tomorrow morning, about sixty. If we spend tomorrow in the tunnel and go the next day, maybe fifty. The day after that, forty-two or so. Of course we absorb a few rems daily in the tunnel. There's a point of diminishing returns, but it's after we run out of food and water."

"I just want to do the safest thing," Cammie wailed. She had taken her lumps with few complaints, but my niece was distraught to find her decision makers unsure on a vital decision.

"I say we eat our last meal three mornings from now and run for it on full stomachs," Kate said. I agreed with her.

Ern wanted to go in two days, taking our last tins of juice and beef.

Lance wanted to go now, now, now. He was fed up with toeing a tight line in a hole with no chewing gum.

Shar sided with Ern; Cammie didn't know what she wanted; and Devon just looked at us, blinking, fighting a resurgence of stomach cramps. Of course we ended by taking another secret ballot. I figured Cammie would do what she thought her parents wanted.

We counted one vote for leaving the next day, two for leaving in three days, and four for leaving in two days. So it was settled: we'd spend the following day getting the bikes fixed up with their generators and any other maintenance they needed, and I would replace the battery in the Lotus, taking a half-dozen rems while getting it fueled and ready.

We would be all set to run for the border, so to speak, on the morning of D + 9.

And we would have been, if the decision hadn't been snatched from our hands.

VI. Doomsday Plus Eight

I waited until after brunch—Lord God, how I learned to loathe noodles and tomato paste!—to dress for my trip to the garage to prepare the Lotus. Ern knew I would be packing heavy heat, the twelve-gauge, when I drove away as their escort. To conserve fuel I intended to drive behind them, catching up and then coasting until they were well ahead before I eased ahead again. But none of them left the tunnel to watch me collect my hardware and spare ammo. I made a second trip for the battery and the jerrycan with the remainder of my fuel.

Fully dressed in my Halloween outfit, I hauled the second load across my lawn in bright sunshine, through an ankle-deep layer of dead leaves, to the garage. Here and there I saw the fresh green of tender young weeds, prodded into unseasonal growth by irradiation. The twelve-gauge wouldn't fit under the Lotus's dash so I stashed it more or less out of sight in the foot well, where my left thigh would keep it company.

The fuel went in quickly; the battery, not so quickly. My damned rubber gloves and the fogging of my goggles made me a prize klutz.

I was afraid I'd have to push-start my little bolide, but eventually it coughed, cleared its throat in a healthy rasp, then began to purr. I let it idle and knelt with my tire gauge to see if pressures were okay. I'd been outside about ten minutes, two rems' worth, and figured on running back in another minute or so if the right rear tire was as healthy as the others. Kneeling with my head near the exhaust pipe, I heard muffled staccato reports and simultaneous metallic clangs, and I fell back on my keester. With the scarf over my ears I didn't interpret the sounds correctly; I thought the engine had munched a valve.

But my Lotus continued its quiet purr. I scrambled up,

leaned over the doorsill, shut off the ignition. That's when I heard the throb of a big V-eight heading toward the house.

For the space of a heartbeat I felt the joy of unexpected good fortune; and then remembered that my gate had been locked, and reassessed the sounds I'd thought were engine trouble. Someone had used an automatic weapon on my gate.

I stepped near the window, I let my goggles hang at my throat, and picked up the mattock Devon had shouldered a week before. A mattock handle fits loosely into the steel head, unlike an ax. I slipped the hickory shaft from the head, watching through a crack in the old garage door while the pickup followed my gravel drive and stopped near the garage. The pickup had a Contra Costa County logo on the driver's door, but it also had several indented holes through the side panels. They were just about the size of rifle slugs. One headlight had been shattered.

Four men were crammed in the cab. The first to get out was obviously the man in charge, a big sturdy loafer wearing khakis that were too small for him and a shiny badge that looked wrong on him. He carried a pump shotgun in one hand and a long-barreled police .38 in a holster.

The man who emerged after him wore khakis and badge too; a tall, slow-moving fellow without a sidearm. The leader commanded, "Move it, Ellis, and this time remember not to point this thing until you're ready to use it." With that he handed the shotgun to Ellis. Both men swept my acreage with their eyes as the third man scrambled out. The driver stayed put. Someone had taped around the windows, and the three dudes who got out all wore gloves and sunglasses. No respirators or masks of any kind; if these guys were sheriff's deputies, I was a teenage werewolf.

The third man out wore slacks and pullover and carried one of the little vintage Air Force carbines. Not much of a threat at two hundred yards, but closer in on auto fire it could rattle you full of thirty-caliber holes. He glanced toward the Lotus, then said, "You want me for backup, Dennison?"

Dennison, the leader, waved an arm in my general direction. "Look for fuel, whatever you can boost in there. Then come to the door and give us a roust. Hell, you know the procedure, Riley; the smoke from the standpipe says there's somebody in the house. If we can make this sweep without wasting any ammo, that's ammo we won't have to replace later."

"Got it," said Riley, the carbine toter. He moved in my direction. In the cab the fourth man was rolling himself a cigarette. Not many jail-farm employees rolled their own— maybe because so many inmates *did*.

I knew my clownish garb made a lot of noise when I moved, and there was no place to hide and no time to reach into the car for my artillery because I would have to do it in full view of the approaching Riley. I did the only thing I could, an ancient time-honored ploy: I stepped as quietly as possible to the near wall next to the open door and raised my hunk of hickory on high. If he glanced my way, it could be all over for ol' Uncle Harve.

Then a soft pop, no louder than the snap of a fingernail, spanged from the cooling guts of the Lotus. I saw the man's shadow jerk and shorten as he crouched, intent on my car, peering hard into the gloom of my garage.

Another snap of cooling metal. He kept the carbine aimed into the shadow one-handed and knelt to feel my exhaust pipe, and he must have heard the rustle of my clothes because he began to swing the little carbine toward me as I connected with the mattock handle against his receiver mechanism with an impact that bashed the weapon completely from his grasp and knocked it clattering against a wall.

I took three fast steps. The first brought my right foot into range of his belly; the second was a kick just under his sternum to paralyze his hollering apparatus; and the third was a hop to regain my balance as I crossed the doorway in full view of anyone who might be looking toward the garage. He had time to declaim one wordless syllable, ending in a plosive grunt.

Riley, knees drawn up, clutched his belly and rolled to face me, mouth gaping like a carp. I squatted low and menaced him with the mattock handle while risking a peek outside. Dennison and Ellis were approaching my seldom-used front door as coolly and confidently as if on official business. The driver addressed a paperback, still in the pickup. I grabbed the hapless Riley by one ankle and jerked him into shadow so hard his head bumped concrete.

A solid kick to the solar plexus can render a professional athlete helpless for a half-minute. While Riley groveled and gasped, I circled around the front of the Lotus, keeping in shadow, and slung my twelve-gauge on my back by its sling before returning to stand over the man who now lay on his back, eyes rolling at me.

I gave him a quick pat-down and found the five-inch switch-blade thrust down the inside of his high-top boot. I let the blade flick open. "Nice and quiet," I growled, placing the flat of the blade under his jaw. "I won't even have to pull a trigger if you try anything louder than a whisper, Master Riley. Now: down on your face if you want to live. Arms and legs spread."

He needed help to roll over, uttering croupy wheezes as his diaphragm muscles began to unkink. Ever since the ice-pick routine years ago, I've had a loathing for knives. I wasn't about to let Riley know that because then he might make me shoot him. And my twelve-gauge announces itself like a multiple boiler explosion, and I didn't want to alert those two on my front porch. Now, I wish I had.

Spread-eagled on his face, he couldn't help but feel the prick of his own stiletto near his carotid artery. I asked it softly: "What is Dennis on after?"

"Food. Guns. Booze. Jewelry," he wheezed. Then, "Broads. He's a deputy sheriff. If you're smart you'll let me—"

I raised his head by the hair and whacked it lightly against concrete. "Try again, Riley. He's a scuffler from the rock-hockey farm. If I'm *really* smart, I'll just slit your throat and take out your buddy in the pickup and drive away whistling. Or just wait for your pals. Each lie earns you a fresh headache. Now: what's Dennison's procedure here? Quickly," I added, grasping him by his hair again.

A long breath, a short curse. "Dennison and Ellis go in— very polite, asking—who needs help. Then they say—they're searching for escapees—from the county farm. Sorry, citizen, but that's—how it is, and—whoever looks like trouble—gets asked to lead the way—to search the rest of the house. And then down comes the sap—on the back of his head, and strapping tape—to hogtie him while we—shake the place down. Anybody gets antsy, we—mention we've got a hostage."

Slick; too slick by a damned sight. But he'd left a loose end, and it dangled in the back of my mind. "Why did he want you to give him a roust?"

Pause; sigh. "So I can call him Deputy Dennison. It's supposed to make everybody—sure we're legit."

I took a chance. "Didn't work too well last night, did it?"

Riley stiffened, then shrugged. "Not very. Are you The

Man?" If he thought I was a cop, he probably figured I knew something about what his bunch had already done. Which, I suspected, included homicide within a half-mile of my place.

I said I was The Man, all right. "Sit up, facing away from me, and strip out your bootlaces. If I have to speed you up, I'll brain you and do it myself." Still working just to breathe, he tugged the heavy laces from his boots. I leaned the mattock handle against the wall without taking my gaze from Riley.

"Your driver's name," I prompted when I had the laces.

"Oliver."

I could see the two men on my front porch, and at that point I probably could still have averted a tragedy. Then I saw Shar inviting them in, and the moment passed into the oblivion reserved for wasted chances. I wondered how long it would be before Shar called to me, canceling my hope of surprise.

I unslung my terrible hole card and held it ready. To Riley I said, "Your life depends on suckering Oliver in here without making a fuss. I'm just itching to blow you away and I've got as many rounds of double-ought buck here as you had in that carbine. Turn around and see for yourself."

He did, gulping as he saw the fat magazine and stubby barrel of my weapon. "What the fuck is *that?*"

"Enough death to go around, little man. Now stand up and call Oliver in here. Bear in mind that if you can't get him in here or if you take one step toward the outside, you get your ticket canceled."

I could see his arms and legs trembling as he stood. I stepped up next to the mattock handle with my back to the wall near the open door; gestured with my gun barrel for him to move near the Lotus.

He nearly fell, but leaned against the rear fender; licked his lips; gave a low hoarse call. No response. He called again.

I heard a door open. A bored tenor called a sullen, "Yeah?"

The briefest of pauses. I clicked the safety. Riley called urgently, "I never seen a stash like this in my life! You wanta take your cut now, before Dennison hogs it?" Riley was trying to keep from glancing my way; trying so hard his eyelids fluttered.

The door slammed. I didn't risk a glance as I heard footsteps approach. I used the gun barrel to urge Riley away from my car and he stumbled back, both arms jerking as he started to raise them and then thought better of it.

A few yards away, approaching: "What the hell's with you, man? You on a bad trip?" And then Riley essayed the sickest smile I ever witnessed and a silent, palms-out gesture of helplessness, and Oliver stepped into view, frowning intently at Riley. He took two more steps into the garage before he saw me, and for all I know he didn't even notice the twelve-gauge in the hands of what must've seemed like a towering bogeyman in the shadows.

"Sweet*shit*," Oliver screamed, leaping sideways to rebound from a fender.

"No no no," Riley begged me, arms thrust high as he squeezed his eyes shut in anticipation of death. It saved his life. I snatched up the mattock handle and brought it humming in a sidearm swoop as Oliver whirled, and it took him flush across the bridge of his nose and swept on over his forehead as his head snapped back. Another second and he would've been outside, and I would've been obliged to bisect him instead of just giving him the great-grandsire of all concussions. He fell on his back, legs twitching, blood beginning to rivulet from his nostrils.

"Like you said, Riley," I breathed. "No. Keep this up and you may get a reduced sentence." That was bullshit, of course, but I wanted him to see a carrot as well as a stick.

Riley spread-eagled himself again while I trussed Oliver's ankles and wrists with bootlaces, bound behind him so that he lay on his side out of sight. He bled a lot and breathed in snorts. I took a long-barreled revolver from his belt and snapped the blade off his sheath knife between the jaws of my blacksmith's vise. I could claim I hoped I hadn't killed Oliver, but I wasn't even thinking about him. I was furiously considering my next move.

I retrieved the little carbine, pocketed all its ammo, jacked out the chambered round, and reinserted the empty clip. Then I took the second full clip from Riley's hip pocket and gave him another frisk to make sure he hadn't hidden a singleton round on him. I'd heard about a hit man who used to carry one round each of twenty-two long, parabellum, and forty-five ACP in his change pocket, just in case. Riley wasn't that farsighted. He accepted the carbine, blinking nervously.

"That's just window dressing," I told him. "Keep it in view. You'll have an alarm signal—maybe several. Shots? What? And while you're wondering if you should lie about it, think about this: if anybody in that house gets hurt, you get the same."

He licked dry lips. "The horn. One toot for an alert. Two means stay put. Three means haul ass. That was Oliver's job." Enough scorn leaked into that last phrase to make me believe him.

I nodded, considering an assault past the root cellar stairs, which meant bulling through the book barrier. But I wouldn't be able to see into there and I'd be impossible to miss by anyone standing in the cellar. Or I could just wait behind the pickup, or go into the house with Riley. Better still, *behind* Riley.

But too many things could go wrong, and those badged bastards thought in terms of hostages. Besides, they might spot me coming across the yard from a window while they separated Ern from the others. I wondered if I could make use of the unconscious Oliver, then noticed that his hair was nearly black. Scrunched down while I—literally!—rode shotgun, my head might look like his from the back. That was important, because now I decided to draw those bogus lawmen from the house toward me. My place was infected, and I sought to draw the pus to the surface.

The county pickup was parked so that with a ten-yard sprint, I could put it between me and the house. I gave Riley his orders and made sure he knew I'd be only a pace behind, then whacked his shoulder. He scuttled for the passenger's side, the harmless carbine in one hand, and piled into the pickup while I squatted, my twelve-gauge at ready, and let him slide behind the steering wheel. Only then did I ease into the cab with him, sliding down, stuffing my rain hat in my belt. "Okay, Riley," I said. "Roll down your window, give one toot, and start the engine."

He did it, no longer shaking as he stripped tape from the side window, his face impassive. I liked him shaky so I said, "Did I mention that this thing is semiauto? With sixteen rounds?" He blinked, whispered something to himself, shook his head. "Now give one toot again." He did. I thought I saw movement at one of the upstairs windows. "Aim the carbine up the slope toward the garden," I said.

He did it. I heard him mutter, "Bang bang; this ain't gonna fool anybody."

"Hand me the carbine slowly and burn rubber for the gate," I replied, "and give three toots on the way." I snatched the little weapon as he swung it into the cab, wondering if he entertained ideas of using it as a club. But he did a fine job of spewing gravel as I braced myself, leaning against the far door, aiming my persuader at his middle while we accelerated away.

I called for three more toots and got them, then told Riley to stop at the gate. "No panic braking! You don't want *me* to panic, do you?"

The pickup stopped. I made Riley give another three toots, had him gun the engine a few times. Nothing—at least nothing I had hoped to see.

I opened my door and eased out, keeping the cab between me and my house. My adrenal pump insisted that hours were whistling past me in a gale of confusion, so I spoke with deliberation. "Don't open your door but lean out and wave and shout," I told Riley. "As if a posse were coming from up the hill. I'm going to fire for effect."

Mine was a delicate problem in personnel management; if Riley thought I was shooting at him without provocation, sure as hell he'd panic. As Riley waved and hollered, I reached in and shifted the gear lever to neutral, then took the revolver from my raincoat and squeezed off three rounds toward my garden plot three hundred yards distant.

Almost immediately the lank Ellis appeared on my porch, swiveling his head and his scattergun, seeking the source of Riley's excitement. "Get 'em here on the double," I snarled.

"They're coming," Riley shouted, waving and pointing. "Let's go, let's go!" He pounded on the side of his door and gunned the engine, darting a glance at me, getting my nod. I should've expected that, in doing a little more than the minimum, the little scuffler was conning me, awaiting a lapse on my part. "Let's *go*," he repeated.

Ellis shouted something in reply, ducked into my house, and reappeared a moment later with Dennison right behind him. My heart pounded against my throat as I saw what Dennison dragged with him.

Naturally he would choose the hostage who seemed most likely to be manageable, but Dennison had made a mistake. He held Lance McKay by the hair with one hand, his sidearm drawn in the other. Both men began to run toward me crabwise, searching behind them, scanning for enemies as they came. Half-squatting, I thrust the revolver into my belt as Ellis came into range of my twelve-gauge. Dennison lagged behind, wrenching my nephew's head, Lance stumbling behind him as a shield against an imagined enemy. Squalling and cursing,

Lance was anything but tractable.

I suppose Riley was waiting until he knew my attention was focused on Ellis, for without warning he gunned the pickup hard and let the clutch pedal thump upward. But Riley hadn't seen me snick the gear lever into neutral and of course the pickup didn't budge. I did, in a half-pivot toward Riley, who tumbled out the other side of the cab and hit running.

"Get 'im, Ellis, he's behind the cab!" Riley sang it over his shoulder as he loped down my access road toward distant blacktop. Ellis stared at him in astonishment, then caught sight of me as I peered over the side of the pickup. He made a stutter-step sideways, heading for a sycamore ten paces from me, and brought up his pumpgun.

My first round of double-ought buck took Ellis just above the belt buckle at a range of ten yards and jerked him backward like a marionette. Recoil aimed my second round higher, partly deflected by the airborne pumpgun, but the rest of the big pellets left him with no skull above the eyebrows. Ellis was already dead as he slid across the carpet of sycamore leaves.

Dennison had struggled within extreme range of my scattergun by now, but the twin thunderclaps of my twelve-gauge and Ellis's rag-doll collapse sent him scurrying behind the largest of my nearby sycamores. I had no confidence in a handgun I'd never sighted in and no time to cram the full clip into the carbine that lay on the floor of the pickup. Lacking pinpoint accuracy, I couldn't risk a shot while Lance screeched and flailed against his tormentor; at twenty-five yards a sawed-off shotgun's pattern is much too broad for precision shooting.

Dennison tried to quell Lance by shouting at him. I knew I had the bastard stopped if I could only get a moment to ransom his freedom for Lance's. "Lance!" I put every decibel I had behind it, making the same mistake as Dennison. "Lance, it's Uncle Harve! Calm down; you'll be okay!"

"Come beat him up! Owww, you better—" replied my nephew before Dennison whacked him with his pistol barrel. Lance heard me, all right; it was his tragedy that he never truly believed in ultimate control or ultimate punishment. But he believed in that pistol barrel and grabbed his head in both hands while screaming his head off.

Dennison's arms were possible targets. So was Lance. Then my nephew slumped, still squalling. From behind the tree came Dennison's voice, harsh with command: "You try for me and the kid gets it!" His muscular forearm clamped under Lance's chin, the pistol held to the boy's head.

"Stop it, Lance," I shouted and added, "Dennison, you won't outlive him by five seconds."

"Settle him down, then," the man responded, and it was as much a plea as demand. I felt an instant of hope, realizing that Dennison wanted to negotiate.

But only for that instant. Maybe Lance saw his father leap from my front porch, silver shreds of duct tape flapping at his ankles, jacking the slide of my big .45 Colt as he ran for the cover of a walnut tree. Or maybe Lance was only getting his second wind. I'll say this, with a lump in my throat: the little bugger never gave up. I think he bit down on Dennison's wrist.

The man snarled and jerked his left arm up, and then Lance was on all fours, slipping on leaves, and whether Dennison intended to merely wing my nephew or not, he fired from a range of ten feet. Shot through the back, Lance fell heavily and lay still.

I needed a clear shot, but as I stepped away from the safety of the pickup, Dennison backpedaled fast, keeping the sycamore between us, angling for a middle-size oak farther from me. There was a sizable chance that he'd make it until he heard the heavy bark of the Colt in Ern's hands.

Dennison turned toward the sound—a very long shot for a handgun; no wonder Ern missed—and I pulled my trigger again. It didn't nail Dennison but it sent him sprinting away. Ern advanced firing two-handed, each blast of the Colt a second after the last.

Dennison knew his weapons, all right. He managed to get thirty yards from my scattergun and then made a desperate lunge for the top of my eight-foot fence, snapping a shot at Ern before tossing his revolver aside. Ern did not flinch but raced forward. He had already fired five rounds without a strike, but number six caught Dennison just at the base of his neck as he struggled at the top of my fence. Dennison jerked, fell, then hung facing us with one sleeve caught on the top of the wire. Ern, eyes wide in a face whitened by rage, ran without hesitation to point-blank range and put his last round squarely into Dennison's heart.

By this time I had Lance in my arms, and as I ran to the house, I called, "Leave that garbage, Ern! Lance may not be hurt too badly."

My twelve-gauge slapping my back as I ran, I got Lance to the house, where Shar met me wailing. I relinquished her son to her and stood aside for Ern, who ran several paces behind me, sobbing.

Kate stood ashen-faced, my little target pistol in her hand, just inside my front door. The added weapon made me think of Riley, whose defection might not last. "Kate, we'll have to get Lance to a doctor," I said, breathing hard. "Can you tear down the book barrier double-quick?"

"I can try. Is Lance hurt badly?"

"Moaning and breathing. That's all I know," I said and wheeled back toward the pickup, checking the target pistol as I ran. I fairly clanked with my arsenal, but weapons weren't the items of hardware that concerned me most. I wanted that pickup.

The engine was still bumbling along, waiting for whoever got there first. I backed it furiously past two deaders, wondering how much radiation I'd taken during the attack.

When I ripped the plastic cover from my root cellar doors, I found Kate and Devon toppling a bookcase. Devon claimed he could shoot, so I stationed him in the pickup two paces from the root cellar entrance with the carbine, its full clip, and orders to fire one warning round if he saw anything suspicious. Then I hotfooted through my tunnel to the basement and to the keening little group of McKays surrounding my waterbed.

Lance lay on his back, breathing but glassy-eyed with shock. Midway up his naked breast on the right was a small purplish crater, trickling crimson, which Cammie kept wiping away with facial tissue while Shar tore at a roll of adhesive tape. It was good to know that the bullet wasn't lodged in Lance's body. It was very bad that the exit wound was bubbling as he breathed.

Lance's punctured lung canceled any thoughts I'd had of sealing my place up. In fifteen minutes we had all dressed as thoroughly as possible with our food in slender blanket rolls and a few other necessaries thrown into my old backpack. At my request, Kate scribbled directions to her place at Yountville, which I pocketed knowing I might never get that far.

The pickup had room for all the McKays, Devon, and the bikes as well. Devon kept the carbine in sight for the edification of any lurking 'jackers. Before backing the Lotus out I cut the bonds of Oliver, who lay still unconscious on my garage floor.

Maybe I should've dumped him into the pickup, but on my list of priorities he was as expendable as a hangnail.

Kate didn't like sharing my passenger seat with two shovels, a backpack, and a hundred pounds of Spot—but then neither did he. I led the way past my gate, Ern driving the pickup while Shar cradled Lance in the cab. Poor kid was coughing some blood. Our plan, or more accurately Shar's decision, was for me to lead the way to Kaiser Hospital in Antioch in the forlorn hope that we would find it open. If not, Martinez also had a Kaiser Hospital. Wherever we found medical help, Shar would stay there with Lance while Ern and the rest of us headed for Yountville.

But those plans proved fruitless. I wasted five minutes trying to find a route to the hospital in Antioch, and it seemed to me that the number of wrecks and abandoned vehicles increased as we got within a mile of the place, as if they were deliberately aligned as roadblocks. It *would* look that way, of course, after fifty thousand people converged on the same point with life-threatening emergencies.

I might've got to the hospital by some judicious hops in the Lotus, but not with Lance and Shar both. And since I couldn't raise Kaiser/Antioch on the phone, we didn't know whether it still offered any hope.

We lit out for Martinez, using sidewalks and road shoulders when necessary and trying steadily to get the Martinez hospital on the phone. Kate said all she got was interference. Then we tried emergency numbers and got multiple busy signals. Ditto with police numbers. That was strange because we saw nobody on the streets, and it seemed unlikely that police circuits would be overloaded in a dead township. We finally got through to an emergency fire number, an exchange now manned by army engineers.

"Kaiser/Martinez was evacuated to Petaluma yesterday," said the sergeant, ready to break the connection.

I tried to picture that in my head; it would've been a big operation. "What route did they take, sergeant?"

"Staging area in Martinez just south of the railroad bridge. We ran a bunch of boxcars in and hauled everything movable in one load. There's another train scheduled late today into Concord, but with all those burn cases it's gonna be late. Don't expect to find any medical staff; we had to forcibly evacuate some. Can't risk losing trained people to fallout residuals."

I said, "We're in a pickup. Can we get across at Martinez? Ferry boat? Anything?"

"Not a chance. We're clearing the traffic bridges with 'dozers and wheel-loaders, just dumping vehicles into the bay, and with all that heavy equipment thrashing around, we can't allow any foot traffic. You get conscripted to a work detail for trying." His brusque rumble lowered slightly. "Off the record, I hear they're allowing foot traffic and bikes over the railroad bridge except when there's rolling stock on it. But if you try that with a car you'll wind up on a work detail. Just 'cause you don't see a sentry don't mean he don't see *you*. Signing off," he said, and the line went dead.

I waved Ern to a stop and told him what I'd learned. We could get to the railroad tracks near the bridge, but Lance would have to be my solitary passenger as I wave-hopped across Suisun Bay in the Lotus. Assuming I made it across, I would await the rest of the group on the Vallejo side, then take Shar and Lance to Napa at all possible speed.

Before leaving my place, I had buckled Spot's heavy ID collar on him, more as a mark of his domesticity than anything else. I didn't want him shot as a zoo runaway. Now I saw that the collar would come in handy, because Spot might not take kindly to seeing me drive away without him. True enough, Spot was a watchcat, not an attack cat. But if Cammie's soothing hands and voice weren't enough, he might put clawmarks on somebody when he saw me drive away. I gave that a lot of thought while seeking the nearest approach to the railroad bridge, that great greasy black steel span running parallel to the freeway bridge out of Martinez.

Our little convoy stopped about a mile short of the bridge near a welter of abandoned cars, clothing, even bedding and kitchenware. We saw not one human form—only a few rats, seemingly unaffected by fallout. No doubt they lived far down in sewers; theirs was a holocaust life-style. Ern judged that the place looked like the aftermath of a railroad staging area but intended to keep going as near as possible to the railroad bridge before abandoning the pickup.

While Cammie and Shar placed Lance into my passenger seat, I borrowed belts from Devon and Ern, passing them through Spot's collar and looping them through tie-downs on the pickup. I didn't want to use my own belt because my pants would've been at half-mast in an instant. That's how much weight I'd lost in nine days.

I said, "Cammie, try and keep him calm, but if he gets out of control, stand away until I'm out of sight. Ern, you start off for the bridge first. Spot might not get antsy if he's the one who's moving instead of me."

Kate, darkly: "And what if he won't follow us over the bridge?"

"Just don't leave him tied up," I sighed. "I can't ask you to waste a second worrying about him." I wasn't prepared for the lingering hug she gave me; I was too intent on leaving. My sister's eyes were wet but steady on me as I slipped into the car.

"I love you, bubba," she said, her chin quivering as she nodded toward her son. "Get him across for me; okay?"

I gave her our old childhood horsewink because I didn't want to cry, then waved her away. I watched my rearview as Ern steered, jouncing, over tracks and headed toward the bridge. Cammie knelt near Spot, scratching him and talking, and though he yipped and watched me with what may have been yearning, he didn't try to break free. I had underestimated his liking for Cammie—or maybe I'd just underrated my quadruped pal.

With a look at Lance, I squirted the Lotus away in search of boat ramps. My nephew drooled bloody spit into a towel, and his normally ruddy color had faded to pallor. I tried to minimize bumps without using the fans; a Cellular's fans are notoriously short-lived if used for more than momentary jumping, and I'd already made one open-water crossing on them.

From Waterfront Road I turned toward the bay at my first chance, resolved to find a ramp westward, to my left. To my right lay the Naval Weapons Station, and new signs warned that I could expect to be shot if I continued in that direction. Would the sentries be adequately protected against radiation? I doubted it. Would they be at their posts? That I did not doubt. But I saw no one in the open. Martinez lay silent and dusty and dead around me.

A mile of fruitless driving took me past warehouses and loading docks, but finally, almost in the shadow of the railroad bridge, I found a small boat ramp. The fans eased us up and shrilled a song of short life as I studied the opposite shore.

The ramp I aimed for was clogged by a deep-keeled sloop

which had somehow rolled off its trailer and now lay like a beached whale, mast thrusting into the water. I continued to within a few yards of shore—if the fans packed up now, I could tow Lance to dry land—and scooted toward the little state park where I'd gone skimming with Kate a week, and an era, before. The keening of fans and wail of my little engine masked the distant bang-clatter of Caterpillar diesels high overhead, and I never thought to look up as I skimmed under the high bridges. Until, of course, the Pontiac hurtled into the bay fifty yards in front of me.

The Army Corps of Engineers was as good as its word, using huge log-fork-equipped behemoths to toss everything off the bridge. No, I didn't wallop the damned sedan, but I passed it two seconds after it struck and its splash nearly swamped us. By some miracle my fans digested the spray without complaint and then I could see the park to my right, and three minutes later I plopped the Lotus down on dry land, grateful for the chance to disengage the fans.

I needed the fans again to jump a fence and a jam of cars before finding a route through Benicia's waterfront to the railroad tracks. Then I drove slowly back toward the bridge and shut my engine down a few yards from the tracks. My nephew's breath sounded rattly to me but I didn't know what to do about it. Cradling my twelve-gauge, staring down the tracks, I could barely make out the bobbing of tiny figures nearly a mile away. Nearer, on the freeway bridge, I could see a white-clad man in the enclosed cab of an enormous D-10 bulldozer, maneuvering a semi trailer over the rail with his front blade. He was the first stranger I'd seen who spelled "help" instead of "trouble."

Ern needed a car and I had ten minutes to kill, so I spent it inspecting the dozen vehicles nearby. Three of them still had keys in the ignition but none would run. Someone had drained their tanks, just as I would've done. I pondered transferring a gallon of my fuel to a VW transporter that was surely old enough to vote. Then I squinted toward the bridge again and waved a circled thumb and forefinger. My brother-in-law stumbled as he thrust his bike over the cinders, but filling his cargo basket was a hefty fuel can he'd taken from the pickup. What I'd forgotten, Ern had remembered, and vice versa. Spot heard my hail and briefly proved that he was the world's fastest sprinter.

I hugged the fool, ran toward my struggling little group, grabbed the fuel can from the exhausted Ern, and hoofed it toward that old transporter, cursing Spot as he gamboled beside me. Lucky for us, the old VW had no siphon-proof inlet pipe; the fuel thief hadn't needed to cut its fuel line. I got a gallon of fuel into it before the others arrived panting, Devon far in arrears. Ern got it running while I tossed backpack and shovels from the Lotus.

We were breathless from our labors but: "There'll be message centers in Napa and Yountville," Ern husked, pouring the rest of his fuel into the transporter. His eyes flicked toward Shar, who tenderly eased into the Lotus with Lance. "We'll be in touch."

Cammie urged Spot into the VW as I slid into my car. We wasted no time in farewells, and a moment later I chirped rubber heading north. I patted my sis on the knee after circling one barricade. "We'll get there," I reassured her over the engine's snarl, and saw her nod before I drifted the Lotus through a curve. That was the extent of our conversation en route to Napa; if I was quick enough with the Lotus, maybe we wouldn't lose my nephew.

Life is hard, but death is easy. For bullheaded, valiant little Lance it was as easy as slipping away from us in a game of permanent hookey from the school of hard knocks. He was still with us when the police shunted me to Napa State Hospital, a facility near the town now crammed with thousands of trauma cases and not enough medical staff.

Lance seemed to rally, they said, after a third-year med student drained all that blood from his lung cavity and rigged Shar for a whole-blood transfusion. But Dennison's slug had ruptured too much lung tissue; shocked his system too hard; and we had no thoracic surgeon on call. The hospital had no remaining supply of oxygen or adrenalin and goddammit, the kid never had a chance. . . .

My sis and I wept quietly that afternoon, holding each other as we had when mom died, in a basement hall filled with others whose own miseries insulated them from ours. Eventually I left Shar long enough to send a brief message from the emergency comm center to Napa's message center. I agonized over the content of that message but finally spoke for my allotted twenty seconds. Past the lump in my larynx I said, "They're doing all they can here at Napa State Hospital but it doesn't look good, Ern. Shar is coping." Then I added, "No great hurry; he can't have visitors." That way Ern might prepare himself for what I already knew without his hearing it all at once. And maybe he wouldn't take crazy chances driving to us if he knew he couldn't literally race to Lance's side.

After midnight Ern arrived with Cammie, already suspecting the truth. They let me handle the burial arrangements through a massive graves registration system—one of those horrendous details the Surgeon General's Office had worked out long before as a public health measure.

While waiting in line I learned that the almost negligible radiation in Napa was marginally rising, no thanks to vagrant winds that swept up and borrowed fallout particles from San Rafael. I calculated that we had spent less than two hours between my place and Napa and hoped that the gradual rise in background count would not extend to Yountville. Kate and Devon waited for us there with Spot, working their buns off to get the Gallo house ready for long-term occupation. By "long-term" I was thinking about several weeks. I missed it by a bunch.

VII. Doomsday Plus One Hundred and Seventy-six

I may as well put the bad news first: Devon Baird didn't make it through the winter. Cammie took it hardest, though she, like the rest of us, knew what was coming after his hair fell out and the chelate medicine wasn't available to the public until after his bone marrow had quit producing red corpuscles. It seemed that I wasn't destined to have a foster son after all.

But "destiny," I believe, is a word we use to hide incompetence. I may have a son or daughter one day, because in Kate I've found one hell of a wife.

It hadn't occurred to me that I might ring any chimes for a young woman until early December when I was in Napa, registering the old VW transporter in case its prewar owner showed up. I recognized Dana Martin instantly as she slid the forms to me. She had been an FBI intermediary cutout years before, but sleek and sharp as she was, Dana didn't recognize me at first.

When she did: "Good Lord, Harve," she marveled. "You're a hell of a specimen—and ten years younger, minus the beard and thirty kilos of suet." Same old Dana; even her compliments came with a built-in backhand.

"Living off the land isn't easy even in a mild winter," I reminded her. She seemed interested in prolonging our chance encounter and wondered out loud how often I got into Napa. I said not often, and she constructed an ingenue's pout for me, and I bugged out feeling like an escapee from a small predator—which was more truth than fancy. I kidded myself that I was only in a hurry to barter my three bushels of processed acorns for seed and a plow attachment for our third-hand garden tractor. But on my way back to our place near Yountville, I thought about Dana Martin some more and the comparison with Kate came unbidden, and from that moment forward I was a lapsed bachelor.

I said as much to Kate that evening. She only smiled and said, "I was beginning to wonder about you," and her mouth was warm and hungry. We legalized it in January.

Why a woman of Kate's youth and vitality would want to make such a commitment to me was a mystery until the night she asked me what I knew about the bouillon ballot.

"You might not want to know," I said.

"Which means that you *do*. I thought as much. That lonesome vote for Devon the first time; that was you, wasn't it?"

I cocked an eyebrow, enjoying her quest and the way she went about it. "That would be telling on Ern and Shar."

"Screw the tenants, buster. I'm dead sure it was you. You're not the kind to weasel out of a tough decision—but I wanted to hear it from you."

"All right. It was me; but the way you hollered afterward, the others must've thought it was you."

"I don't care. It wasn't right that three of us placed the burden on one. But I damn sure voted the second time, Harve. Not that it matters, but I bet the second abstention was Ern's."

"You lose."

"Then Shar—"

"Shar, nothing. It was mine."

For once Kate was astonished. "Do you mean to sit here under my fanny and tell me you abstained just to teach us a lesson? That's petty!"

"Not to teach anything," I protested. How the hell did I let myself get into these things? "Kate, after your protest, I saw shame on three faces. I felt sure you would all toughen yourselves on the next ballot—and if you felt tough, chances were you'd vote for tough logic. For Devon. But if all four were the same there'd be no secret to the ballot, and you three were obviously touchy about making your decisions known. So . . ."

"So you gave us something to hide behind." Her head was wagging sideways, but on her face was loving acceptance.

"If you wanted it," I shrugged.

"I want it still. Very few men realize how much a woman will do for a man she can depend on. Long legs and a tight gut are nice, but give me a man I can depend on. Fortunately I can have it all unless you start eating too much again." And then she found my mouth and used it mercilessly, I'm happy to say.

We—not only three surviving McKays and two Rackhams

but the surviving eighty million Americans—aren't out of trouble yet, though the armistice is a month old now and the radiation count is slowly receding from a small fraction of a rem in many regions. The chance of bone tumors, leukemia, and other long-term damage has leaped by an order of magnitude, which means we have a small chance of dying that way within the next twenty years. Compared to life expectancy when this republic was young, those odds look bearable. Since the depletion of stored blood, accident victims get whole-blood transfusions or none at all. That's why a blood-group tattoo on the inner forearm is becoming popular. During the past winter there was a shortage of protein, and we see very few cats or dogs these days. Spot is one of those few, because he doesn't solo very far from our designated turf.

You could say with too much justification that Spot is a perfect example of the kind of luxury nobody can afford in this postwar world. If I'd expected the war, perhaps I'd have turned him over to the people at Oregon's Wildlife Safari.

Well, I didn't; and I won't. In the past few months he has learned to maul an intruder and to dodge strangers with sticks that go bang, and he patrols our tender new crops to bag the beasties that would otherwise damage them. That's the only protein supplement he gets, and if he doesn't like living on cereal grains, well, tough; neither do the rest of us. But soybeans will grow here, and by this fall we may not need to boil acorns or find new ways to flavor alfalfa sprouts.

Do I feel defensive about Spot? Yes. Does he pull his weight? Probably not, but maybe so. Gaunt as he is, he submits to the small saddlebags Cammie sewed for him. They'll hold the seine and the fish when we hike to the reservoir, or twenty pounds of whatever else we don't want to tote when one of us goes foraging. Besides, he's becoming known. Anyone who has seen him cover a hundred yards in three seconds will tend to be circumspect at double that distance.

High-tech luxuries like holovision and many medicines will be in short supply for a long time, and as Bay Area suburbs cool down, they become vast junkyards ripe for reckless foragers. City stripping can be downright foolhardy even in some places the bombs missed. Like Milwaukee, where typhus ran its course; and Lexington, where typhoid began in a public shelter and swept the county. I suspect we're through building beehive cities, those great complex organisms that proved so dreadfully vulnerable. If the current plans are any guide, the feds and state officials will rebuild many sites as ring cities surrounding the ruins.

The federal gummint doesn't interfere much with a state's regional decisions now, and since the rural population pulled through in such good shape, the political climate is just what you'd guess: conservative. Kate and I persuaded the McKays to stay on here at the Gallo acreage because that makes us all one household, and taxes are easier on us this way. Currently we're required to pay twenty-four hours of labor into the skills bank every seven days—two twelve-hour days each week. If you think I put my time in as a part-time cop, think again; I cussed and cajoled a wood stove for years, and on the days when I cook for Napa County nabobs, they look forward to gourmet meals. Of *course* I always bring some of it home! Why should a planning commissioner eat better than my wife does?

As for the McKays? Cammie's in school again, training in radiology, which is going to be a crucial skill. Shar is a lab technician in the nearby hospital that used to be a veteran's home and now manufactures its own coarse penicillin. So we don't lack for some basic pharmaceuticals. And Ern, when he isn't engineering the new water-purification plant, is scrounging materials on his own to convert timber by-products into fuel and lubricants. If any one of us becomes a plutocrat during reconstruction, it'll be Ern McKay. I figure he's earned it.

When anyone asks Kate what she does, she says she's my physical therapist; keeps me skinny. God knows that's true enough, and no complaint, but she has a very special talent with little kids. Anyone who thinks a Yountville first-grader can't be adept at postwar survival skills simply hasn't watched her students dress out a chicken, or repair a bike, or create sandals from worn-out tire casings. An intriguing progression of skills there: Kate got some of it from counterculture folks, who got it from travels among the Mexicans, who learned it by rummaging among the castoffs of the rich yanquis.

So it's my wife Kate, more than any of us, who'll be the key to the future of this country. We adults are survivors by definition; our first priority now is to make our next generations expert at pulling through.

NUCLEAR SURVIVAL

Gimme Shelter!

A generation ago Herman Kahn urged us to think about the unthinkable: nuclear war. He then proceeded to scare the hell out of us with his own scenarios on megadeath and civil defense (CD). Soon afterward we were deluged with plans, arguments for and against fallout shelters, and an open letter to the public by then-President John Kennedy. The President, New York Governor Nelson Rockefeller, Kahn, and many others were strongly in favor of public shelter programs in view of the awesome destructive power of nuclear weapons.

A loyal opposition quickly emerged, notably from a phalanx of educators in the Boston area and in the pages of the *Bulletin of the Atomic Scientists*. Freeman Dyson's argument was succinct: nuclear nations should *not* build shelters on a large scale, because while a lack of effective shelters may mean death for a warring nation, effective shelters may mean death for the entire human race. Dyson reasoned that effectively sheltered antagonists would go on pounding away at each other until not only the duelists but the whole world was fatally contaminated. Better that the warring nations die alone, he concluded, than to drag all mankind down with them.

Dyson did not deal with the obvious, e.g., what happens when one duelist is protected and the other is not. We must deal with it now. Relatively speaking, the USSR is effectively protected. The United States is not.

Now that we have your full attention, let us remind you that Dyson warned us against shelters *on a large scale*. If a few thousand or million of us choose to survive on a small scale, it shouldn't affect first-order terms of the megadeath equation very much. And even if we *do* go in for shelters on a large

145

scale, we don't have to share Dyson's opinion. Lots of experts don't.

No one can know today whether our lives would be worth living after a nuclear war, and we won't dwell on the moral questions of the individual's responsibility to oneself and to others. For the ultimate amorality, the survivor who envies the dead can join them any time he chooses. But you ought to have the option of nuclear survival, and that option starts with information. We can't expect to be as effective as the USSR has been in training tens of millions of Soviet citizens as a survival cadre, but we can help a few train themselves. Much of the information is basic. For many of us, particularly urbanites, it begins *before* we step into a fallout shelter. This article is a beginning. Subsequent articles will show how, with a little foresight, you might reverse the odds against yourself once a shelter is reached.

In the 1950s we knew that the 20 KT (equivalent to twenty thousand tons of TNT) Hiroshima blast was almost insignificantly small compared to the 20 MT—*mega*ton—and larger weapons then in development. Was the public interested? Not much, until Kahn popularized the mathematics of annihilation and helped provoke the great shelter debate of the sixties. Suddenly in 1961 we were more than interested; we were fascinated, and then inundated by a tsunami of articles, pamphlets, and books. Like the European tulip craze of the seventeenth century and our Muckraker Era after 1900, the topic blazed into focus. It didn't stay long; anyone can see by checking the *Readers' Guide to Periodicals* that by 1963 the topic was plummeting from public view. By 1979 it had fallen almost out of sight.

For several reasons the US public largely abandoned CD until very recently; and now the rules have changed! Government agencies spent most of a billion dollars in the 1950s locating and stocking potential fallout shelters in urban areas. With all those signs telling us where to go, we'd be okay when we got there; right?

Wrong. Language sets its own tripwires, and in our focal effort to find fallout shelters, we concentrated altogether too much on only one danger, i.e., fallout. Quick, now: how many victims in Hiroshima and Nagasaki succumbed to fallout? Evidently none. The bombs were detonated high in the air for maximum effect against the two cities. An airburst does its damage as a one-two-three-four punch. First comes the thermal radiation, moving out from the fireball core at light speed and lasting something under one minute. Next comes the blast wave, a hammer blow of air moving a bit faster than Mach 1 that can reduce nearby concrete structures to powder, the range of blast destructiveness weakening with the cube root of the bomb's energy. This means that a 20 MT bomb's blast effect reaches only (!) ten times as far as that of a 20 KT bomb. Third comes the firestorm, a genuine meteorological event caused by the burning of everything ignitable within range—and that encompasses many square miles—of the initial heat effects. Last and most lingering comes the fallout, a rain of deadly radioactive ash from the mushroom cloud that moves downwind.

The bigger the bomb, the more preponderantly it is an incendiary weapon. Victims of conventional Allied incendiary air raids in World War II were found suitably protected from blast effects in shelters—suffocated and cremated by the firestorms that ensued. Even without nukes the toll was 200,000 in Tokyo, 300,000 in Dresden. In New York City fallout shelters the toll might be twenty times as high, because the first bomb targeted against a big city will almost certainly be an airburst with appalling incendiary effects. Suburbanites far downwind may live long enough to worry about fallout.

The ground burst is the one that punches a vast depression in the earth and sends thousands of tons of vaporized dirt into the air. We can expect ground bursts against deeply buried military installations and other "hard" targets. The fallout from a ground burst may be lethal hundreds of miles downwind, because the vaporized dirt will condense and drift down as radioactive ash—thousands of tons of it.

Incidentally, because so much of the ground burst's energy goes into punching that hole in the ground, the blast and initial radiation effects of a ground burst will not be as widespread. Your chances a few miles from a ground burst can be better than the same distance from an airburst, if you're far enough upwind or sheltered well enough to avoid fallout from the ground burst. But that mushroom cloud will be miles across; and if I'm near it, gimme shelter!

But what *is* effective shelter? Not an ordinary urban basement. Probably not even a subway tunnel, unless the tunnel can be hermetically sealed against the firestorm. Imagine a gopher in his tunnel, with openings fifty feet apart, under a bonfire a hundred feet across. The fire will rage for hours, causing updrafts of hurricane force toward the center that suck air right out of the tunnels. It simply withdraws the little varmint's oxygen while the heat gradually builds up deep beneath the bonfire. Well, a big firestorm is a miles-wide bonfire, and our subway commuter is the gopher. The Soviets have given that a lot of thought. Unlike us, according to Leon Gouré, they've done something about it.

Gouré, a RAND Corporation man, emigrated from Moscow in infancy and revisited the USSR in 1960 (he's still one of our top scholars of Soviet strategy). He found huge blast doors set into the floors of Moscow subway tunnels—and we can take hermetic seals for granted. Moscow might burn, but a million or so Muscovites can keep on breathing. Gouré also learned that Soviet civil defense officials, the MPVO (for Mestnaia Protivovozdushnaia Oborona, so from now on we'll just give acronyms; trust us, okay?), can call on twenty or thirty million members of a paramilitary civilian cadre called DOSAAF. DOSAAF people correspond roughly to a national home guard, and they all get compulsory training as population leaders in evacuation and shelter exercises.

The Soviets, with total control over the architecture of apartment buildings as well as municipal structures, have very special building codes for urban basements. Many apartment-building basements have specially reinforced thick ceilings and walls with load-bearing partitions and airtight steel doors. In addition, ventilation tunnels filter incoming air and provide remote emergency escape passages. Gouré cited toilet facilities, stored food and water with other supplies, and implied that bottled air may be provided. Thus protected, Soviet apartment dwellers just might live through all but the fiercest firestorm.

It's possible for us to build better urban shelters than these, but we do not appear to be doing it. Our civil defense posture has regeared itself more toward evacuation than to digging in. More accurately, at the moment we're between gears, idling in neutral.

A recent Boeing study revealed to a congressional committee that with its low-key, continuing civil defense, its carefully dispersed industry, and its less centralized population, the USSR might recover from a war in two to four years, while the United States might need twelve years for recovery. Two percent of the Soviets might die. Sixty percent of Americans might die. *Now* do you see why the Soviets marched into Afghanistan with such confidence?

Anecdote time: we know a scientist who fled the Soviet bloc some years ago. Her eyewitness report on Soviet civil defense is more recent than Gouré's, and perhaps more scarifying. She insists that the USSR and its satellite countries feel confident that their people would easily survive a nuclear war because of their massive compulsory CD programs. Now in the United States, our scientist friend moved as far from local target areas as she could and modified her basement into an acceptable fallout shelter. She's still dismayed that her American friends have no hermetically sealed public tunnels and that they consider her efforts, in a word, weird.

China has her tunnels, too. Less elaborate than Moscow subways, Peking's tunnels are only a few meters below the surface and probably would be employed as an escape route to the countryside. Dairen, a big shipping port, is a likely target and its deep tunnels are stocked for eighty thousand evacuees. The tunnels criss-cross like a bus network and might be marginally suitable if they are effective conduits beyond the firestorm area.

Canada has her National Shelter Plan, several years in arrears of our own and still geared to identifying mass fallout shelters for urbanites. Undeniably Canada harbors fewer prime targets than we do in both major categories: the hardened military sites for which ground bursts are slated, and the soft population targets so vulnerable to airbursts. But Canada's cities are just as vulnerable as ours. She needs an urban public that's drilled as well in evacuation as in cellar dwelling, just as we do.

Almost makes you wish you lived in some small, modern, nonaggressive country like Switzerland, doesn't it? The Swiss were neutral in both world wars and show every sign of maintaining that tradition. Little or no bothersome CD preparations there, right? *Totally* wrong: no country in the Western world has more or better personal shelters per capita. It's written into their building codes.

From all evidence, both United States and USSR civil defense officials count on being alerted many hours or even days before Time Zero, apparently on the basis of judgments of political events and evidence that the other side is battening down its hatches. This is a gamble we take collectively; but you, *personally,* don't have to take all of that gamble.

So how do you reduce the gamble for your immediate family? Being painfully aware that you may find some of the answers very unpleasant, we'll start with some generalizations and some specifics.

1. Talk to your local CD coordinator, who may be making do with absurdly low federal and local funding. Local officials usually have expert guesses as to the nearest target area. What common carriers are earmarked for evacuation? What should you carry with you? Where will you go and what facilities will you find there? Ask for a copy of the 1977 booklet *Protection in the Nuclear Age,* or borrow theirs and copy it. The booklet strongly reflects the shift in emphasis toward evacuation—or, in CD jargon, "crisis relocation." Among other things the booklet describes home shelters of several kinds, a source of free shelter plans, and your best tactics in evacuating a target area.

2. If you live or work in a primary target area, for God's sake seek other stomping grounds. This is far and away the best item in improving your chances—and the toughest one to implement.

3. Do your homework on fallout, prevailing winds, and target areas upwind of you. The November 1976 *Scientific American* is a good departure point.

4. More homework. Make a low-key, consistent hobby of studying survival and technology. Oldies like *Fortunes in Formulas* and any decent encyclopedia set may be more helpful than books on woodcraft. If you wind up in the woods you either know your stuff already or you're up the creek without a scintillator. Mel Tappan's column on survival was a fixture in *Guns & Ammo* magazine since December, 1976, and Tappan was no wild-eyed troglodyte. His argument in favor of living in a smallish town rather than a metropolis or mountaintop is eloquent.

5. Fill a scruffy rucksack with raisins and jerked meat; transistor radio; masking tape and monofilament line; first-aid equipment, including water-purification tablets; a few rolls of dimes; leather gloves; vitamins; steel canteen; thermally reflective mylar blanket from any outfitter; good multipurpose clasp knife; and so on. You might have to change plans and relocate without notice. We spent an evening once

at Poul Anderson's place with several writers, arguing the merits of a survival kit that was originally stored in a certain specially stiffened Porsche coupe. Basically our kit was intended to get a tinkerer across country. It didn't look worth stealing. That's a vital point: when you can't expect a policeman to help, keep a low profile.

The kit had some of the items mentioned already, plus small slide rule, pliers, drill bits, wire and needles, compass, fishhooks, wax-coated matches and candle stub (a plumber's candle is high in stearic acid and burns very slowly), thick plastic bags, pencils and pad, all wrapped in heavy aluminum foil so that it could be swung like a short club. Huge half-inch-wide rubber bands looped around the handle end. Never forget that a slingshot with big rubber bands is quiet and flashless, and ammunition for it is everywhere. Why the masking tape? Whether you stay put or evacuate, you may need to tape cracks around openings to make your quarters as airtight as possible. Freshen the kit annually.

Pamphlets suggest you may have two days' warning. Don't bet your life on it.

No booklet can possibly cover all the problems you're likely to find if you choose crisis relocation, i.e., evacuation after the alert sounds. But another brief list might help you.

1. Keep detailed county and state maps. Decide where you'll go and learn alternative routes; chances are, major arterials will soon be clogged. Consider strapping bikes onto your car as second-stage vehicles. Roads that become impassable by car might still be navigable on a bike.

2. When you already have a good idea which way you will probably go, polish up your friendships with acquaintances who live in that presumably safer region. Establish agreements that they'll accept you, and do your part ahead of time. For example: buy a hundred-gallon water-storage tank and let them have it on permanent loan; furnish them with a survival library; help them build their shelter; and/ or *be* an encyclopedia of survival lore they'd rather be with than without.

3. Get in shape. Stay that way. Regular exercise, particularly jogging, hiking, and bicycling, gives you stamina for that extra klick or edge of alertness when you need it.

Physical exhaustion has its corollary in emotional exhaustion, and a sense of futility is a heavier load than a full backpack. Besides, if you use a cycle regularly you'll keep your bike in good repair. How long since you patched a bike tire at the roadside?

4. Collect a first-stage kit and a second-stage kit in your garage or storage shed, and be ready to stow both in your car. First-stage kits include saw, pick, and shovel; plastic tarps; extra bedding and clothes; all the food you can quickly pack into rugged boxes; a spare fuel supply for your car (store it wisely in the meantime); the contents of your medicine cabinet; tools; sanitation items; and any books you may think especially useful. Second-stage kits include the rucksack we described earlier, small ax or hatchet, sleeping bag, plastic tarp, maps, and medication or other essentials according to your special needs. If you must abandon your car later, you can grab your second-stage kit and keep going afoot or on a bike.

5. Move quickly without panic if the time comes to relocate. Drill your family in the details and obey officials in face-to-face encounters. Law officers coping with the crisis may not be willing to put up with much argument when you're en route. Choose the clothes you'll wear beforehand and dress for a hike.

6. Pretend you've gone halfway to your destination, abandoned your car, and are afoot in a sparsely populated area when you perceive that you're downwind of a mushroom cloud. You may have several hours before you must have shelter, but the time to seek it is right *now!* A homeowner may take you in, especially if you look like you'll be more help than hindrance. If not, don't risk getting shot. Keep going until you find some structure that will shelter you. The more dirt or concrete above and around you, the better; a dry culvert could be much better than a bungalow. Establish your location on the map, seal yourself in for what may be days, and attend to your radio for information on local conditions. If you're one of the few with a radiation counter, you'll know when to stay put and when to move on. Fallout is like lust; it isn't forever, but it colors your decisions.

7. If you're heeled—carrying weapons—cache them securely before you enter any public or communal shelter.

You'll almost certainly be required to give them up anyhow, and you'd be dangerously unpopular if it became known that you didn't surrender them. And you probably wouldn't get them back once you surrendered them. For most of us, weapons are more harmful temptation than useful tools. Of course, a tiny pocket canister of Mace is another matter. Ever notice how some defensive items look like cigarette lighters—especially if spray-painted silver or white?

It's probably not necessary to justify all the points we've listed, but you'll find a rationale behind any advice that's worth hearing. Our embedded biases aren't hard to pin down. We believe that mass evacuation from target areas is a more viable response than most shelters in those areas. We know that our present CD planning is underfunded for the goals it is planning. Translation: your local officials probably won't be able to cope with the evacuation after they call for it.

We also believe that the more actively you study the problems and consider prudent means to avoid bottlenecks in your own relocation, the more likely it is that you'll become part of CD solutions.

And consider the rationales in the details, e.g., bicycling. It does more than improve your stamina and speed your relocation. It can be equipped with a tiny generator and light; it requires no stored fuel; it can be bodily carried or even hauled through water; it is almost noiseless in use; and ultimately it can be abandoned without great financial or emotional loss. It's part of that low profile we mentioned.

By now it should be obvious that for many of us, crisis relocation will precede effective shelter. Once you've relocated to an area where shelter can be effective, you'll need to focus on such things as fallout shielding, air filtration and pumping, hygiene, and other basic life-support needs. In the next article we'll show you how to build simple air-filtration and pump units with a minimum of effort and time.

In the meantime, do yourself a favor. Talk with your local CD people and visit your library for the articles we've mentioned. After you've studied the problem a bit, you'll be prepared to make a better response to an alert than to stand on the courthouse lawn bawling, "Gimme shelter!"

Living Under Pressure

We began this series of articles to update and alert you on the problems of survival after an all-out nuclear exchange. Briefly summarized: in Gimme Shelter we explained that twenty-mile-wide, thermonuclear-kindled firestorms would render many US urban areas utterly uninhabitable. The government—much too quietly, in my opinion—now favors mass evacuation from high-risk areas following an alert. The problems with this new and more sensible civil defense (CD) posture lie in educating us about it; in the likelihood of clogged routes during the evacuation; in improvising shelters in low-risk areas; and in doing anything on a large scale with damnably low CD budgets. We also referenced some publications and promised to give you some tips on making a shelter more effective, starting with air filtration and pump units that you can make on short notice. We're making good on that promise now. In a phrase, one key to clean air is living under pressure.

We assume that you have your free copy of the government's CD pamphlet of February, 1977, *Protection in the Nuclear Age*, which admits the wisdom of "crisis relocation" and suggests that you find a shelter completely surrounded by two or three feet of masonry or dirt. But even if you have such a shelter, you still aren't safe from fallout unless you can make the place airtight.

If you've ever fretted through a dust storm, you know how air supports dust particles and how a breeze sifts the finest ones past infinitesimal cracks around doors and window frames. While a lot of fallout will be large visible ash, too much of the stuff will be invisibly small hunks of airborne grit, settling hundreds of miles downwind of a nuclear strike. They are lethal dust motes if you breathe enough of them during the first two

154

or three weeks after a nuclear strike. That's why a shelter should be stocked with caulking material and tape: so that every crevice in the shelter can be sealed. In short, you must turn the shelter into a pressure vessel and bottle yourself up in it.

Which means that you could swelter in your body heat and asphyxiate in your own carbon-dioxide waste if you stayed inside very long without a fresh air supply. We'll give figures later in this article; for the moment the rationale's the thing.

If your supplies are adequate, you might stay in the shelter for weeks—but almost nobody will have a week's supply of bottled air. What you need is a means of pumping cool filtered air from the outside and for exhausting the stale humid air from your shelter. Believe it or not, the solution isn't necessarily very complex once you've practiced doing it, even on a small-scale model.

We infer from sources on Soviet CD that the first stage of their civilian shelter filters is through something called a blast attenuator—a wide vertical conduit pipe filled with big rocks and gravel. The pipe has a rain cap on top, aboveground, and a removable grille covering one side of its bottom end. The grille is sturdy enough to hold the gravel and coarse enough to let air through. Note that a conduit of twenty-four-inch diameter can be used as an emergency exit, once the grille is removed and the gravel drained out. The gravel lets air through while trapping large fallout particles and baffling concussion waves from any nearby explosions. The Soviets use finer filters for the air that is sucked down through the gravel by pumps. Incidentally, if you're building such a "blast attenuator" for a shelter, specify rounded quartz gravel. Hunks of limestone can eventually become cemented together to become a rigid sponge that impedes airflow.

In extremis you could build a medium-mesh filter by taping a towel over a square-foot-size inlet into the shelter. You might find it clogged after a day or so. A finer-mesh filter can be made with corrugated cardboard, large juice cans, replaceable rolls of toilet paper, and tape.

Our demonstration rig was designed to provide air for two adults. It uses a standard household furnace filter element taped securely over the intake hole of the filter box—because we assume that you *won't* have a yards-long gravel-filled conduit. After you build your air-filtration unit, you'll have to place it in some weatherproof spot just outside the sealed shelter. Thus you can get to the unit quickly in case filter elements become clogged.

The standard furnace filter has a coarse fiberglass element. Particles that get past it will be small, but many would be visible to the naked eye. That calls for a second and finer element.

For its second element our model uses the same stuff employed by a great many industrial air filters: nothing more than a piece of flannel. As it happens, we spent a dollar on a yard of cotton outing flannel, enough for a one-square-foot filter element with eight spares. That might be enough for two weeks, depending on how much fallout is in your area. We could've used a new diaper or a flannel shirt; it's the soft, fuzzy nap of the flannel that traps so much dust. Flannel that's been washed until its fuzz has gone the way of all lint is, ah, washed up. Don't use it, or use two layers. Terry cloth could be used but to less effect.

So far our scheme calls for a coarse fiberglass filter element taped over a shallow frame of some sort, and right behind it, one fuzzy flannel element. In a pinch these elements would probably protect you from 95 percent of the fallout without finer filtration. But the particles that get past these two coarse elements might still zap you if fallout is heavy. What we really need is a still finer element, or a set of them in parallel, to take out particles of micron size. That's where toilet paper rolls come in.

For many years some engine-oil filters employed a roll of toilet paper as the filter element. The oil was forced under pressure to pass between the many circular layers of paper— and the central hole was, of course, plugged. Note well: the oil didn't pass from one *side* of the paper cylinder to the other; it passed from one circular *face* to the other. In the process, even very small solid particles in the oil were trapped in the paper. Only the smallest particles, reportedly on the order of a half-micron, could get through such a filter element.

The same kind of filtration works in extracting tiny fallout particles from air. However, we assume that your air pump (like ours) will be the sort that provides high volume but not much pressure. Since a paper roll restricts the airflow somewhat, it's necessary to use at least four of the rolls simultaneously, in parallel, to allow enough airflow for two adults.

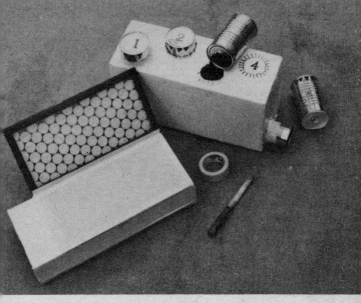

Figure 1

It's worth repeating: a four-roll filter is minimal. Use more if you have the materials.

In Figure 1 we see the filtration unit during assembly. The coarse filter elements with their shallow cardboard frame are ready for mounting, the fiberglass element hinged by masking tape and ready to swing down over the flannel element. The shallow frame will fit over the canisters holding the (fine) paper elements. Our small model uses only four paper roll elements, fitted into juice cans. The can with Fine Element #1 is already taped in place; Fine Element #2 is in place, ready for taping; Fine Element #3 is ready to be thrust into its hole; and the hole for Fine Element #4 hasn't yet been cut. Element #4 lies beside the filter box with the paper roll inside its canister. To prepare the hole for Element #4, first cut out the central hole; then cut the radiating slits; and finally fold the slit tabs of cardboard outward so that the hole allows passage of the juice can, in the same manner as Element #3. The white paint on the unit isn't just cosmetic; a gallon of quick-drying latex paint will seal the pores of lots of corrugated cardboard.

You'll probably find that a roll of toilet paper won't fit in

Figure 2

a juice can until some paper has been unrolled. Strip off the
necessary layers and stuff some of it into the can before you
insert the roll. Stuff the rest of the paper tightly into the central
hole of the tissue roll. Last, insert the roll into the can so that
it's a snug, but not crushed, fit. Of course there must be holes
in the other end of the canister through which air can be drawn.
In the demo model we've punched four triangular holes next
to the closed end of each can, orienting the holes so that when
the filter box lies in its normal position, air must rise through
the holes. This gives fallout particles one more chance to drop
out. In Figure 1 the filter box stands upended so that you can
see assembly details.

In Figure 2, the filter box lies in its normal operating position. The coarse elements and their cardboard frame have
been taped in place on the filter box. Hidden within the coarse
filter frame are the four canisters with the fine-filter rolls, taped
securely in place. Every seam on the unit has been double-
taped, and you can see its size from the meter sticks in the
illustration. The small soup can inserted at one rear corner of
the filter box has both its ends removed. It merely provides a
connection to the air-conduit tube leading from your filter unit
to the pump in your shelter.

• • •

Our pump unit is a simple bellows pump, made from another cardboard box. Obviously if you have a hand-cranked blower, a battery-powered automobile heater blower, or some other commercial pump, you're way ahead. We're taking the position that, like almost everybody else, you failed to buy such equipment and must either make your own at the last minute or die trying.

Before starting on the pump body, make its conduit tube. If you don't have the equivalent of a three-inch-diameter cardboard tube, grab a thick section of old newspaper and roll it into a tube. Tape the long seam and tape the ends to prevent fraying, then slather latex paint over it. Make it no longer than necessary, remembering that the longer it is, the more resistance it has to airflow. Ideally your filtration unit will be only a step from your shelter, so you'll need only a few sections of newspaper conduit. Our demo model uses one section, just to show how simple it is.

Chances are, a newspaper conduit won't be sturdy enough on its own to withstand the partial vacuum created when the pump is working. So why didn't we use a heavy cardboard tube or, more efficient, smooth-walled metal stovepipe? Only because we assumed you won't *have* any. As it happens, there's a quick remedy for the "collapsing conduit" problem. You make a long cruciform stiffener of cardboard, or several short ones, and insert it into the conduit. The conduit might still buckle a bit, but it won't collapse. If you can make conduit that's stiffer, without incurring a heavy time penalty, do it.

Now cut a round hole in your shelter wall near the floor and run the conduit through, taping around the hole, and tape the conduit to the filter unit outside (as we did in Figure 2). At this point you can retreat into your shelter and seal yourself in with tape. You're only half-finished, but you can breathe shelter air while you build the pump.

The pump unit is absurdly simple, really, even with its two flapper valves. In Figure 3 it's half-finished, the inked lines showing where you must fold and cut, including the flat piece that eventually becomes our admittedly gimmicky pump handle. For our bellows material, we used transparent flexible sheeting, so that we could see through it to watch the inlet valve operate; but plain translucent or even black polyethylene

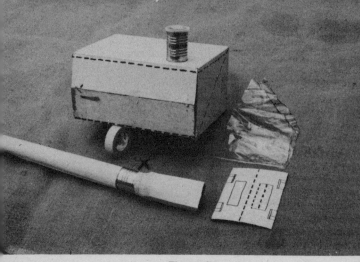

Figure 3

sheeting would do. You should choose four-mil-thick or thicker sheeting.

You can see that the pump begins as a rugged corrugated cardboard box, with seams taped to make it airtight. As the dotted lines show, one rectangular face and the adjoining triangular halves of two other faces must first be cut away. The removed cardboard can be used as a pattern to cut the flexible plastic bellows material. Or you can cut the flexible plastic freehand, as we did. In Figure 3 the flexible stuff is folded double, lying between the box and the pattern for the pump handle.

Next make the pump handle. We like to play with cardboard, so we built a rigid cardboard handle that locked into the top of the pump with tabs, and we taped it around the tab slits to prevent air leakage. It probably would've been quicker merely to punch two holes in the box and to run a rope handle through the holes. Knots in the ends of the rope handle would keep it from pulling through, and tape around the holes would minimize air leaks. The point is, you can do it any of several ways, so long as you don't leave sizable holes in the pump box that would dramatically lower the pump's efficiency.

Now for the moving parts: the two flapper valves. Here, again, we deliberately made them of different materials only to demonstrate that you can use whatever's handy. In Figure 3 the valves aren't yet in place. The outlet valve is sitting atop the pump. The body of the inlet valve has been mated to a conduit tube via a soup can. We made the inlet valve from an empty macaroni carton, a sloppily cut rectangle of cardboard slightly larger than the mouth of the carton, and a piece of masking tape as a hinge. Simply tape the cardboard rectangle— the flapper—at the top only, so that it hangs down over the mouth of the carton. Blow through the carton, and the cardboard flapper swings out to let the air pass. Blow against the face of the flapper, and it swings shut, preventing airflow. That's it; a one-way flapper valve. It isn't completely airtight, of course, but as long as it fits neatly over the mouth of the carton, it's close enough. And it only takes a moment to make.

Cut a hole through the rear face of the pump box to accept the carton, shove the carton halfway through, and tape it in place. The valve works better if you mount the carton at a slight angle, protruding upward into the box. That way gravity makes the flapper lie flat over the carton's mouth. In Figure 4 you can see the inlet valve flapper through the transparent bellows—about which, more later.

Make the outlet valve and install it the same way, except that the outlet valve flapper is mounted on the outside of the box. *Inlet flapper inside; outlet flapper outside.* In our model

Figure 4

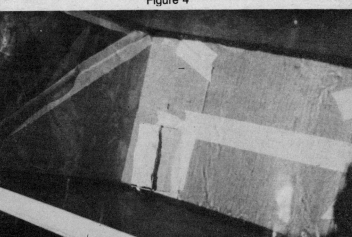

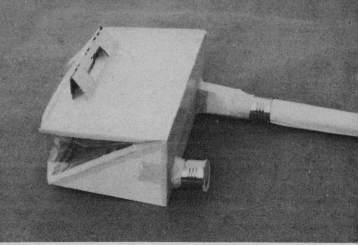

Figure 5

we made the outlet valve from a soup can and a throwaway plastic lid. Even at the risk of boring you, I repeat: there was no special reason why the inlet and outlet valves were different shapes and made from different materials, except to prove that there are lots of ways to do it. For you perfectionists: with rubber faces between flapper and valve body and with very slight spring-loading to help them close, you could make better valves than we made. But it would take longer. Our model worked so well that the observer's typical first response was delighted laughter. The little bugger'll blow your hat off!

You're almost finished when you cut a long trapezoidal piece of flexible plastic sheeting (the same size and shape as the piece of cardboard you cut away along the dotted lines) and then tape the sheeting onto the box in place of the missing cardboard. When you finish double-taping and latex-painting the pump box (you don't have to paint the handle), grab the handle and raise the lid of the box. You should hear the pump draw a mighty breath, then a faint *clack* as the cardboard flapper of the inlet valve drops back into place inside the pump box. Now push down firmly on the handle. The pump should exhale with a whispery *whoosh,* followed by another *clack* as the outlet flapper drops back into place. Check for air leaks; if air is expelled from anyplace besides the outlet valve, those leaks must be sealed. In Figure 5 the completed pump is in "inhale" position and the tape-hinged outlet flapper is visible.

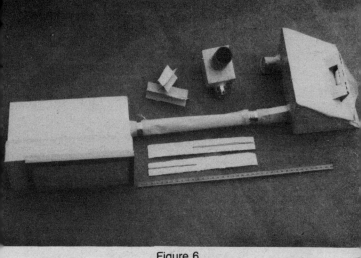

Figure 6

Our small model displaces about two thirds of a cubic foot of air with every inhale/exhale cycle. If you can start with a bigger box, naturally your pump will move more air—which is all to the good, as we'll explain later.

The last step before drawing clean air is simply to mate the conduit from the filter unit to the pump inlet, tape the joint, and start pumping. It may not keep absolutely all radioactive particles out of your shelter, but the little rig assembled for testing in Figure 6 should make your breathing air cleaner than outside air by several orders of magnitude—a thousand times as clean. For somebody who started three hours ago, you're doing pretty well! If two of you are building the units together, it could be closer to two hours. Incidentally, in Figure 6 you can see cruciform conduit stiffeners of various lengths—the longest one not yet assembled—and a stale air valve we haven't yet discussed, because when minutes count, it should be built last.

Though you now have a means to pump clean air into the shelter, you still need to consider how you'll get rid of the stale air you've already breathed. That stale air will normally be a bit warmer than it was when it entered the shelter but it'll be more moist, too, from water vapor given off by every animal in the shelter. The stale air will also be loaded with your exhaled carbon dioxide, which is slightly heavier than air. All in all, you can expect the moist, carbon dioxide–laden stale air to lie

Figure 7

near the floor. Therefore, the stale air exhaust valve inlet should be placed at floor level and far away from the fresh air squirting into your shelter from the pump.

Before you ask how much more mickey-mouse gadgeteering we need for the system, a glance at Figure 7 will show you. The job of the stale air exhaust valve is to permit the escape of stale air when the shelter air pressure is raised by a very small fraction of a pound per square inch—in fact, by a fraction of an *ounce*. This little exhaust valve is the last part of our air supply system.

Our stale air exhaust valve consists of a small box for the valve body, a perforated soup can sticking up into the box from below as an inlet and flapper support, a piece of styrofoam taped atop the soup can as the valve flapper, and a cardboard tube leading from the side of the valve box through a hole in the shelter wall to the "outside." Note the penny glued atop the styrofoam flapper. Styrofoam is so light, it needed a tiny weight to ensure that the flapper would always close. The flapper will rise when shelter pressure is very slightly elevated above ambient, i.e., outside, air pressure. If a windstorm brews up outside and gusty winds try to blow in through the exit tube, the flapper stays put. Little or no unfiltered, fallout-laden air gets in.

By studying Figure 7 you can see that, like the other parts of our system, the stale air exhaust valve can be made from whatever's handy, so long as it's airtight. We punched triangular holes around the bottom of the soup can for stale air to enter. We taped the can securely into the box, then did the same with the cardboard exit tube. We tape-hinged the styrofoam flapper atop the soup can, then taped the box shut so that any air passing out of the shelter must pass through the triangular vents at floor level, up through the flapper, and then out of the shelter via the exit tube.

Finally, in Figure 8, we pushed the end of the exit tube through a hole in the shelter wall and taped it in place so that the valve stands on its inlet tube.

Unlike the valves in the pump, the stale air exhaust valve won't clatter much during operation. In fact, you might want to install a piece of plastic or glass as a window into the little box so that you can inspect it now and then while someone operates the pump. If it never opens at all, start looking for

Figure 8

leaks in the shelter while the pump is in operation. A few wisps of cigarette smoke might help you trace a leak. Otherwise don't smoke!

You now have all the necessary elements for a minimal air supply system for two adults in a small shelter. It's a far cry from an automated system. In fact, if you are alone in your shelter, you could still be in serious trouble if you fall asleep for many hours.

Engineering texts on ventilation systems call for two or more air changes per hour in a meeting room, more for lavatories, locker rooms, or assembly halls. They also call for roughly a thousand cubic feet of air per person *per hour*. Frankly, this approaches the upper airflow limit of our small demo unit even if you kept it going all the time. Luckily, as the texts admit, these figures are greatly in excess of general practice.

How much in excess? Well, you probably needn't worry about CO_2 poisoning or sticky-wet humidity if you manage to get 400 cubic ft. of fresh air into the shelter per person per hour. It's my personal suspicion that you could get by on a fraction of that when sleeping or sitting quietly. But if you begin to feel headachy, dizzy, or drunk, get to work on the pump.

For a rough approximation of your pump's output, measure the outside dimensions of the pump when it is fully open; then find the volume inside. Next, bearing in mind that the pump doesn't entirely close down to half of its maximum volume, multiply the maximum by 0.4; in other words, take 40 percent of the pump's maximum volume. That's roughly how much air the pump gives you every time you open and close it fully.

Example:

> Our pump box dimensions are 20″ × 14″ x 10″.
> Maximum volume, then, is 2800 cubic inches.
> 40% of 2800 cubic inches = 1120 cu. in.
> And since 1 cubic foot = 1728 cubic inches, each pump stroke yields $^{1120}/_{1728}$ cubic feet of air, which is roughly ⅔ cubic feet per stroke.

For those of you who think these calculations are too elementary: please knock it off, you guys. We want to make this clear enough for a smart sixth-grader.

Since we can operate our pump at about twenty strokes per minute without tearing it up we find that our little demo unit will give us 14 cubic feet of fresh air per minute, or 800 cubic feet per hour. I think—but with so many variables of shelters, valve seals, and such I wouldn't swear to it—that you might get by with three adults in a shelter using this little rig half the time. To put it another way: each of you three would probably have to operate our little pump for four or more hours every day to assure a decent air supply. That implies a lot of work, which means heavy breathing, which means elevated humidity.

As we said before, the pump provides more than just oxygen; it also keeps the humidity and temperature down to bearable levels in the sealed shelter by forcing out the stale air.

What if you're alone? There's no one to pump while you sleep, so you should choose a shelter that contains a thousand cubic feet of air or more. And bring an alarm clock with you. Far better to be awakened by a clattering bell every two hours to pump for a while than never to wake at all.

No alarm clock? Lordy, what are we gonna do with you! Just remember that sand or water can be metered to trickle slowly into a container on a seesaw. When the seesaw shifts, it can knock something over noisily in approved Rube Goldberg fashion. Sure, this is all a lot of trouble. Why didn't you invest in good, commercially available equipment *before* the klaxon tooted?

No one is suggesting that the primitive life-support system illustrated here is any match for a commercial unit. To repeat: this article is for the 95 percent of us who may know what we ought to do but aren't doing it. It's easy to critique the system— and to make this one better.

The filter unit could be improved several ways: by being larger, with more fine paper roll elements; by having a quickly resealable panel for fast replacement of paper rolls in case they become clogged; and by being more rugged than cardboard. Duct tape is stronger than the masking tape we used, but much more expensive. Buy some anyhow; tell yourself you're worth it.

The pump is the weakest link in our model; it should've been bigger. But even using the box we used, you could increase its capacity by altering the pattern for the bellows so the pump would open wider. We found that a single thickness of cardboard is almost too flimsy for the top face (the one with the handle) of the pump. A double sheet of cardboard, plywood, or even thin wooden slats taped across the flimsy top face would make it last longer.

You'll find that the pump's light weight can be a problem. It creates so much suction, the whole box wants to rise up when you lift the handle. If you don't want to wedge the pump in place on the floor, you could weigh it down. Just unseal the bellows, lay several bricks down on the pump's bottom face between the valves, then reseal the bellows. In that position the bricks won't reduce the pump's output, and they'll keep the pump from jumping around while you use it.

When we characterized this model as "minimal," we weren't kidding. With only four paper rolls in the filter unit, airflow is so restricted that you must exert some effort to lift the pump handle. You'll be dog-tired after using it awhile. You'll wish you'd built a filter box with more roll elements so you could pump more easily. Well, you still can! Just build another filter unit, go outside briefly, and connect the filter units by a short conduit.

You could elect to build a filter without the paper roll ele-

ments. It won't purify the air as much, but it's much quicker
and it makes pumping much easier. Of course, the flannel
element can be quite large.

We won't go into great detail on the subject of negative-
pressure shelters because they aren't as secure. But you could
opt for such a system, in which the shelter air pressure is very
slightly *lower* than ambient. Essentially, you install a stovepipe
from your shelter to the roof and install a simple, commercial,
wind-driven rotating ventilator atop the pipe. When the wind
blows, the ventilator sucks air up and out of the shelter. If you
taped a couple of layers of flannel over a window-size opening
into your shelter, the ventilator would do your pumping for
you, drawing fresh air in past the flannel elements. The pressure
differential in the shelter would be too low, however, for you
to hope it could suck air in through paper roll elements.

Summarizing the low-pressure shelter scheme: it's attractive
because it doesn't require you to pump by hand. On the other
hand, it won't pull air through a really fine filter element—
and besides, the low shelter pressure can draw unfiltered air
in through crevices. Moreover, when the wind isn't blowing,
your air gets stale anyway.

Whatever system you use to provide fresh, clean air in your
shelter, what do you do if it proves less than adequate? Well,
you trouble-shoot it to check for something clogging any part
of the system. You breathe through a flannel (or something
better) mask while the shelter is open to ambient air. You
remind yourself that you're buying time during the hours when
your system *is* working, because day by day the radioactivity
of fallout particles should diminish. In forays outside the shelter
you wear gloves and all-enveloping rain gear, leaving it just
outside the shelter when you seal yourself in again. You treat
clogged elements as radioactive.

Now we're getting into hygiene. What do we do about
hygiene in a shelter, including disposal of body waste? How
about lights and other niceties? We'll get to those topics in
subsequent articles; for the moment it's enough to know you
can live under pressure.

POSTSCRIPT

Jim Baen pointed out that I could've added an important datum.
"What if I don't have four rolls of toilet paper?" he asked.

"Stay out of Mexico," I said.

"I'll put it another way." He sighed. "What if I'm willing
to spend a few bucks for good commercial filters?"

Good point. Well, HEPA Corp., Flanders, Inc., and Farr
sell high-efficiency fiber cartridges for $20 and up through air
filter vendors. These are the kind of filter elements used by
nuclear labs, industrial clean rooms, and operating rooms. These
luggage-size cartridges must be set into a frame—an enclo-
sure—that you can buy or build, with your conduit leading
from the frame into your shelter.

These commercial filter elements don't resist passage of air
much, so you can pump faster, easier; or you can use a small
fan. Specify a rigid cartridge that removes 99.7 percent or more
of particulates down through the 2-micron range—which means
it'll remove most spores and bacteria, too—and is rated at
hundreds of cubic feet of air per minute. A Farr Riga-Flo 200
cartridge is a good example. If you install a cheap, coarse
furnace filter element in front of such a cartridge, it should
keep you breathin' easy for a month without replacement in
all but the most horrendously lethal fallout area.

Power and Potties to the People

In previous articles, we argued that the average citizen would have fair to excellent survival chances after an all-out nuclear exchange—but only by having certain awarenesses and acting on them. To summarize briefly: the first piece explained that the government now favors mass evacuation from high-risk areas following an alert, since firestorm is a more immediately lethal threat for city dwellers than is fallout. But you will probably be on your own when evacuating and improvising shelter, because no sufficiently powerful lobby group has fought to fund the machinery—software and hardware—of city evacuation. We discussed the logistics in some detail and suggested that you relocate *now* from primary target zones.

The second article showed how to build air filtration and pump devices from household materials in a few hours, so you can breathe relatively uncontaminated air once you find shelter beyond a firestorm-candidate area. Finally we promised some tips in future articles on making your shelter more livable; things like lights, hygiene, and so on.

Okay, it's time to power your shelter. Take heart: even though our premise is that you haven't amassed special equipment, we've tested enough commonplace equipment to prove it's rather easy to generate enough electricity to run lights, radios, even a cassette recorder—from at least one source we'll bet you never thought about.

A moment's thought will remind you that cars, motorcycles, boats, even many bicycles are equipped with subsystems that you could use in a shelter. It's a sorry automobile that doesn't have a complete electrical system with a hefty battery to store electricity; a generator to generate more electricity; many yards of wiring; several electric motors, some connected to fans that

171

you might use for shelter air; and more light bulbs than you'll
need. Of course we don't suggest that you run your car inside
your shelter. We do suggest that you familiarize yourself with
a car that you can park in your garage and then strip of some
life-support items when the time comes. You can always replace the hardware quickly if you need it in the car again.

We won't go into detail on removing car parts because
electrical systems differ a lot. Study your own and ask any
mechanic for details on cannibalizing it. We will mention a
few things that could free you of frustration when you're trying
to set up an emergency power system.

To start with, be advised that a good car battery can strike
sparks if its positive terminal (also called the hot or plus terminal) comes in contact with metal parts of the car. This does
not mean the battery can shock you. Its 12-volt jolt is much
too low. You simply have to remove the cables from the battery
terminals with care.

The average car battery has enough energy stored in it to
operate a small light for a week or more without a generator.
You can find tiny lamps with removable sockets in glove com-
partments, in instrument panels, on roof interiors, and next to
license plates. Many of the interior lights are designed to be
installed and removed instantly, socket and all. In Figure 9 we
have wired a tiny transmission shift selector light, and a slightly
larger light pried out of a glove compartment with its socket,
to the remains of an extension cord. The wires lead to a 12-
volt power source that could be a car battery. Or it could be
something else—about which, more later.

Light bulbs in your brake and taillights, directional and
backup lights, and so on require more power and provide more
light. Finally you could remove a headlight, which sheds tremendous light on the subject but also gobbles up a battery's
stored energy in a few hours.

Generally the brighter the light, the more power it consumes.
You may think you need a high-wattage bulb in your shelter
until you plug off the last window with old books and find out
how dark it gets in a secure shelter. Then you'll see that a 6-
watt glove-compartment light makes the difference between
merely shadowy and downright scary. Remembering that

1 watt = 1 volt × 1 amp, so that
6 watts = 12 volts × 0.5 amps

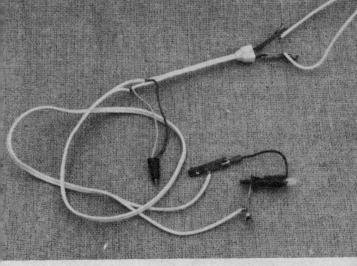

Figure 9

you can see that a half-amp rating for a bulb in a 12-volt system means it draws about 6 watts. When you are considering a 12-volt motor that has a wattage but no amperage on its ID plate, you can solve for the amperage. Select appliances that use little power, so the battery will last longer. If you must do a lot of reading, cuddle up near a small light and put a mirror or other reflection where it will help. If you have a fluorescent drop light intended to plug into a 12-volt system, good. It's stingy with power and doesn't give off much heat. In the days when shoemakers and tailors worked by candlelight, they found a nifty way to concentrate what little light they had. They suspended a water-filled glass globe so that the globe created a lens effect, sending a powerfully concentrated beam of light onto a small working area. Try it with a wineglass; you'll probably get a long, slender patch of light intense enough for threading needles.

If you haven't already noticed: we make a worst-case assumption that you don't have welding equipment, special tools, or arcane talents with you. Probably you won't have rolls of insulated wire or tinkerer's alligator clips for making test connections. But you can use extension cords and, in lieu of alligator clips, hair-curl "clippies." That's what we used to cobble up some power and light devices for this article. You can slice through an extension cord and bare its wires with any kitchen knife. Yes, it'd be better if you could clamp or solder your final connections; but if you tightly twist copper wires together and tape over the connection, it will usually work well. Millions of temporary electrical connections have been made by forcing a sturdy safety pin through insulated wires; this is often done when hooking up trailer lights to the wiring in cars.

We also assume that you can recognize the places where you must connect a wire to a light bulb or its socket. In the simplest use of your system, just bind one naked wire end to a battery terminal and one naked end of your second wire to the other terminal. Then touch the other ends of those wires to the cannibalized lamp and you should have light. Since 12 volts won't shock you, you can even do it by hand.

Don't worry about the battery burning out the tiny lamp if the lamp was taken from a similar 12-volt system; the lamp will draw only the few watts it needs. You could probably have a string of tiny lamps going simultaneously (connected in parallel, not in series) with less use of power than if you used a brake light.

Electric motors usually use electricity faster than several small lamps; be advised. For God's sake don't use a battery to run a heating element, e.g., the little elements that plug into cigarette lighters to keep cups of coffee warm. A heating element really squanders electricity. You'd be better off using a candle for heat.

If you're up to it you might remove the generator from your car and mount it against the rear wheel of a bicycle. Most modern car generators are called alternators because they generate AC, and they're quite efficient. But if you intend to build such stuff, remember that an alternator won't generate any juice at all unless a battery can supply at least a trickle of power to it to energize its field coils. You don't believe me? Disconnect your car battery and get your car going downhill at any speed you like, then try to start your car with the alternator alone. The nice thing about the old DC car generators was that they'd start your car even if your battery had been stolen! Talk to your friendly junkyard man; some old DC car generators are still around.

Now, about that bicycle that took you past the traffic jam. . . . You must somehow jack the rear wheel clear of the floor so you can pedal in place, the rear wheel spinning the generator pulley that's snubbed against it. If you align the pulley against the rubber tire, the friction of tire against pulley will serve as a pulley belt. You may have to dismember a chair or even rip into a wall somewhere for sturdy wood to whittle and bind a frame for mounting your car generator to the bike. Here we're talking about fairly rugged rigs, and at this point many of you may be deciding to forget a generator. Hold it: if you have a bike, you may also have a quicker answer.

The fist-size little DC generators built for bike lights are so cheap, every bike can and should have one. They mount on the bike frame, spring-loaded so they can ride against the tire as it spins, generating enough amperage to run a bike headlamp and tail lamp. If you can, get one that is rated at 12 volts or thereabouts. Because so help me, it can also power an AM/FM radio or cassette player of the sort you can plug into a cigarette lighter. Our kids are the only ones on the block who have had tape decks on bikes! It was just a guess, but we guessed right: the cheap commercial adaptors sold to adapt a car's 12-volt system to 6- or 9-volt hardware can also be wired to the little bike generator.

Figure 10 shows how handily a bike generator can be adapted to power an AM/FM cassette recorder. The only trick is in wiring the generator to an adaptor that was intended to plug into a cigarette lighter, as shown in Figure 11. Our adaptor came with several different plugs, to fit the different kinds of small appliances. For instance, one of the plugs fits a hand calculator. Our adaptor also has a tiny switch that lets you choose 6- or 9-volt output. Our cassette machine uses 6 volts; most hand calculators use 9 volts. Don't try to run both simultaneously.

In Figure 12, the bike's rear end is suspended with pieces of broomstick across the backs of two folding chairs. We bound one broomstick with cord and the other with strapping tape just to show that either will serve. Then we mounted *two* bike generators on the broomsticks so that they engage the bike tire on its tread. If they are mounted on the sidewall as is often done, the toothed generator pulley tends to chew the tire's sidewall up. We could've mounted three or even four of the little generators on that tire. The point is, the generators don't cost much and they don't load the tire down much, either. You can actually recharge a great whopping car battery by trickle-charging it with a bike generator—more quickly using several bike generators wired in parallel.

Figure 10

Figure 11

Figure 12

One brief gimmick: ordinarily a bike generator is grounded against the bike's metal chassis. Of the two terminals protruding from the aft end of the generator in Figure 12, one accepts a wire leading to the weak little tail lamp while the other accepts a wire leading to the headlight. So neither of these terminals is a "ground" terminal. By mounting our generators on non-conducting broomsticks, we made it necessary to supply a ground wire from the generator mount to a ground connection on the adaptor as shown in Figures 10 and 11.

If you buy bike generators for this broad-spectrum use, *don't* get the kind with both lamps built into the generator body. You'll want to run wires here and there in your shelter; to a battery, or to a bike headlight used as a reading lamp, or maybe to that cassette player so you can have Villa-Lobos to keep you company.

A bike generator will light its little bulbs even if you haven't lugged a car battery into your shelter as a storage tank for electrical energy. But without a battery, you'll have to keep pedaling as long as you want light. The pedal effort is slight and does not seem appreciably greater when two generators are mounted against the tire; but even with no generators, the effort will tire you and cause you to use a lot of air during a half-hour of steady pedaling. That's a good reason to have a car battery and to install more than one tiny generator.

We tried some other ideas that didn't work well, so we

didn't illustrate them. One idea was to tape bricks on the bike pedals and turn the bike upside down so you could crank the pedals by hand and use the mass of the bricks to get a flywheel effect. If you could somehow fill a bike tire with lead weights, it might be marginally effective, but the bricks added little inertia because they weren't very heavy and their moment arm was short. Sorry 'bout that.

On the other hand, we're still playing with some other ideas that sprang from the bike generator.

Example 1. Find a way to mount an adult's bike on the end of your roof so that the front wheel minus handlebars can pivot easily. Now cut pieces of venetian-blind slats and, with tape or wire, mount the slats like turbine blades among the front wheel spokes. If the slats have a modest angle of incidence (that is, angled like propeller blades), the wheel should spin in a decent breeze. With a homemade weathervane mounted through the handlebar socket—ours was a mop handle with a cardboard rudder tacked onto it—you can make the device turn itself into the wind, pivoting as it would with handlebars. Voilà: a small windmill. If you use a big 26-inch wheel, it should barely run a bike generator in a good breeze. *Certainly* it's primitive, nowhere near as effective as some other systems; but it's a free power source. Oh: don't forget to mount the generator on the front wheel *fork* so that it pivots with the wheel, as we did in Figure 13. Our experimental rig worked

Figure 13

only when the wind was around 25 mph—but could work in lesser breezes if the generator pulley diameter is somehow enlarged.

Example 2. A wind-driven bike wheel can also let you convert a bike speedometer to a small power drill or other rotary-motion tool.

Example 3. A big-motha' windmill, with 4-meter epoxy-coated high-aspect ratio blades and a capstan drive made from a wheelchair (why didn't Oklahoma State toy with such handy little windmill drives in their development work?) is in development on a ranch near us. But it runs a Chevy alternator, which wouldn't be worth a cent if something happened to the huge truck battery below, because there'd be no initial jolt to energize the alternator field. Well, we're going to put a tiny little bike generator on the site just for emergency engagement to energize the big alternator. We're not saying it will be an optimal answer—only that it may be one very quick answer. We don't even have to mount the bike generator up high; it could be kept on the ground, out of the weather.

So much for those ongoing experiments. Now it's time to inject what we can call an in-text footnote because it isn't really a digression: candles and other combustion devices. Combustion uses up your oxygen; sometimes it stinks, too. Unless you have plenty of air, don't use up much of it with candles or kerosene lamps. If you use a kerosene lamp, trim the wick and keep it adjusted for minimum combustion without smoke. For years we've used a tiny kerosene lamp, a Japanese scale model of the big ones, to read while backpacking. It uses an ounce of fluid every three hours; neither it nor its fuel takes up much room in a pack; and it's a cheery companion when you're on a sierra solo, with a wire gizmo made to let a coffee cup stay warm atop the little lamp. A quart of fluid can keep such a lamp burning for ninety hours, but unless you have air to spare, think twice about it.

Oh, yes; we played with the stubby little candles of the votive or "fondue warmer" type. When they are free-standing, they become a broad puddle of wax all too quickly. Placed in a container that keeps molten wax from running away, one of the little candles can burn for nine hours or more. Just remember, it's using a lot of oxygen and adding to the heat and carbon dioxide in a semiclosed life-support system. Make sure your air supply is adequate.

We also made experiments with flashlights using two D-size cells. Standard heavy-duty cells powered a bulb for eighteen hours, while alkaline cells powered it for thirty hours. We burned out several bulbs before we learned to accept the fact that the duty cycle of most flashlight bulbs is brief. That is, you mustn't expect a common flashlight bulb to burn more than an hour or so in one session. Use it for a while; let it cool awhile; then turn it on again when you must. Flashlight batteries will recover a bit after they've rested for a few hours. But if you depend on flashlight bulbs and batteries, keep spares for both.

A few people will be ahead of us with gasoline-powered electrical systems or windmills. Just remember that even the smallest gasoline engines use a lot of fuel and oxygen, put out a lot of noxious exhaust, and make a lot of noise. You'll almost certainly want to keep such bellowing little brutes outside your living quarters. A windmill is much quieter and uses no precious fuel.

Summarizing your power-and-light options, and presuming you don't have solar cells or a hydroelectric plant handy, a windmill seems a very good bet if you can make one. But for every shelter boasting such a power source, there'll probably be hundreds making do with a bike-powered generator and perhaps a car battery. If you manage to haul two fully charged car batteries into a shelter, you might have enough stored power to dispel the dark for the better part of two weeks without a generator of any kind. And many pundits are guessing that if you can stay put that long, radiation from fallout will have greatly diminished.

In two weeks of continuous occupation, a shelter can get pretty ripe, considering body wastes and other odors. You must find or make a portable potty.

A sturdy bucket or even a cardboard box, with plastic garbage bag for a liner, makes an acceptable john. It is important that you sprinkle household bleach or hydrated lime into the bag after defecating into it. Not only the smell but the danger of disease will be lessened by disinfectants. If possible, train all shelter occupants to do their doo-dahs at roughly the same time. If you have no plastic bags you may have to use brown paper bags or newspaper as a liner. In that case you'll quickly

Figure 14

learn to urinate into an old milk carton or other waterproof container to minimize the mess when emptying the john.

For empty it, you must, and as soon as practicable after use, if you expect to live in an enclosed area for several days. If you have reason to suspect that even a moment outside shelter might be lethal, you'll have to store body wastes in a covered garbage can or the equivalent until the first possible chance to get rid of the waste. It should be dumped in a hole far from the shelter, then covered with dirt.

Figure 14 shows an emergency john made from a wastepaper basket, several layers of cardboard taped together with a hole cut through them, and a plastic bag taped into the hole. Okay, so it ain't the Waldorf; it only took ten minutes to build and it's fast, fast, fast relief. Once the john has been used by all who will, some hardy soul must sprinkle a few ounces of lime into the bag, extract the bag, tape it shut, and dispose of it.

Hygiene is more than simply a system for disposing of fecal material. It involves staying as clean as you can; using dilute bleach solution to clean messes with minimum waste of precious water; donning rain gear for any essential forays outside the shelter; shaking dust particles off yourself before you get to the shelter opening; carefully shucking the rain gear before you enter the shelter itself; and more. Don't forget that your hair is a dandy dust trap; wear a shower cap or other cover to keep from trapping fallout particles in your hair when you're outside. And as we've cautioned before, make a dust mask from flannel or use something even better to avoid breathing unfiltered outside air. All this is hygiene. It keeps you relatively free of contaminants you cannot afford.

Mental hygiene fits in here somewhere. Sensory-deprivation studies suggest that we might get through the shelter ordeal much better if we do have light, some meaningful activity, and games of some sort to occupy us while the clock ticks away. If we don't have playing cards we can make them. The same is true of checkers, chess, dice, and many other games. Anyhow, the sooner we get used to manufacturing what we can't buy, the sooner we'll be back in charge of a high-tech existence.

Each shelter occupant might keep a journal, jotting down any ideas that might be fruitful for the future—including a log the radio provides on daily local and not-so-local survival conditions. In between reading favorite books, you could do worse than read some basic texts on gardening, electricity, food preservation, first aid, and appliance repair, to name only a few. Whatever you need to know that you don't know already: start learning it while you have enforced leisure.

If you've digested the information in the three articles so far, you have a good chance of emerging from a shelter two weeks after a major fallout event without serious illness. A healthy adult *can*, if necessary, live for nearly a week without water, over three weeks without food. If you've provided yourself with food and water, you might survive with no ill effects—except that you might have a mild case of claustrophobia. If personal experience is any guide, we expect that you'll also have a brand-new outlook on life. How sweet it is to be alive when you look back on the nearness of death!

Even if you're breathing through a homemade flannel mask, you're still breathing; planning; making ready for whatever comes next. We hope you've given some previous thought to the day when you emerge from shelter, because, as Freeman Dyson has opined, a lot of people will probably outlast an all-out nuclear war. In the next article we'll suggest some things you should know—for example, that castor oil is easily extracted from beans and is a good engine oil. And we'll mention some things you should have all packed away for the postshelter era.

Not in a hope chest. In a tenacity chest.

Stocking Your Tenacity Chest

In previous articles, we argued that many Americans could survive an all-out nuclear exchange if we knew what to do, and if we did it. We started this series of articles by describing a firestorm, a more lethal and immediate threat than fallout for city dwellers. You can be asphyxiated and roasted in a blast-proof shelter—as three hundred thousand casualties proved in Dresden.

The US government has agreed about firestorm; has suggested that you relocate from target areas if war seems imminent. We suggested that you relocate *now*—or at least prepare for evacuation with a bike rack on your car for your "second stage" vehicle.

Our second article showed you how to build air-filtration and pump devices from household materials, so you can breathe clean air in a shelter beyond the firestorm area. Oak Ridge National Lab (PO Box X, Oak Ridge, TN 37830) has put a little tax money to excellent use in developing and testing other home-built rigs, including jury-rigged shelters and a high-volume air pump. Their pump will not pull air through a fine filter, but without filter restrictions it pumps much more air than ours.

Our third article illustrated ways to rig toilets and lighting systems in a shelter. Briefly summarized: you build a small potty using thin plastic bags to catch solid waste, and sprinkle hydrated lime or Clorox into the bag before sealing it. Small lights, cannibalized from a car, can be run by auto batteries or even by tiny 12-volt bike generators that will also power tape recorders and calculators. Wiring is safe and simple.

Finally we promised to add some tidbits on postfallout survival; call it cottage industry if you will. If you've read our previous articles, our texts and photographs will testify that we've spent a lot of time developing gadgets and trying advice collected from others. Amerinds, settlers, guerrillas, anthropologists—survivalists all—have taught us how to make fuels, treat illness, and scrounge food; well-informed Americans need not face a hand-to-mouth existence when first emerging from fallout shelters. So we promised, in our last article, to suggest some things to store in your "tenacity chest" for the postfallout world. Much of that storage will be in the form of information.

We decided to break our information package down into five groups: shelter, food, health, energy, and utensils. There's a great deal of overlap here; you'll need to build utensils to make your own fuels and lubricants, for example.

Your most intimate shelter is clothing. It was Sylvan Hart, a modern mountain man with an engineering background, who said he was afraid of only one thing: a cold wind. He was talking about hypothermia, the situation in which your body heat is drawn away faster than your body can replace it. When you read that someone died of "exposure," chances are he died of hypothermia.

You can insulate yourself from cold by wearing several layers of clothing, but not if those clothes are wet. The air trapped between clothing layers provides good insulation. Water conducts heat and replaces the air, so your body heat is conducted from your skin through the damp clothes to the cold wind. Conclusion: stay dry in cold weather.

If you can't stay dry, try wearing leather. We found that thick elkhide trousers, though they were soaking wet in mountain snow, provided much more insulation than heavy jeans. But they dry more slowly, and we swear they weigh fifteen pounds wet!

You can dry your damp socks by putting them inside your shirt just above your belt. It takes awhile, but it's worth it for warm, dry feet. Clothes should be vented so body moisture can escape. Rubberized or other entirely moisture-proof fabrics tend to trap moisture inside to make you clammy. Outfitters can steer you to a nylon cloth so densely woven that it will shed rain while allowing water vapor to escape. For that matter, a weekend with a veteran backpacker can lead you to the items you need from an outfitter's shelves. Weatherproofing shoes (mink oil), keeping unlined leather gloves on during chores, and rigging a pack are three things that immediately come to mind.

Need oilcloth? The original stuff was, literally, cloth drenched with linseed oil and sun-dried. The sunlight polymerized the linseed oil to a flexible solid. You can start with plain cloth; just remember not to store it folded. The stuff tends to glue itself together into a useless lump.

We considered clothing as shelter because it's likely that you'll be more mobile—personally mobile, on foot—than you are today. But what if you're afoot and soaking and cold?

If you are more than an hour from known shelter, stop and get warm. It's nice to have a little hemispherical nylon-and-stiffener tent on your pack, preferably one of drab color. Next best might be a rectangle of ten-mil plastic for a tent, big enough so that you can lie on it as well as under it. A down mummybag can be as small as a ten-pound bag of flour. People have also found refuge from that cold wet wind in hollow trees, abandoned cars, haystacks, bridge foundations—even warm compost heaps.

For more permanent shelter, architects are beginning to rediscover the virtues of dirt, citing the "soddy" dugouts that insulated settlers from ferocious Great Plains weather. Oddly they don't often cite Frank Lloyd Wright's berm house of the 1930s, but they should. A berm is an earth ramp. If you build a wooden or stone house, you'll find yourself better protected and insulated with berms shoveled along the outside walls up to the windows or eaves. Since a berm will hold rain and ground water, you should place a water barrier (thin plastic sheet will do, but be careful not to tear it as you shovel dirt against it) between the wall and the dirt berm. A gravel-filled, stone-covered trench at the foot of the wall and under the berm will let ground water percolate away, if your trench leads away downhill. If you build in a depression you're asking for flooding. We know, we know: there's lots more to it, but we're only touching the high spots.

A semipermanent shelter requires amenities like vermin-proof storage, a firepit with smoke hole, and a bough bed or lath-lashed sleeping platform. Study old *National Geographics* to see how the Ashanti or Blackfoot or Polynesians coped with special enviroments similar to yours.

We haven't the space here to dwell on ways to fortify shelters; your best protection is probably camouflage—including a grassy berm—and inconspicuous multiple exits also make sense.

Our second category is food, and we'll start with meat. Recently canned food should be okay, of course. Why waste space on the dressing out of large animals? You probably won't see many. Among common domestic animals, swine and chickens seem to have superior powers to survive high radiation doses. Fish might be plentiful, and the radioactive particles they absorb seem to be concentrated in the organs we normally discard, so fish may be a staple. But remember not to eat shellfish unless you eat only the muscle tissue.

Extrapolating from the known hazards of irradiated fish organs, we suspect you should discard *all* animal organs. And we know the edible meats aren't all represented at Safeway. Frogs and snakes, for example, can be delicacies. Skin the snake and remove the head and organs, cut the flesh into manageable segments, then fry or roast the segments like chicken. Frog legs are skinned, then fried or roasted, the same way.

Insects? Many people have survived on such a diet—but not on insects recently subjected to high radiation. Some edible creepies such as grubs, termites, and night crawlers might be relatively safe because they don't live in the open—but all have organs that might concentrate irradiated particles, and the energy you spend collecting them might surpass the energy you get from digesting them. Several months after the last fallout, it might be safe to dine on those crawly critters. They have been praised as soup stock, but not by us!

Vegetables will probably comprise 95 percent of your diet. We'll admit that corn, wheat, legumes, and other staples will be important and go on to lesser-known foods. The lowly acorn is plentiful, easily shelled, and (aren't we all?) bitter as hell when raw. You must leach out the tannin (a substance also boiled from oak bark for tanning hides) by boiling, say, a pint of shelled acorns in a quart of water, changing the water every five minutes, for about forty minutes. Then let the acorns sundry. They can be munched as is or ground into flour for flatcakes or soup stock. When salted, they're so tasty we wonder why they aren't marketed.

We all know about fruit and nuts, but had you thought of crushing nutmeats and pressing them to get oil for cooking or lamps? If you can't rig a powerful hand press, boil and stir the crushed nutmeats and skim off the oil that floats to the top. Save the nut soup, dry it, and use the dried nutmeats for flour or nutcake.

Fruit "leather" is easy. Boil the fruit whole, drain it, saving the drained liquid to drink, and press the boiled fruit pulp through a sieve—perhaps a metal can with lots of nail holes. The thickish paste can be sweetened with honey or with the boiled-down juice of fruits. Pour the paste onto a flat surface and dry it, protecting it from insects. When it's leathery, roll it into small tubes and store it as candy.

Cattails have a pulpy inner stem you can mash and eat raw or, better still, boil it first. Where the stem joins the root, you'll find a lump that you can peel and eat like a potato.

Learn to identify the salsify weed, or "oyster root," which has a purple or yellow blossom and later a puffball like a huge dandelion. In Europe its root is a delicacy. Pull a double handful of salsify roots, clean and boil them awhile. Big roots can be too fibrous for our taste, but we've seen guests take third helpings of the smaller roots with their faint delicious oysterish taste. The dandelion makes marvelous salad greens, or the leaves can be boiled like spinach. The cleaned, dried, ground-up root makes a tea-color, coffeeish-flavored brew, and the vitamin A in dandelions puts a carrot to shame.

Vitamin C is found in tomatoes and citrus, of course; but also in rose hips, the moderately bitter seed pods of the common rose. We are pampering a tiny "decorative" orange tree two feet high because it winters indoors in Oregon and yields sour fruit the size of Ping-Pong balls. The little zingers are loaded with vitamin C and are fresh in January.

Incidentally, the leaves of mint, blackberry, and strawberry can also be brewed as tea. You might grow spices (sage, thyme, mint, oregano) as a barter crop. A pound of dry oregano might be worth a block of sea salt.

Wine making is an art lauded in many books. Remember that you can make it from berries and fruit, too. It won't be sweet unless you add sugar. Brandy is made by distilling wine to obtain the ethyl alcohol and some of the original wine. If you have the right apparatus, including a sensitive chemical thermometer, you can wind up with almost pure ethyl. If your apparatus includes metals like lead, you can wind up poisoned.

If you aren't a gardener, find a plot of bathtub size or larger and start now. A compost pile is a small art, and the pile can be quite small. The finer the particles of food scraps and decaying grass you start with, the sooner it becomes good plant food; and if it starts to mildew, it's too damp. Some plants like marigolds and mint seem to repel bugs, and you should learn which veggies you can grow best in your locale. Why only in your locale? Because you're not likely to travel very far from it. Long-distance travel may become hazardous for most of us.

We could go on for volumes, rehashing Euell Gibbons and Brad Angier on the subject of common edible plants—but what for, when others have done it so well? Choose a text or two; stalk the wild whatsit for fun—and for longevity.

For health problems: again, you should have advice and texts by experts. We can help a little by parroting them. Aspirin can reduce fever and aching of many kinds from flu to rheumatism. Ethyl and isopropyl (rubbing) alcohols are among the best general disinfectants, without the side effects of iodine and Merthiolate. Disinfectant should be daubed *around* an open wound, not directly into it. Unflavored vodka is about half ethyl alcohol and might serve as an emergency disinfectant. We suspect that germs aren't just wild about acetone, either— and soap and water are among the best cleansers of wounds, especially if you must scrub debris from them.

Bleeding helps cleanse a puncture wound. A clean bandage, *not* airtight, should cover a break in the skin after disinfecting the surrounding skin.

Burns can be relieved first by cold compresses, followed by a gauze bandage smeared with clean petroleum jelly. The jelly helps prevent secondary infection while your body repairs the burn. We've read about mountain men covering a burn with tallow or bear grease—but if you're trying such a remedy with animal products, you'd better cook the stuff first to kill the bacteria it may harbor.

In the special case of a profusely bleeding surface wound, try to pull edges of the wound together and tape them that way. Don't use a tourniquet unless it's absolutely necessary; gangrene from tourniquets has caused as many deaths as has blood loss. You can lose a pint of blood without serious loss of mobility. To prevent shock after a burn or other injury, have the victim sip a quart of water containing a level teaspoon of salt and a half-teaspoon of bicarbonate of soda. No booze!

You can often relieve a cough by sucking hard candy, by inhaling over a bowl of steaming water, or by sipping hot drinks. Constipation can be countered by adding fruit, especially prunes, figs, or raisins, to your diet. If the fruit is dry, soak it in water awhile.

For many skin problems—poison oak, rash, fungus infections—calamine lotion will help. Athlete's foot is a fungus infection, by the way. The fungus thrives on soft, soggy skin, which explains why you must keep your feet and footgear dry—and brings us to an area of special concern: your feet.

When you can no longer buy fuel for your moped and the barter market or paramedic is two klicks away, you will begin to give your feet the respect they always deserved. If you don't think corns or athlete's foot can have you walkin' on your knees, you've led a charmed life. A corn, often from improperly tight shoes, can cause excruciating pain. Commerical preparations can dissolve them, but you may be reduced to shaving one away with a razor blade. Don't imagine that you can get away with wearing a corn pad indefinitely, unless your shoe was designed for that pad—and it wasn't, was it? So treat the symptom (the corn) and correct its source (usually tight or rundown footgear).

Athlete's foot isn't as painful at first, but it can fill your boot with blood and yuchh and may lead to serious systemic infection, and the itch can drive you right across the ceiling. Oh, yes; and if you scratch it with fingernails, you can spread the fungus to other parts of your infection-weakened bod. *Now* will you take athlete's foot seriously? Cotton or wool socks help absorb moisture from your foot, while synthetics don't. You could also put tiny lamb's wool pads between your toes if your feet sweat a lot. Always dry between your toes after a wetting before your socks go on; and a dusting of talc between toes and into shoes will help.

Choose ankle-protecting footgear for ruggedness and reasonably loose fit, and wear two pairs of socks if you need to. Keep shoes pliable and water resistant. If you try to dry them next to a fire, you're risking serious deterioration of the leather. Don't choose the sexy overlap-closure boots that hint of the downhill racer unless you live in snow. Those closures keep snow out, but water doesn't give a damn for any but the most perfect overlap; step into a creek up to the closure and it may mean instant sog in your boot. Instead, choose the accordion-fold closure and inspect the lace D rings to be sure they weren't anchored through the leather in such a way as to leave a path for water to trickle through to your sock. Your walking boots should let you step into water nearly up to the lace tie without letting water in.

If you have a persistent skin sore, whether on your foot or from a hangnail, you might try a last-ditch remedy we've tested: man's best friend. We'd read of people with jungle rot letting a healthy dog treat the wound by licking it but never tried it until 1978. An infected hangnail then defied our two-week treatment with antiseptic. Then our neighbor's canine medic Bozo took a sniff of the offending digit and did everything but write us a prescription. Whatthehell, we thought, and let him treat it twice a day. We can't swear that Bozo licked the swollen hangnail well in a week, but we *can* swear that we used no other medication during "saliva therapy," and it got well in a week. We were only trying what American guerrillas on Leyte tried and got the same excellent results. Hardly a controlled experiment; but it's an idea you might keep on file.

Energy technology, especially alternative sources of heat and fuel, is a fad right now. Pay attention to the simple alternatives. We've seen a cardboard box with sloping clear glass front and foil-lined insulated inner walls cook pastries by sunlight. It could just as easily dry fruit leather or cure meat strips into jerky, even in a light overcast.

Many stored fuels, including gasoline and diesel fuel, are perishable within a year. If you use old stored fuels you risk fouling the engine or carburetor with gums and shellacs. There are special stabilizer chemicals you can add to stored fuel, but you might just use alcohol. Rubbing alcohol is about half water and won't work. Methyl (wood) and ethyl (booze) alcohols are a bit tough to store because they readily evaporate, but they won't foul an engine. For a diesel, alcohol won't work well. For a gasoline engine, it works well *after you modify the carburetor*.

The optimum gasoline-to-air ratio is different from the optimum alcohol-to-air ratio, and there are two ways easily to modify that ratio in the carburetor. You can ream the carburetor's main jet with a drill bit so that its cross-sectional *area* is about half again—i.e., 150 percent the size of the original hole through the jet. That way the tiny hole can supply half again as much liquid fuel to provide roughly the same power as always—though your mileage will be poorer with alcohol. Or you can adjust the choke, a much easier process, by mechanically wiring or jamming the carburetor's "butterfly" air intake valve partly closed. This restricts the carburetor's air intake instead of increasing its alcohol intake—and of course your maximum power will be reduced somewhat. If you don't understand this paragraph, ask any mechanic to show you what we mean.

But where do you get alcohol? You can distill corn mash or wine for ethyl alcohol. You can (because we've done it) distill wood chips or kindling to get methyl alcohol, which is poison if taken internally. Remember that the charcoal left in the container after methyl alcohol distillation is a perfectly good fuel for stoking the next "charge" of the still. Don't use charcoal in a closed room; its carbon monoxide effluent can kill you.

When you begin to produce alcohol, you'll shoot your thirsty Thunderbird in favor of a Honda or moped. Even a five-gallon yield is more than a tabletop operation; you'll need a big metal drum or its equivalent to contain the wood to be heated. An airtight lid on the drum is essential. The condenser of a still may be a coil of tubing or may be simply a long, water-cooled pipe, which is much easier to clean out. Water, acids, wood tars, and turpentine are all recoverable from heated wood, along with the alcohol and acetone that will collect in the condenser. Consider a second distillation to separate the alcohol from the acetone by careful control of temperature. Acetone can fuel an engine with alcohol, but is also a particularly good solvent. You can make quick-drying wood cement by dissolving shavings of many plastics in acetone. When the wood cement is thinned with more acetone, it makes lacquer.

On a more modest level, study fire-kindling techniques. Lint and stored dandelion fluff will kindle from a modest flame, be it flint and steel or some other device. Wooden matches can be waterproofed by a dip in barely molten wax, especially beeswax.

A windmill or watermill can power generators taken from old cars, which in turn can power lots of things, including pumps, blowers, radios, and lights. Yes, clever folks can extract energy from warm springs and chicken flickin's, but your most available energy sources will probably be sunlight, wind, and wood.

Sad to say, you may have your pick of utensils in a post-fallout world. Sad, because you will be picking from the belongings of people who didn't pull through as you did. Stainless-steel utensils will last longer than other metals, which is why they're favored by restaurant kitchens.

You may have to make your own utensils to process soap, for instance. Start with a gallon container with nail holes in the bottom, packed nearly full of white wood ash—*not* black charred ash. Trickle a gallon of water through the ash, catching it in another container, which may take a few days. Sprinkle the sodden ash around the rim of your garden plot to discourage snails and focus on the collected lye water. Filter the lye water if necessary, then boil it or let it evaporate down to a half-pint or so. It's concentrated lye when an egg or a scrap of potato floats in it (specific gravity over 1.2). Meanwhile you've rendered tallow from fat and filtered it clean. A half-pint of lye and a pound of grease make a pound and a half of soap. When the tallow is melted, nearly too hot to touch, and lye is body temperature (feel the container), slowly pour the lye into the tallow, stirring for a half-hour. Then pour it into a shallow pan and let it cure for a week. Sometimes it won't come out perfectly; unmixed tallow will set on top and lye will be on the bottom. But much or all of it will be firm soap. Don't use aluminum containers; the lye will eat them up.

How about glass containers for chemical work of this sort? Learn to cut and smartly rap gallon jugs with a glass cutter so that the top makes a funnel and the bottom a wide-mouth vat. Grind sharp edges with a stone for safety. There's also a grease-soaked, flaming-twine-and-water shock method, too. You'll break several jugs learning these tricks. Hacksaw blades are available today with carbide chips for sawing through glass.

How can you make twine? Soak long pulpy leaves of flax or yucca plants for a week in water, then strip and save the long leaf fibers from the leaf pulp. Fibers can be twisted or braided into twine, thence into rope. The Anasazi braided sandals that way.

Pottery? Find clay that can be squeezed and twisted without crumbling, make it into soup ("slip"), screen it to remove crud, then evaporate it to a plastic solid. Slap a piece repeatedly on a hard surface to remove air bubbles (it's called wedging) before you hand-form it. Let hand-formed pieces sun-dry, then stack them loosely within a specially built chimney. Build a fire gradually to roar right through that chimney for an hour or so. Or stack the pieces on a heavy metal grid over an intense and long-lasting fire. You potters will sigh at the things we've left out; you others might watch a potter sometime. We've seen water pumps, tobacco pipes, and toilets built of clay, then fired and glazed for watertightness. You could build distillation heat exchangers that way, making several parallel tubes instead of a coil, the way metal steam boilers are built.

For strong wood glue, boil and stir shavings of horn or hoof in water until you have a sticky gum. Use it while hot and wet, and give it a day to sun-dry. To save the rest, twirl it on a stick and let it dry, then immerse and boil your glue lollipop the next time you need it, as the Comanches did.

Weaving is too complex an art to detail here; study primitive methods like the simple bow loom as well as modern craft methods. Strips of rabbit fur can be interspersed with fibers to weave a marvelously warm blanket. You can also knot or tie fiber into fishnet, bird trap, or a blanket grid for those fur strips.

If you have the electricity, the expertise, and the need, you can build a mile-long telegraph line as our guerrillas did. They unwound barbed wire and ran the separated strands from tree to tree, using pop bottles for insulators.

If you can't get lubricating oil for an engine, you might try fractionally distilling old oil to reclaim it. Or perhaps you can locate a few castor bushes. Castor beans, though they are poisonous, are easily crushed for castor oil. Process them as you would for nut oil, with one exception: don't breathe the vapor while you are boiling the mush. We found the vapor an all-too-efficient laxative. Don't worry that good castor oil will damage an engine; many a racing engine has thrived on it. It leaves a varnish on parts eventually, but it's an excellent lubricant.

For hunting small game, consider the sling and slingshot. Both are easy to make, they're quiet, and ammunition is plentiful. A longbow will drop a deer but takes a good arm and carefully crafted equipment. If you are pondering which gun to buy, avoid the calibers for which ammunition may be rare. The most commonly available rounds in the United States are the .22, .30-.30, .45 ACP, 12-gauge—and at almost every drugstore, the BB. The .22 won't reliably and immediately drop game over thirty pounds and needs at least an 8-inch barrel for reasonable accuracy. For birds and rabbits, there are some excellent air pistols with rifled barrels that shoot either lead pellets or BBs interchangeably. An air rifle is more accurate but also pretty big to lug around. A pump pistol is relatively quiet, with muzzle velocity up to 500 feet per second, and will sting the bejeezus out of a mean mutt. Perhaps the best thing about a good air pistol is that you can quietly practice using it for pennies inside your house, using plywood or a dozen thicknesses of corrugated cardboard as backstop.

Jerzy Kosinski once described a simple fire carrier made from a big juice can, for travelers without matches who need warmth while traveling. Punch ten spaced holes around the side of the can next to its bottom, and cut its top completely out. Add a long wire handle, borrow some fire, and keep a small bed of coals glowing as you hike along. For a fast fire, drop in a few hunks of wood and kindling and swing the can around in a circle; the forced draft does the rest. Kosinski claimed it was called a comet because of the trail of sparks it makes as it whirls around your head, and we found that the metal can is glowing in less than a minute. If it doesn't discourage an unarmed intruder, he must be desperate. As a small space heater and stove, the "comet" is a lifesaver. Our kids learned to make them at age six. Since then we've developed sophisticated versions, testing new wrinkles by stoking a comet in a handy fireplace. It's a low-profile hobby, and it could save the hobbyist's life.

Perhaps you've noticed: we've begun to segue from the software of your tenacity chest to its hardware. Check on the shelf life of seeds and medicines you keep (even aspirin eventually decays, with a vinegary odor), and next time you spot a sale on needles or injector blades, get a handful. A dime may have more purchasing power than a paper bill, so keep a roll of coins. Get a quarter-mile spool of strong monofilament nylon fishing line for lashings, sewing, traps, and so on.

Pick up a hand-cranked meat grinder at a garage sale. We cut the clamp from one and made a small T-handle so the whole thing, spare grinder heads and all, fits into a bike's handlebar pouch as a mass the size of a grapefruit. It'll grind tough meat or hard corn, and when you have dental trouble, it can make life bearable. It's also useful for processing nut and vegetable oils. Why did primitive plant gatherers seldom live past forty? For one thing, grit from their stone grinders wore their teeth down to the gum line by that age, part of a chain reaction of events that impaired digestion and health. Get the bloody hand grinder! It's more crucial than you think.

There's one item we won't suggest that you buy, because you wouldn't; radiation monitors are expensive. But you can make one for next to nothing! Oak Ridge document ORNL-5040 is a little book that gives astonishingly complete instructions on building a calibrated foil electroscope that measures ionizing radiation—i.e., a fallout meter. Its calibration lets you know how much fallout is in your area so you can judge your tactics better, and the little meter is built entirely of common household materials. We've rarely seen any sophisticated device as well engineered to be built by rank beginners—and have never seen one as potentially crucial to human survival. Copies of the manual have been sent to libraries in Stanford Research Institute, National Technical Information Services, Illinois Institute of Technology, and defense documentation centers. Your congressbody can probably locate one that could be reproduced for you. Newspaper editors please copy; the document is in the public domain.

We've covered only some bare necessities to be packed into your tenacity chest, but we must stop somewhere. The one thing you must keep stored, above all, is your own tenacity. If you weren't interested in the history of technology before, you'd be wise to get interested now. Herbert Hoover and wife translated Agricola's mining/smelting treatise, *De Re Metallica*, into English. The conquistadores processed nitrates from horse manure to make gunpowder and might have used bat guano from caves as well. Platinum jewelry can make catalyst grids for making industrial chemicals, including acids. What do you care about thumb-pumped hairspray? Well, the spring-loaded ball check valve is visible inside and can teach you how larger pumps can be built.

Presuming a postfallout world, you'll find yourself becoming a generalist, much more self-sufficient—but you'll be smart to specialize as well, so you can trade special skills and products. Concrete begins with mortar from crushed, kiln-baked seashells. Repeated flooding and evaporation of sea water yields acres of edible salt. Sugar can be extracted from beets or cane.

Smokeless powder begins with cotton steeped in a mixture of nitric and sulfuric acids for guncotton, which is then washed, dried, dissolved in solvent such as acetone, and extruded to dry as flakes or tiny pellets. It has its dangerous moments, just as producing nitric acid from sulfuric acid and nitrates does. You'd best leave the production of primer explosives to chemists—though guncotton, in its dry, fluffy form before solvent processing, can be detonated by a blasting cap or shotgun-shell primer and might have brief popularity as a commercial explosive.

Commercial? Positively, yes. Even if governments fail and most citizens die, survivors will clear away the debris and eventually build a new commerce, a new government, a new society. If you've stored enough tenacity with your information and hardware, you may find that life can still be long and sweet and useful. And if you would be fondly remembered, you could hardly do more than demonstrate the pleasures of a life that's long, sweet, and useful.

A HOMEMADE FALLOUT METER, THE KFM: HOW TO MAKE AND USE IT

FOLLOWING THESE INSTRUCTIONS MAY SAVE YOUR LIFE

I. The Need for Accurate and Dependable Fallout Meters

If a nuclear war ever strikes the United States, survivors of the blast and fire effects would need to have reliable means of knowing when the radiation in the environment around their shelters had dropped enough to let them venture safely outside. Civil defense teams could use broadcasts of surviving radio stations to give listeners a general idea of the fallout radiation in some broadcast areas. However, the fallout radiation would vary widely from point to point and the measurements would be made too far from most shelters to make them accurate enough to use safely. Therefore, each shelter should have some dependable method of measuring the changing radiation dangers in its own area.

During a possible nuclear crisis that was rapidly worsening, or after a nuclear attack, most unprepared Americans could not buy or otherwise obtain a fallout meter—an instrument that would greatly improve their chances of surviving a nuclear war. The fact that the dangers from fallout radiation—best expressed in terms of the radiation dose rate, roentgens per hour (R/hr)—quite rapidly decrease during the first few days, and then decrease more and more slowly, makes it very important to have a fallout meter capable of accurately measuring the unseen, unfelt and changing fallout dangers. Occupants of a fallout shelter should be able to control the radiation doses they receive. In order to effectively control the radiation doses, a dependable measuring instrument is needed to determine the doses they receive while they are in the shelter and while they are outside for emergency tasks, such as going out to get badly needed water. Also, such an instrument would permit them to determine when it is safe to leave the shelter for good.

Untrained families, guided only by these written instructions and using only low cost materials and tools found in most homes, have been able to make a KFM by working 3 or 4 hours. By studying the operating sections of these instructions for about 1½ hours, average untrained families have been able to successfully use this fallout meter to measure dose rates and to calculate radiation doses received, permissible times of exposure, etc.

The KFM (Kearny Fallout Meter) was developed at Oak Ridge National Laboratory. It is understandable, easily repairable, and as accurate as most civil defense fallout meters. In the United Sates in 1976 a commercially available ion chamber fallout meter that has as high a range as a KFM for gamma radiation dose-rate measurements retailed for $600.

Before a nuclear attack occurs is the best time to build, test and learn how to use a KFM. However, this instrument is so simple that it could be made even after fallout arrives **provided** that all the materials and tools needed (see lists given in Sections V, VI, and VII) and a copy of these instructions have been carried into the shelter.

II. Survival Work Priorities During a Crisis

Before building a KFM, persons expecting a nuclear attack within a few hours or days and already in the place where they intend to await attack should work with the following priorities: (1) build or improve a high-protection-factor shelter (if possible, a shelter covered with 2 or 3 feet of earth and separate from flammable buildings); (2) make and install a KAP (a homemade shelter-ventilating pump)—if instructions and materials are available; (3) store at least 15 gallons of water for each shelter occupant—if containers are available; (4) assemble all materials for one or two KFM's; and (5) make and store the drying agent (by heating wallboard gypsum, as later described) for both the KFM and its dry-bucket.

III. How to Use These Instructions to Best Advantage

1. Read ALOUD all of these instructions **through Section VII,** "Tools Needed," before doing anything else.

2. Next assemble all of the needed materials and tools.
3. Then read ALOUD ALL of each section following Section VII before beginning to make the part described in that section.

> A FAMILY THAT FAILS TO READ ALOUD ALL OF EACH
> SECTION DESCRIBING HOW TO MAKE A PART, BE-
> FORE BEGINNING TO MAKE THAT PART, WILL MAKE
> AVOIDABLE MISTAKES AND WILL WASTE TIME.

4. Have different workers, or pairs of workers, make the parts they are best qualified to make. For example, a less skilled worker should start making the drying agent (as described in Section VIII) before other workers start making other parts. The most skilled worker should make and install the aluminum-foil leaves (Sections X and XI).
5. Give workers the sections of the instructions covering the parts they are to build—so they can follow the step-by-step instructions, checking off with a pencil each step as it is completed.
6. Discuss the problems that arise. The head of the family often can give better answers if he first discusses the different possible interpretations of some instructions with other family members, including teenagers.
7. After completing one KFM and learning to use it, if time permits make a second KFM—that should be a better instrument.

IV. What a KFM Is and How It Works

A KFM is a simple electroscope fallout meter with which fallout radiation can be measured accurately. To use a KFM, an electrostatic charge must first be placed on its **two** separate aluminum-foil leaves. These leaves are insulated by being suspended separately on clean, dry insulating threads.

To take accurate readings, the air inside a KFM must be kept very dry by means of drying agents such as dehydrated gypsum (easily made by heating gypsum wallboard, "sheet-rock") or silica gel. (Do not use calcium chloride or other salt.) Pieces of drying agent are placed on the bottom of the ionization chamber (the housing can) of a KFM.

An electrostatic charge is transferred from a homemade electrostatic charging device to the two aluminum-foil leaves of a KFM by means of its charging-wire. The charging-wire extends out through the transparent plastic cover of the KFM.

When the two KFM leaves are charged electrostatically, their like charges (both positive or both negative) cause them to be forced apart. When fallout gamma radiation (that is similar to X rays but more energetic) strikes the air inside the ionization chamber of a KFM, it produces charged ions in this enclosed air. These charged ions cause part or all of the electrostatic charge on the aluminum-foil leaves to be discharged. As a result of losing charge, the two KFM leaves move closer together.

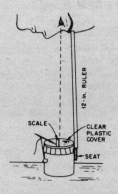

To read the separation of the **lower** edges of the two KFM leaves with one eye, look straight down on the leaves and the scale on the clear plastic cover. Keep the reading eye 12 inches above the SEAT. The KFM should be resting on a horizontal surface. To be sure the reading eye is always at this exact distance, place the lower end of a 12-inch ruler on the SEAT, while the upper end of the ruler touches the eyebrow above the reading eye. It is best to hold the KFM can with one hand and the ruler with the other. Using a flashlight makes the reading more accurate.

If a KFM is made with the specified dimensions and of the specified materials, its accuracy is automatically and permanently established. Unlike most radiation measuring instruments, a KFM never needs to be calibrated or tested with a radiation source, if made and maintained as specified and used with the following table that is based on numerous calibrations made at Oak Ridge National Laboratory.

**TABLE USED TO FIND DOSE RATES (R/HR)
FROM KFM READINGS**

*DIFFERENCE BETWEEN THE READING BEFORE EXPOSURE
AND THE READING AFTER EXPOSURE (8-PLY STANDARD
FOIL LEAVES)*

DIFF.* IN READINGS	TIME INTERVAL OF AN EXPOSURE				
	15 SEC. R/HR	1 MIN. R/HR	4 MIN. R/HR	16 MIN. R/HR	1 HR. R/HR
2 mm	6.2	1.6	0.4	0.1	0.03
4 mm	12.	3.1	0.8	0.2	0.06
6 mm	19.	4.6	1.2	0.3	0.08
8 mm	25.	6.2	1.6	0.4	0.10
10 mm	31.	7.7	2.0	0.5	0.13
12 mm	37.	9.2	2.3	0.6	0.15
14 mm	43.	11.	2.7	0.7	0.18

The millimeter scale is cut out and attached (see photo illustrations on pages 204–207 to the clear plastic cover of the KFM so that its zero mark is directly above the two leaves in their discharged position when the KFM is resting on a horizontal surface. A reading of the separation of the leaves is taken by noting the number of millimeters that the **lower edge** of one leaf appears to be on, on one side of the zero mark on the scale, and almost at the same time noting the number of millimeters the **lower edge** of the other leaf appears to be on, on the other side of the zero mark. The **sum** of these two apparent positions of the lower edges of the two leaves is called a KFM reading. The drawing appearing after the photo illustrations shows the **lower** edges of the leaves of a KFM appearing to be 9 mm on the right and zero and 10 on the left, giving a KFM reading of 19 mm. (Usually the lower edges of the leaves are not at the same distance from the zero mark.)

As will be fully explained later, the radiation dose rate is determined by:

1. charging and reading the KFM before exposure;
2. exposing it to radiation for a specified time in the location where measurement of the dose rate is needed—when outdoors, holding the KFM about 3 ft. above the ground;
3. reading the KFM after its exposure;
4. calculating, by subtraction, the **difference** between the reading taken before exposure and the reading taken after exposure;
5. using this table to find what the dose rate was during the exposure—as will be described later.

Instructions on how to use a KFM are given after those detailing how to make and charge this fallout meter.

To get a clearer idea of the construction and use of a KFM, look carefully at the following photos and read their explanations.

A. An Uncharged KFM. The charging wire has been pulled to one side by its adjustment-thread. This photo was taken

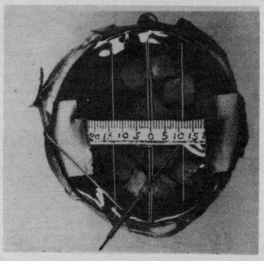

looking straight down at the upper edges of the two flat, 8-ply aluminum leaves. At this angle the leaves are barely visible, hanging vertically side by side directly under the zero mark, touching each other and with their ends even. Their suspension-threads insulate the leaves. These threads are almost parallel and touch (but do not cross) each other where they extend over the top of the rim of the can.

B. Charging a KFM by a Spark-Gap Discharge from a Tape That Has Been Electrostatically Charged by Being Unwound Quickly. Note that the charged tape is moved so that its surface is perpendicular to the charging-wire.

The high-voltage electrostatic charge on the unwound tape (that is an insulator) jumps the spark-gap between the tape and the upper end of the charging-wire, and then flows down the charging-wire to charge the insulated aluminum-foil leaves of the KFM. (Since the upper edges of the two leaves are ¾ inch below the scale and this is a photo taken at an angle, both leaves appear to be under the right side of the scale.)

C. A Charged KFM. Note the separation of the upper edges of its two leaves. The charging-wire has been raised to an almost horizontal position so that its lower end is too far above the aluminum leaves to permit electrical leakage from the leaves back up the charging-wire and into the outside air.

Also note the SEAT, a piece of pencil, taped to the right side of the can, opposite the charging wire.

D. Reading a KFM. A 12-inch ruler rests on the SEAT and is held vertical, while the reader's eyebrow touches the upper end of the ruler. The lower edge of the right leaf is under 8 on the scale and the lower edge of the left leaf is under 6 on the scale, giving a KFM reading of 14.

For accurate radiation measurements, a KFM should be placed on an approximately horizontal surface, but the charges on its two leaves and their displacements do not have to be equal.

V. Materials Needed

A. For the KFM: (In the following list, when more than one alternative material is given, the **best** material is listed first.)

 1. Any type metal can, approximately 2⁹/₁₆ inches in diameter inside and 2⅞ inches high inside, washed clean with soap. (This is the size of a standard 8-ounce can. Since most soup cans, pop cans, and beer cans also are about 2⁹/₁₆ inches in diameter inside, the required size of can can also be made by cutting down the height of more widely available cans—as described in Section IX of these instructions.)

 2. Standard aluminum foil—2 square feet. (In 1977, 2 square feet of a typical American aluminum foil weighed about 8.2 grams—about 0.29 oz.) (If only "Heavy Duty" or "Extra Heavy Duty" aluminum foil is available, make 5-ply leaves rather than 8-ply leaves of standard foil; the resultant fallout meter will be almost as accurate.)

 3. Doorbell-wire, or other light insulated wire (preferably

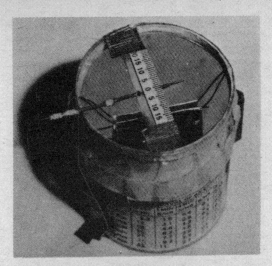

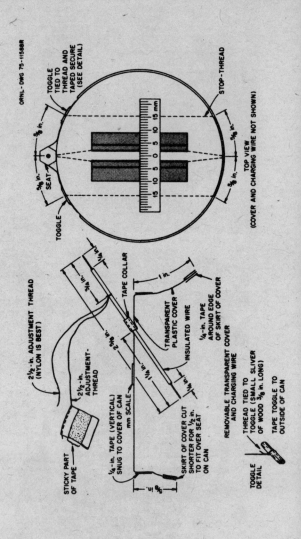

ORNL-DWG 73-11598R

TOP VIEW
(COVER AND CHARGING WIRE NOT SHOWN)

TOGGLE TIED TO THREAD AND TAPED SECURE (SEE DETAIL)

STOP-THREAD

³/₈ in.

SEAT

³/₁₆ in.

³/₁₆ in.

TOGGLE

2½-in. ADJUSTMENT THREAD (NYLON IS BEST)

2½-in. ADJUSTMENT-THREAD

STICKY PART OF TAPE

¼-in. TAPE (VERTICAL) SNUG TO COVER OF CAN

mm SCALE

TAPE COLLAR

TRANSPARENT PLASTIC COVER

INSULATED WIRE

¼-in. TAPE AROUND EDGE OF SKIRT OF COVER

SKIRT OF COVER CUT SHORTER FOR ½ in. TO FIT OVER SEAT ON CAN

REMOVABLE TRANSPARENT COVER AND CHARGING WIRE

THREAD TIED TO TOGGLE (SMALL SLIVER OF WOOD ⅜ in. LONG)

TAPE TOGGLE TO OUTSIDE OF CAN

TOGGLE DETAIL

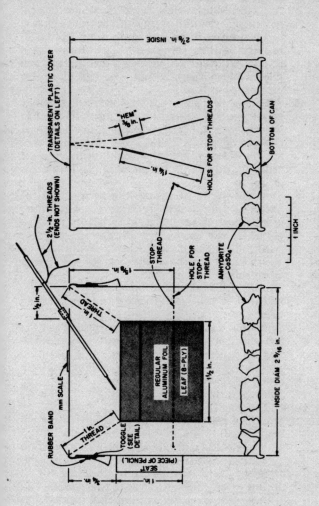

(This is **not** a Full Scale Drawing).

but not necessarily a single-strand wire inside the insulation)—6 inches.

4. Any type of lightweight thread (preferably but not necessarily nylon). (Best is twisted nylon thread; next best, **unwaxed** lightweight nylon dental floss; next best, silk; next best, polyester.)—3 feet. (Thread should be **CLEAN**, preferably not having been touched with fingers. Monofilament nylon is too difficult to see, handle, and mark.)

5. A piece of clear plastic—a 6 x 6 inch square. Strong polyethylene (4 mils thick) used for storm-proofing windows is best, but any reasonably stout and rather clear plastic will serve. The strong clear plastic used to wrap pieces of cheese, if washed with hot water and soap, is good. Do not use weak plastic or cellophane.

6. Cloth duct tape ("silver tape"), or masking tape, or freezer tape, or Scotch-type tape—about 10 square inches. (Save at least 10 feet of Scotch Magic Transparent Tape for the charging device.)

7. Band-Aid tape, or masking tape, or freezer tape, or Scotch transparent tape, or other thin and very flexible tapes—about 2 square inches.

8. Gypsum wallboard (sheetrock)—about ½ square foot, best about ½ inch thick. (To make the essential drying agent.)

9. Glue—not essential, but useful to replace Band-Aid and other thin tapes. "One hour" epoxy is best. Model airplane cement is satisfactory.

10. An ordinary wooden pencil and a small toothpick (or split a small sliver of wood).

11. Two strong rubber bands, or string.

B. For the Charging Devices:

1. Most hard plastic rubbed on **dry** paper. This is the best method.

   a. Plexiglas and most other hard plastics, such as are used in draftsmen's triangles, common smooth plastic rulers, etc.—at least 6 inches long.

   b. **Dry** paper—**Smooth** writing or typing paper. Tissue paper, newspaper, or facial tissue such as Kleenex, or toilet paper are satisfactory for charging, but not as durable.

2. Scotch Magic Transparent Tape (¾ inch width is best), or Scotch Transparent Tape, or P.V.C. (Polyvinyl chloride) insulating electrical tapes, or a few of the other common brands of Scotch-type tapes. (Some plastic tapes do not develop sufficiently high-voltage electrostatic charges when unrolled quickly.) This method cannot be used for charging a KFM inside a dry-bucket, needed for charging when the air is very humid.

C. For Determining Dose Rates and Recording Doses Received:
   1. A watch—preferably with a second hand.
   2. A flashlight or other light, for reading the KFM in a dark shelter or at night.
   3. Pencil and paper—preferably a notebook.

D. For the Dry-Bucket: (A KFM must be charged inside a dry-bucket if the air is very humid, as it often is inside a crowded, long-occupied shelter lacking adequate forced ventilation.)
   1. A large bucket, pot, or can, preferably with a top diameter of at least 11 inches.
   2. Clear plastic (best in 4-mil-thick clear plastic used for storm windows). A square piece 5 inches wider on a side than the diameter of the bucket to be used.
   3. Cloth duct tape, one inch wide and 8 feet long (or 4 ft., if 2 inches wide). Or 16 ft. of freezer tape one inch wide.
   4. Two plastic bags 14 to 16 inches in circumference, such as ordinary plastic bread bags. The original length of these bags should be at least 5 inches greater than the height of the bucket.
   5. About one square foot of wall board (sheetrock), to make anhydrite drying agent.
   6. Two 1-quart Mason jars or other airtight containers, one in which to store anhydrite and another in which to keep dry the KFM charging devices.
   7. Strong rubber bands—enough to make a loop around the bucket. Or string.
   8. Four square feet of aluminum foil, to make a vapor-proof cover—useful, but not essential.

VI. Useful but not Essential Materials
—Which Could be Obtained Before a Crisis—

1. An airtight container (such as a large peanut butter jar) with a mouth at least 4 inches wide, in which to keep a KFM, along with some drying agent, when it is not being used. Keeping a KFM very dry greatly extends the time during which the drying agent **inside** the KFM remains effective.
2. Commercial anhydrite with a color indicator, such as the drying agent Drierite. This granular form of anhydrite remains light blue as long as it is effective as a drying agent. Obtainable from laboratory supply sources.

VII. Tools Needed

Small nail—sharpened
Stick, or a wooden tool handle
   (best 2–2½ inch diameter and at least 12 inches long)
Hammer
Pliers
Scissors
Needle—quite a large sewing needle, but less than 2½ inches long
Knife with a small blade—sharp
Ruler (12 inches)

VIII. Make the Drying Agent
—The Easiest Part to Make, but Time Consuming—

1. For a KFM to measure radiation accurately, the air inside its ionization chamber must be kept **very dry**. An excellent drying agent (anhydrite) can be made by heating the gypsum in ordinary gypsum wallboard (sheetrock). Do NOT use calcium chloride.
2. Take a piece of gypsum wallboard approximately 12 inches by 6 inches, and preferably with its gypsum about ⅜ inches thick. Cut off the paper and glue, easiest done by first wetting the paper. [Since water vapor from normal air penetrates

the plastic cover of a KFM and can dampen the anhydrite and make it ineffective in as short a time as two days, fresh batches of anhydrite must be made before the attack and kept ready inside the shelter for replacement. The useful life of the drying agent inside a KFM can be greatly lengthened by keeping the KFM inside an airtight container (such as a peanut butter jar with a 4-inch-diameter mouth) with some drying agent, when the KFM is not being used.]

3. Break the white gypsum filling into small pieces and make the largest no more than ½ in. across. (The tops of pieces larger than this may be too close to the aluminum foil leaves.) If the gypsum is dry, using a pair of pliers makes breaking it easier. Make the largest **side** of the largest pieces no bigger than this.

4. Dry gypsum is **not** a drying agent. To drive the water out of the gypsum molecules and produce the drying agent (anhydrite), heat the gypsum in an oven at its **highest** temperature (which should be above 400 degrees F) for one hour. Heat the gypsum after placing the small pieces no more than two pieces deep in a pan. Or heat the pieces over a fire for 20 minutes or more in a pan or can heated to a dull red.

5. If sufficient aluminum foil and time are available, it is best to heat the gypsum and store the anhydrite as follows:
   a. So that the right amount of anhydrite can be taken quickly out of its storage jar, put enough pieces of gypsum in a can with the same diameter as the KFM, measuring out a batch of gypsum that almost covers the bottom of the can with a single layer.
   b. Cut a piece of aluminum foil about 8 in x 8 in. square, and fold up its edges to form a bowl-like container in which to heat one batch of gypsum pieces.
   c. Measure out 10 or 12 such batches, and put each batch in its aluminum foil "bowl."

   d. Heat all of these filled "bowls" of gypsum in hottest oven for one hour.

   e. As soon as the aluminum foil is cool enough to touch, fold and crumple the edges of each aluminum foil "bowl" together, to make a rough aluminum-covered "ball" of each batch of anhydrite.

   f. Promptly seal the batches in airtight jars or other airtight containers, and keep containers closed except when taking out an aluminum-covered "ball."

6. Since anhydrite absorbs water from the air very rapidly, quickly put it in a dry airtight container while it is still quite hot. A Mason jar is excellent.

7. To place anhydrite in a KFM, drop in the pieces one by one, being careful not to hit the leaves or the stop-threads. The pieces should almost cover the bottom of the can, with no piece on top of other pieces.

8. To remove anhydrite from a KFM, use a pair of scissors or tweezers as forceps, holding them in a vertical position and not touching the leaves.

IX. Make the Ionization Chamber of the KFM
(To Avoid Mistakes and Save Time,
Read All of This Section ALOUD Before Beginning Work.)

1. Remove the paper label (if any) from an ordinary 8-ounce can from which the top has been smoothly cut. Wash the can with soap and water and dry it. (An 8-ounce can has an inside diameter of about 2⁹⁄₁₆ inches and an inside height of about 2⁷⁄₈ inches.)

2. Skip to step 3 if an 8-ounce can is available. If an 8-ounce can is not available, reduce the height of any other can having an inside diameter of about 2⁹⁄₁₆ inches (such as most soup cans, most pop cans, or most beer cans). To cut off the top part of a can, first measure and mark the line on which to cut. Then to keep from bending the can while cutting, wrap newspaper tightly around a stick or a round wooden tool handle, so that the wood is covered with 20 to 30 thicknesses of paper and the diameter (ideally) is only slightly less than the diameter of the can.

   One person should hold the can over the paper-covered stick while a second person cuts the can little by little along the marked cutting line. If leather gloves are available, wear them. To cut the can off smoothly, use a file, or use a hacksaw drawn backwards along the cutting line. Or cut the can with a sharp, short blade of a pocketknife by: (1) repeatedly stabbing downward vertically through the can into the paper, and (2) repeatedly making a cut about ¼ inch long by moving the knife into a sloping position, while keeping its point still pressed into the paper covering the stick.

Next, smooth the cut edge, and cover it with small pieces of freezer tape or other flexible tape.

3. Cut out the PAPER PATTERN TO WRAP AROUND KFM CAN. (Cut the pattern out of the following Pattern Page A.) Glue (or tape) this pattern to the can, starting with one of the two short sides of the pattern. Secure this starting short side directly over the side seam of the can. Wrap the pattern snugly around the can, gluing or taping it securely as it is being wrapped. (If the pattern is too wide to fit flat between the rims of the can, trim a little off its lower edge.)

4. Sharpen a small nail, by filing or rubbing on concrete, for use as a punch to make the four holes needed to install the stop-threads in the ionization chamber (the can). (The stop-threads are insulators that stop the charged aluminum leaves from touching the can and being discharged.)

5. Have one person hold the can over a horizontal stick or a round wooden tool-handle, that ideally has a diameter about as large as the diameter of the can. Then a second person can use the sharpened nail and a hammer to punch four very small holes through the sides of the can at the points shown by the four crosses on the pattern. Make these holes just large enough to run a needle through them, and then move the needle in the holes so as to bend back the obstructing points of metal.

6. The stop-threads can be installed by using a needle to thread a single thread through all four holes. Use a **very clean** thread, preferably nylon, and do not touch the parts of this thread that will be inside the can and will serve as the insulating stop-threads. Soiled threads are poor insulators. (See illustrations.)

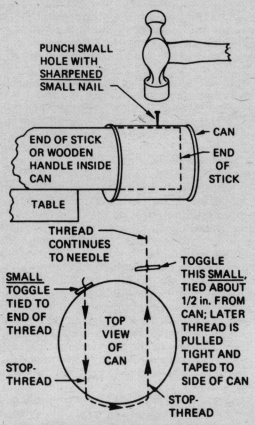

PUNCH SMALL HOLE WITH <u>SHARPENED</u> SMALL NAIL

CAN

END OF STICK OR WOODEN HANDLE INSIDE CAN

END OF STICK

TABLE

THREAD CONTINUES TO NEEDLE

<u>SMALL</u> TOGGLE TIED TO END OF THREAD

TOGGLE THIS <u>SMALL</u>, TIED ABOUT 1/2 in. FROM CAN; LATER THREAD IS PULLED TIGHT AND TAPED TO SIDE OF CAN

STOP-THREAD

TOP VIEW OF CAN

STOP-THREAD

SINGLE THREAD THREADED THROUGH 4 HOLES TO MAKE 2 STOP-THREADS

PATTERN (A)

The paper patterns on the next two pages are the exact size for a KFM. These patterns should be cut out and glued together so that their center lines align exactly. Each page has an overlap area to make this easier. Once glued together this pattern should be wrapped around a KFM can and glued or taped securely to it. *Caution:* Xerox copies of these patterns will be too large.

PATTERN (A)

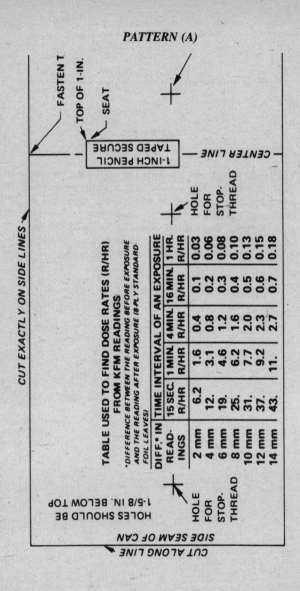

CUT EXACTLY ON SIDE LINES

FASTEN T

TOP OF 1-IN.

SEAT

CENTER LINE

1-INCH PENCIL TAPED SECURE

HOLE FOR STOP-THREAD

TABLE USED TO FIND DOSE RATES (R/HR) FROM KFM READINGS

*DIFFERENCE BETWEEN THE READING BEFORE EXPOSURE AND THE READING AFTER EXPOSURE (8-PLY STANDARD-FOIL LEAVES)

DIFF.* IN READINGS	TIME INTERVAL OF AN EXPOSURE				
	15 SEC. R/HR	1 MIN. R/HR	4 MIN. R/HR	16 MIN. R/HR	1 HR. R/HR
2 mm	6.2	1.6	0.4	0.1	0.03
4 mm	12.	3.1	0.8	0.2	0.06
6 mm	19.	4.6	1.2	0.3	0.08
8 mm	25.	6.2	1.6	0.4	0.10
10 mm	31.	7.7	2.0	0.5	0.13
12 mm	37.	9.2	2.3	0.6	0.15
14 mm	43.	11.	2.7	0.7	0.18

HOLES SHOULD BE 1-5/8 IN. BELOW TOP

HOLE FOR STOP-THREAD

SIDE SEAM OF CAN

CUT ALONG LINE

PATTERN (A)

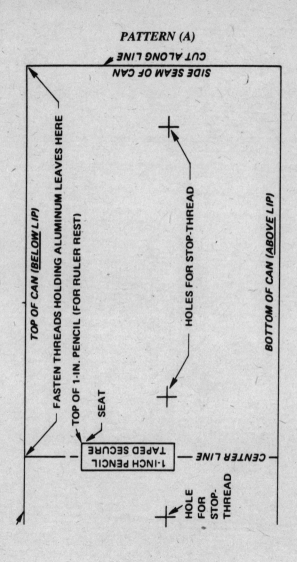

SIDE SEAM OF CAN
CUT ALONG LINE

TOP OF CAN (*BELOW LIP*)

FASTEN THREADS HOLDING ALUMINUM LEAVES HERE

TOP OF 1-IN. PENCIL (FOR RULER REST)

SEAT

1-INCH PENCIL
TAPED SECURE

CENTER LINE

HOLES FOR STOP-THREAD

HOLE
FOR
STOP-
THREAD

BOTTOM OF CAN (*ABOVE LIP*)

Before threading the thread through the four holes, tie a **small** toggle (see the preceding sketch) to the long end of the thread. (This toggle can easily be made of a very small sliver of wood cut about ⅜ in. long.) After the thread has been pulled through the four holes, attach a second toggle to the thread, about ½ inch from the part of the thread that comes out of the fourth hole. Then the thread can be pulled tightly down the side of the can and the second small toggle can be taped securely in place to the side of the can. (If the thread is taped down without a toggle, it is likely to move under the tape.)

The first toggle and all of the four holes also should be covered with tape, to prevent air from leaking into the can after it has been covered and is being used as an ionization chamber.

X. Make Two Separate 8-Ply Leaves of Standard [Not Heavy Duty*] Aluminum Foil

Proceed as follows to make each leaf:

1. Cut out a piece of standard aluminum foil appropriately 4 inches by 8 inches.
2. Fold the aluminum foil to make a 2-ply (= 2 thicknesses) sheet approximately 4 inches by 4 inches.
3. Fold this 2-ply sheet to make a 4-ply sheet approximately 2 inches by 4 inches.

---

*If only heavy duty aluminum foil (sometimes called "extra heavy duty") is available, make 5-ply leaves of the same size, and use the table for the 8-ply KFM to determine radiation dose rates. To make a 5-ply leaf, start by cutting out a piece of foil approximately 4 inches by 4 inches. Fold it to make a 4-ply sheet approximately 2 inches by 2 inches, with one corner exactly square. Next from a single thickness of foil cut a square approximately 2 inches by 2 inches. Slip this square into a 4-ply sheet, thus making a 5-ply sheet. Then make the 5-ply leaf, using the FINISHED-LEAF PATTERN, etc. as described for making an 8-ply leaf.

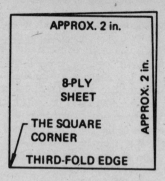

4. Fold this 4-ply sheet to make an 8-ply sheet (8 sheets thick) approximately 2 inches by 2 inches, being **sure** that the two halves of the second-fold edge are exactly together. This third folding makes an 8-ply aluminum foil sheet with **one corner exactly square**.

5. **Cut out** the FINISHED-LEAF PATTERN, found on the following Pattern Page B. Note that this pattern is **NOT** a square and that it is **smaller** than the 8-ply sheet. Flatten the 8 thicknesses of aluminum foil with the fingers until they appear to be a single thin, flat sheet.

6. Hold the FINISHED-LEAF PATTERN **on top of** the 8-ply aluminum foil sheet, with the pattern's THIRD-FOLD EDGE on top of the third-fold edge of the 8-ply aluminum sheet. Be sure that one lower **corner** of the FINISHED-LEAF PATTERN is on top of the **exactly square corner** of the 8-ply aluminum sheet.

7. While holding a straight edge along the THREAD LINE of the pattern, press with a sharp pencil so as to make a shallow groove for the THREAD LINE on the 8-ply aluminum sheet. Also using a sharp pencil, trace around the top and side of the pattern, so as to indent (groove) the 8-ply foil.

8. Remove the pattern, and cut out the 8-ply aluminum foil leaf.

9. While holding a straight edge along the indented THREAD LINE, lift up the OPEN EDGE of the 8-ply sheet (keeping all 8 plies together) until this edge is vertical, as illustrated.

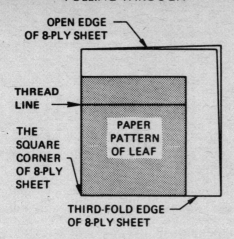

OPEN EDGE
OF 8-PLY SHEET

THREAD
LINE

THE
SQUARE
CORNER
OF 8-PLY
SHEET

PAPER
PATTERN
OF LEAF

THIRD-FOLD EDGE
OF 8-PLY SHEET

Remove the straight edge, and fold the 8-ply aluminum along the THREAD LINE so as to make a **flat-folded** hem.

10. Open the flat-folded hem of the finished leaf until the 8-ply leaf is almost flat again, as shown by the pattern, from which the FINISHED-LEAF PATTERN has already been cut.

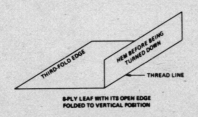

THIRD-FOLD EDGE

HEM BEFORE BEING
TURNED DOWN

THREAD LINE

8-PLY LEAF WITH ITS OPEN EDGE
FOLDED TO VERTICAL POSITION

11. Prepare to attach the aluminum-foil leaf to the thread that will suspend it inside the KFM.

PATTERN (B)

PATTERN FOR CLEAR-PLASTIC COVER FOR KFM CAN

The paper patterns on the next two pages are the exact size for the clear plastic cover for a KFM can. Cut out these patterns and glue them together so that the center line between the two leaves aligns exactly. Overlap areas on both pages should make this easier.

Caution: Xerox copies will be slightly too large.

PATTERN (B)

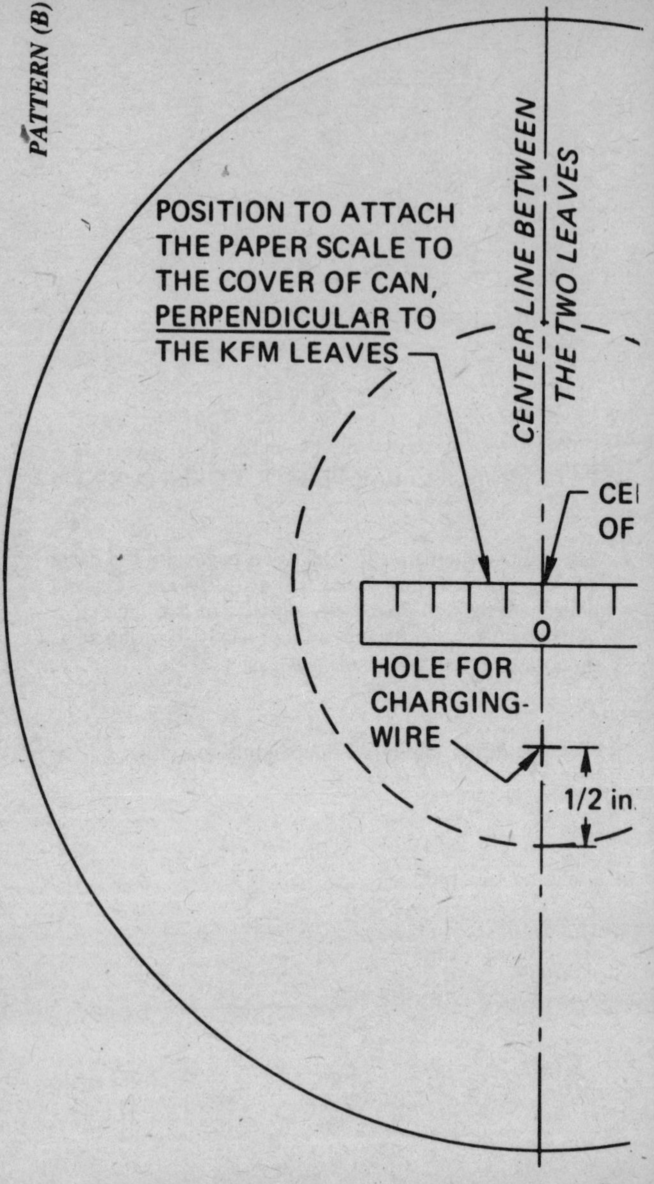

POSITION TO ATTACH
THE PAPER SCALE TO
THE COVER OF CAN,
PERPENDICULAR TO
THE KFM LEAVES ─

CENTER LINE BETWEEN
THE TWO LEAVES

CE
OF

HOLE FOR
CHARGING-
WIRE

1/2 in.

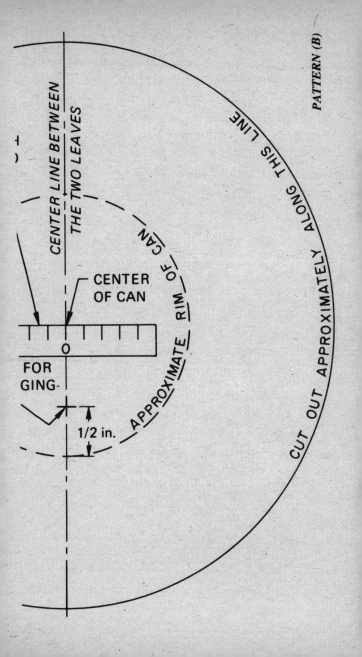

PATTERN (B)

CENTER LINE BETWEEN
THE TWO LEAVES

CENTER
OF CAN

O

FOR
GING-

1/2 in.

APPROXIMATE RIM OF CAN

CUT OUT APPROXIMATELY ALONG THIS LINE

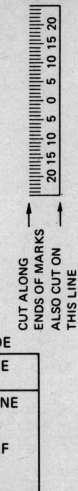

CUT ALONG
ENDS OF MARKS

ALSO CUT ON
THIS LINE

20 15 10 5 0 5 10 15 20

PAPER SCALE (TO BE CUT OUT)

CAUTION: XEROX COPIES OF THE FINISHED-LEAF AND THE
SCALE PATTERNS WILL BE SLIGHTLY TOO LARGE.

SHORT SIDE

| OPEN EDGE |
| THREAD LINE |
| 8-PLY LEAF |
| THIRD-FOLD EDGE |

LONG SIDE

FINISHED-LEAF PATTERN
(CUT OUT EXACTLY ON SIDE LINES)

If no epoxy glue* is available to hold down the hem and prevent the thread from slipping in the hem, cut two pieces of tape (Band-Aid tape is best; next best is masking or freezer tape; next best, Scotch tape). After first peeling off the paper backing of Band-Aid tape, cut each piece of tape ⅛ inch by 1 inch long. Attach these two pieces of tape to the finished 8-ply aluminum leaf with the sticky sides up, except for their ends. As shown by the pattern on the following pattern page, secure ⅛ inch of one end of a tape strip near one corner of the 8-ply aluminum foil leaf by first turning under this ⅛-inch end; that is, with this end's sticky side down. Then turn under the other ⅛-inch-long end, and attach this end below the THREAD LINE. **Slant** each tape strip as illustrated on Pattern (C).

Be sure you have read through step 18 before you do anything else.

12. Cut an 8-½-inch piece of fine, unwaxed, very clean thread. (Nylon twisted thread, unwaxed extra-fine nylon dental floss, or silk thread are best in this order. Nylon monofilament "invisible" thread is an excellent insulator but is too difficult for most people to handle.)

Cut out Pattern (C), the guide sheet used when attaching a leaf to its suspending thread. Then tape Pattern (C) to the top of a work table. Cover the two "TAPE HERE" rectangles on Pattern (C) with pieces of tape, each piece the size of the rectangle. Then cut two other pieces of tape each the same size and use them to **tape the thread ONTO the guide sheet**, on top of the "TAPE HERE" rectangles.

Be very careful **not to touch** the two 1-inch parts of the thread next to the outline of the finished leaf, since oil

*If using epoxy or other glue, use only a **very** little to hold down the hem, to attach the thread securely to the leaf and to glue together any open edges of the plied foil. Most convenient is "one hour" epoxy, applied with a toothpick. Model airplane cement requires hours to harden when applied between sheets of aluminum foil. To make sure no glue stiffens the free thread beyond the upper corners of the finished leaf, put no glue within ¼ inch of a point where thread will go out from the folded hem of the leaf.

The instructions in step 11 are for persons lacking "one hour" epoxy or the time required to dry other types of glue. Persons using glue instead of tape to attach the leaf to its thread should make appropriate use of the pattern on the following page and of some of the procedures detailed in steps 12 through 18.

and dirt even on clean fingers will reduce the electrical insulating value of the thread between the leaf and the top rim of the can.

13. With the thread still taped to the paper pattern and while slightly lifting the thread with a knife tip held under the center of the thread, slip the finished leaf **under** the thread and into position exactly on the top of the leaf outlined on the pattern page. Hold the leaf in this position with two fingers.

14. While keeping the thread straight between its two taped-down ends, lower the thread so that it sticks to the two plastic strips. Then press the thread against the plastic strips.

15. With the point of the knife, hold down the center of the thread against the center of the THREAD LINE of the leaf. Then, with two fingers, carefully fold over the hem and press it almost flat. Be sure that the thread comes out of the corners of the hem. Remove the knife, and press the hem down completely flat against the rest of the leaf.

16. Make **small** marks on the thread at the two points shown on the pattern page. Use a ballpoint pen if available.

17. Loosen the second two small pieces of tape from the pattern paper, but leave these tapes stuck to the thread.

18. Cut 5 pieces of Band-Aid tape, each approximately ⅛ inch by ¼ inch, this small.

Use 3 of these pieces of tape to secure the centers of the side edges of the leaf. Place the 5 pieces as illustrated in the SIDE VIEW sketch on the next page.

ORNL-DWG 76-6542

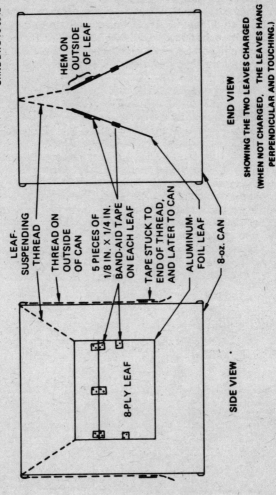

LEAF-SUSPENDING THREAD

THREAD ON OUTSIDE OF CAN

5 PIECES OF 1/8 IN. X 1/4 IN. BAND-AID TAPE ON EACH LEAF

TAPE STUCK TO END OF THREAD, AND LATER TO CAN

ALUMINUM-FOIL LEAF

8-oz. CAN

8-PLY LEAF

SIDE VIEW

HEM ON OUTSIDE OF LEAF

END VIEW

SHOWING THE TWO LEAVES CHARGED
(WHEN NOT CHARGED, THE LEAVES HANG
PERPENDICULAR AND TOUCHING.)

PATTERN (C)

The paper patterns on the next two pages must be cut out and glued together so that they align exactly. Then tape the entire pattern to the top of a work table. Cover the two "TAPE HERE" rectangles with same-sized pieces of tape, in order to keep from tearing this pattern when removing two additional pieces of tape. Then, by putting two other pieces of tape this same size on top of the first two pieces, tape the thread ONTO this pattern, and later attach a leaf to the taped-down thread.

Warning: The parts of the thread that will be inside the can and on which the leaf will be suspended must serve to insulate the high-voltage electrical charges to be placed on the leaf. Therefore, the suspended parts of the thread *must be kept clean.*

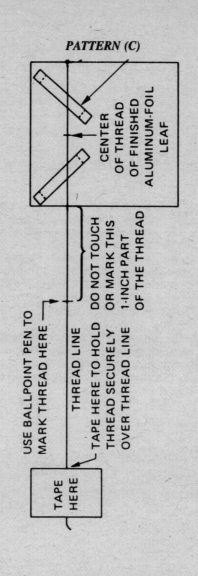

PATTERN (C)

CENTER
OF THREAD
OF FINISHED
ALUMINUM-FOIL
LEAF

DO NOT TOUCH
OR MARK THIS
1-INCH PART
OF THE THREAD

USE BALLPOINT PEN TO
MARK THREAD HERE

THREAD LINE

TAPE HERE TO HOLD
THREAD SECURELY
OVER THREAD LINE

TAPE
HERE

PATTERN (C)

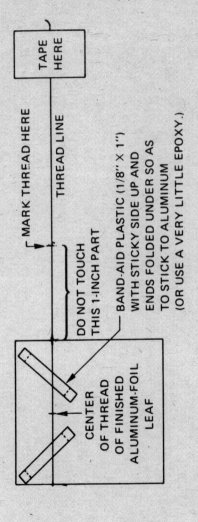

TAPE HERE

MARK THREAD HERE

THREAD LINE

DO NOT TOUCH THIS 1-INCH PART

BAND-AID PLASTIC (1/8" × 1") WITH STICKY SIDE UP AND ENDS FOLDED UNDER SO AS TO STICK TO ALUMINUM (OR USE A VERY LITTLE EPOXY.)

CENTER OF THREAD OF FINISHED ALUMINUM-FOIL LEAF

XI. Install the Aluminum-Foil Leaves

1. Use the two small pieces of tape stuck to the ends of a leaf-suspend the leaf inside the can. See END VIEW sketch, page 233. Each of the two **marks** on the attached thread MUST **rest exactly on the top of the rim of the can**, preferably in two **very small** notches filed in the top of the rim of the can. Each of these two marks on a thread should be positioned exactly above one of the two points shown on the pattern wrapped around the can. Be sure that the hem-side of each of the two leaves faces outward. See END VIEW sketch.

2. Next, the suspending thread of the first leaf should be taped to the top of the rim. Use a piece of Band-Aid only about ⅛ in. x ¼ in., sticking it to the rim of the can so as barely to cover the thread on the side where the second leaf will be suspended. Make sure no parts of the tapes are inside the can.

3. Position and secure the second leaf, being sure that:
   a. The smooth sides of the two leaves are smooth (not bent) and face each other and are flush (= "right together") when not charged. See END VIEW sketch and study the first photo illustration, page 204, "An Uncharged KFM."
   b. The upper edges of the two leaves are suspended side by side and at the same distance below the top of the can.
   c. The leaf-suspending threads are taped with Band-Aid to the top of the rim of the can (so that putting the cover on will not move the threads).
   d. No parts of the leaf-suspending threads inside the can are taped down to the can or otherwise restricted.
   e. The leaf-suspending parts of the threads inside the can do not cross over, entangle or restrict each other.
   f. The threads come together on the top of the rim of the can, and that the leaves are flat and hang together as shown in the first photo illustration. "An Uncharged KFM."
   g. If the leaves do not look like these photographed leaves, make new, better leaves and install them.

4. Cover with tape the parts of the threads that extend down

the **outside** of the can, and also cover with more tape the small pieces of tape near the ends of the threads on the outside of the can.

5. To make the SEAT, cut a piece of a wooden pencil, or a stick, about one inch long and tape it securely to the side of the can along the center line marked SEAT on the pattern. Be sure the upper end of this piece of pencil is at the same position as the top of the location for the SEAT outlined on the pattern. The top of the SEAT is ¾ inch below the top of the can. Be sure not to cover or make illegible any part of the table printed on the paper pattern.

6. Cut out one of the "Reminders for Operators" and glue and/ or tape it to the unused side of the KFM. Then it is best to cover all the sides of the finished KFM with clear plastic tape or varnish. This will keep sticky-tape on the end of an adjustment thread or moisture from damaging the "Reminders" or the table.

XII. Make the Plastic Cover

1. Cut out the paper pattern for the cover from the Pattern Page (B).

2. From a piece of clear, strong plastic, cut a circle approximately the same size as the paper pattern. (Storm-window polyethylene plastic, 4 mils thick, is best.)

3. Stretch the center of this circular piece of clear plastic over the open end of the can, and pull it down to the sides of the can, making small tucks in the "skirt," so that there are no wrinkles in the top cover. Hold the lower part of the "skirt" in place with a strong rubber band or piece of string. (If another can having the same diameter as the KFM can is available, use it to make the cover—to avoid the possibility of disturbing the leaf-suspending threads.)

4. Make the cover so it fits snugly, but can be taken off and replaced readily.

Just below the top of the rim of the can, bind the covering plastic in place with an ¼-inch-wide piece of strong tape. (Cloth duct tape is best. If only freezer or masking tape is available, use two thicknesses.)

Keep vertical the small part of the tape that presses against

REMINDERS FOR OPERATORS

THE DRYING AGENT INSIDE A KFM IS O.K. IF, WHEN THE CHARGED KFM IS NOT EXPOSED TO RADIATION, ITS READINGS DECREASE BY 1 MM OR LESS IN 3 HOURS.

READING: WITH THE READING EYE 12 INCHES VERTICALLY ABOVE THE SEAT, NOTE ON THE MM SCALE THE SEPARATION OF THE LOWER EDGES OF THE LEAVES. IF THE RIGHT LEAF IS AT 10 MM AND THE LEFT LEAF IS AT 7 MM, THE KFM READS 17 MM. NEVER TAKE A READING WHILE A LEAF IS TOUCHING A STOP-THREAD. NEVER USE A KFM READING THAT IS LESS THAN 5MM.

FINDING A DOSE RATE: IF BEFORE EXPOSURE A KFM READS 17 MM AND IF AFTER A 1-MINUTE EXPOSURE IT READS 5 MM, THE DIFFERENCE IN READINGS IS 12 MM. THE ATTACHED TABLE SHOWS THE DOSE RATE WAS 9.6 R/HR DURING THE EXPOSURE.

FINDING A DOSE: IF A PERSON WORKS OUTSIDE FOR 3 HOURS WHERE THE DOSE RATE IS 2 R/HR, WHAT IS HIS RADIATION DOSE? ANSWER: 3 HR x 2 R/HR = 6 R.

FINDING HOW LONG IT TAKES TO GET A CERTAIN R DOSE: IF THE DOSE RATE IS 1.6 R/HR OUTSIDE AND A PERSON IS WILLING TO TAKE A 6 R DOSE, HOW LONG CAN HE REMAIN OUTSIDE? ANSWER:

6 R ÷ 1.6 R/HR = 3.75 HR = 3 HOURS AND 45 MINUTES.

FALLOUT RADIATION GUIDES FOR A HEALTHY PERSON NOT PREVIOUSLY EXPOSED TO A TOTAL RADIATION DOSE OF MORE THAN 100 R DURING A 2-WEEK PERIOD:

6 R PER DAY CAN BE TOLERATED FOR UP TO TWO MONTHS WITHOUT LOSING THE ABILITY TO WORK.

100 R IN A WEEK OR LESS IS NOT LIKELY TO SERIOUSLY SICKEN.

350 R IN A FEW DAYS IS LIKELY TO PROVE FATAL UNDER POST-ATTACK CONDITIONS.

600 R IN A WEEK OR LESS IS ALMOST CERTAIN TO CAUSE DEATH WITHIN A FEW WEEKS.

REMINDERS FOR OPERATORS

THE DRYING AGENT INSIDE A KFM IS O.K. IF, WHEN THE CHARGED KFM IS NOT EXPOSED TO RADIATION, ITS READINGS DECREASE BY 1 MM OR LESS IN 3 HOURS.

READING: WITH THE READING EYE 12 INCHES VERTICALLY ABOVE THE SEAT, NOTE ON THE MM SCALE THE SEPARATION OF THE LOWER EDGES OF THE LEAVES. IF THE RIGHT LEAF IS AT 10 MM AND THE LEFT LEAF IS AT 7 MM, THE KFM READS 17 MM. NEVER TAKE A READING WHILE A LEAF IS TOUCHING A STOP-THREAD. NEVER USE A KFM READING THAT IS LESS THAN 5MM.

FINDING A DOSE RATE: IF BEFORE EXPOSURE A KFM READS 17 MM AND IF AFTER A 1-MINUTE EXPOSURE IT READS 5 MM, THE DIFFERENCE IN READINGS IS 12 MM. THE ATTACHED TABLE SHOWS THE DOSE RATE WAS 9.6 R/HR DURING THE EXPOSURE.

FINDING A DOSE: IF A PERSON WORKS OUTSIDE FOR 3 HOURS WHERE THE DOSE RATE IS 2 R/HR, WHAT IS HIS RADIATION DOSE? ANSWER: 3 HR x 2 R/HR = 6 R.

FINDING HOW LONG IT TAKES TO GET A CERTAIN R DOSE: IF THE DOSE RATE IS 1.6 R/HR OUTSIDE AND A PERSON IS WILLING TO TAKE A 6 R DOSE, HOW LONG CAN HE REMAIN OUTSIDE? ANSWER:

6 R ÷ 1.6 R/HR = 3.75 HR = 3 HOURS AND 45 MINUTES.

FALLOUT RADIATION GUIDES FOR A HEALTHY PERSON NOT PREVIOUSLY EXPOSED TO A TOTAL RADIATION DOSE OF MORE THAN 100 R DURING A 2-WEEK PERIOD:

6 R PER DAY CAN BE TOLERATED FOR UP TO TWO MONTHS WITHOUT LOSING THE ABILITY TO WORK.

100 R IN A WEEK OR LESS IS NOT LIKELY TO SERIOUSLY SICKEN.

350 R IN A FEW DAYS IS LIKELY TO PROVE FATAL UNDER POST-ATTACK CONDITIONS.

600 R IN A WEEK OR LESS IS ALMOST CERTAIN TO CAUSE DEATH WITHIN A FEW WEEKS.

the rim of the can while pulling the length of the tape hor-
izontally around the can so as to bind the top of the plastic
cover snugly to the rim. If this small part of the tape is kept
vertical, the lower edge of the tape will not squeeze the
plastic below the rim of the can to such a small circumference
as to prevent the cover from being removed quite easily.

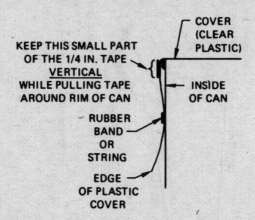

5. With scissors, cut off the "skirt" of the plastic cover until
   it extends only about one inch below the top of the rim of
   the can.
6. Make a notch in the "skirt," about one inch wide, where it
   fits over the pencil SEAT attached to the can. The "skirt"
   in this notched area should be only about ⅝ of an inch long,
   measured down from the top of the rim of the can.
7. Remove the plastic cover, and then tape the lower edges of
   the "skirt," inside and out, using short lengths of ¼-inch-
   wide tape. Before securing each short piece of tape, slightly
   open the tucks that are being taped shut on their edges, so
   that the "skirt" flares slightly outward and the cover can be
   readily removed.
8. Put the plastic cover on the KFM can. From the Pattern
   Page (B) cut out the SCALE. Then tape the SCALE to the
   top of the plastic cover, in the position shown on the pattern
   for the cover, and also by the drawings. Preferably use
   transparent tape.

EXACT SIZE

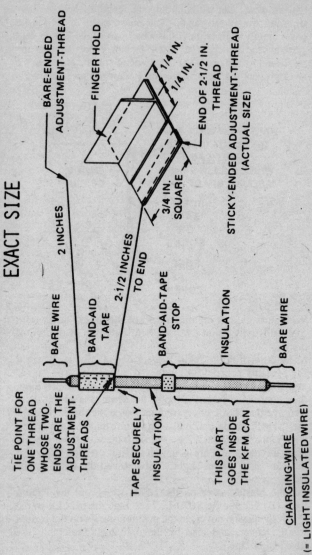

TIE POINT FOR ONE THREAD WHOSE TWO-ENDS ARE THE ADJUSTMENT-THREADS

BARE WIRE

BAND-AID TAPE

TAPE SECURELY

INSULATION

THIS PART GOES INSIDE THE KFM CAN

INSULATION

BARE WIRE

CHARGING-WIRE

(= LIGHT INSULATED WIRE)
(BELL-WIRE IS BEST)

BARE-ENDED ADJUSTMENT-THREAD

FINGER HOLD

2 INCHES

2-1/2 INCHES TO END

1/4 IN.

1/4 IN.

END OF 2-1/2 IN. THREAD

3/4 IN. SQUARE

STICKY-ENDED ADJUSTMENT-THREAD
(ACTUAL SIZE)

BAND-AID-TAPE STOP

STICKY-ENDED ADJUSTMENT—THREAD
(OVERSIZED DRAWING)

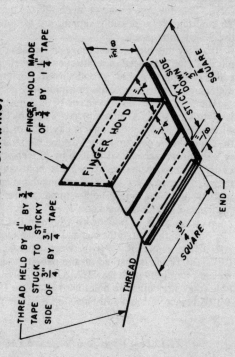

THREAD HELD BY $\frac{1}{8}"$ BY $\frac{3}{4}"$
TAPE STUCK TO STICKY
SIDE OF $\frac{3}{4}"$ BY $\frac{3}{4}"$ TAPE.

FINGER HOLD MADE
OF $\frac{3}{4}"$ BY $1\frac{1}{4}"$ TAPE

$\frac{3}{8}"$

$\frac{1}{4}"$

$\frac{1}{4}"$

FINGER HOLD

STICKY SIDE

DOWN

$\frac{3}{4}"$
SQUARE

$\frac{1}{8}"$

END

THREAD

$\frac{3}{4}"$
SQUARE

Be careful not to cover with tape any of the division lines on the SCALE between 20 on the right and 20 on the left of 0.

9. Make the charging-wire by following the pattern given on page 244 which is **exactly the right size**.

Doorbell wire with an outside diameter of about $\frac{1}{16}$ inch is best, but any lightweight insulated wire, such as part of a lightweight two-wire extension cord split in half, will serve. The illustrated wire is much thicker than bell wire. To stop tape from possibly slipping up or down the wire, use a very little glue.

If a very thin plastic has been used for the cover, a sticky piece of tape may need to be attached to the end of the bare-ended adjustment thread, so both threads can be used to hold the charging wire in a desired position.

The best tape to attach to an end of the adjustment-threads is cloth duct tape. A square piece $\frac{3}{4}$ inch by $\frac{3}{4}$ inch is the sticky base. To keep this tape sticky (free of paper fibers), the paper on the can should be covered with transparent tape or varnish. A piece about $\frac{1}{8}$ inch by $\frac{3}{4}$ inch serves to stick under one end of the sticky base, to hold the adjustment-thread. A $\frac{3}{4}$ inch by $1\frac{1}{4}$ inch rectangular piece of tape is used to make the finger hold—important for making adjustments inside a dry-bucket.

With a needle or pin, make a hole in the plastic cover $\frac{1}{2}$ inch from the rim of the can and directly above the upper end of the CENTER LINE between the two leaves. The CENTER LINE is marked on the pattern wrapped around the can. Carefully push the CHARGING-WIRE through this hole (thus stretching the hole) until all of the CHARGING-WIRE below its Band-Aid-tape stop is inside the can.

XIII. Two Ways to Charge a KFM

1. Charging a KFM with Hard Plastic Rubbed on **Dry** Paper.
   a. Adjust the charging-wire so that its lower end is about $\frac{1}{16}$ inch above the upper edges of the aluminum-foil leaves. Use the sticky-tape at the end of one adjustment-thread to hold the charging-wire in this position. Stick this tape approximately in line with the threads suspending the leaves, either on the side of the can or on top of the plastic

cover. (If the charging-wire is held loosely by the cover, it may be necessary to put a piece of sticky-tape on the end of each adjustment-thread in order to adjust the charging-wire securely. If a charging-wire is not secure, its lower end may be forced up by the like charge on the leaves before the leaves can be fully charged.)

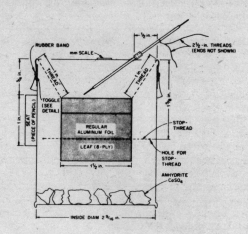

b. Select a piece of Plexiglas, a draftsman's plastic triangle, a smooth plastic ruler, or other piece of hard, smooth plastic. (Unfortunately, not all types of hard plastic can be used to generate a sufficient electrostatic charge.) Be sure the plastic is dry.

For charging a KFM inside a dry-bucket, cut a rectangular piece of hard plastic about 1½ by 5 inches. Sharp corners and edges can be smoothed by rubbing on concrete. To avoid contaminating the charging end with sweaty, oily fingers, it is best to mark the other end with a piece of tape.

c. Fold **DRY** paper (typing paper, writing paper, or other smooth, clean paper) to make an approximate square about 4 inches on a side and about 20 sheets thick. (This many sheets of paper lessens leakage to the fingers of the electrostatic charges to be generated on the hard plastic and on the rubbed paper.)

d. Fold the square of paper in the middle, and move the hard plastic rapidly back and forth so that it is rubbed **vigorously** on the paper in the middle of this folded square—while the outside of this folded square of paper is squeezed firmly between thumb and the ends of **two** fingers. To avoid discharging the charge on the plastic to the fingers. keep them away from the edges of the paper. See photo.

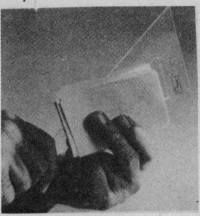

e. Move the electrostatically charged part of the rubbed plastic rather slowly past the upper end of the charging-wire, while looking straight down on the KFM. Keep the hard plastic approximately perpendicular to the charging-wire and about ¼ to ½ inch away from its upper end. The charge jumps the spark gaps and charges the leaves of the KFM.

f. Pull down on an insulating adjustment-thread to raise the lower end of the charging-wire. (If the charging-wire has been held in its charging position by its sticky-ended adjustment-thread being stuck to the top of the clear plastic cover, to avoid possibly damaging the threads: (1) pull down a little on the bare-ended adjustment-thread; and (2) detach, pull down on, and secure the sticky-ended adjustment-thread to the side of the can, so as to raise and keep the lower end of the charging-wire close to the underside of the clear plastic cover.) **Do not touch the charging-wire.**

   g. Put the charging paper and the hard plastic in a container where they will be kept dry—as in a Mason jar with some drying agent.

2. Charging a KFM from a Quickly Unwound Roll of Tape. (Quick unwinding produces a harmless charge of several thousand volts on the tape.)

   a. Adjust the charging-wire so that its lower end is about ¹⁄₁₆ inch above the upper edges of the aluminum-foil leaves. Use the sticky-tape at the end of one adjustment-thread to hold the charging-wire in this position. Stick this tape approximately in line with the leaves, either on the side of the can or on the plastic cover. (If the plastic cover is weak, it may be necessary to put a piece of sticky-tape on the end of each adjustment-thread, in order to hold the charging-wire securely. If a charging-wire is not secure, its lower end may be forced up by the like charge on the leaves before the leaves can be fully charged.)

   b. The sketch shows the "GET SET" position, preparatory to unrolling the Scotch Magic Transparent Tape, P.V.C. electrical tape, or other tape. Be sure to first remove the roll from its dispenser. Some of the other kinds of tape will not produce a high enough voltage.

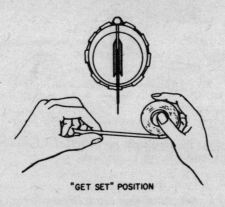

"GET SET" POSITION

   c. **QUICKLY** unroll 10 to 12 inches of tape by pulling its end with the left hand, while the right hand allows the roll to unwind while remaining in about the same "GET SET" position only an inch or two away from the KFM.

d. While holding the unwound tape tight, about perpendicular to the charging-wire, and about ¼ inch away from
the end of the charging-wire, **promptly** move both hands
and the tape to the right **rather slowly**—taking about 2
seconds to move about 8 inches. The electrostatic charge
on the unwound tape "jumps" the spark gaps from the
tape to the upper end of the charging-wire and from the
lower end of the charging-wire to the aluminum leaves,
and charges the aluminum leaves.

   Be sure neither leaf is touching a stop-thread.

   Try to charge the leaves enough to spread them far
enough apart to give a reading of at least 15 mm.

e. Pull down on an insulating adjustment-thread to raise the
lower end of the charging-wire. If the charging-wire has
been held in charging position by its sticky-ended adjustment-thread being stuck to the top of the clear plastic
cover, it is best first to pull down a little on the bare-
ended adjustment-thread, and then to move, pull down
on, and secure the sticky-ended adjustment-thread to the
side of the can so that the lower part of the charging-
wire is close to the underside of the clear plastic cover.

   Do not touch the charging-wire.

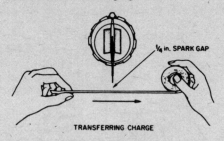

¼ in. SPARK GAP

TRANSFERRING CHARGE

f. Rewind the tape **tight** on its roll, for future use when
other tape may not be available.

XIV. Make and Use a Dry-Bucket

By charging a KFM while it is inside a dry-bucket with a
transparent plastic cover (see illustration), this fallout meter
can be charged and used even if the relative humidity is 100%

outside the dry-bucket. The air inside the dry-bucket is kept very dry by a drying agent placed on its bottom. About a cupful of anhydrite serves very well. The pieces of this dehydrated gypsum need not be as uniform in size as is best for use inside a KFM, but do not use powdered anhydrite.

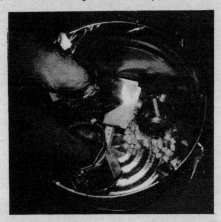

A dry-bucket can be readily made in about an hour by proceeding as follows:

1. Remove the handle of a large bucket, pot, or can preferably with a top diameter of at least 11 inches. A 4-gallon bucket having a top diameter of about 14 inches is ideal. If the handle-supports interfere with stretching a piece of clear plastic film across the top of the bucket, remove them, being sure no sharp points remain.

2. Cut out a circular piece of clear plastic with a diameter about 5 inches larger than the diameter of the top of the bucket. Clear polyethylene 4 mils thick, used for storm windows, etc., is best. Stretch the plastic smooth across the top of the bucket, and tie it in place, preferably with strong rubber bands looped together to form a circle.

3. Make a plastic top that fits snugly but is easily removable, by taping over and around the plastic just below the top of the bucket. **One**-inch-wide cloth duct tape, or **one**-inch-wide glass-reinforced strapping tape, serves well. When taping, do not permit the lower edge of the tape to be pulled inward below the rim of the bucket.

3/4 in.

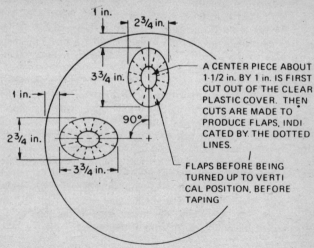

1 in.

2¾ in.

3¾ in.

3¾ in.

1 in.

1 in.

2¾ in.

3¾ in.

90°

A CENTER PIECE ABOUT 1-1/2 in. BY 1 in. IS FIRST CUT OUT OF THE CLEAR PLASTIC COVER. THEN CUTS ARE MADE TO PRODUCE FLAPS, INDICATED BY THE DOTTED LINES.

FLAPS BEFORE BEING TURNED UP TO VERTICAL POSITION, BEFORE TAPING

4. Cut two small holes (about 1 inch by 2 inches) in the plastic cover, as illustrated. Then make the radial cuts (shown by dotted lines) outward from the small holes, out to the solid-line outlines of the 3 inch by 4 inch hand-holes, so as to form small flaps.

5. Fold the small flaps upward, so they are vertical. Then tape them on their outer sides, so they form a vertical "wall" about ¾ inch high around each hand-hole.

6. Reduce the length of two ordinary plastic bread bags (or similar plastic bags) to a length that is 5 inches greater than the height of the bucket. (Do not use rubber gloves in place of bags; gloves so used result in much more humid outside air being unintentionally pumped into a dry-bucket when it is being used while charging a KFM inside it.)

7. Insert a plastic bag into each hand-hole, and fold the edge of the plastic bag about ½ inch over the taped vertical "wall" around each hand-hole.

8. Strengthen the upper parts of the plastic bags by folding 2-inch pieces of tape over the top of the "wall" around each hand-hole.

9. Make about a quart of anhydrite by heating small pieces of wall-board gypsum, and keep this anhydrite dry in a Mason jar or other airtight container with a rubber or plastic sealer.

10. Make a circular aluminum-foil cover to place over the plastic cover when the dry-bucket is not being used for minutes to hours. Make this cover with a diameter about 4 inches greater than the diameter of the top of the bucket, and make it fit more snugly with an encircling loop of rubber bands, or with string. Although not essential, an aluminum-foil cover reduces the amount of water vapor that can reach and pass through the plastic cover, thus extending the life of the drying agent.

11. Charge a KFM inside a dry-bucket by:
    a. Taking off wrist watch and sharp-pointed rings that might tear the plastic bags.
    b. Placing inside the dry-bucket:
       (1) About a cup of anhydrite or silica gel;
       (2) the KFM, with its charging-wire adjusted in its charging position; and
       (3) dry, folded paper and the electrostatic charging device, best a 5-inch-long piece of Plexiglas with

smoothed edges, to be rubbed between dry paper folded about 4 inches square and about 20 sheets thick. (Unrolling a roll of tape inside a dry-bucket is an impractical charging method.)

c. Replacing the plastic cover, that is best held in place with a loop of rubber bands.

d. Charging the KFM with your hands inside the plastic bags, operating the charging device. Have another person illuminate the KFM with a flashlight. When adjusting the charging-wire, move your hands very slowly. See the dry-bucket photos.

12. Expose the KFM to fallout radiation **either** by:

a. Leaving the KFM inside the dry-bucket while exposing it to fallout radiation for one of the listed time intervals, and reading the KFM before and after the exposure while it remains inside the dry-bucket. (The reading eye should be a measured 12 inches above the SEAT of the KFM, and a flashlight or other light should be used.)

b. Taking the charged KFM out of the dry-bucket to read it, expose it, and read it after the exposure. (If this is done repeatedly, especially in a humid shelter, the drying agent will not be effective for many KFM chargings, and will have to be replaced.)

XV. How to Use a KFM after a Nuclear Attack

A. Background Information

If during a rapidly worsening crisis threatening nuclear war you are in the place where you plan to take shelter, postpone studying the instructions following this sentence until after you have:

(1) built or improved a high-protection-factor shelter (if possible, a shelter covered with 2 or 3 ft of earth and separate from flammable buildings), and

(2) made a KAP (homemade shelter-ventilating pump) if you have the instructions and materials, and

(3) stored at least 15 gallons of water for each shelter occupant if you can obtain containers.

Having a KFM or any other dependable fallout meter and knowing how to operate it will enable you to minimize radiation injuries and possible fatalities, especially by skillfully using a high-protection-factor fallout shelter to control and limit exposures to radiation. By studying this section you first will learn how to measure radiation **dose rates** (roentgens per hour = R/hr), how to calculate **doses [R]** received in different time intervals, and how to determine **time intervals** (hours and/or minutes) in which specified doses would be received. Then this section lists the sizes of doses (number of R) that the average person can tolerate without being sickened, that he is likely to survive, and that he is likely to be killed by.

Most fortunately for the future of all living things, the decay of radioactivity causes the sandlike fallout particles to become less and less dangerous with the passage of time. Each fallout particle acts much like a tiny X-ray machine would if it were made so that its rays, shooting out from it like invisible light, became weaker and weaker with time.

Contrary to exaggerated accounts of fallout dangers, the radiation **dose rate** from fallout particles when they reach the ground in the areas of the heaviest fallout **will decrease quite rapidly**. For example, consider the decay of fallout from a relatively nearby, large surface burst, at a place where the fallout particles are deposited on the ground one hour after the explosion. At this time one hour after the explosion, assume that the radiation dose rate (the best measure of radiation danger at a particular time) measures 2,000 roentgens per hour (2,000 R/hr) outdoors. Seven hours later the dose rate is reduced to 200 R/hr by normal radioactive decay. Two days after the explosion, the dose rate outdoors is reduced by radioactive decay to 20 R/hr. After two weeks, the dose rate is less than 2 R/hr. When the dose rate is 2 R/hr, people can go out of a good shelter and work outdoors for 3 hours a day, receiving a daily dose of 6 roentgens, without being sickened.

In places where fallout arrives several hours after the explosion, the radioactivity of the fallout will have gone through its time period of most rapid decay while the fallout particles were still airborne. If you are in a location so distant from the explosion that fallout arrives 8 hours after the explosion, two days must pass before the initial dose rate measured at your location will decay to $\frac{1}{10}$ its initial intensity.

B. Finding the **Dose Rate**

    1. Reread Section IV, "What a KFM Is and How it Works." Also reread Section XIII, "Two Ways to Charge a KFM," and actually do each step immediately after reading it.

    2. Charge the KFM, raise the lower end of its charging-wire and read the apparent separation of the **lower** edges of its leaves while the KFM rests on an approximately horizontal surface. Never take a reading while a leaf is touching a stop-thread.

    3. Expose the KFM to fallout radiation for one of the time intervals shown in the vertical columns of the table attached to the KFM. (Study the table on page 257.) If the dose rate is not known even approximately, first expose the fully charged KFM for one minute. For dependable measurements outdoors, expose the charged KFM about three feet above the ground. For most exposures, connect the KFM to a stick or pole (best done with two rubber bands), and expose it about three feet above the ground. Be careful not to tilt the KFM too much.

    4. Read the KFM after the exposure, while the KFM rests on an approximately horizontal surface.

    5. Find the time interval that gives a dependable reading—by exposing the fully charged KFM for one or more of the listed time intervals until the **reading after the exposure is:**

        (a) Not less than **5 mm.**

        (b) At least **2 mm** less than the reading before the exposure.

    6. Calculate by simple subtraction the **difference** in the apparent separation of the **lower** edges of the leaves before the exposure and after the exposure. An example: If the reading before the exposure is 18 mm and the reading after the exposure is 6 mm, the **difference** in readings is 18mm–6 mm = 12 mm.

    7. If an exposure results in a difference in readings of **less than 2 mm**, recharge the KFM and expose it again for one of the **longer** time intervals listed. (If there appears to be **no** difference in the readings taken before and

after an exposure for one minute, this does not prove there is absolutely no fallout danger.)

8. If an exposure results in the **reading** after the exposure being **less than 5 mm**, recharge the KFM and expose it again for one of the **shorter** time intervals listed.

9. Use the table attached to the KFM to find the **dose rate** (R/hr) during the time of exposure. The dose rate (R/hr) is found at the intersection of the vertical column of numbers under the time interval used and of the horizontal line of numbers that lists the calculated difference in readings at its left end.

   An example: If the time interval of the exposure was **1 MIN.** and the difference in readings was **12 mm**, the table shows that the **dose rate** during the time interval of the exposure was **9.2 R/HR** (9.2 roentgens per hour).

**TABLE USED TO FIND DOSE RATES (R/HR.
FROM KFM READINGS**
*·DIFFERENCE BETWEEN THE READING BEFORE EXPOSURE
AND THE READING AFTER EXPOSURE IS PLY STANDARD
FOIL LEAVES)*

DIFF.* IN READINGS	TIME INTERVAL OF AN EXPOSURE				
	15 SEC. R/HR	1 MIN. R/HR	4 MIN. R/HR	16 MIN. R/HR	1 HR. R/Hh
2 mm	6.2	1.6	0.4	0.1	0.03
4 mm	12.	3.1	0.8	0.2	0.06
6 mm	19.	4.6	1.2	0.3	0.08
8 mm	25.	6.2	1.6	0.4	0.10
10 mm	31.	7.7	2.0	0.5	0.13
12 mm	37.	9.2	2.3	0:6	0.15
14 mm	43.	11.	2.7	0.7	0.18

   Another example: If the time interval of the exposure was **15 SEC.** and the difference in readings was **11 mm**, the table shows that the dose rate during the exposure was halfway between **31 R/HR** and **37 R/HR** that is, the **dose rate** was 34 R/hr.

10. Note in the table that if an exposure for one of the listed time intervals causes the **difference** in readings to be 2 mm or 3 mm, then an exposure 4 times as long reveals the same dose rate. An example: If a 1- min exposure results in a difference in readings of 2 mm, the table shows the dose rate was 1.6 R/hr; then if the KFM is exposed for 4 minutes at this same dose rate

of 1.6 R/hr, the table shows that the resultant difference in readings is 8 mm.

The longer exposure results in a more accurate determination of the dose rate.

11. If the dose rate is found to be greater than 0.2 R/hr and time is available, recharge the KFM and repeat the dose-rate measurement—to avoid possible mistakes.

C. Calculating the **Dose Received**

The dose of fallout radiation—that is, the **amount** of fallout radiation received—determines the harmful effects on men and animals. Being exposed to a high **dose rate** is not always dangerous—provided the exposure is short enough to result in only a small **dose** being received. For example, if the **dose rate** outside an excellent fallout shelter is 1200 R/hr and a shelter occupant goes outside for 30 seconds, he would be exposed for ½ of 1 minute, or ½ of ¹⁄₆₀ of an hour, which equals ¹⁄₁₂₀ hour. Therefore, since the dose he would receive if he stayed outside for 1 hour would be 1200 R, in 30 seconds he would receive ¹⁄₁₂₀ of 1200, which equals 10 R (1200 R divided by 120 = 10 R). A total daily **dose** of 10 R (10 roentgens) will not cause any symptoms if it is not repeated day after day for a week or more.

In contrast, if the average dose rate of an area were found to be 12 R/hr and if a person remained exposed in that particular area for 24 hours, he would receive a **dose** of 288 R (12 R/hr x 24 hr = 288 R). Even assuming that this person had been exposed previously to very little radiation, there would still be a serious risk that this 288 R **dose** would be fatal under the difficult conditions that would follow a heavy nuclear attack.

Another example: Assume that three days after an attack the occupants of a dry, hot cave giving almost complete protection against fallout are in desperate need of water. The dose rate outside is found to be 20 R/hr. To backpack water from a source 3 miles away is estimated to take 2–½ hours. The cave occupants estimate that the water backpackers will receive a dose in 2–½ hours of 50 R (2.5 hr x 20 R/hr = 50 R). A dose of 50 R will cause only mild symptoms (nausea in about 10% of persons receiving a 50 R dose) for persons who previously have received only very small doses. Therefore, one of the cave occupants makes a rapid radiation survey for about

1-½ miles along the proposed route, stopping to charge and read a KFM about every quarter of a mile. He finds no dose rates much higher than 20 R/hr.

So, the cave occupants decide the risk is small enough to justify some of them leaving shelter for about 2-½ hours to get water.

D. Estimating the **Dangers** from Different Radiation Doses

Fortunately, the human body—if given enough time—can repair most of the damage caused by radiation. An historic example: A healthy man accidently received a daily **dose** of 9.3 R (or somewhat more) of fallout-type radiation each day for a period of 106 days. His total accumulated **dose** was at least 1000 R. A dose of one thousand roentgens, if received in a few days, is almost three times the dose likely to kill the average man if he receives the whole dose in a few days and after a nuclear attack cannot get medical treatment, adequate rest, etc. However, the only symptom this man noted was serious fatigue.

The occupants of a high-protection-factor shelter (such as a trench shelter covered with 2 or 3 feet of earth and having crawlway entrances) would receive less than ½00 of the radiation dose they would receive outside. Even in most areas of very heavy fallout, persons who remain continuously in such a shelter would receive a total accumulated **dose** of less than 25 R in the first day after the attack, and less than 100 R in the first two weeks. At the end of the first two weeks, such shelter occupants could start working outside for an increasing length of time each day, receiving a **daily dose** of no more than **6 R** for up to two months without being sickened.

To control radiation exposure in this way, each shelter must have a fallout meter, and a daily record must be kept of the approximate total dose received each day by every shelter occupant, both while inside and outside the shelter. The long-term penalty which would result from a dose of 100 R received within a few weeks is much less than many Americans fear. If 100 average persons received an external dose of 100 R during and shortly after a nuclear attack, the studies of the Japanese A-bomb survivors indicate that no more than one of them is likely to die during the following 30 years as a result of this 100 R radiation dose. These delayed radiation deaths would be due to leukemia and other cancers. In the desperate crisis period following a major nuclear attack, such a relatively small shortening of life expectancy during the following 30 years should not keep people from starting recovery work to save themselves and their fellow citizens from death due to lack of food and other essentials.

A healthy person who previously has received a total accumulated dose of no more than 100 R distributed over a 2-week period should realize that:

100 R, even if all received in a day or less, is unlikely to require medical care—provided during the next 2 weeks a total additional dose of no more than a few R is received.

350 R received in a few days or less is likely to prove fatal after a large nuclear attack when few survivors could get medical care, sanitary surroundings, a well-balanced diet, or adequate rest.

600 R received in a few days or less is almost certain to cause death within a few days.

E. Using a KFM to Reduce the Doses Received Inside a Shelter

Inside most shelters, the dose received by an occupant varies considerably, depending on the occupant's location. For example, inside an expedient covered-trench shelter the dose rate is higher near the entrance than in the middle of the trench. In a typical basement shelter the best protection is found in one corner. Especially during the first several hours after the arrival of fallout, when the dose rates and doses received are highest, shelter occupants should use their fallout meters to determine where to place themselves to minimize the doses they receive. They should use available tools and materials to reduce the doses they receive, especially during the first day, by digging deeper (if practical) and reducing the size of openings by partially blocking them with earth, water containers, etc.—while maintaining adequate ventilation. To greatly reduce the danger from fallout particles entering the body through nose or mouth, shelter occupants should at least cover their nose and mouth with a towel or other cloth while the fallout is being deposited outside their shelter.

The air inside an occupied shelter often becomes very humid. If a good flow of outdoor air is flowing into a shelter—

especially if pumped by briefly operating a KAP or other ventilating pump—a KFM usually can be charged at the air intake of the shelter room without putting it inside a dry-bucket. However, if the air to which a KFM is exposed has a relative humidity of 90% or higher, the instrument cannot be charged, even by quickly unrolling a roll of tape.

In extensive areas of heavy fallout, the occupants of most home basements, that provide inadequate shielding against heavy fallout radiation, would be in deadly danger. By using a dependable fallout meter, occupants would find that persons lying on the floor in certain locations would receive the smallest doses, and that, if they improvise additional shielding in these locations, the doses received could be greatly reduced. Additional shielding can be provided by placing a double layer of doors, positioned about two feet above the floor and strongly supported near their ends, and by putting books, containers full of water and other heavy objects on top of these doors. Or, if tools are available, breaking through the basement floor and digging a shelter trench will greatly increase available protection against radiation. If a second expedient ventilating pump, a KAP, is made and used as a fan, such an extremely cramped shelter inside a shelter usually can be occupied by several times as many persons.

BEST-SELLING
Science Fiction
and
Fantasy

Fantasy from Ace
fanciful and fantastic!